CONSTANTINOPLE

APRIL 1915

First published in Great Britain by Black Apollo Press, 2009
Copyright © Haig Tahta 2009
A CIP catalogue record of this book is available at the British Library.
All rights reserved; no part of this publication may be reproduced or transmitted by any means electronic, mechanical, photocopying or otherwise without the prior permission of the publisher.
ISBN: 9781900355698

CONSTANTINOPLE
April 1915

Haig Tahta

BLACK
APOLLO
PRESS

The four families in *April 1915*

The Avakians of Makrikoy

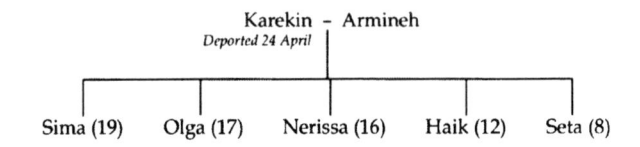

Karekin - Armineh
Deported 24 April

Sima (19) Olga (17) Nerissa (16) Haik (12) Seta (8)

The Asadourians of Cæsaria

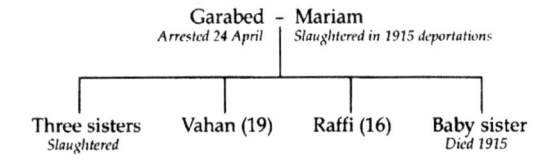

Garabed - Mariam
Arrested 24 April *Slaughtered in 1915 deportations*

Three sisters Vahan (19) Raffi (16) Baby sister
Slaughtered   *Died 1915*

The family of Dr Nazim Kemal

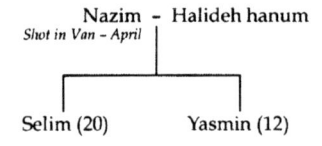

Nazim - Halideh hanum
Shot in Van - April

Selim (20) Yasmin (12)

The Sarafians of Makrikoy

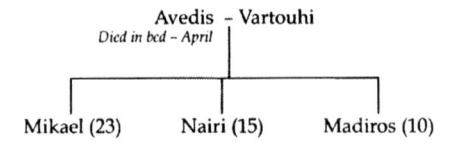

Avedis - Vartouhi
Died in bed - April

Mikael (23) Nairi (15) Madiros (10)

CONTENTS

Prologue		7
1	Makrikoy, breakfast at the Avakians	11
2	Vahan and his father	20
3	The family of Dr. Nazim Kemal	34
4	Harry and his father	45
5	Harry's report	53
6	Olga	68
7	Garabed Asadourian	74
8	Breakfast at the Avakians	83
9	The Siege of Van	89
10	Tea at Tokatlian's	112
11	André, Harry and the invasion force	118
12	Guests at the Avakians	130
13	The 24th April dawns	142
14	Karekin	151
15	Sima	159
16	Vahan in Makrikoy	166
17	Armineh and Sima	180
18	Raffi, and the arrest of Garabed	187
19	Van, the last effort	195
20	Haik	202
21	The last hours of the 24th April	213
22	Harry at Gallipoli	224
23	Garabed's escape	230
24	Karekin's escape	237
25	Mikael and his father	244

26	Garabed in flight	260
27	The Avakians without Kerakin	275
28	Raffi faces life and death	287
29	Garabed drives on	298
30	Selim and the Arab dimension	306
31	Harry and the Arab Bureau	313
32	Mikael and Olga	323
33	Raffi hangs on	337
34	Olga and Selim	345
35	Vahan Survives	354
36	Garabed finally arrives	364
37	Karekin and Aram return	373
38	Olga decides	386
39	Makrikoy. The Avakians	394

PROLOGUE

1915 - the world was still living in the final twilight years of the era known as the 'long' nineteenth century. The slaughter of the first few months of the Great War had still not triggered those enormous changes which were soon to come.

1915 - the Ottoman Empire - the so-called 'sick man of Europe' was not really as sick as the vultures surrounding it liked to make out. In this year, this reputedly moribund Empire was to inflict on the proud British Navy a major defeat for the first time in over one hundred years. The world would never be the same again.

1915 - the Austrian Empire was in some ways a state even more entitled to be considered as the sick man of Europe, with its equally diverse and fascinating collection of peoples and cultures and ways of life. Throughout the Great War it scarcely ever managed to win a single major campaign, except perhaps against the unfortunate Italians, who only just made it as a major power anyway.

But were either of these two generally tolerant though inefficient, multiracial and multicultural organisations, the real 'sick men'. Hard and virulent unicultural nationalism was the growing creed in the world, and neither of these old and anachronistic empires sat comfortably with the seething tribal passions of the sovereign territorial nation-state. But who in truth were the really sick men? What after all actually happened in the Twentieth Century, which established in any way that the Hapsburgs or the Ottomans were so hopelessly 'sick', when compared with their powerful neighbours?

Russia gave way to a materialistic Revolution, which within not much more than ten years resulted in the massacre, death and misery of millions upon millions of uncomprehending peasants. The German Empire -so much more efficient, monocultural and monoracial than the Austrian Empire - gave way to a tribal nation-state in arms, whose hysterical demand for uniformity and racial 'purity' resulted in one of the greatest crimes in history. The other petty nation-states that sprang up on the ruins of the two, so-called 'sick', Empires consistently had a history throughout the century, of tyranny, pogroms, and in the end 'ethnic cleansing', far outweighing the evils of the bureacratic inequalities and random cruelties of the old empires.

After the Ittihad revolution of 1908 in the Ottoman Empire, the Young Turks impatiently thrust aside the multi-national and tolerant legacy of the old Ottoman Sultans, substituting for it the narrow prejudiced exclusiveness of the tribal nation-state. This then resulted in the first of the great massacres leading to ethnic cleansing, of which this so-called enlightened century has been so full.

In August 1914, Europe entered into the destructive, purely European, war, which was known then, and for its first few months, as 'the Third Balkan War'. It was the entry into this war of the Ottoman Empire in November 1914 which turned it into the First 'World' War.

Finally – April 1915 - The Dardanelles campaign, fought within actual sight of that very first epic war of Western tradition - the Trojan War – was one of the great 'what-ifs' of history. It was also one of the greatest disasters suffered by the British Army until the fall of Singapore, twenty-five years or so later. Both defeats, ironically, were at the hands not of any recognised traditional European rival, but of a despised oriental foe. The world was changing, and here was the pivot.

Constantinople - Stamboul - Bolis .... The City.

Final note - In the Ottoman world people referred to their loved ones by many differing endearments which go far beyond 'my dear' or 'darling''. These endearments, when translated literally into English, may appear somewhat stilted and artificial. Armenians, for example, use the word 'hokis', when addressing their children, or spouse. This translates as 'my soul', and has been used here throughout, as has 'my lovely father' or 'my little father' rather than always just 'Darling' or 'Dad', which would perhaps be the truer translations.

CONSTANTINOPLE AND THE STRAITS

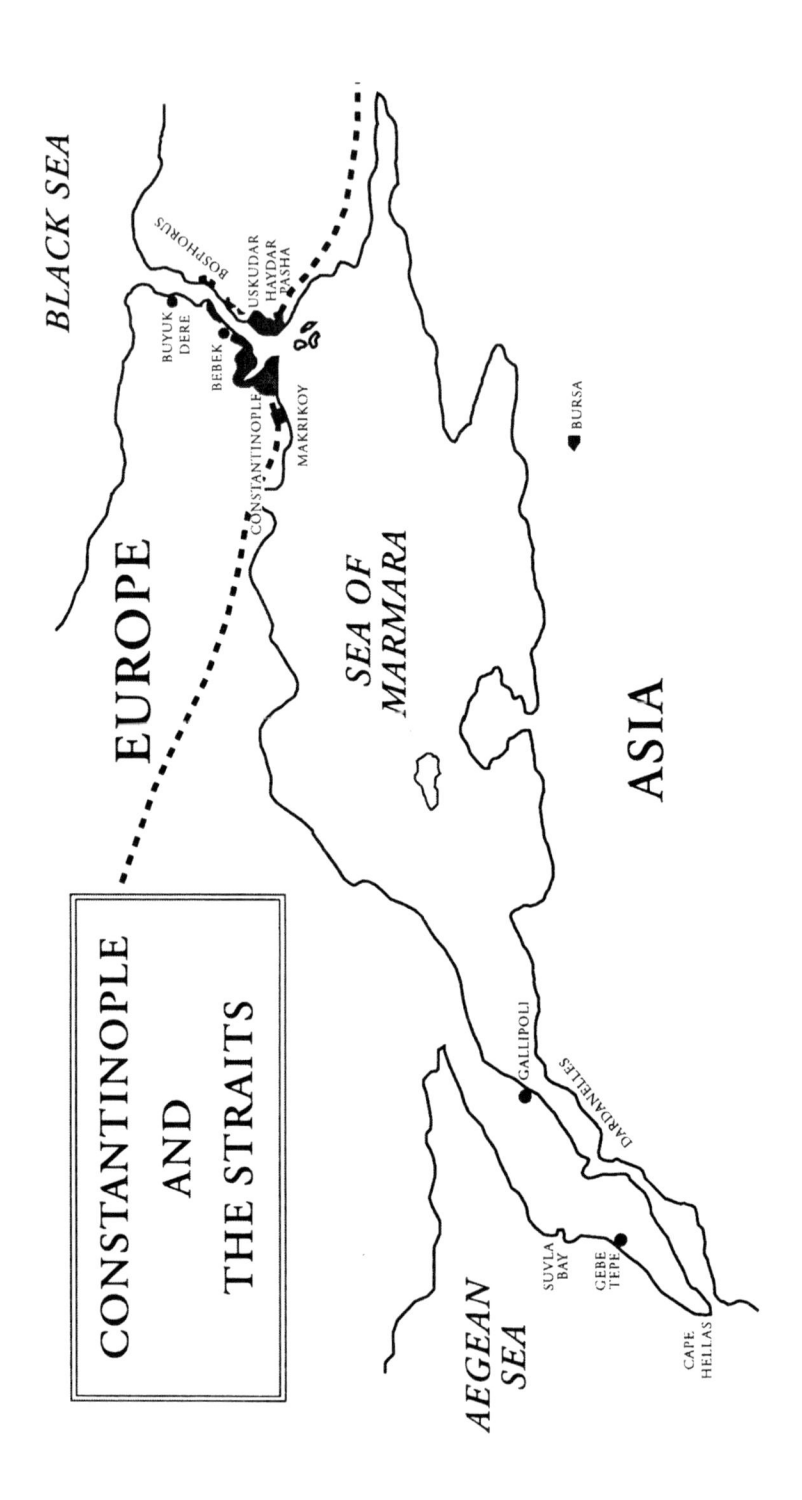

CHAPTER 1

Makrikoy, Breakfast at the Avakians

"I don't agree with you at all, Nerissa."

Sima, 19 years-old, the tall, eldest daughter of the Avakian family, haughtily addressed her younger sister. Sitting bolt upright at the breakfast table with a stiff straight back as she had been taught, dressed in a flowing white summer frock, Sima continued-

"I see no reason at all why we ever came into this war in the first place, so why should the British, or the French for that matter, bother to attack us? Their real enemies, surely, are the Germans. What have we ever done to harm them?"

"But Sima, my darling," replied Nerissa, as she sipped her tea, "don't you see that all that bombardment by the British navy in the straits last month must surely be the preliminary of something – another attack – or, I don't know, – something?"

"For heavens sake, can't you two talk about something more interesting," said Olga, the family's second daughter. "I'm getting thoroughly bored with all this talk of war. It's all happening so far away from us, anyway. The only thing we've seen, is that there are no longer any decent clothes to buy in the shops."

Dressed simply in her college uniform, Olga nevertheless managed to display an elegance in the simple lines of her green skirt, which Sima, in her expensive white muslins, failed to achieve. Quite outstandingly pretty, Olga had a stunning smile, which, coupled with her large inquisitive brown eyes, she used shamelessly on all and sundry. Her charms were to no avail on her sisters, who ignored her comment and continued their discussion as if she hadn't spoken.

"Haik, will you please eat something instead of your mindless chatter. For heaven's sake, a piece of toast and honey isn't so difficult to swallow," snapped Armineh, as she pushed his neglected plate back at him. She knew perfectly well that continually nagging at her thin and wiry 12 year-old son about his hopeless incapacity to eat anything at mealtimes, was a totally pointless exercise. However, she couldn't help herself.

Armineh was beginning, at last, to look older than the 38 years she was prepared to acknowledge publicly, and her noisy family was trying her patience more and more often in these difficult days. Her figure had always been round and short, but the birth of five children had made her increasingly dumpy. Armineh drew a deep breath, firmly trying to put out of her mind all irritation at the sight of her son toying with his food, and surveyed the rest of her family at the breakfast table.

Karekin, her husband, had not yet come down, and she glanced at the stairs that curved up impressively from the middle of the large hall where most of the family's activities took place. Here, in the centre of the house, immediately beyond the main entrance door, stood the table and chairs where the family took all their meals. On one side of this great room, beyond the dining area, was the door to the kitchens, and on the other side, doors to the formal sitting rooms. Dotted about the marble floor were settees and comfortable sofas and some large slightly faded but still beautiful Persian carpets.

The family's long-time nanny, Marie – a large and comfortable figure – was bustling round the table, from the kitchen and back, pouring tea and helping 8 year-old Seta, the youngest of the Avakian family. It was never entirely clear whether the lively Seta was eating or talking, sitting still or ready to jump up and run off, as she seemed to be in a constant state of motion.

Breakfast at the Avakians was never silent, but on this beautiful spring morning on the 1st day of April 1915, it was particularly noisy.

Everyone was talking at once, when Karekin appeared at the top of the stairs.

It would be an unjustified exaggeration to suggest that his appearance was followed by any sort of respectful silence as he walked purposefully down the stairs. There was, perhaps, a tiny imperceptible drop in the decibel level, but the animated conversation carried cheerfully on. Sima smiled up at her father, whilst Olga turned round, jumped up and gave her father a great kiss and a hug as he arrived at the bottom of the stairs.

Karekin was a tall and upright figure, almost always dressed formally in a grey suit of English cut. He was never seen in public, and indeed rarely even outside his bedroom, without an impeccably knotted tie. Every inch of his tall frame, with his long prematurely bald head, was stiff and dignified. He walked ramrod tall with his hands often clasped behind his back. Underneath all this formality, however, was an ultra-liberal with outstanding ideas about education for girls. His wife, Armineh, was not at all so sure, and regularly complained to Karekin that formal education for the girls was an expensive irrelevance.

It was, in fact, unusual for the daughter of an Armenian merchant family to be sent for her education to one of the Western schools in the City of Constantinople, and, in this respect, Karekin had always been considered eccentric by his business friends and neighbors.

Armineh, who was more traditional in her outlook, had not been so happy about all this book-learning, and was relieved that Sima had left school and was no longer exposed to temptation by the daily trips into the city during the school terms. By being at home, Sima could also help Armineh in dealing with the hypersensitive Haik and lively Seta. Marie could no longer cope alone, and servants were getting more difficult to find.

That very morning, in the privacy of their bedroom before coming down to breakfast, Karekin and Armineh had had one of their discussions about the girls,

"Karekin, my soul, this war has dulled your responsibility to family matters."

"Oh, my love, are we going to have to go through all this

again? You worry too much, and in any case ..."

"Karekin, you must look at the situation here in your own home and stop spending your time with those political friends of yours ... and those ..."

"Armineh, my love ..."

"No, just listen. We have three problems. First you must consider Sima's marriage prospects. She's 19 and it is time you started thinking about this. Times haven't changed so much that you can shirk this duty, war or no war. Then there's Haik. He's 12, Karekin, and he's unusually naïve, but he's well into puberty – oh Karekin, pay attention – you know perfectly well what I'm talking about. He still runs about in the garden naked. You have to talk to him; find out what he knows and what he doesn't."

"You mean you want me to tell him to start feeling guilty about his body," replied Karekin, rather absently, as he stretched his neck to knot his tie.

"Karekin, don't be obtuse. We're not talking high philosophy here. We're talking about your son, and what he should be made aware of."

"Armineh, very well – that's enough – I do agree with you, and I'll think about it, I promise. And now, my dear, what is your third problem?"

"I can't put my finger on it, but Olga is up to something – I know – I just know it in my bones that she is hiding something from us, but what it is I have no idea ..."

"Come on Armineh, my soul, this is you panicking as usual, a vague anxiety about everyone in your brood. Relax! There's nothing wrong with her. Look, Haik is my problem, I accept that, but you deal with Olga. She's getting a good education, and she knows wrong from right – which is more than can be said for most of the 17 year-old girls around here. As for Sima, we'll deal with her marriage prospects during the next month, so long as the British leave us alone."

"Karekin, honestly, you always ..."

"Armineh, my sweet, don't stamp your foot in vexation. I'll be down to breakfast shortly, and that's an end to it."

On arriving at breakfast, Karekin sat at the top end of the

table, and was immediately served with his usual light Russian tea with a slice of lemon by Marie. This was invariably followed by olives and white cheese, and usually ended with him taking a slice of toast with the family's own honey.

"Baba, Nerissa and I were talking about the possibility of a Western allied attack here at Bolis. What do you think? Do you really think it likely? I myself can't believe that there's any reason why the British should attack us. Along with the French, they have always been supporters of the Ottomans, haven't they?" Sima asked, as she passed the toast to her father.

"Sima, my soul – Marie some more tea please – I think Nerissa is right. Now that the British have failed to get their battleships through the Dardanelles, they're surely going to try something else, but don't ask me what."

"But, Baba, the French and the British have always been friendly to the Ottomans and …"

"Yes, but they aren't now, and as they can't seem to get at the Germans, they're going to come at us. I'm afraid, girls, we are likely to be facing some sort of attack – near here – sooner or later. Olga, where are you off to in such a hurry?"

"Oh father," Olga said as she rose from the table and went round giving everyone a quick kiss, "you know that I have to get an earlier train than you. Come, Haik, why don't you keep me company on the walk down to the station, then you can go on to school after the train goes."

Haik shook his head, while Armineh looked at Karekin meaningfully, as if to suggest that Olga's hurry to get away showed she was hiding something. Karekin merely waved his hand at her, making it clear that he wasn't in agreement, and dismissing the whole subject. Meanwhile Olga, grabbed her bag, flashed her smile at everyone, and hurried out to catch her train to the city.

When Karekin at last rose to take his hat and stick, Nerissa and Seta came and kissed him, as always, before he went to work. Haik finally pushed his plate away, grinning at his exasperated mother, and went to give his father a hug.

"Baba – is there actually going to be any fighting here – are we going to see the British battleships firing their guns... I mean at us even...can their shells actually reach us here ...?"

Karekin turned, returning his son's hug and replied, as he reached the front door,

"No, my son, that's pretty unlikely. In any case, things are never quite so exciting as they might seem when they are actually happening. We will just have to wait and see."

Having received a kiss from everyone, he straightened up even more, if that was possible, and walked out of the front door.

Karekin usually caught the 8.15 a.m. local train from Makrikoy to the city. Before the outbreak of this interminable war, he used to make a point of getting the later train so that he could stand on the platform and watch the slow passage of the magnificent train from Paris – the Simplon-Orient Express – with its long line of mysterious, dark blue, Wagon-Lits sleeping coaches, often with the blinds still down in the windows, although the city was now only twenty minutes away.

Trains and ships were often late or delayed in the Ottoman world, but it was rare for the Simplon-Orient not to be dead on time every day. Some of the smart conductors in dark brown uniforms, even as early as Makrikoy, would already be pulling down the windows of their carriage door, preparatory to opening the door as the train pulled into the European terminus at Sirkeci Station. The sight of the great train never ceased to give Karekin a frisson of simple childish delight, as the coaches passed slowly by the little station, most marked as originating from Paris, but some from Rome and other great cities, and even one each day all the way from London.

Karekin, whose main business activity was the importation of fine muslins largely from Lancashire in England, had once traveled to Manchester before the war with his eldest daughter, Sima, to set up a direct personal contact with his main supplier. He was not completely fluent in English, apart from the few necessary words required for conducting business in shipping and commerce all over the world; English was the lingua franca for all the great trading houses of Europe. Sima had attended the

English High School for Girls in the City, and had gone on the trip with her father to help him with the language. The journey to Western Europe had been on this same inter-continental service, and on that same once-a-day sleeper coach that would be shunted across Paris, eased onto the train ferry across the Channel, finally arriving at Victoria Station in London, three days after setting out from the City.

But now, in April 1915, there were no more trains coming from Europe, with the exception of the occasional German freight train, routed through neutral Rumania and the wavering Bulgaria. So he had taken to catching the earlier train to town in order to get back to his family in the early afternoon while it was still light.

Karekin hadn't hesitated, seven years ago, in placing the then 12 year-old Sima in the prestigious English High School for Girls. However, Constantinople was a city in which the influence of the European Great Powers waxed and waned throughout these years. Wealthy Greek and Armenian families tended to put their sons into the schools of the dominant, and currently most highly regarded, European Power. The influence of France and England had been slipping, as they both got ever closer to Russia in their anti-German alliance. Russia, of course, was the permanent, age-old enemy of the Ottomans. The corollary of all this was a rise in influence and prestige of Imperial Germany in Constantinople, and the popularity of new German schools. Karekin, who was not enamoured of Prussian militarism and values, had decided to place Olga, his flirtatious and sprightly second daughter, in the American School – Robert College – where she was still flourishing.

The long walk to the station was Karekin's main daily exercise and he strode along, occasionally raising his hat to neighbors and acquaintances, but with nothing more than a muttered morning greeting. His large house, with its walled garden and orchards, lay just south of the new district of Osman Aga. He rarely took the short direct road alongside the Valli Effendi racecourse, but preferred the longer road which went above the little town, past a vantage point where he could look down on Makrikoy – the ancient Hebdomen of the Eastern Roman Empire – seven miles from the city walls.

Here Karekin would sit on an old wooden bench for a few moments and muse about his family in the warm morning sunshine. It was not that he didn't discuss matters with his wife, Armineh; he did, and he often took her into his confidence. However, he was much older than her, and they had married in the old arranged style when she was barely sixteen. Sharp, intelligent and formidably strong-willed, nevertheless her upbringing in the Armenian heartlands of Erzerum in Anatolia, had been traditional, and, like most girls, she had little formal education. Within his own household, on the other hand, he had encouraged his four lively daughters to discuss and express their views volubly, with spirit and without fear. He had, as a result, paid the inevitable price of heading a fairly noisy and not entirely peaceful household.

Here, however, sitting on the old bench staring down at the old Ottoman town houses, crumbling away among the ruins of the ancient Hebdomen palaces, he could let his thoughts wander in peace. Whilst musing, he could pick out the old Palace of Magnaurus and see the old granite column which had carried the statue of the Emperor Theodosius, and which stood, now ruined, right by the shore. All along the coast lay the ruins of more decrepit cisterns, ivy-creepered walls and the old Imperial Byzantine jetty, now almost entirely collapsed into the water.

Karekin's perspective wasn't dominated by a romantic view of the past. The old ruins were simply there – they were an absolute part of the accepted background to his life and those of his friends. In the end, he thought little about them. He had his own life to lead, his family to raise, and the fact that he was doing it in one of the oldest and most historically significant cities in the world, was coincidental.

So, as he sat on the old bench and stared out at the little town and the ruined palaces, his thoughts were on other things. He mused on his two elder daughters, Sima and Olga. The question of the marriage for Sima was looming, and Armineh had been quite right to draw his attention to it this morning. Already two or three of his business colleagues had referred fairly openly to eligible sons, already in business with their fathers, and looking for another good merchant house with which to join forces. Yes, it was time that the proud Sima was introduced to some suitable young men.

The position with Olga was quite different. Vivacious and full of a rather self-absorbed determination, Olga, he felt, was already meeting far too many young men at Robert College.

Karekin sighed. He had no real fears in his own mind that any of his daughters would go too far. Under all the froth, even Olga, he was sure, had a clear understanding of what was right and wrong. However, as he had already seen this morning, Armineh didn't see it that way at all, and worried when Olga returned home on a later train than usual, having stayed on for tea at some friend's house in the city.

Karekin rose. Even in early April, the sun was coming up fast and he had little time left to get to Cobancesme station – the local station for this end of Makrikoy – to catch his train. He strode down, putting aside all thoughts of Olga and Sima, his mind now turning to the business needs of the day. He crossed the line and walked into the little station and onto the platform. There, standing with others waiting for the next local train, he saw his old friend Doctor Manuelian.

"Parev, Doctor," he greeted, pleased, as always, whenever he met his friend Aram, with whom he regularly played backgammon on Sunday mornings after Church. They stood together waiting for the train.

"What news, Aram?"

"Well, you know that concert of local culture that was held in Galata in the city a couple of nights ago. Both Talaat Bey and Djavid Pasha were there. The enthusiasm for the performance of our own Father Komidas was enormous, Karekin."

"No, I wasn't meaning that. I meant whether you had any news about the War."

"Oh, it's the same old stuff, large numbers of young men dying just to gain a few more yards for one side or the other. Let them get on with it, its not going to affect us here in our little backwater. Ever since the failure of Enver's Caucasian campaign last year, even he must be sorry we joined in the War. No, no, my dear friend, all we need to do is to sit tight and let them all exhaust themselves. Don't worry man, you'll soon be getting your precious Lancashire cotton again."

At this point the local train pulled in. Nodding to each other, Dr Aram Manuelian clambered into his first-class carriage, while Karekin walked down and got into a second-class compartment.

"Stubborn old bachelor," thought Karekin, "why won't he change his habits of a lifetime and join me on this short trip to town."

"What a ridiculously rigid fellow Karekin is," thought the Doctor at the same time, "he could easily afford to come with me and forget his liberal, egalitarian principles for once."

Stopping at every small station on the way, trundling along beside the Sea of Marmara, the train passed through the gap cut into the ancient great Theodosian Walls of the City, and, skirting round the Topkapi Palace, found its way into the European terminus of the railway – Sirkeci Station.

CHAPTER 2

Vahan and his father

On that same 1st day of April, 1915, Vahan bounced, rather than walked, down the road to the Galata bridge, on his way to his classes at the University. Ever since his arrival in this wonderful city, from his provincial home in Caesaria in Central Anatolia, to take up his scholarship place at the Music and Drama Department of the university, he had been in a state of high excitement. The world belonged to him, and to whoever was currently his best friend.

The Galata bridge!

This, one of the great bridges of the world, connected old Stamboul – the original city of Constantinople – to Pera and

Galata, the original European trading suburbs. The crossing was as usual teeming with life. Turkish porters trotted past with a leather thong around their foreheads attached to huge loads carried on their backs, calling out to the passers-by – 'make way, make way'. A few gentlemen with Panama hats and walking sticks, strode along dressed in Western fashion. One or two old-fashioned Ottoman gentlemen, still dressed in the Stambuliya long coat, with a high collar and reaching down to the knees, walked slowly by. The occasional veiled lady passed from one side of the bridge to the other.

Then, there were the one-horse carriages, waiting beside the pavement to pick up passengers coming up the steps from the quayside under the bridge. The ferries themselves, hooting and jostling against each other as they drew up below, trying to nudge into a spot against the quayside to discharge all their fares coming in from further up the Bosphorus, or across the straits from the Asian side. The ubiquitous red fez was everywhere, on Moslem and Christian head alike. Old and new, European and Asian, Christian and Moslem, Jew and Gentile, all thronging together in a noisy and jubilant mass. The only group under-represented at this time in the morning, was women.

Vahan was a stocky square-set young man. He had silky light brown hair and soft eyes with a permanently questioning look. He was currently dressed in the uniform of the Harbiye military academy. He stood leaning against the iron railings, looking down at the ferries and the crowds tumbling up the steps. Staring across the waters, not so full of ships as might have been the case a year before, now that Turkey was at war, he could just make out the looming, grey shapes of the two German battle-ships, sitting out in the roadstead, towering over all the other ships, with their long heavy guns, pointing straight ahead. He could not restrain a self-satisfied smile of sheer joy as he mused over the events of the last year.

Nine months ago, at the height of the summer of 1914, he had heard that he had won a scholarship to the Music Department of the University of Constantinople. His mother, Mariam, hiding her tears, had immediately started work on all the little things that he was going to need when he left home. His father Garabed, bursting with pride, had taken him to the main bazaar of the provincial town – ostensibly to buy necessities for the journey, but really to show off his son's achievements to all his business friends and associates. Vahan was unaware of his mother's private tears, but he had felt and even revelled secretly in his father's pride.

Just turned 18, Vahan had never been anywhere beyond the province of Caesaria. His father had travelled regularly on horseback into the Eastern highlands to visit the many village families, from whom he commissioned wonderful and intricate carpets, worked entirely by hand and made with bright, vegetable-dyed wool. Garabed would sometimes take his second son, Raffi, with him on these trips, but his eldest son would always be left behind.

Vahan, still staring out at the bustle around him, recalled the last occasion a year ago when this had occurred, and the sharp words that had been exchanged between himself and his father, as they had stood facing each other in the dark entrance hall of their house. The actual words sprung to his mind as he stared down at the bustling ferries below –

"Baba, it's not right – you took Raffi with you last time. It's my turn to go with you and meet all these families with whom you do business. Look, I can take my violin with me, and I can play at night – they'll love it."

"My son, I need you to stay at home to look after your mother and sisters in case anything happens to me on the trip. Vahan, also consider, life is hard in the highlands, these people have no time for music."

"Oh, father, believe me that that, at least, is not right. Even the most deprived people appreciate and make time for folk music and melodies, to relieve their tensions and worries after a hard day's work. In any case, both mother and grandma are far more capable than me of managing the house."

`"Vahan, you may be right about music, I don't know, but you don't understand the real issue," said Garabed, and Vahan recalled the mounting anger in his father's eyes at being contradicted.

"We live in a Muslim society. However competent your mother may be, a male head of the family is vital. Officials, or indeed anybody coming to this house, are trained to ignore the women – sometimes even to look away from them if they are in the same room. A male is essential in any household, even if he is totally manipulated by the women behind the arras. Enough, Vahan, I will not listen to any more of this thoughtless and childish nonsense. That's enough, you will do as you are told"

Garabed Asadourian was a strict man liable to lose his temper easily and Vahan had immediately acquiesced. Like most of his generation in Central Anatolia, Garabed had missed out on the great renaissance of Armenian culture and education of the late nineteenth century. He could speak only Turkish and whilst of course he attended Church and was an active member of the Armenian community, he had not been overwhelmed by the nationalist fervour led by teachers and academics from the great cities, who flocked into the local schools, teaching the language, the culture, the poetry and the history of their people to their young pupils.

This strident ethnic nationalism appeared and flourished throughout the old, 19th century empires. Suddenly all over Europe, something unique and special was found in a 'German' forest, or a 'Czech' river. A Bulgarian poem became superior in some indefinable way to a Rumanian one. A Welsh song had a special quality, which other songs – particularly English – did not possess. But where did all this fervour leave the old multi-lingual and multi-cultural Empires of old Europe.

Garabed had had his children educated by these new enthusiastic teachers. His children, even his daughters, all now spoke Armenian well. He was very proud of them, and he was proud in a rather casual and unstructured way of the architecture and poetry of his people. However, he was equally aware that, below the surface, nationalistic and ethnic passions could easily be aroused on both sides by all these well-meaning and enthusiastic academics, and that Armenian nationalism could easily arouse a backlash from a much more dangerous Turkish nationalism. For him there was a lot to be said for the easy-going tolerance and stability of the old multi-ethnic Empires, and the Ottomans in particular.

Vahan's father had had no problem in acting as a 'Mukhtar' or local headman in the town and cooperating as well as he could with the Ottoman authorities. Like most educated Ottoman citizens Garabed deplored the vicious and unstable character of the odious Sultan Abdul Hamid II. However, this did not prevent him from trying to work the system, or from cooperating with those of his Turkish Muslim neighbours with whom he had fairly good relations; relations, which admittedly did not extend to much family contact, but which certainly included having coffee and smoking a pipe together in the local street-cafe.

Garabed had welcomed the great revolution of 1908, which eventually resulted in the deposition of the paranoid Sultan, and he had been prepared to see Vahan – then only twelve – joining with the other boys dancing together in the streets in celebration. He had not objected or made any comment when Vahan had joined with more of his school friends later – both Turkish and Armenian – to collect coins on street corners to help pay for the two great new Dreadnought-type battleships ordered by the government from the shipyards of Great Britain.

Vahan, still daydreaming on the bridge, realised with a feeling of guilt that Garabed had known perfectly well, that Vahan's move to the University at Constantinople would almost certainly estrange him from his eldest son. The difference between life in the great cosmopolitan centre of the Empire and out in the remote provinces was enormous. But Vahan reflected, with a feeling of love, that this had been a price his father was prepared to pay for the inestimable benefits likely to arise in the future for his first-born.

He had left Caesaria early in September with 30 gold coins sewn by his mother into a belt he was to wear under his clothes. He had travelled on his own horse with a servant riding alongside, to the nearest railhead, which was some five days ride away. He had taken some books, his violin, some basic clothes, a bible, which his mother insisted he take, some ready money and his rolled up bedding.

At nights, he and the servant would stay at a *khan*, the traditional resting points for travellers, hardly changed since medieval times. These were almost always large square courtyards, usually with a well in the middle, where the animals would be tethered. These courtyards were surrounded by low buildings; on the first storey were connected balconies with rooms leading off, their windows and doors looking out onto the courtyard below. There were no women of any kind. Washing and other facilities scarcely existed, and the smells were strong and pungent – but the food served was usually surprisingly good and filling. The atmosphere in these *khans* was nearly always hostile, aggressive and sexually charged. As a young lad, Vahan was well aware that he had to be very careful, eye contact being a particular danger.

On his arrival at Eregli, the railhead, he had handed his bedding and his horse to old Mahmud who had then ridden back to Caesaria. Vahan had never seen a railway or a steam engine before, and when he arrived, after two days on the train, at Hayder Pasha station on the Asian side of Constantinople, he also had his first sight of the sea on the ferry ride across the Bosporus. He remembered standing on the white steps of the newly completed station looking out at the Straits for the first time – full of other ferries chugging back and forth between Europe and Asia – and all the shipping of the world as it passed into and out of the Black Sea. He boarded the first ferry going across to Europe with only the haziest idea of where his uncle's house was, too excited to care.

Then, as he passed Leander's Tower, the vista opened out to reveal the magnificent panorama of the Constantinople skyline, with its wonderful domes, minarets and palaces. Also visible were the two great German battle-cruisers – riding at anchor – grey and sleek in the water and both with the Ottoman flag flying from their mastheads. As the ferry passed nearby, Vahan saw the German sailors, wearing the red fez, but otherwise dressed in smart, white, German uniforms. He had noted the impressive 11" guns pointing unmistakably at the Byzantine shoreline and the Sultan's palaces. Both ships dwarfed everything else on the waters. Even in his excitement at everything around him, Vahan recalled the feeling of wonder at how it had come about that these two magnificent ships had appeared in Constantinople. The Empire had not then been at war, and all enlightened opinion was united in the belief that the Ottomans had to avoid another war at all costs.

At only 18 years of age on his arrival, Vahan could not have been aware of the menace implied by the guns of these two ships – but other more sophisticated observers certainly could.

Within a month of his arrival in Constantinople, he had managed to find himself a room in the home of a Greek family where he took lodgings and could enjoy his independence. But within three months, the *Goeben* and the *Breslau* battle cruisers, now renamed the *Sultan Selim* and the *Medilli*, had sallied out into the Black Sea and had bombarded the Crimean coastline under the Ottoman flag, but still commanded by the German Admiral Souchon. The two ships had demonstrated their power by arrogantly sailing outside Sevastopol itself, daring the weaker old pre-dreadnought Russian battleships to come out. Partly as a result of this, Turkey had been dragged into the war against Russia and the West. The entry of the Ottoman Empire into the Great War, had transformed a basically European war into the first World War.

Vahan finally gave up his musing, and ran to jump on a tram taking him to the University building to which he was heading. This was not the Music and Drama Department, but the military academy attached to the university to which he was now seconded. As a student in the university he had automatically become an officer in the Ottoman Army, and had to spend two mornings a week learning about the theory of warfare, and the esoteric art of drilling. It was all a lot of fun, and far removed from the stories of what appeared to be happening in Europe in the trenches of France. If he found it a bit odd that he was a citizen of an Empire that was fighting a war against countries he had always admired, he certainly did not let it worry him – that was life and he was prepared to fight if necessary, like everyone else. Did he but know it, it was a feeling that applied to millions of young men throughout Europe on all sides in that year of 1914-1915.

He was unaware, even now, of the effect that the two battle-cruisers standing high and proud in the waters of the Bosporus had already had on his life and those of countless others.

On his first day in the city, eight months ago, Vahan had eventually found his uncles. But it had soon become apparent to him that he simply could not stay with either of them. Family relationships and obligations were always paramount in Armenian culture, and neither uncle would have ever considered asking Vahan to stay anywhere else. However, they had their own lives and families to think about, and the relatively unknown Vahan would have been bound to be a strain. Finance was of course no problem. His father's contacts with the two or three carpet merchants of the city, with whom he had business arrangements, ensured that Vahan could collect the allowance arranged by Garabed regularly and without difficulty.

Accordingly, within a month of his arrival, Vahan had found lodgings on the Stamboul side of the city with a Greek family which appeared to have fallen on difficult times and who were looking for a lodger. The family owned a small but delightful old Ottoman house set in a quiet cul-de-sac in old Stamboul. This house overlooked the railway line running round the old sea walls, which led round below the Topkapi Palace and into Sirkeci station. It was not possible from even from the top storey of the house to see the Sea of Marmara, but it could be heard below on quiet evenings.

Having avoided all the Armenian families his uncles had suggested, he moved in with the Greek family after much searching. All this had been taking place during the crucial month of August 1914. Vahan was intelligent, well-educated and fully aware of what was then going on in Europe; however it was all far away, and none of it appeared to him to be half as important as the vital and absorbing matter of finding himself a suitable place to live.

The Patakis family consisted only of females. The family

comprised two daughters – Elena and Marisa; a heavy and overdressed mother Christina, and a formidable and sharp-tongued old grandmother. Christina's husband, the father of the two girls, had died recently, and it was his recent death, and the subsequent collapse of his retail business selling lokum and other sweets, that had resulted in the family having to take in a lodger.

Vahan had been brought up in a large, extended family with several sisters. Nevertheless, the somewhat puritanical atmosphere of provincial Armenian life in the country had left him without any experiences of dealing with girls of his own age. Marisa Patakis was only fifteen, but she was a bright and lively girl, aware of everything going on around her. Elena, five years older, was quite different. She was a heavy woman with thick, sensual lips, hooded languorous eyes and large well-developed breasts. She was dark, slow and ponderous, and highly sexed. She was immediately challenged by the arrival in the house of this young, shy and reserved Armenian boy from the provinces.

Vahan had arranged that he would take breakfast and the evening meal with the family, but that he would be out most of the day at the university. He was always punctilious in letting Christina know when he would not be at home for the evening meal. Father Komitas was reciting and lecturing on Armenian liturgical music in the city during those months, and Vahan, a student of music, often attended these evening recitals.

The day after his half-hour reverie on the bridge, Vahan raced downstairs, late for breakfast as usual. He didn't have to be at the university for a couple of hours, and relished, for once, a quiet lengthy breakfast by himself. Vahan sat and thought about the chats that had been taking place round the Patakis dinner table in those weeks before the Ottomans joined in the war. Marisa, always bubbling away with questions about the momentous events taking place around them; Elena, who couldn't say anything at all without some sort of sexual innuendo; Christina, who appeared to have her own agenda where the young Vahan was concerned; and the usually silent, but occasionally vituperative, old grandmother, always dressed in black, sitting toothlessly at the far end of the table.

It was nearly always Marisa who would start up a discussion about something she had heard that day at school. He recalled specifically the day he first heard about the German battleship – *Goeben*:

"Listen everybody – did you hear that the *Goeben* raised anchor this morning, sailed up the Bosphorus, and then stopped opposite the Russian Ambassador's new house – you know the one that used to be used as a summer house for the Khedive of Egypt. Well, it seems the ship turned round, broadside on to the road alongside. All the sailors stood in a line facing the house – took off their red fezzes – put on their German sailor's caps – and then sang 'Deutschland uber Alles' at the top of their voices. We heard that the Russian ambassador was furious, and put in an official complaint to the old Grand Vizier. Isn't it all absolutely priceless?"

"Oh dear! What could the poor old man do about it anyway," Christina asked. "Enver and Talaat decide everything that goes on nowadays, and they aren't going to raise a finger."

"What do you think, Vahan?" ignoring her mother, Marisa turned towards Vahan. "Will we go to war with Russia?"

"I don't know, Marisa, but it certainly looks more and more like it, but surely it would be a terrible mistake if we did. For centuries we've balanced Russia against France and Great Britain. Surely our present leaders wouldn't make the basic error of antagonising all three at the same time. No, no, surely not even our little Napoleon – Enver – would make that mistake, although heaven knows he has made just about every other possible mistake he could – the little jerk."

"Vahan," interjected Christina, "you really must be more careful how you speak about our current leaders, you can get into trouble."

"But, Vahan, although we won't have the French or English helping us this time, Germany will be with us, and they can deal with Russia far better than the others. There's always those two ships with those great guns sitting in the harbour – no stupid Russki is going to get past them," Marisa continued.

"But, for heaven's sake consider! Why should Turkey go to

war – what can we possibly gain?"

"Oh well, everyone else is tripping off gaily to war so why not us. The silly old Russians think that after this war, if they win, they're going to grab Constantinople – so wouldn't it be better to get the Germans to stop them."

Vahan chuckled to himself as he recalled all the conversations he'd had along these lines during those fateful months leading up to the fatal entry into the war of the Empire. But then he remembered the very last dinner before the arrival in the house of André Tarkowski. Once again the conversation had been about whether to enter the War or not.

"Vahan, by the way, what do you say," Elena had interrupted, clearly bored by the discussion, "will you come with me to Church on Sunday? Afterwards, we can walk to the Square and have a sherbet or something."

"Marisa – just think about it." **Vahan**, trying to ignore Elena's remark and instead start up a general conversation, "The Russians would only be able to grab the City if we made the mistake of abandoning our neutrality."

"Vahan, you never answered – are you going to come with me on Sunday or not? You know you haven't even been to your own church once, since you've been here – so why don't you accompany me to mine?"

"Er ... " Vahan had mumbled looking down at his plate, as Elena grumbled on at him, trying to catch his gaze.

"I'm not much of a church-goer," he continued lamely, not having the courage to answer firmly that he was fast losing the simple faith of his mother each day that he remained in this town, the centre of so many different faiths.

Christina was well aware of Elena's interest in Vahan, and was happy to join her daughter in ensnaring this young man, despite her being at least two years older than him. With Elena now dowry-less, and getting on, she worried about her future. Here was a young man who clearly had a good allowance from his provincial parents, and who in any case was registered at the prestigious University. She pulled at his slender arm to get his attention and fixed her black eyes on him.

"Yes, Vahan, I would be most grateful if you could accompany Elena to church on Sunday, as I have to take Marisa to meet her aunt, and clearly Elena must have an escort."

Vahan sat there at the empty breakfast table musing on the fact that he had then started mumbling again, but had known when he was beaten. He had realised that he really could not get out of it. He recalled that he had nodded, and then turning to Marisa had burst out with some political opinions which had been simmering in him for some time. He somehow found himself giving in to youthful enthusiasm in front of a group of people who really could not have cared less about his passionately held, if somewhat confused, views about nationalism and the dangers of abandoning their multi-racial Empire for a string of intolerant nation-states.

Vahan recalled how they had all looked at him, surprised at his vehemence, as if he had been giving a lecture. His feelings of inadequacy at having failed to parry Elena and her mother's manipulation, to which he had tamely submitted, probably prompted his outburst. At this point the old grandmother had got up and turned to Vahan.

"And that, my dear young man, is the view of a person who belongs to a people who have no hope of ever achieving a nation-state of their own in the first place. Sour grapes, my lad – sour grapes! It's the sort of talk the Jews here in this city indulge in".

Vahan watched the retreating back of the spiteful old lady and whispered, half to himself.

"Well, you never know, even the Jews might create a nation-state for themselves one day – the question then will only be whether or not it will end up the same as all the others, with the same intolerance and exclusivity."

The old lady, always capable of hearing even the quietest words when she wanted to, turned and snapped back at the increasingly anxious and confused Vahan, who was not used to speaking like this to his elders –

"That comment, young man, applies equally to any tin-pot nation-state that your lot might one day manage to create." And with that she had sailed out.

The very next day, Christina having previously announced that the other attic room opposite Vahan's had now been let, the new lodger – André Tarkowski – had arrived at the house.

André turned out to be a Pole from Germany. He was a slim handsome young man, five years older than Vahan, with fair hair and grey eyes, with a slight military bearing. Vahan never really discovered what he was doing or where he came from. André never denied that he was a German citizen, Vahan presumed that he must either be in some sort of government employ, or a deserter or conscientious objector. He had turned up with two cheap suitcases, one of which remained locked and unopened under his bed. There was, in addition, an unusual tin case, also left locked under the bed.

Sitting alone drinking his tea, he laughed out loud as he recalled how Elena had almost immediately transferred her attentions from the shy Armenian boy to the confident Polish man. Right from the start this had let him off the hook. Even though he was presumably a Catholic, André had duly accompanied Elena that first Sunday to the Church, instead of Vahan. He had been escorting her on and off on a similar basis for the next few weeks.

André had exuded sexuality in every movement of his eyes and body. He and Elena, without any great objections from the complaisant Christina, often stayed out late. Their heavy flirtation took over the household, leaving Marisa confused and silent. For his part, Vahan was fascinated and overawed by André. He was the first Catholic and Westerner that Vahan had ever come to know at all intimately. He used to come wandering into Vahan's room across the corridor in the evenings after getting back from being out with Elena. He would talk about general subjects, never politics or his own past. In particular he would chat about girls and life in the great European cities, while Vahan listened with rapt attention.

One evening, arriving late from a Komitas recital, Vahan surprised Elena and André in the little space between the two rooms at the top of the staircase. They were passionately embracing, and André's hand was hidden somewhere around what Vahan could not help but see was Elena's dishevelled skirt.

Both of them turned and stared at him as he came up the narrow stairs. Vahan had had no idea where to look or what to say. His somewhat puritanical nature made him deeply embarrassed. They, on the other hand, did not appear to be the slightest bit put out and made no effort to hide the circumstances in which they had been found. Vahan had mumbled 'goodnight' and slipped past them into his room.

That night, as he was undressing, André had come barging into Vahan's room – his eyes alight with sexual mischief and violence. "You're a virgin, aren't you, Vahan?" You've never been with any kind of woman, have you? Good heavens, I bet you haven't even kissed a girl yet." André laughed out loud, whilst the half-naked Vahan stared back mutely.

"Oh, for heavens sake don't look so solemn – laugh, man, laugh. You're a good kid and I like you. You'll be all right one day. Look, have a look at this."

He pulled out two passports – both of which had recently been issued by the British Embassy. Still unsure what was going on, Vahan saw that one appeared to be in the name of André Tarkowski, and the other in the name of Elena Patakis. Vahan remembered the shock he had felt, and his sheer incapacity to understand what was going on.

"Elena and I are leaving very early tomorrow morning from Haydar Pasha station for Jerusalem, from where we are going to go on to Egypt."

Vahan had just stood and stared at him shivering slightly as he was without shirt or vest. André, eyes glittering with sly malice and a hint of sadistic pleasure, had suddenly grabbed hold of him and drawing him close up to his body he had kissed him fully, passionately and violently, on his lips, holding the astonished Vahan tight against him for several seconds. Then with a laugh he had pushed him back onto the bed, and strode out.

Vahan had never seen either him or Elena again.

That next morning, after a night in which Vahan had scarcely slept, and during which he had heard his neighbour slipping downstairs, Christina, looking like an old woman, with her dark eyes red from weeping, had come up and cleared the room opposite, saying not a word to Vahan. She had broken open the cheap suitcase under the bed, and dragged it down, but the tin case had disappeared. Vahan had offered to help, but had been waved away. As he glanced at the half-open case as she dragged it down, he had noticed that it seemed to contain a German naval uniform.

Three weeks later the *Goeben* and the *Breslau* had sailed into the Black Sea and Turkey had entered the War.

Vahan finished his tea, called out 'goodbye' to the now always quiet and subdued Christina in the kitchen, and left for the University.

CHAPTER 3

The family of Dr. Nazim Kemal

By 8 o'clock on this same early April morning, the Galata district, on the north side of Halic – the Golden Horn, was already teeming with the hustle and bustle of crowds walking up the hill from the Galata Bridge. Businessmen and merchants of all kinds walked briskly to their offices off the hooting ferries arriving at the quays below the bridge.

Doctor Nazim Kemal lived in a modern flat at the top of the road that led up from the bridge towards the Grande Rue de Pera. A sparse, thin man with a sharp, well-groomed moustache, he worked in the German Hospital at Siraselviler in Beyoglu, not far from Taksim and well within walking distance of his flat. This morning, as always, he was carefully shaving himself.

Nazim considered himself to be at the forefront of the modernising influences at work in the Empire. Like almost everyone else in the city – Turk, Jew, Greek or Armenian – he had welcomed the Ittihad Revolution of 1908, when the more exuberant of the citizens had gathered in the streets and danced together, regardless of their racial background. Nazim had not deemed it proper to join in such exhibitionist behavior, but he had not objected when his eldest son Selim – then 13 years-old – had asked to be allowed to join in with the happy crowds in the streets.

Things had gone badly wrong since that early, confident start. The detestable Abdul Hamid had been forced to abdicate, but not before there had been several coups and counter-coups. The loss of yet more Christian provinces during the two Balkan wars, had resulted in an ugly and confused mood amongst the normally tolerant Ottoman elite of the city.

A month earlier, Nazim, with a group of like-minded friends in a literary circle, loosely referred to as the Liberal Book Club, had decided to organise an evening of music and poetry. Nazim had a deep loyalty to the ideal of tolerance of the old Ottoman Empire, and had persuaded his friends that this recital should not only include the great Turkish poets and singers, but should also be representative of the other minorities in the Empire – the Greeks and Armenians on the one hand, and even the Arabs on the other.

The Club had contacted figures in the new government, who had all expressed enthusiasm. The new rulers saw this as a way of promoting specifically Turkish national identity, as opposed to the cosmopolitanism of the old Ottoman Empire – a multi-ethnicism which the new government were, in fact, planning to repudiate. Accordingly they were not so happy with the suggestion that there might be some Greek or Armenian input into the concert. From the start, there was a contradiction between the ideals of Nazim and his associates, and the Young Turk government.

As far as their international profile was concerned, the Ittihad leaders accepted that a concert and recital of this sort would be seen as a good example of the fresh modern outlook fostered by the new government. Ironically, modernizers like Nazim and his friends, were much closer in spirit to the tolerant Ottoman Sultans of the past.

Nazim had worked hard on the details of this celebration of the diverse cultures of the empire. At the opening of the concert he had stood at the entrance to the hall as the guests arrived, welcoming the many dignitaries of the Ittihad party currently running the government, including Talaat Bey himself, in addition to two elderly Ottoman princes and numerous writers, poets and Muslim dignitaries. The Greeks were largely absent, but dotted around the hall were several Armenians, including the four current Armenian Members of Parliament, together with the Ambassadors of the allied powers of Germany and Austria.

As Nazim continued to muse on the evening concert, his hand uncharacteristically slipped a little, and he winced as his razor cut into his chin too deeply and a small scar appeared. He tut-tutted impatiently – he hated any blemish on his person – but continued shaving.

One of the minority performers, whom it had been Nazim's task to persuade to attend was the Armenian priest – Father Komitas – who was currently working at the Armenian Church in Galata, where he was re-organising and improving the choir. Nazim knew that Komitas had for many years been working on the collation and transcription of Armenian folk songs collected from all over the highlands of Eastern Anatolia. He had also worked on the core of Armenian medieval church music, rewriting a lot of the old musical liturgy in modern notation.

Komitas had only just returned from a trip to Berlin. There he had attended, almost daily, performances of Wagner's music at the Opera House. He had met and made friends with a German colleague friend of Nazim, with whom he had found a common interest in Wagner's music. Komitas was unable to talk freely with other Armenians about such a secular preference as this love of Wagner. Already the Armenian National Church Assembly had published a biting criticism of the mild and gentle Komitas in a Constantinople journal, with the following words amongst many other adverse comments-

"Father Komitas has in addition commercialised and popularised sacred songs and dirges of the Holy Armenian Church, and we ask the leaders of the Church severely to reprimand him for this disgraceful behaviour".

Nazim, who like any other intellectual in Constantinople was well aware of all this ferment in the Armenian press, had found this all faintly amusing. He prided himself on his own secular attitudes. However, he was not an atheist, and he certainly admired and even loved the simple virtues of Islam, even though he could not bring himself to the fever-pitch of his humbler compatriots.

For Nazim, the tolerant nature of the old Ottoman Empire, multi-cultural and open to all talents within the Empire, was the ideal to which he would have liked the new state to aspire. He despised both the passions aroused by religion on the one hand, and the nationalistic fervour of the teachers and rabble-rousers on the other. His weakness was his failure to understand the power that these feelings had on other people.

The cultural evening had gone well. The introduction of the pale and sad-looking Komitas had been a masterpiece of modern liberal Turkish sentiment. The Armenians had been referred to as a people who had always been on the frontier of Turkish cultural life, and it had ended with the words -

"These are the people with and amongst whom we have lived for centuries".

Komitas had then sat at the piano and sang and played his mainly melancholy songs. Nazim recalled that the Hall had reverberated with ovations and applause. The old Turkish phrase – "May Allah save him from all evil eyes" rang out from all sides.

Nazim grinned to himself at the recollection. Many of his Christian acquaintances had come up to congratulate him on the part he had played in arranging the evening. How could these people, he thought, spend so much time and energy, and even violence, on their interminable discussions about the nature of their prophet – Jesus Christ. Nazim may have been a liberal intellectual, but he still found it difficult to comprehend what he thought of as a typically Greek attitude to life and philosophy. His mind contrasted the subtle Greek concept of 'three-in-one' godhead with the simple pure tenets of his own father's faith. To think that the Armenians and Greeks – to him simply infidels together – were insuperably separated by an argument stretching back centuries, as to whether the nature of the Son was 'similar to' or 'the same as' the Father. The whole argument seemed to him to be utterly ludicrous.

Nazim laughed out loud at his thoughts. He was disconcerted as his son Selim, now a young man of 20, poked his head round the door –

"What's funny, baba"

"Nothing, nothing my son – just a recollection. Are you ready."

"Yes father – I'm just going. I will be home late this evening, as I'm doing some extra study with a friend. I've told Mama. Good bye."

Nazim nodded. His decision not to send Selim to the old Sultan Abdul Mecit University in Bayazit, but to the American College – Robert College – in the north of the city seemed to him to have been a success. Selim was growing up with modern, liberal ideas, but did not appear to have rejected any of the old values which Nazim still felt were important.

Nazim finished all his morning rituals and went down to join his wife Halideh for breakfast.

"Husband, come, your tea is ready. Selim has already left. I sent him upstairs to say goodbye to you."

Nazim grunted and began on his usual breakfast of thin Stambouli bread, olives and cheese and weak tea. He eyed Halideh, who was clearly anxious to tell him something important, though not wanting to disturb his first mouthfuls. He showed her sympathetically that he was ready to listen.

"Husband of mine, I am worried about Selim. I do believe that your decision to send him to that infidel College was a great gamble. Who knows what immoral ideas he will pick up there. Yesterday he told me that he and a group of his friends had sat and had a little picnic in the College grounds with some of the young girl students. Nazim, it seems they talked together for about two hours. Nazim, my lord, what self-respecting girl would stoop to such a thing."

Nazim said nothing, continuing to eat his breakfast, and

extending his glass for another tea. However, he was listening carefully. Halideh took a breath and continued –

" I understand that they all spoke together, seven or eight boys and about six girls. Can you believe it? He tells me they spoke about the war, and how badly Enver Pasha's offensives in the Caucasus had been managed. Nazim, listen, they actually openly criticized our government. I suppose I don't mind that so much, though it could be dangerous – but above all what sort of girls are they to talk so freely with young men."

"Halideh, my beloved one, once I made the decision to send Selim to a western-style College, I accepted that that decision must necessarily expose him to many different influences. I, also, believe that Enver and the others in the Ittihad party are driving this country fatally in the wrong political and moral direction, so I really have no concern if this turns out to be the view held by Selim and his friends. However, my beloved, I agree that he should be more careful about publicly voicing his criticisms, and I will certainly warn him about this tonight."

"But Nazim, you have said nothing of this disgraceful mixing of the sexes."

"I agree that unsupervised contact between impressionable young men and women could be dangerous, but it is not our daughter who is involved, and I have every faith in the good sense and honour of our son. He will not be tempted into any wrong-doing, of that I am quite certain. Meanwhile, my beloved, please do not be anxious about our own young girl. I have no intention whatsoever of sending her to any of these smart modern Western schools, and on this point I will surely follow your preferences, if I can."

Rising from his seat, Nazim saluted his wife, and stepped out into the busy street, heading for the Hospital.

Selim, Nazim's son, was a tall young man of 20, with broad shoulders and powerful rather long arms. He had black curly hair which he let grow long. He was dark and swarthy and had difficulty controlling stubble on his chin, often shaving twice during the day. He had deep-set black eyes, which usually looked out rather sleepily from under thick eyebrows. Like all the other students, he sported the usual Enver-style moustache. He never wore a fez or a hat. Whilst the father was one of the few men in Stamboul who was always completely clean-shaven, the son was one of the few who always went around without any head covering

Selim was peripherally aware of the enormous political issues facing the Empire in which he lived. Like any educated Turk, he resented the humiliations imposed on the Ottomans as a result of the recent Balkan Wars. However, he and his friends had not been directly affected. These wars had been fought as always by the patient long-suffering Anatolian peasants, led by inefficient and effete Stambouli officers. What could you expect?

Only the day before, Selim and his father had had one of their long discussions at the family breakfast table over the direction the Turkish state was currently taking.

"Father, you must admit that now that all our European Empire has been lost, probably for ever, there are no longer as many Christians as Turks. Don't you think that the state should now concentrate on its Turkish identity, rather than continuing to try to be all things to all men, by retaining its multi-national character."

"My son, what you say sounds logical, but what about all the Greeks and Armenians still left in Anatolia, and who have been there as long as we have – what about all the Arabs who have lived under Ottoman rule, benign or otherwise for centuries. At least they haven't spent their time murdering each other during the time that the Ottomans have been the dominant power."

"Oh, Baba – forget about the Arabs – they're no problem, they're irrelevant as far as we're concerned. I often think that it would be a good idea if we abolished the Caliphate. It's an anomaly in this modern world – it's an old-fashioned Arab concept that hinders rather than helps us. We are a vibrant Turkish people – what need do we have for this ancient Arab institution."

"My dear boy, even if you are right about removing the title of Caliph from our Sultan, be careful of what you may find taking its place. By having a Caliph – old-fashioned concept though it may be – our faith did at least contrive to respect a single head. Even if sometimes it has proved a broken reed, it has acted as a restraining force on extremists, fundamentalists and crackpots, claiming to have some sort of divine revelation for whatever happens to be their current brand of murderous ideology."

"Well father, let the crackpots get on with it. What we want here is a Turkish state which happens to be mainly Moslem, rather than a Moslem state that happens to be mainly Turkish."

"Well put, my boy, well put. But the original Ottomans were not like either of those. What we had, until the odious Abdul Hamid ruined it all, was a universal empire based on geography and economic convenience, which tried to accommodate many different people, many different customs and many different religions. It may have been somewhat inefficient, but it did at least prevent people trying to eliminate each other in the name of some religious or national unity."

"Father, I know that you disapprove of the current direction that the Ittihad rulers are taking – I know you don't like their exclusive nationalism – but, baba, the Empire is dying, and we must start thinking of putting something new in its place. A state should be based on a 'people' – in this case Turkish."

"Beware, my son, of the passions of the 'people' when they are aroused as a tribal force. However, my loved one, you give me much to ponder over, and your points are well put and clear."

Like any thoughtful father, Nazim broke off the discussion, leaving his eager son the full honours of the argument. He disagreed with Selim, much more fundamentally than he had admitted, but he recognised the factor of his own slightly world-weary conservatism, and above all he had no desire to squash his son's enthusiasms in any way.

As a young lad, Selim had gathered enthusiastically with his friends in the streets persuading passers-by to donate their paras and odd coins to the collection for the purchase of the two Dreadnoughts, intended to recreate Ottoman seapower in the Eastern Mediterranean. But whether he was collecting for the glory of the multi-ethnic Ottoman Empire, of which he was a citizen, or for a new Turkish nation state, which seemed to be emerging from the Ittihad party line, he could not have said.

The people had raised the money by popular subscription to build these two ships in British shipyards. Agents had gone from house to house painfully collecting small sums of money. There had been entertainments and fairs all over the country, and women had sold their hair for the benefit of the common fund. These two ships therefore represented an outburst of popular feeling, affecting every community, that was unusual in the Empire.

The Ottoman Empire was not Turkish in the way that France was French or Germany German. The Ottoman ruling class, all born and bred in Stamboul, were Turkish only in that they knew and spoke Ottoman Turkish – itself a literary and upper-class language somewhat different to the common Turkish spoken on the Anatolian farms. The very word 'turk' was often used pejoratively by these well-born pashas, to refer to the simple Anatolian peasants of the interior, the cannon-fodder of the old Ottoman armies

Yet in these proudly collected pennies, like everything in those last few years of the Ottoman Empire, there was a fatal paradox. For whom did all these eager people think that these two great ships were being built – the Muslim Caliphate – a nationalistic new Turkish state – or the old Ottoman Empire?

An immense anger had swept over Selim and his friends during August 1914, when they heard that the British government, far away on the other side of Europe, had impounded the two battleships. This confiscation had been carried out by an anxious British government at the very moment the bill had been fully paid with the hard-earned pennies of ordinary people, and at the very moment when Turkish crews had already arrived in England to take over the completed ships. In the long run, it had been a terrible mistake on the part of the British. The British fleet was already immeasurably superior to the German, and two dreadnoughts, more or less, could not have made any great difference. Yet, as always when war loomed, alleged military concerns took precedence over what was likely to become a diplomatic disaster.

Unlike the masses throughout Western Europe, the young men of the Ottoman Empire were not bellicose nor did they look upon war with 'excitement'. Turkey had been at war, on and off, for several years already. Ottoman youths were much more aware of the dreadful side of modern warfare than their French, English or German counterparts.

On the 10th August 1914, just before Selim was about to start at Robert College, the two great German battleships -the *'Goeben* and the *Breslau* had passed through the Dardanelles and anchored in the Bosporus opposite the Dolmabahce Palace. Selim had never realized for a moment how these two ships were going to have such a profound effect on him and his contemporaries. Above all, when he heard that in order to maintain their neutrality the two ships had been "sold" by the German government to the Sultan, and had been renamed the *Sultan Selim*, and the *Medilli*, complete with their full crew, he fell about with all his friends in exuberant joy, enjoying the embarrassed discomfiture and objections of the British Ambassador, all of which had been fully reported in the Press.

Actually for once, it did not matter whether you were a youthful Turkish student, or a young Greek or Armenian one. The 'one in the eye' delivered by the government to the arrogant British Empire gave everyone an immense satisfaction. This seemed to be the first time for years that Constantinople had dared to stand up to the Westerners. The fact that Turkey had virtually tied itself to an alternative Western power, Germany, was overlooked.

On the day of the announcement of the 'sale', the students flocked to the road along the waterfront and saw the German sailors parading, each with a fez on their heads, and with the Sultan's emblem at the masthead. They cheered and cheered, but with no idea as to how or why the ships had got there in the first place, nor what it would mean to them in the long run.

Selim knew that his father belonged to the school of thought which believed strongly that the Empire should stay out of the war. "Let them get on with killing each other – why should we care if one *giavour* beats up another *giavour*" was his continual refrain. Nazim's feelings were of course more complex than that, but it was what he said to his son, and Selim and his friends basically agreed.

In November 1914, whilst Selim was enjoying every moment of his new life at the College, the two great ships sailed out of the Bosporus, and into the Black Sea, where they totally dominated the old-fashioned Russian fleet which had no ship which could even match the *Breslau*, never mind the superb *Goeben*. The Crimean coast was bombarded, and the Ottoman Empire found itself at war with Russia and the Western Powers, and in alliance with Germany and Austria. The ability of a few German sailors, the failure of the British and their much-vaunted fleet to stop them, and the amateurish arrogance of the Young Turk leaders, had succeeded in pushing the empire into a lethal death-struggle, which the wisdom of traditional Ottoman statesmen had always managed to avert for over a hundred years. The unthinkable had at last happened. The one fatal error that generations of old Pashas and Viziers – Greek, Albanian and Turkish – had studiously avoided, namely a simultaneous war with Russia and the western maritime powers, had come to pass.

But it had hardly yet affected Selim at all. The ambitious, dapper Enver Pasha had gone off to the Caucasus, with an army largely still composed of Anatolian recruits and officered by the old Regular Army officers. Everyone, the old Sultan, the German attaché and most of the Ottoman elite, had advised strongly against a winter campaign in that terrible terrain. But the arrogant Enver had overridden them all, as he had at each critical step throughout the year, and had led the army to a major disaster.

But Selim's mind was on none of these matters as he ran down the street, having just left his father shaving. All he could think of was the meeting he had arranged with a girl from the

American Girl's College whom he had met during a recent picnic. He simply could not get her out of his mind. He had been shy at meeting all these girls, several of whom were clearly not Muslims. But this girl – he only knew then that her name was Olga – had looked at him with her huge dark eyes, and had smiled so naturally and warmly that his heart had turned over, and he had almost cried out with a feeling of tenderness.

He had discovered after they had all separated, that her name was Olga Avakian, which meant that she must be an Armenian – but what was that to him. Through another student at the College he had met her fleetingly again, inevitably in yet another large group, and they had actually exchanged a few words, painful in their banality.

However, today on this glorious first day of April, he was going to ask her to meet him again at some future date at Tokatlian's for tea, after the end of the usual college day – he, at any rate, proposing to be on his own. The butterflies in his stomach at the thought of this proposed invitation were worse than any he had previously had in anticipation of a childhood punishment or an academic test. He didn't know how he was going to get through the rest of the day – though of course he did.

CHAPTER 4

Harry and his father

The whole question of the arrival in Constantinople of the two German battle cruisers at the start of the War, was at this moment, on this same first day of April, in the forefront of Lieutenant Harry Bridgeman's mind. He was currently stationed at the Admiralty, employed in the process of analysing, in depth, the reasons for the recent failures of the British Navy. This research was needed as evidence in the forthcoming court-martial of those commanders, who were ostensibly responsible. His work was based both on his own recollections, having been present at the very first contact with the two ships, as well as on a series of documents surrounding the incident.

It was an equally bright spring morning in London, when Harry Bridgeman left his parents' house in Chelsea and strode off to his work at the Admiralty. Harry was a product of the public school system and Oxford, where the children of the confident English upper-middle classes were marked out for one of the Guards' regiments. However, his sharp mathematical brain, and his own inclinations, led him instead towards the Navy. He had tentatively put his views to his intimidating father – Colonel William Bridgeman – where he met considerable opposition. Despite this, in his own more diffident way, Harry was as obstinate as his father, and had stood up to him each time the subject was broached.

Harry was an only son. The Colonel had harrumphed and blustered, and the discussions had gone on between them, usually at the breakfast table in their small suburban house in West London. His father would get red in the face and start shouting at him to the effect that the Bridgemans had always gone into the Guards. He would emphatically declare that he could get Harry into any regiment he might choose – but it had to be the army, as he had no influence in Navy circles.

Inevitably, Harry would reply that he was not cut out to be a Guards officer, claiming that he was more of a technician, and his interests were more scientific. Above all, he was sure that he would be no good in the cut and thrust of army life.

And so it would go on, over and over and round in circles, with the Colonel calling on family history, and Harry stubbornly and quietly resisting. In the end, the Colonel had referred his problem to a member of his club, a respected acquaintance.

"Look, Smithson, I am at my wit's end with my son Harry. What the blazes are children coming to these days. I wouldn't have dreamt of contradicting my father on a matter of such importance. I really can't understand him at all. You know that the Bridgemans have always been in the army – now the little idiot wants to go into the Navy – the Navy damn it – I've no influence there at all, and it goes against one hundred years of tradition."

"My dear Sir," the urbane Smithson replied, "you should consider yourself lucky. Harry might easily have ended up wanting to be a poet or something. Could you have coped with that? Look man, he does at least want to go into one of the services. God, he might even have wanted to go into the teaching profession. Think of the horror of that old chap. Let him do as he wants, and be thankful."

William Bridgeman was an unnervingly direct man, without any doubts about his own opinions or of what was right or wrong in the world around him, but he was not stupid. He immediately saw the sense of his friend's point, but he wasn't going to give in that easily, so made Harry repeat his arguments for a little longer, until he finally, and grumpily, conceded.

Harry was 24 years old, tall, somewhat angular, with rather dreamy soft blue eyes, which belied his sharp brain when he felt like using it. He respected his father but he also feared him, and looked to his gentle, and somewhat careworn, mother, for expressions of parental love. Harry didn't have a sister, and like so many of his class and time, he had as little contact with the opposite sex, as a young man of his age would have had in the Muslim East.

Harry was outwardly conformist. He had excelled at sports at his minor public school and had been fairly popular with his peers. He had often been invited to the large house parties of the period, and had little difficulty mixing with his contemporaries, but he never invited any of these friends back to his parents' own modest house. He knew how to behave towards others in the way they expected with impeccably good manners, without pretension or hypocrisy, and though he could occasionally surprise his peers by quoting poetry or expressing some alarmingly liberal views, he had no difficulty in keeping up his 'good chap' image. Lacking the arrogance to impose his own view of life on others, he simply did not have the confidence to act in any other way than conformity.

So far everything he had done at school or at university, all that he had tried to be in his 'public' life, was an attempt to win his father's approval. He was not consciously aware of this. He would lie awake at nights wondering why neither his mother's unstinting love, nor the fact that he had many good friends, all of whom in their way loved and respected him, was ever quite enough.

Harry was in awe of his father, plucking up the courage to contradict him as he grew older. It never occurred to him that what he craved, his father was incapable of giving. Harry was forever hoping for his father's approval, that he would be a source of pride to his father, but more than this, he wanted his father's love.

William Bridgeman, on the other hand, believed that bringing up a son required that the boy respect him and learn to be self-sufficient, and to that end, he should show no vulnerability of any kind, particularly to an eldest son. Over the course of his life, he had scarcely ever said the words "I love you" to anyone – not even to his own mother or his wife. Only his wife knew that secretly, and only on rare occasions – when Harry was a young boy – William Bridgeman would steal upstairs, stare down at his sleeping son, and give him a light kiss on the forehead – tip-toeing away, fearful that Harry might awake, catching him in this moment of weakness.

Harry's step, on this bright spring day, was brisk and his spirit was undimmed by the depressing news of the stalemate on the Western Front. He avoided the Underground, preferring to walk all the way to work. On this April morning – the first day of sunshine since the end of the winter – he recalled the crowds on this very route, on that gloriously sunny day in August 1914 when war was declared. The crowds had surged up and down in an ecstasy of patriotic fervour and delight. The war would be over in a few months. Meanwhile what a joy it was for all these eager young men to embark on the greatest adventure of the century – leaving behind the drudgery of their boring daily lives.

For once the ordinary people – the so-called man and woman in the street – were well ahead of their leaders in the cry for battle. This was never a matter of old men frivolously putting the lives of the young in jeopardy, a myth to be fostered in a later and more cynical age, but of young men and women impatiently urging their elders on. It was all very well for Sir Edward Grey to stare bleakly out of the windows of the Foreign Office, and mutter about 'lamps going out all over Europe', but Harry and his friends had been in high spirits at the thought of flexing their muscles in a stirring camaraderie of danger and honour.

Harry grinned to himself as he strolled on to work – what was it that his friend, the young poet Rupert Brooke, had written. He considered and then recited to himself as he walked on –

"Now, God be thanked who has matched us with His hour,
And caught our youth, and wakened us from sleeping,
With hand made sure, clear eye, and sharpened power,
To turn, as swimmers into cleanness leaping,
Glad from a world grown old and cold and weary,
Leave the sick hearts that honour could not move,
And half-men, and their dirty songs and dreary,
And all the little emptiness of love." *

Harry was only three years younger than Brooke, and had himself met the young poet, having several friends who were mutual acquaintances. He had found Brooke to be not only an extraordinarily handsome young man, but also intensely witty and alive. Brooke had marked left-wing sympathies, and this had disconcerted Harry's circle. However, his youthful, exuberant patriotism had endeared him to all sections of the social class to which they all belonged.

Harry was not due at his office in the Admiralty before 9.30, even though there was a war on. He decided to sit for a few moments in St. James' Park and watch the ducks whilst he reflected on the report he was compiling on the unfortunate event that had occurred in the first few days of the War in the Mediterranean, a failure of the Royal Navy that was destined to become one of the few really decisive moments of the Great War. His task was to put the events into perspective from his own personal involvement and that of the central office of the

Admiralty, for submission to the forthcoming Court Martial.

He was understandably nervous about this task, as he had come to the conclusion that his superiors at the Admiralty were themselves partly to blame for the predicament which had been so badly handled by the men on the spot. He was reflecting, of course, on the escape of the two German battle cruisers – the *Goeben* and the *Breslau* – and the failure of the Navy to catch them before they finally arrived in Constantinople and by so doing, altering the course of the war.

On his arrival at the office, waiting for him on his desk, Henry found a copy of a memorandum – marked Top Secret – clearly written some time ago by Sir Thomas Hankey, the Secretary to the War Cabinet, and addressed to the War Council. It read:

"The remarkable deadlock which has occurred in the Western Theatre of War invites consideration of the question whether some other outlet can be found for the employment of our forces. In the Western Front any advance must be costly and slow. Days are required to capture a single line of trenches – the losses are heavy, and as often as not the enemy recaptures his lost ground on the next day. Any gains are negligible. Moreover, the advance is so slow that the enemy has time to prepare fresh lines of defense to his rearguard. Germany can surely be struck most effectively, and with the most lasting results for the peace of the world, through her allies, and particularly through Turkey. We could, without in any way endangering our position in France, devote three Army Corps to a campaign in Turkey. This should surely be sufficient to capture Constantinople. The capture of this city would force Turkey out of the war, and in addition we would then be in a position to supply Russia directly with all the goods and exchange she so desperately needs, and which is causing such unrest and hardship there."

Attached to this was a note scribbled by Harry's immediate superior in rather poor handwriting –

"Harry! Jack Fisher has asked me to pass this highly confidential memorandum on to you, as he thinks that you ought to bear it in mind when preparing your own report on the *Goeben* and the *Breslau*. The court martial proceedings are not of course interested directly in the far-reaching results of Troubridge's failure, but Jack thought you ought to be aware of the way current official circles are thinking, so far as this area of the war is concerned.

Incidentally, Harry, Jack has also indicated that he has had enough formal reports from many people in respect of this matter, and he would therefore like your comments to be entirely informal and a pure reflection of your own personal experience. Attach any other documents separately."

Harry cleared his desk – completed once more his monthly request to be posted back to an active station – then sat down to write out the final draft of his report on the decisive events of the previous August.

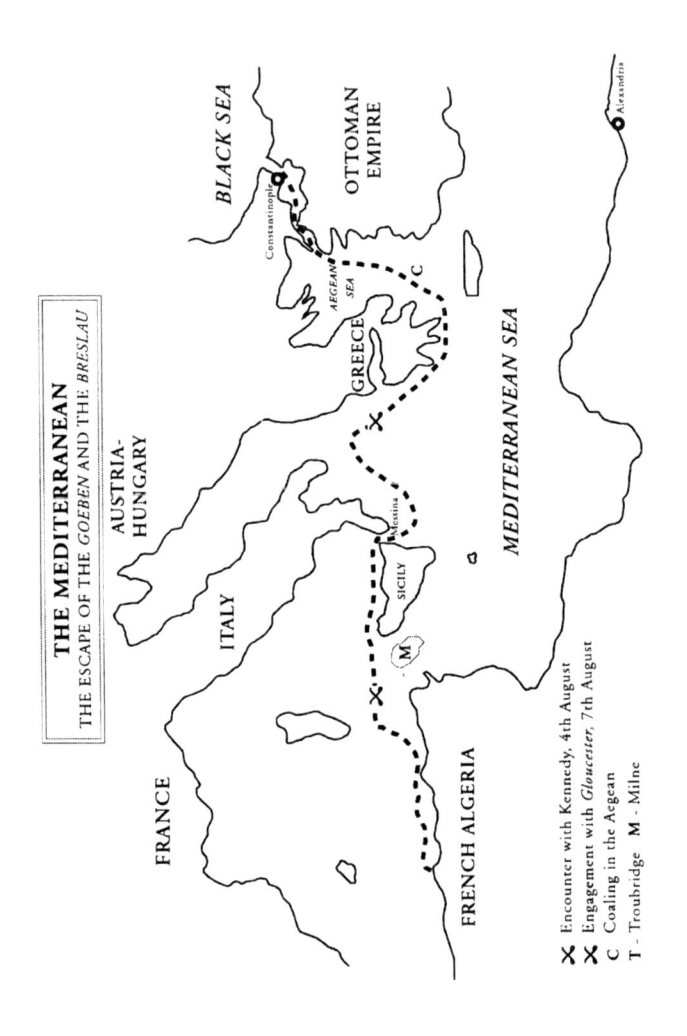

THE MEDITERRANEAN
THE ESCAPE OF THE *GOEBEN* AND THE *BRESLAU*

✗ Encounter with *Kennedy*, 4th August
✗ Engagement with *Gloucester*, 7th August
C Coaling in the Aegean
T - Troubridge   M - Milne

CHAPTER 5

Harry's Report

At the time of the events on which I have been asked to give a personal report, I was stationed on HMS *Indefatigable*, a cruiser commanded by Captain Kennedy. In those first few days of August 1914, we were all aware of the growing tensions in Europe arising from the assassination of the Archduke Franz Ferdinand in Sarajevo.

It was not, however, clear to us, even though we were in touch with the Admiralty through the radio, exactly what our priorities were in the Mediterranean area. Indeed on that first critical day of the 4th August 1914, we were not even sure who we were at war with, if anyone at all.

What we did know was that the powerful German 'dreadnought' type battle cruiser, the *Goeben*, accompanied by its sister ship the *Breslau*, was cruising in the Mediterranean, commanded by the experienced Admiral Souchon. Captain Kennedy had remarked to me on the previous evening, when we heard that an ultimatum had been sent to Germany, that the *Goeben* was undoubtedly the most powerful ship at present in the whole Mediterranean.

On the morning of the 4th August we heard that the *Goeben* and *Breslau* had appeared outside the ports of Phillipeville and Bone in Algeria. Both these harbours were the embarkation ports for the French army stationed in Algeria, an army which was destined to be slotted into the Western front for the vital first two months of the War. Everyone believed that these first few weeks would be decisive, and the Admiralty had conveyed to Sir Berkely Milne – the admiral commanding the whole Mediterranean fleet – that his priority must be to give help to the French Fleet covering the crucial convoys of troops from Algeria to France.

So, that evening, commanded by Captain Kennedy, and with the *Indomitable* alongside, we were sailing fast due west, with orders to help cover the French convoys, and later to block the

Straits of Gibraltar to prevent the *Goeben* and *Breslau* from escaping into the Atlantic. As we sailed west to the setting sun, we suddenly sighted the two German ships sailing straight toward us due east. I was on the bridge, next to Captain Kennedy, as the four ships moved inexorably towards each other.

"Sir – My God, it's the *Goeben* and the *Breslau*," I called out as I studied the approaching ships through the binoculars.

To the cry of "Action Stations", the gun crews swung into position below us as the Alarm bells rang out all over the ship. The rest of the crew also moved briskly to their required locations in the event of hostilities. The whole ship went into a heightened state of alert as everyone became aware that this might well be the first shots of the war.

Captain Kennedy waited calmly, once the ship was fully ready for action, and we watched carefully as the two ships came closer. We knew we were now within range of the *Goeben's* guns, while our own guns still required minutes to be effectively deployed. Neither flotilla altered their direction in any way, and, on present course, would pass each other about half a mile apart.

"Sir, what are your orders? Shall I ready the Gunnery Master?"

"Look, Lieutenant, we have to be very careful. This could be a decisive moment. We musn't take any action which could jeopardise any government initiatives. The ultimatum delivered by the Foreign Secretary to Germany is not due to expire until eleven o'clock this evening – and whether that is London time or Berlin time makes no difference, there are still some hours to go. We cannot fire the first shot. Make sure, however, that everyone is on top alert."

The four ships passed each other at speed, but all that immense firepower gathered on each ship stayed ominously silent. My binoculars were trained on the opposing bridge, and I clearly saw the little German Admiral – Admiral Souchon, staring straight ahead, and next to him, a lieutenant, my counterpart, who was staring through his binoculars at me.

The moment after we passed by, with both sets of crews standing on the decks staring at each other, Kennedy immediately gave the orders to turn around. Our ships swung round slewing over heavily at speed and we set off to shadow the Germans. Captain Kennedy ordered me to go down to the boiler room and inform the stokers of the crisis. But when I got below into the hot sweaty inferno of the boiler rooms, I saw that the news had already preceded me, and the stokers were already frantically trying to raise additional steam to increase our speed.

On paper we should have been able to keep up with the *Goeben* – our respective top speeds, when fully manned, were the same. But it was then that I discovered, for the first time, that we were short of 90 stokers. I was not sure if Kennedy was aware of this, and hurried back up to the bridge to report on the position. I could already see that the two German ships – smoke pouring from their funnels – very slowly but surely pulling away from us.

"Sir, we are short of 90 stokers down below, and even working flat out those available won't be able to increase the present speed".

"Well, they've just got to do their best." replied the Captain gloomily.

At this, one of the other officers gathered on the bridge, staring through his binoculars.

"Sir, if we deputise some of the gunners to go down, we'll be able to keep up. Our boilers are in fairly good trim, and surely it's vital to keep the ships in sight".

"But what if they should suddenly stop and turn a broadside on us. If a shooting match was to start, and 90 of our gunners were down below shoveling, we are going to be caught with our pant's down for god's sake. I can't possibly risk it. Anyway the priority issued by the Admiralty was that the crossing of the French troops from Algeria is to be protected at all costs. Now the one thing that is absolutely certain about the present situation is that the bloody *Goeben* is currently going in the completely opposite direction."

It was unclear to all of us standing on that bridge where Admiral Souchon was aiming for. Neither Kennedy, nor the rest of us gathered there, were aware of exactly who was going to be at war with whom. Our training indicated that Italy and Austria would be allied with Germany, and that our Mediterranean fleet would have to face the two navies, stiffened by the two German battle cruisers. Even if Italy remained neutral, a possibility which the Admiralty had already intimated to the Captain on the radio might be the case, it seemed important not to allow Souchon to join up with the Austrian fleet.

All sorts of conjectures went back and forth between us all on the bridge. But, as we spoke, in the dying light of that summer day, we watched helplessly as the two German ships disappeared over the horizon, until at last we could not even see any distant plumes of smoke. Our Radio Officer had already signaled the news to the Admiralty, but by 11.00 pm at night, we had to report that whilst we could be absolutely certain that the German ships were heading due east and thus away from the French crossings, we had, nevertheless, lost sight of them.

I am adding to this personal account evidence obtained as to what was happening on the *Goeben* during these critical few days. This comes from a Polish officer, Lieutenant André Tarkowski, who was born in Miastiko in the German province of Posen. He came from a family which had lived in this part of Prussia for centuries, and to whom speaking German came as naturally as speaking Polish.

Tarkowski, who is the same age as I, was interviewed by our military intelligence officer in Constantinople about four weeks after the arrival there of the *Goeben,* and the following statement was taken down by the interviewing officer. The Ottoman Empire was then still neutral, and our embassy was functioning normally.

Tarkowski appeared at the Embassy out of nowhere, dressed as a civilian, and asked for an interview. He claimed that he was a Radio Officer on the *Goeben*, that he was currently on a week's official leave, and that he was proposing to desert as a result of discrimination towards Polish officers. He said that he was acting on his convictions as a Polish patriot.

In return for British Travel documents, for himself and a certain young lady, he was prepared to give a series of interviews detailing as much information as he could about the *Goeben*, its systems and armaments. The Ambassador agreed, on condition that the interviews did not take place at the embassy, and that he had nothing to do with it, officially.

Our Naval attaché accordingly interviewed Tarkowski in a private house and obtained some information, most of which has been sent on to our technical department here in London. I have extracted from his long statement those parts relevant to this enquiry.

I would add that I agree entirely with our attaché in Constantinople that Tarkowski's motivation seems to have had nothing to do with 'discrimination' amongst the other officers of the *Goeben*. We both believe that his motivation was private and personal and that he put those feelings above all considerations of duty and career. I would add that the travel documents and passports he requested were duly issued in his name, and that of one Elena Patakis, for travel to Egypt. I have no idea what happened to them or whether they ever got away. I do know that Tarkowski was posted as missing, and was being sought by the Turkish police as early as November 1914.

The evidence of Lieutenant Tarkowski.

My family come from Miastiko, a small town in the German province of Posen near to the Baltic Sea. As I saw it, when I was younger, my basic allegiance undoubtedly lay with the Imperial German government. As my family had always been associated with the sea, I had no hesitation in joining the Imperial German Navy. It seemed to me as a German speaking Pole, that, in the last resort, a German-dominated Poland had a better future than a Russian- dominated one.

My Polish revolutionary hero was Pilsudski, but despite thrilling to tales of his exploits against the Russian state, I felt that my German identity was as important as my Polish, and when it came to ordinary everyday life, I saw my own future as a sailor in the Kaiser's new and growing Navy. I thought the sense of camaraderie amongst naval officers on a ship, overcame any feelings of racial animosity or superiority that may have existed elsewhere in Prussian-dominated political circles, and which I am told certainly made for tensions in the Imperial Army.

I was fascinated in the new technique of radio, and it was as a Radio Officer that I found myself on the *Goeben* at the beginning of August 1914, when war broke out with Russia and France. The commander of our little flotilla operating in the Mediterranean, consisting of the *Goeben*, and a sister ship the *Breslau*, was Admiral Souchon. Souchon was a man of French Huguenot descent; a short, dapper, astute and intelligent sailor to whom his men were devoted. I myself saw and spoke to him frequently, as he would often come to the Radio room to check up on the latest messages from the Kriegsmarine Headquarters at Kiel.

On the declaration of war with France and Russia, we were cruising in the western Mediterranean, and were immediately ordered to approach the French Algerian coastline with a view to disrupting the preparations for the convoy of French troops to mainland France, before the French fleet could arrive from Toulon. Whilst we all knew that the *Goeben* was more than a match for any single ship in the whole French fleet, nevertheless the French had enough ships in total, particularly if they were reinforced by any British ships, to be able to take us on with some possibility of success.

We bombarded the ports of Phillipeville and Bone, but eventually sailed away. Our engines were in poor repair. Furthermore we were already running out of coal.

Souchon informed a gathering of his officers that he was intending to make for Italy to take on more coal.

"Gentlemen, we will head for the port of Messina in Sicily, but I must warn you that I have no idea – nor yet has the Kriegsmarine – where Italy will be standing in this conflict. Above all we must avoid any enemy patrols at this stage until we can refuel."

In the early afternoon of the 4th August, as we slipped away towards Sicily, we encountered two British cruisers coming towards us in the opposite direction – the *Indefatigable*, and, I believe, the *Intrepid*. I came out of the Radio Room and stood and watched as the two sleek grey warships passed us steaming westwards at top speed, less than half a mile away. The tension amongst us was electric. The order to man the guns had already been given by the time I came out, but the whole ship seemed enveloped in a deep silence. I could see Souchon standing stiffly on the bridge, eyes firmly ahead, almost as if he was afraid to make eye contact with any British officer, though at that distance that was a ridiculous proposition.

An uneasy quiet hung on the air all around me. Clearly I must be exaggerating, as all ships ploughing through any kind of seas always generate background noise – but the tension of all around me created a strange feeling of stillness. It was not fear – but uncertainty.

Nothing happened. Each ship held to its course without any of the usual courtesies exchanged by passing ships, but also without any guns booming in anger. However, within seconds of the ships passing, we saw the British cruisers swinging round without slackening speed, and clearly starting to follow us.

"Full steam ahead," was ordered from the bridge, as an Engineering officer came racing down to go to the boiler rooms to press for more steam.

The ship seemed to shudder, though this was more psychological than real, as they strained to reach their top speed of 27 knots. But I heard later that we never got above 24 knots, while, as the light began to fade, three of our engines failed one by one and our speed dropped even further.

Stokers began to fall unconscious in the enormous effort to raise enough steam, in a climate already heavy with midsummer heat. We were informed later that four stokers had died during this chase. We knew that the two British battle cruisers were perfectly capable of reaching 22 to 24 knots, but to our great surprise we saw that we were slowly pulling away, mile by mile, until we had got away from them completely.

On the 5th August, we steamed into Messina. Here Admiral Souchon went ashore to seek out the situation. Although we had heard rumours of the pending Italian declaration of neutrality, nobody on board was at all clear what was going to happen. I believe that Souchon himself had been warned of the Italian withdrawal from our alliance even whilst we were bombarding Bone, but he had not passed this on to us, nor did we have any idea of what the British position was going to be.

Coaling was already taking place when Souchon returned and informed his officers in some irritation, that in accordance with the rules of neutrality, the Italian authorities had granted us only 24 hours in which to refuel, after which we had to leave. This was clearly not enough time to refill our bunkers. The combination of our leaking unrepaired boilers, and the burst of very high speed which we had raised to get free from the two British capital ships, had depleted our coal beyond normal consumption.

I must say that neither I nor any of my junior colleagues had any idea what Souchon would do now. However, we all assumed that we were going to make a dash for the Adriatic in order to join the Austrian fleet, where we could complete our repairs at leisure and refill our coal bunkers. The alternative of another dash to the Algerian coast to try and cause havoc to the French troop movements, seemed impossible without sufficient coal.

Souchon was informed by the Admiralstab that the Austrian Foreign Ministry, in a vain attempt to try and avoid war with Great Britain if possible, had given orders that the *Goeben* and *Breslau* were only to be supported once they were actually under the protection of the Austrian fleet by being physically in Austrian territorial waters. However Admiral Haus, the Austrian Naval commander, indicated in a personal reply to us, that despite foreign ministry wishes, he was prepared to sail as far south as Brindisi, and would await Souchon there. We later heard that he did in fact sail out on the morning of the 7th, but by then we were miles away.

We sailed out of Messina harbour on the evening of the 6th, and I, for one, had no idea where we were going, but on the evidence of the radio messages going to the Austrians I assumed we were still heading for the Adriatic. As we pulled away from Italian territorial waters we did indeed seem to be heading for the Adriatic, but fairly soon we changed course decisively and began heading south towards Greece.

None of us had the slightest idea where we going ...

I am now attaching to this report a copy of a letter from a Mrs. Maurice Wertheim to her father Henry Morganthau, the American Ambassador in Constantinople. I have no idea how this copy got into the hands of British naval intelligence, but it is clearly authentic.

Dear Father ... We all went aboard the Sicilia, *at Venice, as scheduled, on our way to come and see you. We had the most beautiful summer days as we sailed down the Adriatic. The company aboard was aware that there was some sort of crisis between the European powers, but most of the passengers happened to be compatriot Americans, and we were all in cheerful mood. Entertaining our three little daughters took up most of my time, so I failed to notice what was happening around us, and you had, in any case, assured us that Turkey would keep out of any European War.*

We were lunching on deck somewhere between the coasts of Greece and Italy on the 6th or 7th August when I saw two strange looking vessels on the horizon. I ran for the glasses and made out two large battleships. We watched and saw another ship coming up behind them fast. She came nearer and nearer and then we heard guns booming. Pillars of water sprang up in the air along with many little puffs of white smoke. It took me some time to realise what it was all about, and then it burst upon me that we were actually witnessing a naval engagement. The ships were continually shifting position. The two big ones turned and rushed furiously at the little one, and then apparently changed their minds and turned away again. Eventually the little one, which turned out to be a British light cruiser, turned around and calmly steamed in our direction. At first I was somewhat alarmed by this, but all that happened was that she circled round us, with her tars excited and grinning, and somewhat grimy. They signaled and exchanged converse with our captain, then turned and finally disappeared. The Captain told us that the two big ships were German, caught in the Mediterranean, and were trying to escape from the British ...

The rest of the statement of Lieutenant Tarkowski.

... Shortly after we made the dramatic change of course to the south away from the Adriatic, we were spotted by a small British light cruiser, which I now understand was the HMS *Gloucester*. I was tapping away at my radio when I heard the sound of firing coming from the *Breslau*. I could not immediately leave my desk, but after a few moments I went up on deck and saw that the *Breslau* was in a furious engagement with the little *Gloucester*, which kept darting in and out until eventually turning away. It was clear that our change of course had been spotted and we assumed that the British would shortly be upon us.

Whilst we all knew by that time that the French fleet had finally arrived on the Algerian coast, and that it was now busy covering the crossing of French troops, we were also painfully aware that the British had several powerful cruisers in the vicinity. It was therefore with a sense of mounting surprise and elation to find ourselves, over the next few days, in a calm and quiet sea, sailing unmolested round the tip of Greece, without sight of any other ship of any nationality on the whole horizon.

That day or the next – I begin to forget the actual sequence of days – we sailed up the Aegean and made a rendezvous with a German coaling ship, which met us at the little island of Denusa near to Naxos. I must say that we all felt proud of our fierce little commander with this turn of events. Souchon had obviously arranged the rendezvous whilst he had been ashore in Messina, and the entire might of the British Navy had been unable to prevent it. We spent almost three days coaling, with the three ships, our *Goeben* and *Breslau*, and the stocky little coaling ship alongside each other in the beautiful blue waters of the Aegean. Here, like everywhere else in Europe in that fateful month of August 1914, the sun shone from a clear blue sky every day. Looking over the side, we could see the little Greek island with its white villages and its timeless quality. Those of us not on coaling duty even had time to swim. The war seemed far away and at no time did any enemy ship appear.

We set off on the evening of the 9th, this time on a northward course. I was on duty when we arrived at the start of the narrow Straits of the Dardanelles on the morning of the 10th. I was aware of an enormous amount of coming and going – the arrival of Turkish officials ferried from the shore on small white boats, and eventually the arrival of two clearly high-ranking Turkish naval officers who were closeted with Souchon for hours. I spent the morning watching the shoreline on both sides through my binoculars: the Gallipoli peninsula – with its high cliffs on the European side, and the site of ancient Troy on the flatter Asian side.

To the north lay the historic waterway of the Dardanelles – Europe, perhaps the most significant stretch of water in history, bristling with modern fortifications and guns on all sides. It lay just beyond the tip of the bows of our two great ships, and we were all aware that behind us, the British fleet must surely by now be closing in fast. The Ottoman Empire was neutral, and we all knew that during times of war, by long-standing treaties, the state was not allowed to agree to any war vessels passing through these narrow waters. So where were we to go?

I will now continue to trace the events as they appeared through the Admiralty records from the moment the *Goeben* docked in Messina. By the afternoon of the 5th August, even after the two German battle cruisers had been lost by Captain Kennedy's force the evening before, Admiral Milne, commanding the whole British Mediterranean fleet, had a pretty good idea of the probable whereabouts of the two German capital ships in Sicily. However he had no idea of their intentions.

Aware now of the declaration of Italian neutrality, the Admiral considered, and it seems to me a fair decision, that after leaving Sicily, Souchon would probably turn west again and resume his attempts to disrupt the slow French convoys carrying valuable troops across the Mediterranean to Marseille. However, he was also aware of the other possibility – namely that Souchon might try to join the Austrian fleet in the Adriatic. Accordingly, he deployed his heavy battle cruisers west of Sicily, in order to prevent Souchon doubling back to attack the French convoys. At the same time, to prevent Souchon escaping into the Adriatic, Rear-Admiral Troubridge, with four armoured cruisers, would steam to the east, just off the island of Corfu, in case Souchon came out that way and turned north towards the Adriatic.

Just before the outbreak of the war, Churchill, the First Lord of the Admiralty, had signaled that Troubridge, in particular, was not to attack a 'superior force'. By this, the Admiralty had meant the combined fleets of Austria and Italy. At the same time, the Admiralty had made it clear that the *Goeben* was to be Milne's principal objective. Troubridge, who was in command of armoured cruisers, not fully capable of standing up to the *Goeben*, misunderstood, and assumed that the 'superior force' referred to by the Admiralty was the *Goeben*, particularly as he was now aware of Italian neutrality.

So, as the *Goeben* and *Breslau* steamed out from Messina the British fleets were positioned as follows –

Milne with the main Mediterranean fleet was west of Sicily covering the route to the Algerian coast:

Troubridge with his four armoured cruisers lay waiting near Corfu at the entrance to the Adriatic;

Several light cruisers, including the *Gloucester*, commanded by Captain Kelly, were patrolling between Malta and Corfu;

All were poised and ready to catch the two Germans between them.

When the Germans came out of Messina they were spotted by one of the light cruisers – the HMS *Gloucester*. Kelly immediately set off in pursuit, though keeping out of range of the *Goeben's* big 11-inch guns. By the time night fell on the evening of the 6th, it had become clear that Souchon was not heading for the Adriatic at all, but had turned south. This news was duly radioed back to Milne sitting north and west of Sicily, and to Troubridge sitting to the east.

The gallant Captain Kelly could see that if he could delay the two German ships, Troubridge's squadron of four cruisers could sail down and join in intercepting them. Although enormously inferior in armament, though not in speed, Kelly engaged the *Breslau*, and undoubtedly this was the engagement witnessed by Mrs. Wertheim on the *Sicilia*. Like a gnat irritating a great beast, the *Gloucester* darted in and out, causing no damage in view of its relatively tiny guns, but all the time holding back the Germans who twice turned back on him.

But Troubridge did not follow suit or come to his aid.

Worried by the Admiralty's slightly ambiguous instructions not to attack a superior force, he allowed prudence to override the Nelsonian principle – always to close with the enemy. Instead, at 3.47 on the morning of the 7th, he took the decision to turn away, and he signaled to Admiral Milne that he had abandoned the chase. It was said by one of his officers that he was in tears when these orders were given – and well he might be – as the consequences of his decision could be said to have had the most far-reaching strategic consequences of almost any naval decision ever made.

The responsibility for stopping the *Goeben* now passed to Admiral Milne. He, however, continued in the belief that the greater danger was the possibility of Souchon doubling back towards the Algerian coast and the vital French troopships. But by the same night of the 6th and 7th, he was informed by the Admiralty that the French Navy were now, at last, sufficiently organised to counter this threat themselves, so he was free to single-mindedly pursue the *Goeben*. All his battle cruisers were fully coaled, and he could have set off in hot pursuit of the Germans without any difficulty, but once again the Admiralty intervened, warning that hostilities had now begun against the Austrians. Milne delayed, and once again the two ships were saved, by fortuitous coincidence, to make their decisive impact on history.

With the fairly recent advent of Radio, the desk men at Whitehall were suddenly finding that they could influence the fleet in a way that had never been possible before. As can be seen, this was not always with happy results. In the event, whatever the cause, Admiral Milne hung about at the entrance to the Adriatic, while Souchon enjoyed nearly three whole days quietly coaling in the Aegean. As British activity finally resumed, and Milne began moving to the East, Souchon sailed for the Dardanelles. He had nowhere else to go, but nevertheless he was taking a fairly major risk, as he had no idea what attitude the neutral Turks were going to take.

Admiral Milne was, of course, fully aware of the Treaty obligations involving any navigation by belligerents in the Straits, and he knew that the Dardanelles was heavily mined and barred to all warships. He might well have thought that Treaty arrangements would be honoured by the Ottomans, and that all he needed to do was to bring his own three battle cruisers into the Aegean, which, when added to Troubridge's four armoured cruisers, would be certain to catch and destroy the *Goeben*. So he did not hurry!

Thus, it was in the afternoon of the 10th August, that the two great German ships, still completely untouched by the British, anchored at the entrance to the Dardanelles. The British Navy, with seven large ships, was at last moving up fast behind them; ahead of them, was a barred and mined passage.

I have discovered in the naval intelligence archives a copy of a surprisingly uncensored letter from an unknown German sailor to a girlfriend in Basel, intercepted by agents, which, quite pithily, puts the situation as it seemed to an ordinary German sailor on that morning of the 10th August, which I attach here.

"On that morning of the 10th I was on duty on the deck of my ship – the Breslau *– and I could see a hive of activity of small boats going backwards and forwards between the shore and the* Goeben. *My mates and I had no idea what our pipsqueak Admiral was up to, but we all had great faith in the little bastard.*

We could see the big guns of the Turkish fortifications on the Asian shore. We also knew that the Brits could not be far behind. It looked to us as if we were between the devil and the deep blue sea. But just after midday, the Goeben *began to steam slowly up the twisting Dardanelles, and I could see the Turkish pilots and naval officers on their bridge – and by now on ours as well. We moved ever so slowly right behind. These were narrow waters, which we all knew were heavily mined, and to begin with, we were all fairly tense.*

We got through all right. We then sailed up to Constantinople.

Believe me, our arrival there in the late afternoon, and our dropping anchor at the entrance to the Golden Horn, just before that wedding cake seaside Palace – I don't know its name – with the sun beginning to set in the West behind the domes and minarets of old Stamboul, was a sight and experience I will never forget."

Finally, I have been given permission to quote from the diary of His Excellency Henry Morgenthau, the American Ambassador to the Sublime Porte, which deals with the events from the 10th August after the *Goeben* arrived in Constantinople:

10th August

I went to visit Baron von Wangenheim at the German embassy on official business. From his animated manner, edginess and excitement, it was clear he had no interest in our routine discussion. Eventually I got up to go, saying

"Look, something is distracting you, I'll go and come back some other time."

"No, no, my dear Morganthau," he declaimed, "You stay right where you are. This will be a great day for Germany! I believe I will be able to give you a great piece of news that will have the utmost bearing upon Turkey's relation to the war."

Then he rushed out, and came back a few moments later waving a wireless message, with all the enthusiasm of a college boy whose football team has just won a victory.

"We've got them – we've got them, the Goeben *and the* Breslau *have just passed through the Dardanelles."*

I immediately understood his excitement. The voyage of these two ships was very much his personal triumph, for it was he who arranged with the Turkish cabinet for their passage through the straits. By safely getting the Goeben *and* Breslau *into Constantinople, he had all but clinched Turkey's eventual entry into the war as a German ally. But however much I admired Wangenheim's work as a professional diplomat in getting the two ships into Constantinople, I remain amazed that the large British fleet, dominating as it did the eastern Mediterranean, had failed to prevent this result.*

16th August

The Ottoman government, that had earlier announced that it had 'purchased' the two ships, today hosted a formal ceremony in which both ships hoisted the Turkish flag with great pomp. The sailors, all immaculately dressed in white, wore brand new red fezes, and some German officers were in full Turkish naval uniform. The Turks announced that the ships were substitutes for the two dreadnoughts seized by the British government some 12 days earlier. At a stroke, the Turkish navy had become stronger than the Russian Black Sea fleet, and the ultimate entry into war of the Ottoman Empire became almost inevitable. I, myself, doubt if any two individual ships have exercised a greater influence upon history than these two German cruisers.

20th August

Today I heard that Djavid Bey – the finance minister – met the Belgian military attaché in the street, and, stopping him, said, "I have terrible news for you – the Germans have captured Brussels."

The Belgian, a large figure more than six feet tall, put his arm soothingly on the shoulder of the little Turk.

"I have even more terrible news for you." Pointing out to the stream where the Goeben *and* Breslau *lay anchored, "The Germans have captured the whole of Turkey."*

CHAPTER 6

Olga

It was still early in April, on a bright afternoon, when Olga returned home to Makrikoy earlier than usual from the city. She and the young Turkish student – Selim Kemal – had had several further chance meetings and conversations at the College, though always in the company of others in their group. On the 1st April, Selim had finally caught her alone and drummed up the courage to ask her to come out to tea with him after college. To her own astonishment she had agreed to meet him for tea on a day to be arranged at the fashionable Tokatlian Café.

Olga was much the most beautiful of the four Avakian girls, with a delicate, thin nose, fine sensitive features, huge eyes, and a devastating smile. She was also normally socially composed and confident. However, she was not entirely sure of her real feelings towards Selim. Selim was certainly a good looking, darkly handsome, young man, without any trace of the usual young Turkish male's flamboyant arrogance. But she was aware that some of her interest was the result of the excitement of doing something she knew was completely forbidden? She knew that what she was proposing to do was not just a matter of ignoring inevitable parental disapproval, but went deeply against centuries old tribal and religious taboos affecting both communities. Olga was playing with fire and she knew it.

Her sexuality was aroused, but that had happened with her often enough before, and she had always kept it under control. However, she was sensible enough to try not to go to the proposed rendezvous alone. But if not alone, then with whom? Who could she possibly ask to accompany her. If she went with any of her friends, it would be round the college in a flash. Clearly it would have to be one of her sisters.

As she sat in the train on the way home she thought of her three sisters, considering first her elder sister Sima. It did not take her long to dismiss that possibility.

'Oh no for heaven's sake,' she thought, 'she's far too bossy, and over-emotional as well. Afterwards, she'll talk about it the whole time. She'll get excited and sentimental, and above all she will take it all far too seriously. Oh dear, on top of that, she is likely to take over and dominate the whole thing, even at the tea table. No, it must be one of the others. Little Seta is only eight and obviously far too young and she is bound to blurt something out to mother – even if she manages not to shout it out from the rooftops.'

That left Nerissa – poor Nerissa – but yes, hang on, she will do fine. All she does all day is to sit curled up in the corner reading English novels. She hardly says a word to anyone, and she will leave me free to talk to Selim, without trying to butt in and take over like Sima would. But will she come – she's still far too shy with strangers – how am I going to persuade her.?

When the train arrived at the Cobancesme station, Olga alighted and hailed Abdul, the sleepy old driver, head nodding, sitting in his one-horse droshky waiting for fares. Not for Olga any hot dusty walk home like her father – it had to be the arrabiya. Her thoughts on tjhe problem of a chaperone ran on as she clambered into the warm, horsey-smelling, carriage, asking Abdul to open the hood.

When she walked in at the front door and into the marbled hall, she found herself in the middle of a typical Avakian crisis. Her mother, Armineh, was standing in the middle of the hall holding a largish bottle of what looked like yellow liquid. She had on her outdoor clothes but was not yet wearing a hat, and she was looking rather vexed.

Olga immediately recalled that earlier on in the week, there had been talk of the possibility that her mother might be pregnant. In order to make quite sure that there was nothing wrong, her doctor had asked her to provide a urine sample for him to analyse. For several days now, therefore, the whole household had been thrown into turmoil by this entire procedure, much to Olga's delight, causing a great deal of fuss in the household. Anyway, at last all was ready – the urine bottle had been filled, a stopper had been fitted, and the indomitable Armineh was holding it in her hand outside the sitting room waiting to put on her hat ready to sally out into the street and face the world.

At this point, however, it appeared that Armineh had suddenly thought that she really could not be seen walking down the street with a bottle of urine in her hand. So, she had arranged to wrap the bottle in a newspaper which on Olga's arrival had just been accomplished. Then there had arisen the question of which of the four girls should accompany her and carry the bottle. There they all were, standing in the hall – with Armineh holding the wrapped-up bottle, waiting to hand it over while she put on her coat and hat, when Olga walked in.

Seta was grinning all over and hopping about with excitement, assuring her mother that she would be more than happy to take the bottle and accompany her on this small, but significant, expedition. Of course Sima was far too grand to carry a urine bottle down the street. Olga was not about to volunteer for such an undignified task either, and immediately claimed that she was far too tired, having only just got back. Nerissa? – well, she was sitting curled up in the corner reading one of her interminable books, and did not appear to have heard, or even be aware, of what was going on. So there Seta was – eager and willing – indeed jumping up and down in anticipation, whilst Armineh desperately sought some alternative solution.

"Oh mother," Olga spoke, once the matter had been fully explained to her, "for heaven's sake, get Marie to take it down – or even Abdul can take it, he's still outside with the carriage if we are quick about it."

"Never, you silly girl. You don't know what you are saying – it has taken me days to collect all this – I am going to see it safely into the hands of the Doctor or the Nurse at least. Come on Olga, do something useful for once and walk with me."

But even as she asked, she knew that she did not need to await a reply, well aware that Olga would be most unlikely to help. "Nerissa...," she called out. However, Sima standing at the kitchen door interrupted as Armineh turned to call Nerissa again,

"Oh Mother, leave Nerissa be! Olga why don't you help Mother for a change"

"Well, what about you – you've been sitting at home all day," snapped back Olga.

At this juncture, Armineh, who was about to lose patience and issue a diktat, instead stopped herself from making another caustic remark. She wasn't going to trust any servant to take the valuable bottle, and she was not going to walk down the street holding a bottle of urine herself. Finally, she realised that it might be equally undignified to have one of her elder daughters do it for her in full public view.

"Well, well," she sighed, "Seta, you'll have to come with me after all", and still grumbling to herself, she handed the bottle to Seta and went to put on her hat.

All were now in the tiled hall. The irrepressible Seta, clenching the wrapped bottle tightly in its discreet cover, waited patiently by the door for her mother to get herself ready, proud to be the one chosen to accompany her mother on this important occasion. Suddenly, to her horror, she felt the bottle slipping. The harder she clutched at the paper, the quicker the bottle seemed to slip through her hands until gravity took over, and it fell, right out of the wrapped-up newspaper, and crashed to the floor. All that carefully collected liquid poured out over the hall. Armineh took one look – plonked herself down on the seat in the hall and wailed, "Oh my God, my God, even in my peepee, I'm not lucky."

In the chaos that followed, while the elderly Marie came bustling in out of the kitchen to help clear up the mess, Olga grabbed the surprised Nerissa who had finally left her book and come out to see what was happening, and dragged her upstairs, pulling her into her room.

"Nerissa, my love, I have arranged to meet a friend for tea at Tokatlians next week on the day the schools shut early – will you come to town and join us – it'll be fun for you."

"Why me, Olga, who is your friend, do I know her?"

"Oh, my dear, just come and have a nice afternoon – we can go to the Bedestan together before, and look at what's in the shops."

"Olga – you're up to something, I can tell. You know that I'd love to come, but you must tell me what it's all about."

Olga sat on her bed and thought a little. Although Nerissa was just 16, Olga knew she was young for her age and sometimes rather shy. She read voraciously, mainly English novels of the previous century, and had romantic notions, but Olga did not think that she had any real idea of what it was like to feel the thrill of courtship. She had never had any really serious chats with Nerissa, so had no idea how Nerissa would react to the truth.

"Look – I'll tell you, but my darling you must keep it to yourself. I've arranged to have tea with a student friend – a young man."

Nerissa's already large brown eyes opened wide as she looked steadily at her sister.

"You mean, without anyone else there, just you and – er – him."

"No, silly, that's why I want you to come along too. We'll just have tea, listen to the music a bit, and come home."

"Olga, you can't – do Father and Mother know?"

"Certainly not – don't be a ninny, Nerissa – it'll be an adventure. I'll tell mother that I am taking you shopping, and that we will stay out for tea together. She'll be well pleased that you're going out for a change – and with me. Come on Nerissa – there's nothing wrong with it. It's exciting – there'll be lots of army officers there."

Nerissa knew that her mother would be happy to let her go out for an afternoon with Olga. She had had a bad attack of rheumatic fever when she was eleven, and had had to stay at home for long months. As a result, she tired easily, and rarely went out, whilst her shyness with strangers left her somewhat isolated, even at the occasional dinner parties she attended with the rest of the family. She had been well looked after during her illness, and she always had the absolute certainty of her parents' love for her, like all the Avakian children. Nevertheless, she felt that, with so much excitement and exuberance emanating from her sisters, her mother in a sense neglected her. It was clear that she would probably be pleased to be told that one of the two elder sisters was proposing to take her out.

Between Nerissa and Seta came the only boy in the family – Haik – now twelve. It was natural that attention would focus on Haik, and then on Seta, the charming and easy-going baby of the family. This left the rather solemn Nerissa on her own, and this accentuated the introverted side of her character. However, although still rather shy with people outside the family, she was perceptive enough to know there was more in this matter than she was being told.

"Olga – have I met this young man – does he come to our church here, or does he go to one in town."

Olga, suddenly thoughtful, looked at Nerissa steadily. Here in

Nerissa's simple, unthinking words was the first time that she was being confronted with the real issue. A little cold shiver ran through her, but it lasted only a few seconds. Then with a toss of the head and a smile, she dismissed the thoughts from her head, leant forward and planted a big kiss on the astonished Nerissa.

"Oh Nerissa, my soul, you're priceless – I love you."

"All right, Olga, all right – but you must sort it all out with Mother."

"I'll look after everything – you'll have a lovely day,", Olga sang out, as she bounced out of the room, dragging Nerissa by the hand behind her.

CHAPTER 7

Garabed Asadourian

Garabed Asadourian was in every way a big man, both physically and morally. Though his marriage to his gentle wife, Mariam, had softened some of the rougher elements of his character, he remained a forceful man with a quick temper which he had difficulty controlling.

He had set his hand to many different trades and businesses during his life, but it was as an entrepreneur in the carpet trade that he was best known. At the turn of the century, Armenian and Persian carpets were still made by hand, with pure vegetable dyes, in the mountain villages of the Armenian and Persian highlands. They often took families more than a year to make; the really large ones, which would eventually grace public rooms in London or Paris, could take several years to complete.

The loom would be set up for the carpet according to the size required. Looms were built by the father of the family or some other male relative and were fashioned in the traditional form of the area, depending on the type of wood available. The basic design of the carpet would be drawn out and left alongside the loom. It was often only a piece of paper tucked into a crack in the wood. Then the slow, painstaking, task of weaving would be carried out, usually by the women and children, after returning from work in the fields, and all day during the winter, whilst there was light to work by.

The question of money to support the living expenses of the family and for the costs of preparing the cloth and dyes during the carpet's production was usually resolved by an arrangement between the family and their preferred entrepreneur-merchant. For his part, the merchant would commission a carpet according to his own idea of the market currently available; he would agree a price with the family and then pay sums on account as the work progressed, until the carpet was finished. He rarely discussed or questioned the design or colours, unless there was a specific request from a client. There was often a close and mutually respectful relationship between the family and the *effendi* or *bey* from the city, who would often be asked on many matters, when he visited, such as how to write a letter, or how to deal with some Ottoman official or other. Problems with the growing children in the family were discussed between the *effendi* and the parents in the evening. Unlike the Christian families, the womenfolk in the Muslim families of the local Kurds and Turks, would not be present or involved in such matters, even though they may well have had the last word, once alone with their husbands.

"*Effendim* – please remain and accept my poor hospitality," would be the phrase which would signal the close of the purely business aspect of the meeting. Garabed, and latterly with his younger son Raffi alongside him, would then sit cross-legged on the villager's own faded carpet in their one big main room. Bowls of hot water would be brought in and hands and faces would be washed. The children would be introduced and led up to shake hands – it being known that Garabed was opposed to the older, more servile, hand-kissing.

Once the evening food was prepared and brought in, the women would join them – but unlike women in the city they would remain mainly silent. The night would be rounded off with the men smoking a communal 'narghilé', tobacco smoked through bubbling rose water. Raffi would try manfully to join in, but never really managed it, and would splutter and cough and only pretend to inhale. The guests would remain with their own bedding in the main room to sleep, and leave early the next morning with any completed carpets piled on the back of the donkeys.

The carpets, when finished and taken back to Caesaria, would then be sold at a fair profit to traders from Constantinople, who would often deal almost exclusively with their own favourite middle-man whom they might well have met at some stage. They would then send them to Western Europe with huge mark-ups. Needless to say, once the goods left the Empire, the biggest mark-ups of all would be added in the smart carpet houses in Paris and London.

One of Garabed's more carefully cultivated families was that of Sarkis, son of Shahan. Sarkis farmed land in the mountains near the town of Malatya, about a hundred miles away from Caesaria. He had a large family, large even by local standards, with two boys aged eight and eleven, two older girls of fourteen and twelve, and two more girls both under seven. The nimble fingers of his children, and the native artistic intuition of his wife – Adrineh – meant that the carpets commissioned from this family were of a very high standard, and Garabed paid accordingly.

The cash generated had put Sarkis in a favourable position as far as his land-holding was concerned. He had accumulated the necessary capital to be able to purchase many of the tools and animals that his neighbours could not afford.

On the last occasion that Garabed had made one of these expeditions, just before the outbreak of the war, he had stayed the night with Sarkis, who had now registered a surname – Shahanian. In the evening, after the other children had left, Adrineh had indicated to her eldest daughter – Anna – that she could remain with the adults. Despite having borne six children, Adrineh was still an attractive, buxom woman. Anna was thrilled at being able to stay and, nestling up to her mother, listened as Sarkis raised one of his concerns with Garabed.

"Garabed, agha, whilst our relations with the local Turks

whom I have known all my life remain perfectly amicable as always, we are having more and more difficulty with the officials from the town. My neighbour, Mustapha Mahmud, and his family have lived next to us all my life, and we work together at harvest time, and there have never been any difficulties between us. However he told me that last month, when an Ittihad party official came on a tax assessment visit to our village, he had said to Mustapha and some others that we were not to be trusted, and that one day he hoped that we would no longer be here. What does it all mean, Garabed agha? Both my family and Mustapha's have been here living alongside each other for generations."

"What does Mustapha himself say?" asked Garabed.

"Oh! he just laughed and told me not to concern myself about what the educated city slickers said – they know nothing about the real way of life of we farmers, and the way the rhythm of the seasons and nature shapes our lives. He said we should ignore all this shit about races."

"Well, he must be a wise man, this Mustapha. Keep him close to your heart, Sarkis *effendi*. What about the Kurds here."

"Ah, well, sir, they are a different matter, I'm afraid. Many of them are landless, and are easily persuaded to go about in groups harassing the settled population. I try to keep away from them. You know how it is – they shout '*giavour*', '*giavour*' mindlessly and get excited and violent."

"I am afraid that I cannot give you much comfort my old friend. We are in the midst of a great crisis in the affairs of the Ottomans, affecting Turks and Christians alike. I can only advise that you try and keep a low profile and stay on as friendly terms as possible with all your neighbours."

Garabed became a fairly influential man in Caesaria. During the violence which occurred in 1896, the mob, having been incited with full official sanction during the Friday prayers, rampaged through the town for two days killing as many Armenians as they could lay their hands on. Many local Armenians gathered in Garabed's house for safety. Garabed was the local mukhtar – headman – for the district. His house had two-foot thick walls, with only a few windows looking onto the street – and those had iron bars across them. Most of the windows and rooms, like so many of the houses in the town, looked into the inner courtyard, which was totally private and used very like a sitting room during the summer. The courtyard had a deep well situated in the middle, always providing clear fresh water.

This general massacre, unquestionably ordered and arranged from the office of the odious and vindictive Sultan, Abdul Hamid, lasted only three days, during which time Garabed's house remained full of women and children, together with a few young men well-armed with many kinds of firearms. The three larger churches in Caesaria were all also filled with people who had locked themselves in. These churches were solidly built, almost like castles, with large high walls all round and which could be entered only through one or two heavy iron-clad doors. The mobs attacked all three, but armed with only axes and sticks and stones, were unsuccessful. Nevertheless, many people, numbering in the thousands, were killed in Caesaria, and many more in other cities in Anatolia during those three days.

On the third day, the town crier began to go round the Armenian quarter shouting out – "All slaughter and pillage must end – this is on the direct order of the Sultan, our great Padishah – Abdul Hamid."

Then, within an hour, Turkish soldiers and gendarmes began for the first time to appear again on the streets. As always, this allowed Abdul Hamid's supine ministers to claim that the pogrom was spontaneous and ended only because of the arrival of the police. The crowds melted away even before the soldiers arrived, and thus the orders of the great and 'glorious' Padishah were obeyed, in all particulars.

Garabed had two sons – Vahan and Raffi, neither of whom were alive at the time of these 1896 massacres. Each boy later recalled a different aspect of the story as to what had happened to Garabed at that time. The recollection of each boy, reflected their own character. Thus even a mere twenty years later the events had already achieved the status of a family myth, with the truth lost forever. Vahan, in one of his many evening chats with his Polish acquaintance, Andre, told him about these events.

"My father spent the afternoon of the first day going round warning his business friends of the rumours he had heard from Turkish associates of the coming storm. Hurrying home, as the officially sanctioned rioting started, he had to pass through a narrow lane with high walls on each side. Most of the old quarters of Caesaria were like this – Andre – the houses showing bare walls to the outside world, whilst the windows all opened out to the private inner courtyards. Standing at the end of the lane he saw some Turks, including the local seller of meat, who were all hate-filled and bloodthirsty, looking for *giavours* to murder. However on recognising my Dad, who was the mukhtar of the district, the butcher called out to the others who were clearly not locals, "Let him pass, let him pass," and shouted at Garabed, "Go through man, go through, and for God's sake keep your head down."

According to Raffi, however, on his way home on that day his father indeed had to pass through this narrow lane. However, here at the end of the lane, he saw the local grocer, a mean and vindictive character, standing alone. According to Raffi this man, standing there with a large knife, clearly blood-crazed, knew very well that Garabed was a brave man likely to put up a fight. Now he was sixteen, Raffi would then tell his listeners proudly :-

"So even with a big crazy knife in his hand, instead of risking his own life in a fight with father, he turned and faced the wall and called out "Go away man – pass through."

As Garabed himself no longer spoke of these events, it was clearly impossible to distinguish any truth in these two stories. Probably in all that excitement and anxiety, Garabed returned home to his panicky family and blurted out what had just happened to him. In turn, much later, the story was repeated by their mother or one of their sisters to the two boys. Then, as they began to grow up, the story was embellished in their minds in two different ways, reflecting their distinctive views of their father. Both boys end up giving their father great credit, but in different ways; Vahan, by suggesting that it was respect towards his father's character and position which made the local butcher turn away, and Raffi, by suggesting that it was fear of his father which made the local grocer turn away. In the end it gives an insight into the respective character of the two boys, rather than saying anything about Garabed himself.

As well as his two sons – Vahan and Raffi – Garabed had several daughters, who however much he loved them, simply did not count in a provincial Ottoman family. He already had three daughters before the birth of Vahan, and on the day that this his fourth child was born, he had gone off to work as usual, leaving instructions with the servants that if his wife gave birth to a baby boy they must send for him at once. If, however, it was another daughter, it would be all right for him to hear about it when he got home that evening.

That morning in all the excitement of the birth of the first boy in the family, everyone forgot to send any message to Garabed. Accordingly, as he returned home that evening through the narrow streets, he was thinking that once again his wife had borne a girl.

Life in Caesaria revolved strictly round the seasons. The summers were very hot, and without much possibility of any relief. The winters, on the other hand, were bitterly cold, and in the Armenian highlands to the east, it could stay as low as minus 40 ºC for long periods. There would be three months of heavy snow in Caesaria, and Garabed would often return home on winter evenings with threads of icicles hanging from his moustaches.

During the depth of winter, Vahan and Raffi would fill the large well in the middle of the central courtyard, which was about 25-feet deep, with snow. They would then put on their boots and jump about, and stamp down the snow until the well again became half empty – at which they would call for a ladder which would be let down to them and they would clamber out. The next day, they would again refill the well with fresh snow and repeat the process, stamping it down, as if they were pressing grapes, till once again they were below the level of the lip of the well. This would go on for several days until the well was full of hard packed ice and they could stamp it down no further. The well would then be covered up.

During the hot months of the following summer it would provide the household for a long time with ice and cold sweet water. When Garabed took the family off to the country house that he would hire on the slopes of Mt. Erciyas during those boiling two months, he would instruct the servants who remained, to allow any of the neighbors in the little street in which the house stood, to come in and take as much ice as they might need whenever they wanted.

Those long summer months were wonderful times for Garabed's two boys. The country villa was about two hours ride away from the town centre. Garabed would go in to work for two or three days a week, often taking either one of the boys with him, riding on the back of the horse, holding Garabed tightly round his waist. There they would help – Vahan in the office with the books – Raffi, when it was his turn, in the cloth mill. The cloth was woven on fairly primitive wooden machines run entirely by hand, and worked by about a dozen men and boys – all Turkish. Raffi would join them on the days it was his turn to accompany his father, and work away with all the other young men who became his friends.

The relationship between the Greeks and Armenians with the Turks, was quite different to that in the sophisticated city of Constantinople. In this provincial town, the Christian minority comprised, almost exclusively, the middle class of the town – both the professionals and the businessmen. As against this, again unlike in the capital city, the governors and the political leaders of the town were exclusively Turkish, without any minority representation, whether Christian or Jewish. The Turkish leaders here had a particular aversion to the Armenians, who were by far the largest of the minorities, whom they oppressed in minor irritating ways. There was an obvious irony in this, in that they often had more in common with the Greek merchants and Armenian bankers of the town, than with the Turkish underclass – often peasants, who were newly come to the town.

On this early April day, still cold and wet in Central Anatolia, Garabed was becoming anxious and worried by the developing political situation. A deep unease was in the air. The Russians, enthusiastically supported by their own Armenian population, were moving towards the cities of Van and Erzurum. There was uncertainty in the official mind about the loyalty of the Ottoman Armenian population. Could the Ottomans continue to think of their Armenian subjects as loyal citizens of the empire? This was particularly questionable now as a result of the regular failures of the previous Hamidian regime to accept them as such, or to give them the ordinary civil rights and protections afforded the rest of the population. Garabed continued to believe, against increasing evidence to the contrary, that the old Ottoman views would prevail.

He accepted, however, that another 'pogrom', like the three days of officially provoked rioting, could break out again, as in the 1890's. He thought he could take sensible personal precautions to protect his family. Surely, he felt, now that there was a more modern attitude at the heart of the Ottoman government, he did not need to fear anything worse. Surely?

In the summer of 1914, Vahan had got his place at the University of Constantinople to study Music and Drama, and had left for the city. He had never returned. Meanwhile, the rest of the family continued life as before – going to the summer house on the slopes of Mt. Erciyas at the height of the summer, and battening down the hatches for the bitter winters. They gave little thought as to how those two shots in Sarajevo were going to change their lives forever.

CHAPTER 8

Breakfast at the Avakians

Once again, as this clear and sunny April advanced, the Avakians were gathering, as they did every morning, for the family breakfast in the great room in the centre of the house.

Nerissa, the third and most reflective of Karekin's four clever daughters, was usually fairly calm. She would listen to her noisy family, putting in the odd pertinent comment every so often. She helped her mother with the younger children and she chatted to the servants.

There was a small Armenian school in the town which she still attended during the mornings. She was a voracious reader, particularly of English literature, Shakespeare and the Victorian romantic novelists. She had an excellent command of the language itself, which had not been missed by Karekin. Karekin had accordingly already enrolled her in the sixth-form classes at the English High School for Girls in the city, where she would be starting in the Summer. Armineh was not so easily impressed. In her opinion, Nerissa already wasted far too much time reading books and dreaming about impossibly romantic, and to Armineh's mind, rather feeble, young male heroes.

Karekin was unquestionably the centre of the household round whom everything revolved. But it was Armineh who had to face the daily problems of plain ordinary living – all the silly pains and stresses of her children and their many emotional crises. In addition she managed the running of the house – all of which Karekin took for granted. As for all the reading and discussions, Armineh's own feelings were that it was all very well for girls to have a liberal education, but what about husbands – and families!

Like all her sisters, Nerissa adored and hero-worshipped her father, though not without a small tinge of fear. She had just reached the age of sixteen. Still rather young for her age, she had a special affection for her younger brother Haik, with whom she played and chatted in the large garden and walled orchard at the rear of their house. Olga and Sima were far too old and sophisticated for her. They rarely talked seriously to her, and this had thrown her back on the unaffected love and simple affection of her young brother.

Haik, was a lively lad, as quick and as responsive as his clever sisters. He was however somewhat delicate physically, and although now 12, he had retained childish, somewhat pretty and delicate features, with huge brown eyes, a clear pale skin and a thin, peaky long nose. He had only ever known unbounded love and adoration from a household of sensitive and comforting women, and consequently he trusted everyone, almost to the point of naiveté.

Despite being the quietest and most introverted of the children, Nerissa had a complex character. She was not conventionally pretty, having inherited her mother's rather dumpy figure. Her nose was a touch too large, her lips too full. She was, however, the cleverest of all the children. She tended to be critical of what she saw as the social ambition of Sima, her eldest sister, and also what she viewed as the shallow flirtatiousness of Olga, whom she regarded as a complete lightweight. She was fairly unjustified in both cases – and it only reflected the intellectual arrogance of a clever 16 year-old, who had not yet learned to accept other people's faults. She was filled with the romantic ideals of the great English novelists of the previous century, but, so far, these ideas did not attach themselves to any specific male figure.

Nerissa was used to Olga's on-again, off-again ways, so never really expected to be called upon to fulfill the arrangements to which she had tentatively agreed. It was therefore with real surprise that she heard from Olga, on this very morning, that they were to go that afternoon to tea at Tokatlians as agreed.

"Nerissa, my love, there is no need for you to walk home from school this afternoon – I'm going to pick you up, and we're going to go to tea at Tokatlians'."

"Olga – what do you mean – it's going to be this afternoon? What shall I wear?" wailed Nerissa.

"My dear – you'll be coming from school – just take a scarf or a shawl or something with you – for heaven's sake we're only going to have some tea and cakes and a chat."

Nerissa looked across at her mother Armineh who was as usual fussing around the spare and delicate Haik, trying to get him to do more than just peck at his food.

"Mother, did you know that Olga has invited me to go to tea with a friend of hers at Tokatlians this afternoon, after school?"

"My girl," replied Armineh somewhat distractedly, "Olga has already told me – do go if you want to, it'll be a change for you. Now, Olga, mind you make sure that you are both back before seven o'clock, and don't walk up from the station, wait for Abdul or Mustafa, even if they are not there when you get off the train."

Nerissa was half hoping that her mother would object. She had been careful not to tell a lie, but she was aware that there was an element of deception in what Olga was planning, and it made her uncomfortable.

Karekin, as always already fully dressed for the outside world, came down and sat at the end of the table in front of his plate of home-made bread, cheese and olives, with a little honey. Maria poured out tea into his usual glass with a slice of lemon already in it. This was a beautifully engraved example of of an old Ottoman tea-glass, used only by him.

"Haik, my boy – don't give your mother such a hard time – just eat up. Armineh, stop fussing over him – he's not going to waste away."

"Father," piped up Haik "when are you going to take me to the office as you promised."

"I told you – you'll have to wait until the summer holidays. In any case, with this dreadful war there is precious little to do. Armineh, did I tell you that I've had to let Leon and Berge go – there's just not enough work. In any case the government are tightening up on young men with deferment, and the army is certainly going to have them soon in any case."

"Is there any news in the papers of what is happening in Van and Erzerum?" asked Armineh.

"It's serious, my dear, that I can certainly tell you. I'm going to go down to the Patriarchate this morning to find out if there is any more hard news – but the regime is extremely jumpy, the general atmosphere is tense and I don't like the signs at all. I think for the next few days, Sima, you must go with Haik when he goes to school, and either you or one of the servants must go in the afternoon to pick him up. There was an anti-Armenian demonstration yesterday outside the Bazaar. It was broken up by the police eventually – but only half-heartedly, and only after several shop windows had been smashed."

He turned to Olga – "Now Olga, listen, I must say that....."

"Oh father, Oh dear is that the time? I'm sorry I've simply got to dash – you know I've got to catch the earlier train than you."

Olga jumped up before Karekin could finish, and ran out grabbing her coat and bags in the hall. She called back to Nerissa, "Remember Nerissa, I will be at your school to pick you up- at about two o'clock this afternoon."

Karekin looked vexed, and was again about to make a comment towards Olga's vanishing figure, when Sima forestalled him with a hint of anxiety, rising from her seat.

"Come on, Haiky – finish up – let's go."

"Aw, Baba – I'm 12 – I don't need to be taken to school by anyone any more. The other boys will all laugh at me," wailed Haik.

Karekin rose from his seat. He was clearly angry and at the end of his tether. His face darkened as he felt a deep anger rising in him, an anger which was probably rooted in the vague disquiet he was feeling about Olga, a disquiet he could not quite pinpoint. This was coupled to the perpetual nagging worries about the worsening political situation that was threatening not only his family circumstances, but even their very lives and that now lay at the pit of his stomach every day.

Karekin never raised a hand to any of his children, but when roused he exerted authority absolutely and automatically, and he tended to be very much harder on his only son than on his four clever girls. Nerissa, sensitive as always to the charged atmosphere, opened her eyes wide, fearful of the coming explosion. But Armineh and Sima were quicker and a good deal more practical than Nerissa. Armineh, pretending that Karekin had risen to prepare for his departure, quickly handed him a list of things she had already prepared and which she wished him to fetch on his return from the market, whilst Sima jumped up, tweaked Haik's ears and ushered him quickly out of the room, complaining vociferously as he went.

"Come on, little man – let's get you ready. Don't worry Haik, my mouse, I'll leave you well before the school gates."

Haik had no idea that he had narrowly avoided a very uncomfortable five minutes, due to the efforts of his mother and eldest sister.

Karekin, realising that he had just been the victim of manipulation by his wife and eldest daughter, quietly took his hat and coat from Armineh, who looked straight into his eyes, and then gave him a kiss – to his surprise – right on his lips, in front of everyone. The tide of anger that had come over him and which he had been about to unleash on Haik, had had nothing really to do with the boy at all. His worries and anxieties seemed to be multiplying, and he didn't know on which one to concentrate. The news from the Caucasian front during January and February had been bad enough, but that coming from Van was devastating, if true. He determined to check the latest position at the Patriarchate that very morning. Karekin hurried out and walked straight to the station – no sitting on benches and musing these days.

He arrived at the city ignoring, as best he could, the tense atmosphere now ever present in the streets of Stamboul – as if the town was waiting for a storm to burst. Karekin hurried to the quiet calm of the Patriarchate buildings. Crossing the quiet, tree-lined courtyard, he knocked at the door of Father Haroutune, one of the secretaries to the Patriarch and a personal friend. He walked into the little room, where the Priest was seated at a small desk in front of an old typewriter and several bundles of paper.

"Hello my good friend – I am here for news."

"God be with you Karekin agha."

"Look, enough of these rumours, Haroutune, hard news – hard news!. The patriarchate must know what is actually happening in Van and the Armenian vilayets?."

The little priest looked up – his eyes were red, and he was shaking and his voice quavered –

" My dear friend, I don't know for sure as the news from Van is clearly being censored – but there is obviously some sort of insurrection or trouble there and the army is involved in some way. But Karekin it is not only Van. I do believe that something really terrible is about to happen in the interior, even if it has not already started. If the reports I am seeing are true, nothing like it has ever been seen before. Believe me, Karekin, we're going to look back on Abdul Hamid and his whimsical and random barbarities with nostalgia, when faced with what may be the beginning of a deliberate official policy of getting rid of a whole population! The more I read of the decrees and proposals emanating from Talaat's office, the more I fear for for the future."

"For heaven's sakes, man – pull yourself together – all you clerics are the same – you just can't help yourselves making grand moral statements. Just give me the facts – I'll decide if we have anything to fear. For God's sake, Turks have been killing Armenians for centuries, and for all I know, probably the other way round as well, so what's different now?"

Haroutune said nothing for a moment and hung his head in his hands.

"I don't know, Karekin, there's no word for it at the moment. Perhaps the world will make up a word if it ever happens again to someone else, but believe me something evil is about to happen in the villages and little towns of the interior. Here, I have prepared a precis of the reports we have been receiving from our priests in the interior. But it is not only from them, but from German and American missionaries. Here, take the whole file, read it and let me know what you think."

Karekin always balked at the word 'evil'. A good, well-educated liberal did not believe in evil as such.

"Father, everyone is jumpy and nervous. With the failure of the British fleet to break through the Dardanelles a few weeks ago, we all know that they are going to try again with their army soon. So, of course we're all treading delicately on eggs. But,

Father, this isn't the time to talk about 'evil', and start thinking about 'terror', or 'apocalyptic visions'. We're at war and this sort of panic and rumour happens in such circumstances. One of the prices of living in, and being part of, a multi-national empire like ours is the danger of racial tensions arising like this at moments of crisis. However, we have a duty to try and minimize it. Talking about evil can have the effect of making it happen."

"Karekin, I do hope you're right and I fervently pray that I am wrong. I know I'm a timid and fearful man, but I do sense something different about our new masters, something totally alien to the old Ottoman ruling class under whom we have muddled along for so long."

Karekin straightened up. He looked down at the little man and picked up the bundle of papers. Then on instinct he bent down and planted a strong and heartfelt kiss on the man's forehead, and walked out, deliberately ignoring the sign of the cross raised towards his retreating back by the nervous priest.

CHAPTER 9

The Siege of Van

I. The uncontested historical background.

The much vaunted winter offensive by the Turkish 3rd Army into the Caucasus had been a complete catastrophe. Against the advice, not only of the admittedly weary but canny old Ottoman generals, but also of the German military mission, Enver Pasha had overridden all opposition, and marched a badly supplied, and totally unmotivated army, into some of the most difficult terrain in the world. It had been a devastating experience for the Third Army, which had lost all its artillery and about 75,000 men, leaving only a small force of about 30,000 demoralised men, covering the whole of the Erzerum region.

Enver Pasha returned to Constantinople towards the end of January, his arrogance and Napoleonic pretensions intact. On his return, he made every effort to conceal the truth and to represent the catastrophe as nothing more than a local setback. He was totally indifferent to the dreadful suffering of the ordinary soldiers, huge numbers of whom died of frostbite. On the matter of the possible political fall-out, however, he was much more sensitive, and he immediately began searching for some scapegoat to take the blame for his own ineptitude.

In London, the Russian victory had strengthened the position of those who favoured an attack on Turkey. The scale of the disaster to Enver's 3rd Army seemed to make the proposal for a direct attack on Constantinople more attractive in London breaking the current stalemate. The fall of their capital would throw Turkey out of the war, whilst the opening of the Straits to allied shipping would aid the Russians and stave off any possible internal unrest. By February, the British government was ready to take up some offensive option against Constantinople. Approaches were made to the Russians to supply some sort of diversionary operation – perhaps towards the Bosporus, the northern approach to the great city.

The Russians appeared ready to comply, except for the Russian naval commander in the Black Sea, Admiral Eberhardt, who remained cowed by the presence of the *Goeben* and the *Breslau* in the Straits. The Russians faced a dilemma. On the one hand, their long-standing obsession with Constantinople as the centre of their Orthodox faith, as well as the controller of the vital narrows which led to the only Russian outlet to ice-free, warm seas and the great sea-lanes of the world. On the other hand, this had to be balanced against the ability of the two great battleships to cripple the Russian fleet and disperse, with enormous loss of life, any expeditionary force the Russians might send to come to the aid of any British initiative.

In the end, the Admiral's view prevailed. The continuation of a 'fleet in being' seemed to be more important than any help to the British. From the Russian point of view, a successful capture by the British of the great city might be almost as bad as a dramatic failure. Once again, simply by being there, the two battleships had decisively affected history.

Meanwhile, back on the Caucasian front, as the harsh winter gave way to a fairly mild April, the Russians began to make a tentative advance towards the city of Erzerum, to take advantage of the much depleted Ottoman forces. This was wild and inhospitable country, farmed mainly by tenacious Armenian peasantry settled there for centuries, while the main towns were fairly evenly split between Turks and Armenians. Interspersed with these, lawless bands of nomadic Kurdish tribesmen roamed. As the Russians advanced, they naturally tried to exploit these age-old differences to obtain as much support as possible.

The Armenian situation in the high plateau heartlands of the Caucasus and Eastern Anatolia, was very difficult. They were only in a clear majority in one or two of the great cities. The practice of the Ottoman ideal of a tolerant and multi-cultural empire, was merely a chimera here. The situation for the peasantry of the wild and mountainous areas of Eastern Anatolia was quite different. Here the mixture of races and religions, coupled to the poor soil and harsh conditions, had led to intolerance and tribal hatred. Here, petty officials could and did stoop to trivial tyrannies against a generally peaceful minority. With the same people straddling the border of Imperial Russia, loyalties, impossibly strained by the terrible Hamidian pogroms of the 1890's, were much more complicated.

As always, the majority of the population were passive, tilling the soil, weaving their carpets, and celebrating age-old traditions at Easter and Christmas, without too much regard to the political events taking place around them. But if trouble was to come, it would inevitably fall on this patient, uncommitted majority, the family men and their wives and children, who just wanted to get on with their lives. It would not fall on the revolutionaries or nationalist activists seeking change.

Early in April, the Turkish High Command, aware of the worst-kept secret of the whole war – namely the likelihood of an Anglo-French landing somewhere in or near Constantinople – realised that they needed to shore up the Caucasian front. The remnants of the Turkish 3rd Army were now being led by an irascible old Ottoman general – Halil Bey – not a member of the

Ittihad, but connected to Enver by marriage. He led a scratch force of several battalions of regulars, some bits of artillery and a great mob of Kurds. He had already complained that the lack of proper medical services for his forces was threatening their effectiveness.

General Yudenich, on the Russian side, gave the greatest attention, like all good commanders, to the welfare of his troops. Supplies and sanitary and medical services were mainly excellent. This had not been the case with Enver Pasha. Full of such high-minded philosophical ideals as Pan-Turanism and western-style modernisation, the Young Turks were relying on the dumb, unquestioning endurance of the Turkish peasant, without any concern for their welfare. Whatever the faults of the old regime – and they were many – the old Ottoman Pashas had understood the importance of adequately supplied and maintained armies.

In the area of Lake Van, and the valley of the upper Euphrates, the mob of irregular Kurdish tribesmen, ostensibly part of Halil's force, had put the whole countryside into a state of tense anarchy. No one – villagers, townsmen, tenant farmers, Armenians or even Turks felt safe, although it was the Christians who were the principle sufferers.

Meanwhile in the city of Van itself, a particularly vicious Ittihad Governor, Djevdet Bey, had been deliberately goading the Armenian majority by acts of petty tyranny and worse. At last the exasperated and increasingly desperate population of the city of Van, driven to extremity by the tyrannies of the Ittihad Governor and the lawlessness in the countryside around, rose in what appeared to be a revolt. Exploding out of the narrow streets of their quarter, young armed Armenian men commenced a fierce fight against the demoralised garrison and gendarmerie of the town. After only a day or two, the Armenians took possession of most of this ancient city and were in control by the end of the second week in April.

This revolt had nothing to do with Enver's retreat earlier in the year, but was a spontaneous uprising of a population driven to despair. The different elements within the rising were as diverse as most spontaneous revolts tend to be, but after its success, the professional nationalists and revolutionaries inevitably took over. General Yudenich, well informed of the situation, decided to take immediate advantage, and ordered infantry units of his advancing 4th Caucasian Army group to turn their advance towards the beautiful town on the lake. At the same time, he mounted a large Cossack cavalry raid through the Kurdish tribal areas to clear away some of the brigands in his path, who were rife in the area.

Halil Bey, hearing of the revolt, moved his 6,000 regulars up to take back control of the city, before the Russians could arrive, starting the siege of Van, which was to last for weeks. By the time Halil's regulars moved up to take over the siege from the Governor's scratch forces, his large contingent of Kurds had deserted, abandoning him and his Turkish regulars. These Kurdish tribesmen were prepared to harry defenceless peasant settlers – a favourite pastime of nomadic people throughout the ages – but were not prepared to act as docile cannon fodder for the Turkish government. Accordingly, they had disappeared to join and profit from the general anarchy as soon as they could. Meanwhile, both sides dug into their fortified positions and began to fight it out.

II. Doctor Nazim Kemal. The Turkish point of view.

Back in the capital, Doctor Nazim had continued his work at the German hospital. The closure of the French hospital had added to the workload, and he was continually in demand. His criticisms of the Ittihad in general, and Enver and Talaat in particular, had not changed. However he came to modify his comments in public, as he felt that as the Empire was in such difficulties, the government should be supported as far as possible. However, in private and over the breakfast table, he was more outspoken and remained critical.

""Nazim," said Halideh one morning early in April, "I heard in the hammam yesterday that Enver is claiming nothing happened in the Caucasus during the winter."

"Well, my dear, that is clearly not true, as many of our soldiers died. The number of our men suffering and dying from frostbite was enormous, and several of my colleagues in the medical service have confirmed this, quite apart from the the enormous number of men still in pretty bad conditions at the military hospital at Scutari."

"I also heard that he is claiming that Armenian irregulars operating in the area gave a lot of help to the Russians, even some who were of Ottoman nationality, and that explains the defeats."

"Oh, mother, that sounds like pure propaganda, and even downright lies. In any case, isn't he saying that there were no major defeats in any case?"

"Yes that could be so," said Nazim, who suddenly had the fleeting thought that Selim seemed to be always on the defensive these days whenever Armenians were mentioned. "Frankly, I'm convinced that Enver made a real mess of the whole offensive. I think that General Yudenich out-manoeuvred him from the start. So now he's looking for scapegoats to blame for his own shortcomings. That's not to say that the Armenians, themselves, aren't making it easier for him by their ambivalence towards this war. My son, I believe that it was a fatal error to get into this war at all – but now we are in it, we must all rally round the only government we have. They are our soldiers – they must be supported. And that reminds me, son, what we say together at home between us can be as outspoken as we may wish – but not outside! Look, son you must learn to keep your opinions to yourself a bit more. We live in difficult and dangerous times. Abdul Hamid's secret police might have been disbanded, but instead we have a mindless mob, listening out for treasonous talk."

"Oh, baba, you know I'm all in favour of the Ittihad ideas in principle. I don't even think it was all that wrong to get into this war – we've been pushed around enough by those arrogant Westerners already. No, it's those idiots – Enver and Talaat!"

It was some days after this conversation that Nazim heard he was to be drafted into the Army as a Major; his medical and administrative services were going to be required on the

Caucasian front. It appeared that the irascible Halil Bey – a Moslem gentleman of the old school – had insisted on an increase in the medical services for his small force stationed near Lake Van.

There had been little time for Nazim to deal with all his affairs. Since receiving his commission, he had hardly been at home, while he gathered together, supplied and outfitted a scratch medical team to accompany him. On the day he left, he had hugged Halideh hard as they parted in the little hall of their flat in Galata. She had run to the window as the front door closed. She looked down into the street, as he emerged from the entrance of the building. Dressed in his clean new uniform, Nazim carried his own personal medical bag of surgical instruments, while Selim carried his father's bags.

Selim hailed a passing gharry, and stepped in, taking the bags with him. Nazim turned and looked up at the window, behind which he knew that Halideh would be standing, looking down at him. He made no grand gesture, save ever so slightly to raise the palm of his right hand in a discreet salute. He then stepped into the carriage next to Selim.

"The ferry station for Haydar pasha station – driver" he called out.

They were both silent as they drove down the hill to the Galata bridge. They remained largely silent as the ferry chugged its way across the straits and pulled up alongside the ferry landing stage for the Haydar Pasha terminus of the Asian railway system.

They got off and slowly began walking up to the station.

"My son, when we get to the station I will be distracted and busy, sorting out a couple of doctors and several staff. We won't be able to talk. My boy, in case anything happens – you know what I mean – your first duty must be to your mother and sister; however once that is done, your next duty is to fulfil yourself. Don't hurry to give up your deferment, my son – make sure you complete your education before rushing off to war – if you have the chance that is."

Selim shuffled. His heart welled up, and he felt a little sick as he looked at his dapper, well-groomed father.

"Baba, are we fighting a religious war... our enemies, Russians or ... whatever ... are Christians, aren't they. I mean ...

"No, my son, not at all. This war is totally secular; it has nothing to do with religion. The Ittihad may have made a bad mistake in joining in – but there's no doubt that the Empire is beset by predators all round, and we simply have to defend our way of life."

"Father, are we obliged to hate as well? I mean, suppose I knew a Russian lady who was a friend, would it be. ... I mean ... I don't know, wrong to be friendly with an enemy of the state?"

"Don't be silly son, there's nothing wrong with friendship at any level with anyone, so long as it goes no further than that. Life is changing, I accept that, and there's no reason why you can't converse with girls of your own age and class, and make friends. For god's sake don't repeat this to your mother, by the way! I know that you will always be honourable and just in your dealings, and that is all that matters."

"Yes, Father, that's all very well, but what ...

"Major Kemal," a soldier addressed him, coming forward and saluting, as they stood in front of the station at the top of the steps up from the ferry station, "Your unit is awaiting on Platform 2. The medical supplies are currently being loaded at the freight depot, and your supervision is required, Sir."

Nazim turned to Selim – smiled – clasped his shoulder, and, without another word, turned and strode into the station followed by the young soldier now carrying the bag, reluctantly relinquished by an emotional Selim, who stood fighting back his tears as his father walked away

The train made its way slowly to the east, where Nazim had been ordered to join Halil Bey, whom, he believed, was engaged in holding back the Russians who were moving towards the towns of Erzerum and Van.

On his arrival, Nazim reported directly to Halil Bey, whose HQ was in Bitlis, some miles away from Van.

"Your Excellency, I have the honour to present myself –

Major Nazim Kemal, Doctor and Surgeon, with a small medical team raised in Stamboul about a week ago."

"Sit down, Major, sit down. I'm sure you would like to have a coffee." Halil called out to his orderly "Khaveh – shekerli?"

Nazim nodded and sat down.

"I am not sure, Major, how much you know of the situation here. I doubt if the government has been at all open in its reporting in the capital. In fact, I know the news has been carefully censored. The Provincial Governor here is an arrogant bastard by the name of Djevdet Bey – the new Ittihad breed you understand – who has made a mess of his relations with the infidel Armenians, who, incidentally, are in the majority in this town. Can't stand the fellow myself – but of course, this is no excuse for the cursed infidels to revolt. Infamous traitors the lot of them, when you think that the Russian army is close by and moving forward daily."

"What forces do we have available, Sir?" asked Nazim.

"Well, I have a military gendarme division, together with four battalions of regulars. Until a few days ago, I also commanded a mob of Kurdish irregulars: undisciplined and frankly pretty useless except for terrifying women and children. For better or worse, they have all melted away and are over in the east pillaging everything they can lay their hands on, which at least gives the pesky Russkis and the Armenians something to think about. Look, this leaves me with about six thousand men, of which over a half are now manning the siege lines we have drawn round the city."

"Well sir, I'm amazed. I have some Armenian acquaintances in Stamboul, and I had always supposed them to be fairly loyal to the state, despite their awful experiences under the regime of Abdul Hamid. However, a revolt like this in the face of an invading enemy army is totally inexcusable whatever the provocation. I'm appalled. What numbers and strength are we talking about?"

"I don't know, Major. They certainly can't have much ammunition, and they must be using boys and old men. So far as my Intelligence officers have been able to gather, the actual numbers facing us with weapons are not much more than about a thousand. Frankly, Major, once we get fully organised we should be able to deal with them in a couple of days. For the moment, they are simply being contained, and that ridiculous strutting idiot the Governor is still in charge. I want you to move your detachment up to the lines as soon as possible, after which I am going to open up a proper military offensive, with a final push to eliminate the bastards. You may dismiss, Major, but please report any problems directly to me."

The next day, when Nazim arrived at the lakeside behind the Turkish siege lines, he looked across at the town, with its walled old city dominated by a castle on a rock, perched by the beautiful deep blue lake, and bordered by magnificent mountains, still lightly covered with snow. He pinpointed the spot where he would set up his headquarters and went to work.

In his customary cool and efficient way, he busied himself with the setting up of his main tent as a military hospital, and spent the following day inspecting the Turkish front lines drawn around the Armenian quarter of the town. He made many recommendations as to the primitive sanitary arrangements, and slowly, by dint of persuasion, he managed to improve the conditions for the rank and file soldiers in many small but significant ways. The Turkish artillery, meanwhile, continued to unleash shell after shell into the old town below.

Nazim worked tirelessly – day and night – tending the wounds and disfigurements of the Turkish soldiers returning from the continuous gunfire around the old city. Unlike the Ittihad leaders, he slowly came to learn a new respect, which he had never felt before, for the illiterate and inarticulate Anatolian soldiers, who bore their pains so uncomplainingly. Night after night, the talk would turn on the question of when the city would fall, and how or why the rebels were still holding on, when their ammunition must surely be exhausted.

Punctilious as ever, Nazim shaved carefully every day. He spent his spare time writing letters home to Selim and his wife. He never complained of anything more than the days of boredom, interspersed with days of violent action. He did, however, sadly report to his son that the rebellion of the inhabitants of Van, right in front of the Ottoman's historic enemy, had soured his attitude to the Armenians. It was clear to him that there could be no excuse at all, regardless of any provocation, for raising a revolt right in front of an advancing enemy army, when your country was in mortal danger.

III. Clarence Ussher – A neutral position.

Van was one of the most beautiful cities in the whole Ottoman Empire, surrounded by well tended and prosperous gardens and vineyards. It stood on ground that gently sloped down to the deep blue lake – Lake Van – which is itself surrounded by gaunt and steep mountains. Some miles from the shore lies the island of Akhtamar, covered in greenery, with a serene and beautiful old Armenian church set amongst the trees in the centre, where families, Turks as well as Armenians, would go to picnic in the warm summers.

Just outside the old walled town, in the middle of the Armenian quarter, lay the American Protestant Mission. The buildings were surrounded by a high stone wall, and comprised a Protestant church, several schools, a hospital and dispensary, and residences for the staff. Five minutes walk away was the German orphanage run by two old ladies. All around them, were old Ottoman houses, in various stages of picturesque dilapidation, with their wooden lattice bay windows, jutting out over the street.

The American Mission was led by Doctor Clarence Ussher, who was not only in charge of the hospital and the medical supplies, but was also in overall control of the whole Mission. He was helped by his wife, an elder sister, and several Armenian nurses.

Clarence Ussher was the son of a Canadian Episcopalian bishop from a family of devout Christians who had provided Church leaders for generations. A large bearded man with a soft round face and gentle eyes, he nevertheless possessed a clear, hard, inner core of moral certainty. Like so many in the missionary world, he was never at a loss as to what was the right course of action. Doubt never crossed his mind, and this gave him an inner conviction, which carried him benignly through circumstances which would have broken many others.

He was a competent general doctor with fairly good surgical skills. An efficient administrator, he was supremely confident and self-controlled. His wife, the daughter of a missionary, had been born in Caesaria in Central Anatolia. They both spoke Turkish fluently, and they both had that narrow, focussed intensity, so often seen amongst 'driven' 19th-century missionaries everywhere. Having failed to convert more than a handful of Turks, over the years, they turned their attention to good works and trying to convert one of the oldest Christian communities in the world to their own protestant beliefs. Ironically, this had not endeared them to Armenian clerics. Furthermore, it had contributed to the nationalistic fervour, which had been irresponsibly aroused in the vulnerable Armenian peasantry.

Dr. Ussher had been a fairly close friend of the previous Turkish governor – Ahmed Fari Pasha. Fari had been anxious to maintain good relations between all his subjects. Before the secular Young Turks had deprived him of his post at the start of the war, the old Vali, always interested in theological subjects, had delighted in evening dinner parties with the clerics of the various religious sects in the town. On one occasion, the guests were taking their coffee after a meal given by the Vali, at which Clarence Ussher was one of the guests, along with a Nestorian deacon, a Chaldaean Catholic bishop, and a Sufi divine, amongst others. The Vali turned to the Bishop.

"My Lord Bishop, what then must I do to be sure of getting into Paradise?"

The good but rather simple Bishop, who had imbibed far too much of the excellent wine which the Vali had thoughtfully provided, replied-

"I believe your excellency, that for Jesus' sake, the Lord will pardon my sins and allow me into paradise in all circumstances."

The Vali was clearly disappointed at what he considered a facile response. Ussher immediately intervened, and taking the

Vali's comment seriously, went into a long monologue into the theological differences between Christians and Moslems on this all-important matter. The two of them then debated late into the night, much to the boredom of the other three clerical guests.

This old Vali was immediately suspect in the eyes of the Ittihad Committee of Union and Progress, once they had achieved clear power over the old Ottoman bureaucracy.

The Ittihad leaders knew, without the need for spies, who would be reliable, if and when they decided to have a showdown with the minority populations. They knew they would first have to get rid of the old Ottoman ruling class. This was not just because these conservative rulers were unable to come to terms with the new Westernised Turkey they wished to create, but that however inefficient and lazy the old Ottoman ruling class may have been, their instincts would not have allowed them to connive at the terrible solution which was being planned.

Accordingly, after the take-over by the Committee of Union and Progress, the old Ottoman Governor, Ahmed Fari, had been dismissed, and replaced by Djevdet Bey, a cold and arrogant official of the new nationalist school – and brother-in-law of Enver Pasha.

On his return from Enver's disastrous offensive, Djevdet Bey immediately began developing a confrontational policy towards the majority Armenian population. In the second week of April when disturbances broke out in a suburban part of the town, he arranged for four Armenian leaders to go and try to pacify the area. There, he had them murdered by a special police detachment under his direct orders, and he then arrested the Armenian Member of Parliament who was in the town, and sent him back under arrest to Constantinople.

At this juncture, the remaining Armenian leaders, desperately seeking a compromise, offered Djevdet Bey a large bribe to make up for the current shortfall of recruits from the city of which he was complaining. At the same time, they approached Dr. Ussher asking him to intercede. He agreed to visit the new Governor, whose family he had known in happier days. Djevdet Bey, however, remained obdurate, and professing to be worried about the security of the American Mission then stated that he proposed sending eighty soldiers to occupy the American compound.

"Your Excellency," said Ussher, "I am greatly in debt to you for your suggestion, but I do feel that such a large force appearing in the middle of the Armenian quarter at such a tense moment would be a disaster and likely to lead to bloodshed. Perhaps if your Excellency sent a token force of say five askaris, this would be more than enough to guarantee the safety of the compound."

"I am sorry, but I intend sending a fully armed detachment to occupy the Mission for your own safety," replied the Vali coldly.

"Your Excellency, I am most anxious that this meeting should not result in our falling out. The American government is neutral in this war and I will be doing my utmost to make certain that we remain so. However, I would remind you that by arrangement with the Turkish government over many decades, the Mission here has full diplomatic status, as clear as a consulate: I cannot allow the entry of a large body of soldiers into what is technically American territory."

Djevdet Bet, clearly irritated and, with rising temper, blurted out, "In that case, Doctor, I demand a written note absolving me of any responsibility for your safety." Ussher nodded, confirmed that he would be happy to provide a note to this effect and left the office.

During the mobilisation that had taken place over the previous winter, the Armenians had been relentlessly plundered under the guise of requisitioning. The rich had been ruined, whilst the poor, though willingly joining the Army when called up, had been deprived of any arms, and had been forced into doing all the menial tasks for the military. This had resulted in a high degree of tension throughout the city.

On the day of the outbreak of the so-called 'rebellion' – the excuse for this and all later barbarities as well as the new policy of total ethnic cleansing – some Turkish soldiers tried to seize one of a group of Armenian village women who were on their way to the city. She fled. Two Armenian soldiers came up to investigate, and at that point the Turkish soldiers opened fire and killed them. The Turkish entrenchments which Djevdet Bey had been drawing up round the Armenian quarter during the previous three days, then opened up an intense barrage of fire into the residential quarter. The old cannons on Castle Rock began pouring a slow but murderous fire on the houses below. The siege of Van, destined to last for several weeks, had begun.

During the whole of the siege, Dr. Ussher would allow no armed men to enter the compound. The Armenians, understanding this neutrality, gave orders, after the third day, that no wounded soldiers were to be brought to the American hospital. Instead, Dr Ussher would go down with the nurses to the temporary hospital, set up by the Armenians in the church hall, at least once a day. Even so, only a few days after the siege had begun, and before the arrival of Halil Bey's regulars – Djevdet Bey wrote to Ussher claiming that armed men had been seen entering the American compound, and as a result he would be opening fire on the hospital.

Djevdet Bey and Dr. Ussher corresponded with each other during the siege by sending letters to the Italian consular agent – Italy still being neutral. These letters were taken through the lines by old women carrying a flag of truce. At least four of these ladies lost their lives acting as postmen during the siege. It was a feature of the siege that a volunteer replacement was always quickly found. Ussher's note back stated clearly and explicitly -

"Your Excellency, I must make it crystal clear that at no time have I or any of my staff treated any armed, or previously armed men at my hospital. My mission is to preserve the neutrality of our premises by every means in our power. I accept that I have taken in refugees from the villages around, where both regular soldiers and their wild Kurdish allies have been sweeping the countryside – massacring men, women and children, and burning down their homes. Not one of these villagers had any arms. Our hospital, with a normal capacity of 50, now accommodates 187. I remain Your Excellency's faithful servant."

Despite this, the direct bombardment of the American

Mission started on the next day.

It was painfully apparent to Ussher, that in the event of a collapse of the Armenian defenders, the compound would be overrun, and that the chances of survival of the American staff in the bloody massacre that would inevitably follow, would be slight indeed. Despite this, as well as the fact that he had a wife and young children present, who would inevitably be caught up in the slaughter, he remained absolutely steadfast throughout the siege, continuing with his humanitarian work. As always, he was totally confidant in the morality of his stance.

There was never any doubt that Ussher could have left, with his wife and three children, at any time during the siege. The Turks would have let them through their lines, while the Armenians often pressed him to escape. But neither Ussher nor his equally staunch wife ever wavered from what they considered to be their moral duty.

It has been argued that the terrible killings and massacres of the helpless Armenian population in Anatolia, which began soon after these events in Van, were triggered by what Doctors Ussher and Nazim saw from their different viewpoints. However, it cannot explain how the first genocide of the 20th century came to pass. Djevdet Bey was unquestionably the wrong man in the wrong place at the wrong time. But his actions and reactions had in many ways been foreordained by factors which had shaped his formation as an adult, and which, by the coincidence of events, had ended up in this siege.

Clarence Ussher had lived in Van many years before the siege. He had known Djevdet Bay as a growing boy, and had been interested in, and followed his development, into an adult. He had seen the slow erosion in this one individual, of the old Ottoman values.

First had come the paranoid suspicions and random cruelties of the odious and blood-crazed Abdul Hamid. His incredible hatred towards the people who had lived amongst the Turks for generations, had deepened the distrust between the two ethnic groups to breaking point during his thirty year rule. Raised in the closed claustrophobic world of the Harem, there was surprisingly some uncertainty as to whether Abdul Hamid's mother had been a Circassian or an Armenian girl, and this may have aggravated his paranoia. Certainly he himself had had an Armenian look about him as a young man, and sneers to this effect may well have poisoned his mind. Normally the eunuchs in charge of the Harem were particularly careful to note the times and dates and pedigree of any girl who had shared the Padishah's bed. It was accordingly doubly unfortunate that there was a small element of doubt in respect of Abdul Hamid's conception.

So deeply suspicious was this horrific little man who had ordered so many tortures and pogroms, that his personal servants were all trained to move exceptionally slowly in his presence, so as not to alarm him by making sudden movements. He was an excellent shot, and always kept at least two loaded pistols about his person, and is known to have shot at least three palace servants who had inadvertently moved suddenly in his presence.

Djevdet had been brought up in this atmosphere of suspicion and hatred, and had, from childhood, witnessed the regular pogroms and humiliations visited on his Armenian neighbours. The harm Abdul Hamid had done to the minds and attitudes of his subjects, Christian and Moslem alike, was beyond calculation, and that harm had penetrated the mind of the young Djevdet as much as any other.

Ussher reflected that then, following this awful thirty-year reign, had come the 1908 revolution, and the rise of the Ittihad. With this there had arisen a drive towards secularisation, and the erosion now of the older and deeper virtues and values of Islam, for whom 'people of the book' were neighbours, and not racial enemies. Djevdet Bey had been influenced by the impatience of these men with the pashas who had previously run the Empire. These revolutionaries were impatient for reforms and anxious to repudiate the Arab-Islamic element in the Empire and instead promulgate the efficiency of a modern westernised nation-state. Of course Ussher himself had a greater natural sympathy for Muslim gentlemen like the previous governor Vali, than for those he saw as a godless new generation.

Finally, to put the last touch to the development of Djevdet's character came the domination within the Ittihad of Enver, Talaat and Djemal, all preaching a hard nationalistic creed so alien to the great Padishahs of the past. The Western European style 'nation-state' with all its vicious hatreds and contradictions, had at last arrived in the Islamic world, and Djevdet Bey was the final political product of that movement.

Meanwhile, the siege, started in the second week of April, dragged on day by day without resolution, as Ussher went patiently about his mission.

IV. Nevart's situation.

Nevart, an Armenian born and bred in Van, was tired. Now a wizened shrunken old lady dressed always in black, she had lived over 70 years in Van, and apart from trips to the beautiful island of Achtamar in the Lake, had never left the city. Two husbands had come and gone, and her only remaining family was a widowed daughter, now living with her in her ancient Ottoman-style house in the garden city. The house, in the middle of the urban Armenian quarter not far from the American Mission, was cluttered with the detritus of a long life. The leaning and creaking building was made of wood, terraced with others of similar type on either side, all with the ubiquitous latticed windows on the first and second floors. These bay windows stuck out over the street, reducing the view of the sun and sky from below, but giving welcome shade during the day in the hot summers.

Neither Nevart, nor her daughter Sona, ever really knew what was going on during those April days. They felt the tension in the streets, and they noticed there was less mixing between Armenians and Turks in the bazaars, hammams and cafés in the centre.

"What is happening Sona, where have all the young men got to? What is going on?"

"I'm not sure mother, but I have heard that our Governor is angry because the town hasn't produced its full tally of conscripts for the army."

"On top of all that," grumbled Nevart, not taking much notice of Sona's comment, "the price of fresh vegetables has gone through the roof. There must be fewer villagers coming in to town to sell their produce. The open markets are getting more and more bare. I had to traipse around for almost two hours yesterday just to get a few onions, and the price they asked was ridiculous, I got quite angry and was going to refuse, when the woman behind me called out – 'come on grandma I'll take them if you don't want them'. She was a great fat Armenian lady, and I told her to wash her mouth out – but I paid up and took the onions after that. I walked back with old Yevret Hanum – you remember her, the wife of Agop's old Turkish friend and partner. She told me that bands of Kurds are roaming the countryside, disrupting the villagers lives, killing and robbing, so the villagers are frightened to bring in their produce."

"Well, mother, I don't know. Look, I have to go to work. No doubt it's all just rumours." Sona grabbed her hat and coat and hurried out of the house.

Nevart sighed, and picking up her big straw basket, she got ready to spend the whole morning, if necessary, trying to get some vegetables and replenish her stock of rice. She stepped out into the fresh morning air, hoping that she could make her purchases before the hot midday sun. The whole street seemed to consist of little old women, dressed like her in black, hurrying about chasing provisions of one kind or another.

She had just walked into the little square where the country folk usually came to spread their wares out on the pavements, when she heard the first shots ring out. These were quickly followed by a frenzy of shooting that were the opening salvos of the siege – the reasons for which she never came to understand, and which she never expected would go on for so long.

Suddenly the great gun on the Castle rock boomed out, and there was an explosion just ahead of her. Screams rang out, and people began scattering in different directions. Nevart stood quite still not knowing what to do. The other old women had mostly disappeared – though some were on their knees on the pavement crossing themselves and muttering prayers. She saw some young men run past shouting unintelligibly to each other. Their eyes looked ablaze with excitement, and she could see that some were armed. Another shell burst very close by, and she felt the earth shake – and then a piece of masonry or something flew past her ear grazing her cheek deeply. Blood began to flow.

This suddenly woke her up to the reality of her perilous situation. She started running – not exactly in a panic – but no clear direction. Within a minute or so she was already out of breath, and found herself outside the Protestant mission. The great doors of the compound were closed, as they usually were except on Sundays. Recollecting that there was an excellent medical clinic inside, she leant against the wall, gulping down breaths of air. She pulled the knob of the door-bell, and was immediately let in by the small side door by the Turkish porter, who seeing her bloody face gestured to the little hospital building across the court.

Here, she was immediately taken in by a nurse with the name Alicia pinned to her white coat.

"What's happening, mamoushka?" asked the nurse, and Nevart recognised the accent of an Armenian from the Russian side of the divide.

"I have no idea, no idea at all," replied Nevart, who by now had recovered both her breath and her senses. "There were a couple of loud explosions – some buildings were hit, and a lot of shooting. A stone or piece of falling masonry must have hit me. Then there were a lot of young men, who haven't been seen around town for some time, running about and shouting to each other."

While she listened, the nurse, who seemed to understand better than Nevart what was going on, continued calmly treating the wound on Nevart's wrinkled cheek.

"Well, the whole town has been getting more and more tense over the last week or so. It will be some sort of riot I suppose, though I did hear the boom of the castle gun, several times. You won't need any stitches, mamoushka, just be very careful and don't wash there for a few days," she went on, as she stuck a plaster on Nevart's cheek. "You better get home now, and try not to go out in the streets until whatever is going on, dies down."

Nevart walked out of the little hospital still bewildered, but more her usual self. She could still hear shooting, and the occasional boom of the bigger guns. The great doors of the compound were now flung wide open, and she saw the American Mission's leader standing by the gate. She recognised him though she did not know his name – a big man with a beard, at least big in comparison with everyone around him. A small stream of women and an occasional old man, all with similar wounds to hers, were just beginning to walk or be carried in to the compound.

As Nevart passed by, she saw the American stop a young man who had been hopping in on an improvised crutch, and had a rifle in his hands. His leg was clearly badly crushed and incapable of supporting him. The American murmured a few words to the boy who nodded, and he then beckoned over one of the Turkish employees of the Mission. The young lad leant on the porter's shoulder and they shuffled away down the street. Clearly he had been denied entrance to the Hospital. Nevart stumbled home, still in a daze as the shooting was intensifying, and many of the old buildings which had appeared so solid only a few moments before, had crumbled to dust. She was totally disorientated.

Nevart had spent her entire life in the town, mixing with her Turkish neighbours, both as a girl and as a woman. In the Hammams – the baths – she had always joined in the usual rituals in the women's section of the baths. As a naked young girl she had duly scrubbed the backs of the older women, and listened to their gossip; she had endured and giggled as they made sly comments once she had reached and passed puberty. Then as an older woman herself, she too had had her back scrubbed and lathered by other young women in her turn, and she had indulged in the usual banter and gossip about young men who were available as husbands. Both of her own two husbands had been found as a result of discussions between mothers in these same baths.

The point of all this was that there was no difference between a plump naked Turkish woman and an even plumper naked Armenian one. There might be tensions arising from time to time reflecting local political clashes in the outside world, but these racial tensions were dealt with sensibly by the women. They would simply keep apart for a few days until all that male energy outside had spent itself and would then drift back to their usual comfortable tolerance of each other.

As she turned the corner into the street on which her house stood, she saw a knot of women standing outside and just inside her house, the door of which was open. She knew. She knew instinctively at once what had happened. With a cry she ran forward. Two women ran forward and held her. Sona's broken body lay where she had been reverently placed in the doorway – the victim of the very first shell of the first day of the siege.

Nevart stood and stared, held up by the women. The sobs refused to come. Her last contact with life seemed to have disappeared. She allowed herself to be led into the house. Her neighbours took over the necessary practical details. Nevart, herself, simply drifted into a state of numb indifference.

Once the siege got under way, the Armenians in Van were eventually gathered into a district about a mile square, with the American Hospital right in the middle. Protecting themselves against the entrenchments pinning them down, several of the old solid stone houses on the edges of the area had been turned into mined and barricaded defenses. Dr. Ussher's daughter had recounted to her father that despite the terrible shortage of all the material necessary for warfare, the young fighters, numbering about 1,400 men were extraordinarily cheerful, and with a very high morale. They were hopeful of being able to keep the 6,000 Turkish soldiers at bay. They were, after all, fighting for their homes and their very lives.

During those first few hours, as Nevart had stared at the body of her daughter, she was comforted and cosseted by those same black-clad women, all well versed in dealing with grief in all its forms. But Nevart had now finally lost everything that she had ever valued and had lost her capacity to deal with life anymore.

However, eventually, a deep atavistic strength, emanating from generations of female ancestors learning to cope with tragedy, came to her aid, and overcame the apathy, which had gripped her. With no one left for her to feed or care for, she locked up her house, which lay close to where all the shooting seemed to be coming from, took her few saved gold piastres, and walked down to the American Mission.

On her way, she picked up a notice on the street printed on recycled paper, which appeared to have been issued to all the young men, which read –

"Keep clean. Do not drink. Tell the truth.
Do not curse or denigrate the religion of the enemy."

The doors of the compound were now permanently open, and she walked straight in. The formerly neat and tidy courtyard looked totally different from the day she had first visited the place. A large number of people were now sitting about, some under the shade of tattered umbrellas, and some on faded carpets. These were mainly women and old men, although there was a sprinkling of middle-aged men, obviously villagers from the surrounding countryside. The women seemed to be coping fairly well, chatting and gossiping to each other, but the men looked listless and sad.

Nevart picked her way through to the hospital, where she saw several women in white coats bustling about. She sought and eventually found Alicia, the nurse who had treated her on that first day.

"Madam Nurse ..." she began, addressing Alicia, and then went on to explain the death of her daughter Sona, her last remaining relative.

"I would like to help you here. I can cook. I can help in treating wounds. I am prepared to do anything at all."

Alicia looked hard at her. "Mother are you sure, even if it was a question of risking your life."

Nevart smiled, looked straight into the young woman's eyes.

"Yes! Yes! Anything at all. It would be a blessing."

Alicia looked a bit doubtful, but then smiled. "Well – I'll take you to see Dr. Ussher –he needs someone to deliver a letter to an address on the other side of the lines, as the last messenger hasn't returned. He cannot send a man. Nevart, you must understand, it is dangerous. Come, he can explain."

And so it was that Nevart became the last of Dr. Ussher's volunteer postal ladies, in his almost daily correspondence with the authorities on the other side of the lines.

CHAPTER 10

Tea at Tokatlian's

True to her word, Olga arrived early at the gates of Nerissa's school that afternoon. The longer she had been anticipating this meeting with Selim, the more thrilling it had become in Olga's mind. Although she had seen and spoken to Selim many times at college since they first arranged the rendezvous, her strong physical attraction had been compounded by an increasing certainty that this was a man of great personal honour and kindness, with whom she felt immediately at ease. They had never been alone together, but his smile, whenever he saw her, turned her feelings inside out.

Nerissa came out of school, ahead of any of her friends, wrapping a silk scarf round her neck, as she removed the rather dowdy round school hat, and put it into her bag. She too was excited. This was a major event for her, and she was looking forward to going to the Bedestan – the old antique bazaar – with Olga. She wasn't worried about the rendezvous – she knew she wouldn't be called upon to say much, and she could simply sit back and listen to the little orchestra which always played, and let Olga and the young man talk together.

As they walked along, Nerissa realised that in all the excitement of planning this trip, Olga had never told her the name of the young man with whom they were about to have tea. By this time, they were already at the station, and they could see the train approaching down the line. Karekin, although travelling second class, always insisted that his wife and daughters went first class when they travelled without him, and Nerissa and Olga duly climbed into their first class carriage and settled down for the 20-minute ride to the city.

Nerissa snuggled into her window seat, smiling at Olga, ready at last to enjoy this novel experience. Olga was looking so beautiful, she thought, dreamy but clearly so excited, that Nerissa found herself catching her breath with a mixture of pleasure and sadness. She was not, nor had ever been, envious of Olga's beauty and social confidence, but she was painfully aware that these were characteristics to which she herself could never aspire.

"Well now Olga, my darling, – what is the name of your new friend – you know you've never got round to telling me".

The moment had come at last. Olga had always known in her heart that what she was doing would be unacceptable to her parents, as the mild deception she had been practising clearly showed. But she had not really considered the deeper implications within the wider social structure in which she lived. For her – authority simply meant 'mother and father', and a rebellion against such authority was acceptable, daring and without personal costs. But now, for the first time in weeks, Olga was going to have to face up to the actual disclosure of her relationship.

"Selim Kemal," – Olga replied simply, saying nothing more.

Nerissa stopped smiling. She sat there, totally stunned. What could she say? Although only just 16, she saw at once, with great clarity, all the implications contained in those two words. A Turkish boy! In the two minutes of silence that stretched between the two sisters, she analysed the impossibility of this situation – difficulties which, in almost two months of thinking about her feelings, Olga had not even considered.

However shy and introverted Nerissa was, she remained the most studious, intelligent, and reflective of the four girls. Her native intelligence came to her aid. She sat in her corner seat, wondering what her father's reaction might be in such a situation. She reflected that so far as she had understood, his principles had always been never to immediately reject any proposal, without first calmly considering everything from all angles. However, he would also have added that once you have made your mind up on the moral position – you must not compromise or fudge the issues, but take your stance with courage and honesty.

She forced a smile back onto her face. Olga, whose thoughts were entirely on the coming rendezvous, had not even been aware of the two-minute silence, or of the flurry of thoughts passing through Nerissa's mind.

"So, Olga, he is Turkish?" Nerissa, made sure that she did not look away from her sister's eyes, or appear to be distressed or anxious.

"Yes – he's a lovely boy, you'll like him Nerissa I feel sure. He's intelligent and thoughtful, and so gentle – not anything like all the other boys. My darling, when he speaks to me I feel so – so – so -warm and good and protected. Oh dear, it's so difficult to explain. He has none of that male arrogance which you see so often in the other Turkish students."

Suddenly Olga couldn't stop talking. All her pent-up feelings – all those unaccustomed strong feelings, which she had kept to herself, began pouring out, as she stared back into Nerissa's big brown eyes. But in all her explanations, in all this display of deep-seated feelings that, despite all her social savoir-faire, she had never actually experienced before, never once did she allude in any way to the looming problems of such a relationship, neither to Nerissa directly, nor, more tellingly, to herself.

Nerissa listened, thrilled by being a party to the feelings of an elder sister, who, in the whirl of her active social life, had until then largely ignored her. At the same time, she found herself appalled at what she increasingly saw as a domestic tragedy in the making. She knew – she absolutely knew for certain – that her beloved sister was going to be badly hurt one way or another, whatever happened.

Nerissa, a keen reader of Shakepeare's plays in the original, found herself thinking of Juliet and her love for Romeo.

"My God," she thought, "Juliet's problem was nothing, compared to what poor Olga has to face. Romeo was the same race as Juliet, he spoke exactly the same language, he had the same cultural background, he belonged to the same religion; for heavens sake, they even went to the same father confessor, they were from the same class, and but for the silly feud between their fathers – and Shakespeare makes quite clear that it was indeed silly – Romeo would have been a perfect match for Juliet."

But what was Olga up against – did she realise it even for a moment? Here was a young man, however gentle and pleasant, who nevertheless spoke a different language at home, was of a totally different religion, belonged to a different race, furthermore a race which had been locked in a fierce and, seemingly, irreconcileable conflict with her own people for over 500 years, since the fall of the old Byzantine Empire.

What was the right thing for her to do and would Olga take the slightest notice? She could see that nothing she could say at this particular moment would make any difference. Meanwhile, now that the floodgates were opened, Olga chattered on oblivious to all but her own all-consuming feelings, and so Nerissa said not a word as the train slowly pulled into Sirkeci Station – the terminus of the whole European railway system.

As they walked from the station to the covered Bazaar, Nerissa finally got round tentatively to raising the issue foremost in her mind.

"Olga, how far has your friendship with this young man gone?"

"Nerissa, listen, all I know is that this is a good man – a man of truth and honour whom I believe I will be able to trust, if necessary. But, Nerissa, I really don't know how deep my own feelings are, never mind being sure of his."

"But Olga, aren't you aware of the difficulties? What about when it comes to meeting his family?"

"Poof – who cares. For the moment all I want to do is to get to know him better. I don't care a hoot what other people may think. We're two individuals, why should we carry the weight of the past on our shoulders all the time? I am first and foremost a woman – not a representative of my ethnicity or religion. What difference would it make if we were all on a desert island."

"But Olga, my soul, we are not on a desert island – nor in that metaphorical sense, could we ever be."

An hour or so later, after a short somewhat distracted visit to the Bedestan, which for different reasons, had lost its attraction, they came out of the Tunel and took the tram up that deposited them at the front entrance of Tokatlians on the Grande Rue. Here a fairly brisk crowd of fashionable ladies and gentlemen, mixed with a good sprinkling of smartly turned out Army Officers and Cadets, were passing in and out of its Art Nouveau glass doors. Olga and Nerissa walked into the busy vestibule. Here, just inside the door, Selim was waiting, looking rather lost.

A sudden surge of excitement, coupled with a strong feeling of affection, sprang up in Olga, as she saw and appreciated his nervousness. At the same time, she felt a confidence in her own ability to manage the occasion. It was as if Selim's nervousness had sparked in her a calm certainty. Nerissa glanced at her sister and saw her face break into a really natural, warm smile; a smile unlike any of the superficial and consciously charming smiles her sister could so easily produce. Nerissa's heart lurched and nearly drowned in inward tears, as Olga stretched out her hand.

"Oh hello Selim. This is my young sister, Nerissa."

To which Selim, taking Olga's hand into his own, and holding it without making any attempt at shaking it, replied -

"Hello, Nerissa, Salaam! Shall we go in and get a table?"

It took several seconds before Selim became aware that he was still holding Olga's hand. By contrast, Olga had been aware of every second of his grasp, as had Nerissa. Selim, blushing deeply, let go as they moved, somewhat self-consciously, into the tea-room at Tokatlians.

Here, in the large and airy glass-roofed room, Nerissa stared at the noisy crowd of men with a surprisingly large number of women, chatting animatedly at small round tables dotted about the place. The room – or was it a theatre – was liberally sprinkled with potted palms and other plants placed strategically, often shielding the tables from one another. A huge chandelier, magnificent enough to have graced the new Paris Opera House, hung from the ceiling. The setting was grand, though perhaps not very tasteful. No Oriental opulence here, but dark mahogany walls, heavy green foliage, some tall palm trees at the side, small white wrought-iron tables and chairs, and the glittering chandelier hanging over all. A tiny stage at the side of the large hall held a small string orchestra, in front of which was a minuscule polished wooden floor for dancing.

The room was filled with Turkish officers. Nerissa wondered what they were all doing here in the City. Enver Pasha, despite the defeats on the Caucasian front, was clearly still the style of the day. The men were all clean-shaven, save for the same neat, clipped, moustache. They all affected a pose of nonchalant arrogance, with cold eyes and a supercilious regard. Male predators – all of them. As they sat down, Nerissa noticed a young man in the uniform of the officer-cadet school – the Harbiye – clearly an Armenian – sitting nearby with a small group of friends, who was looking at her with soft brown eyes, smiling when he caught her gaze, and then shyly turned away.

Nerissa smiled back and then tried to concentrate on what Selim and Olga were saying to each other, though it was quite clear that the real conversation was going on between their eyes. The little orchestra began playing a Strauss waltz with that absurd late 19th-century sentimental rhythm, and a few couples rose to dance.

To her dying day, and despite the drama of the tragic days that followed, Nerissa would never be able to recall any of the actual words that passed between the three of them on that hazy afternoon in the old *thé dansant* room at the Tokatlian Hotel. She looked and listened, as Olga and Selim, chatted together inconsequentially, and touched hands under the table, with an innocent wonder at the intensity of their own feelings. The atmosphere was dream-like, hazy at the edges – a moment of complete calm, yet only a few days before the storm that was due to burst over them all.

Deeply anxious for her sister, but at the same time thrilled by the occasion, Nerissa sat and watched as this last bastion of the old and elegant Europe seemed to be dancing its last waltz; all these young officers and their companions unconscious that their world was about to die forever, as a result of the same two fatal shots that had assassinated an Archduke and his lady, only nine months earlier. Nerissa said scarcely a word, but she took it all in, and in those three magical hours, she moved inexorably from a shy 16 year-old girl into a young woman.

CHAPTER 11

André, Harry and the invasion force

When the wind blows from the north in Alexandria, blustery and damp, the old trams running along the Corniche clatter and shake about as they proceed from east to west and back again. The ill-fitting windows in all the houses facing the sea shiver and rattle. All the weekend visitors from Cairo smile at each other and take bracing walks along the seafront, feeling pleased that they had taken the trouble to come. When, however, the winds blow from the south, they seem to bring with them the hot, enervating and sultry smells of the rest of Africa looming oppressively beyond the town – a town which normally turns its back firmly against the continent behind it. Then those same weekend visitors from Cairo wonder why they bothered to come at all.

André Tarkowski and his Greek girl-friend Elena Patakis had managed, as planned, to get to Egypt before the Turkish entry into the war closed the frontiers, and turned the British Empire for the first time into an enemy. André had eventually arrived in Alexandria, where he had somehow been able to lay his hands on more than sufficient funds. André's passport, issued to him by the Embassy in Constantinople following what appeared to be his desertion from the *Goeben*, skirted over his German citizenship by referring to him as Polish. Once arrived, he made a great effort to get work with the British naval administration as an expert in the relatively new field of radio.

By dint of perseverance, and by continually improving his command of English, he finally got a job as a civilian radio operator with Naval Intelligence in their radio transmissions department. His knowledge of four further languages – German, Turkish, Polish and Russian was the factor which helped his cause, without too many questions being asked. He was never actually given a full security clearance on sensitive matters, but managed nevertheless to hear a lot of what was going on, in all of which he took a great interest.

André was getting more and more bored by Elena, who, on arrival without any contacts of any kind with the large Greek community in this city, had had to start constructing her own entertainment. She had little in the way of intellectual reserves of her own; without much education, she had acquired few outside interests. André was always out at work or wandering round the town, and whilst their sexual relationship remained passionate and satisfactory, even the highly sensual Elena began to feel the lack of any common activity beyond the bedroom. The atmosphere between the sexes in Alexandria was however much freer than in Constantinople, and fairly soon Elena, ostensibly unmarried, began to attract the attention of the young Greek men, whom she glimpsed in church, and with whom she began to arrange café meetings. Socialising in this way even led to invitations from their families, though these were less frequent. She was always careful to mention these meetings to André, but he seemed uninterested, and indeed even encouraged her.

As April advanced, Alexandria and Cairo began to fill with nationalities from all over the British Empire. In particular, there were the bronzed and athletic young Australians, so much bigger and stronger than the stunted English working-class soldiers. André worked in the Navy's special Radio Telegraph room at the end of the tramline near the seaside Montazah Palace. He would often stand and stare at these glorious men, stripped to the waist on the sands by the sea. André, whose perverse and brutal bisexuality never caused him a moment's thought, would wonder at the simplicity and beauty of these young men. As they rough-housed on the beach, calling each other 'mate' – a colloquialism which appeared to be without the slightest homoerotic overtone. These 'mates' had enlisted together, went into the same regiment together, and in the end went over the top to their deaths together.

André couldn't understand why these young men were here, and what they were doing in a war, which despite all the propaganda, was basically an old-fashioned European 'balance of power' contest.

"Hello, my name is Andrew, what's yours," he would say, initiating a conversation.

"Jimmy?" Smiling with his infectious grin, André would ask, "Tell me Jimmy, what are you doing here? What are you fighting for?"

"Well, sport, it's like we're here to play a game of rugby, but with the bloody Turks rather than each other," answered a New Zealander, meaning it sarcastically, but nevertheless unconsciously putting his finger on their own insouciance and frivolity in joining up in the first place.

The Australians would usually answer as follows.

"Never mind what that Sheepshagger says, we all just reckoned it beat sitting around swatting flies off your face. Hey – Geoff – This bloke wants to know why we're here – well, cobber, I'm here because he's here," and with that, the Aussies would laugh and clap André on the shoulder.

André would usually end up getting details of their regiments.

He reflected on how his seduction of Elena and the affair that followed had already soured. Sexual contact remained satisfactory for both of them, but beyond that, they had very little left to say to each other. Their only common language – the language they had all spoken together in the Patakis household – was of course Turkish. However André, though a natural linguist, was not all that comfortable in Turkish, and, in any case, it didn't seem worth the effort.

Elena was already enjoying the attentions of Greek lads she

was meeting at the Church and in the wider Greek community. André had no feelings of jealousy – much to Elena's surprise, and irritation. Their little two-room apartment was at the top of a large 19th-century building standing opposite the Sports Club grounds, and whilst adequate, was constricting. The building itself housed Greek, Italian, French, and even an Egyptian family.

This was the middle of April – the landings in Gallipoli were due to take place within a week – and meanwhile André was flabbergasted at the total lack of any security throughout Egypt. No military expedition since the Trojan War had ever been more loudly trumpeted and discussed. First the fleet had bombarded the Dardanelles Forts, and had then been pulled back. That pinpointed exactly where a future effort was going to take place. Then, news of the arrival and departure of all the great battleships and the hundreds of transports became common knowledge throughout Alexandria and Port Said, and was reported daily in Cairo. The names and numbers of all the British, French and Anzac divisions were freely referred to in the newspapers throughout Egypt. There were even official references to "the Constantinople Field Force". The word Gallipoli was on everyone's lips. Everyone knew what was coming, as ponies, horses, camels, water lighters, shipping of all kind, were hastily purchased and gathered together in the Egyptian ports.

André simply could not credit this, in view of his experience of the secretive world of Prussian military security. In the end, he came to only one conclusion – they simply did not know what they were doing. From top to bottom, they were going into this campaign like a debutante going to her first ball. Excited, but with no clear idea of what it was all about. Above all, it seemed their leaders had made the cardinal error of ignoring their history. They were failing to take the Turks seriously, or, indeed, to take any account of them at all.

The Turks, after all, had a long tradition of military prowess. Whilst they had long since lost the brilliance in aggressive offensive warfare of their nomadic ancestors, they had instead acquired a dogged, patient, stonewalling, defensive strategy that had always been their strength, even in the days of Byzantium before there were any Turks in Anatolia at all. The Anatolian peasants, who were the bedrock of the army, were mainly illiterate; they were misused and despised, and badly led by their Pashas and officers from Constantinople, but they were used to hardship, to terrible conditions and to bad food. They could endure with patience and stubbonness in much the same way as the Russian mouzhik.

The Ottoman Empire, eventually including Greece, the Balkans, most of Hungary, and the whole of the Arab world including the holy cities of Islam, contained an enormous number of different races, creeds, languages and religions. By the 18th century, it had grown soft, and the question increasingly being raised was what exactly united all these disparate peoples. The Ottoman Empire was the ultimate multi-cultural and multi-racial society, and right up to this very month, despite some notably tragic moments, the Ottoman Empire had treated their many different minorities better than most of the so-called civilised nations to the north.

But as André could see, British officers, army and navy, were unable to conceive of soldiers, who didn't dress like them or look like them, being of any value at all. Hence their unconsciously racist dismissal of the poor Anatolian peasant reinforced their extraordinarily light-hearted attitude to security. Who cares if the Turks know we are coming – 'our chaps' will still give the rotters a good hiding, was the unconscious thought of all of them, from the generals down to the ordinary Tommies.

Finally, and to cap it all, André knew something that, with all the intelligence at their disposal, General Hamilton and the planners at Whitehall did not know. The ridiculous and vainglorious Enver Pasha, would not be facing them at Gallipoli. He had only managed to emulate his hero Napoleon in one regard, by retreating in a winter campaign with only a tiny proportion of his original force left alive. The General who had hurriedly been placed in charge, and with almost a month to prepare the defences, was Mustapha Kemal. Enver, with his smooth face and delicate feminine hands, hopelessly vain and self-confident, with a remorseless lack of pity or empathy, was a gambler. Kemal, by contrast, was a cool chess player, who knew his men well, and who, whilst equally ruthless, never lost his essential humanity.

André would get home fairly late and had begun resisting Elena's demands to be taken out – not that there was much to do in the evenings in Alexandria apart from socialising.

"Andre, come on please, let's go out. There is going to be a concert of Strauss waltzes with dancing at the Cecil Hotel."

"No, Elena, I'm too busy, I've got things to do. I've got some translating work that the Navy wants completed by tomorrow. But look, there's no reason why you shouldn't go."

"Oh, André, I can't go on my own."

"No, but what about that guy Gianni – you were talking about yesterday – Why not go with him?"

"But André, I really would rather go with you – don't you mind my going out with someone else."

"Not at all, Elena, for heaven's sake go and enjoy yourself."

Conversations like this seemed to be taking place more and more often. Elena was becoming concerned by the indifference shown by André and would end up trying to rile him in an attempt to get a reaction; any reaction, even anger, was better than this total neglect.

The flat was tiny, and sitting under the bed, up against the wall, taking up space which was in short supply, was a rather battered locked tin case, which André had brought with him, through all their travels, all the way from the house in Stamboul. Elena had never seen the inside. Elena's references to it seemed to irritate André unduly, and unfortunately Elena had reached the stage where irritating him seemed to be the only way she could reach him. It would often end in a sort of ritualised violence, during the sexual act, in a way which seemed to satisfy both of them.

It was on that last night, at the start of the third week in April, before all the naval transports left, that Elena returned home unexpectedly early from supper with a Greek family she had met. André had been invited but had said that he was far too tired to go, encouraging her to go without him. On arrival, Elena found that the family were in a domestic crisis in regard to an elderly Aunt who had just died, and after giving her condolences and exchanging some polite conversation, she left. She walked into their little sitting room to see the tin case open on the desk, and Andre tapping at some keys on some machine or other, with what looked like muffs over his ears.

"Whatever is that thing, André – it's a funny kind of typewriter," said Elena, as she walked in putting down her hat.

André, who hadn't heard her coming in, carefully lifted off the ear pieces, and turned to face her – his eyes hard, glittering and full of that violence, which on this occasion suddenly caused her to feel a real stab of fear.

"Just one of my toys, Elena – come here," he answered, as he slowly rose from the desk and came towards her.

Harry too was now in Egypt.

Within a week of submitting his report on the events which had led to the escape of the *Goeben* and the *Breslau*, and their arrival in Constantinople, Harry had got his wish and had been posted to an active post on the destroyer, HMS *Leicester*. As the days drew on towards the end of April, the ship made its way, at speed, to Port Said. The *Leicester* was scheduled to escort the transports of the Royal Naval Division due to participate in the forthcoming landings at Gallipoli.

By the end of 1914, the war in Europe had already become an inferno of hundreds of miles of trenches of all kinds: front-line trenches, transverse trenches, supply line trenches, rear-return trenches and others, where men lived and fought each other, like rats scurrying around in a maze. This was not a war of man against man, but man against the inexorable machine. One man's death, impaled on a bayonet or struck down by a sword, was an unbearable tragedy, but the death of 25,000 men, raked down by machine guns in the first 20 minutes of one of the great 'over the top' offensives, had turned these killing fields into industrialised slaughter.

Harry had fallen back into the easy camaraderie that men share at sea with a feeling of relief. He had never been totally comfortable with a desk job at the Admiralty, but his fellow-officers, on board ship, had a somewhat exaggerated respect for the views of one known to have come straight from the Intelligence section in London. On the very evening before they were due to arrive at Port Said, all the officers gathered in the officer's mess, and began to discuss where they were going and what they were supposed to be doing and why. They asked Harry to give them a quick summary of the position as he saw it.

"Harry – you're in the know about what's going on – tell us what's behind all this – come on man, expound!"

" Yes, yes, very well. The whole idea of a landing at Gallipoli started as an attempt to get round the awful stalemate on the Western front, by mounting a flanking manoeuvre as a purely naval operation, rather than as a direct attack on Constantinople. The plan was an attempt to capture Constantinople by a naval *coup-de-main*. It was the original intention that this would be a naval battle fought on sea. The navy alone, was going to force a way through the straits, and then appear outside Constantinople."

"But Harry, how the hell could the navy on its own take, and above all keep, a great city like Constantinople – it doesn't make sense."

"I'm afraid that no one had actually worked anything out. But the top brass felt that, thus far, the navy hadn't done much to justify its huge expense during the previous ten years. The admirals felt that surely for the first time, the navy could be used as a decisive weapon of war."

"Well – what happened – why didn't it work? I was always taught at staff college that warships, capable of carrying enormous guns, and offering only moving targets, usually defeated fixed coastal forts."

"To be honest, I just don't know. When we finally sailed into the straits we had over 200 heavy guns, against a mere handful in the Turkish forts. The forts were silenced on the very first day. It was reliably reported that the rulers in Constantinople thought they were finished. Talaat is supposed to have had a car ready to take him into the interior at a moment's notice – the

Balkan states suddenly thought of getting a bit of the action – the Russians talked of attacking Constantinople from the Black Sea. However, as day after day passed, nothing further happened. Somehow, the clearing of the old fixed forts didn't seem to prevent the hidden mobile guns of the coastal defences from opening up with accurate fire, whenever our minesweepers sprang into action during the night, trying to clear the mines to enable the great battleships to move on.

At last our admirals decided to make an all-out effort. Seventeen battleships and a host of smaller craft, with a French squadron as well, moved forward. By midday most of the Turkish guns had again fallen silent. We were almost there. But then the mines began to take their toll. Three battleships were sunk and several others crippled – 700 sailors died. I know that these losses are tiny compared with what happens in the trenches every single day, but it was enough to finish off our admirals.

That evening they telegraphed the Admiralty to say that the plan had failed. They reported that they no longer believed that the Navy could force the straits alone. They confirmed that they would need the Army – my God what an admission for a British Admiral!"

It was on the morning after this conversation that the HMS *Leicester* finally docked at Port Said. Harry was in a state of intense excitement. He was sure that he had arrived at one of those great heroic moments in history. Even now, still early in 1915, despite the awful experiences on the western front, war was still thought of by all these young men as a glorious, exciting, even poetic, adventure – the epitome of male virtue. Each of the European nation-states believed that their 'chaps' were plucky and gallant, full of honour and duty, ready to sacrifice themselves for their country, and, of course, for their particular God.

Harry's friend – the poet Rupert Brooke – had joined the Royal Naval Division – the RND – scheduled to go in with the Anzacs. Brooke had written a letter to another acquaintance, a copy of which had been sent on to Harry, when he had been told that his division was bound for Constantinople. In it he had written –

"It's too wonderful for belief. I had not imagined Fate would be so kind... Will Hero's Tower crumble under the fifteen-inch guns? Will the sea be polyphloisbic and wine-dark? Shall I loot mosaics from Santa Sophia, and Turkish Delight and carpets? Should we be witnessing a turning point in History? Oh God! I've never been quite so happy in my life, I think ... I suddenly realise that the ambition of my life has always been since I was two years old to go on a military expedition against Constantinople."

"Oh no," thought Harry, "doesn't he realise that people are going to die? That there is going to be blood and pain, loss and horrific injuries, and most terrible and monstrous deaths?"

But even as Harry thought this, he still thrilled to the same passionate desire for heroic action, never for a moment imagining that he, too, might falter in the face of death.

As an intelligence officer who would be helping in the boarding and disembarkation, Harry went to visit the RND which was camped on the other side of the Canal near Port Fuad. There he found the tents, all in neat rows, and eventually traced the one in which Sub-lieutenant Brooke was living. On arrival, Harry saw that clean-cut and handsome face, now swollen and puffed up – the lips thick and bloated – a wasted body lying in a muck sweat on the meagre camp bed in the dry Egyptian heat.

"Good heavens Rupert, what the blazes has happened to you? What's all this?"

"Harry – Harry Bridgeman? It's those blasted mosquito bites – the blighters got me on the lip."

"Have you seen the medics? You ought to be in hospital. Rupert, frankly you look bloody awful".

"Harry – for god's sake, do shut up. It's only a mosquito bite. I'll be on the mend soon. Do you think I am going to miss a chance like this? This is the very battleground that Homer described in the first great epic of the Western world; Achilles, and Hector, Agamemnon and Priam fought only a mile away from where we are headed. Do you think I am going to miss out on the second instalment."

"But, Rupert, you're not going to be seeing much in that awful mess. Look, let me arrange to send some RAMC orderlies round at least to have a look at you."

"Rupert," said the other young officer who had been standing rather helplessly by and who clearly shared the tent, "He's right – these things can get nasty – please just let someone have a look at you."

"No, Charles – both of you, belt up. Charles, if you want to do something, just go and get some ointment or cream and bring it here – there's a good fellow."

Unable to continue, as he was interrupted by a fit of coughing, he closed his eyes, clearly irritated. Harry felt that he ought not stay much longer. He had a word with the other young officer, said he would look out for both of them on board, clasped the poet's hand for a brief moment, and then left.

The very next day the RND packed up their tents and embarked on the little flotilla which was to take them to the Aegean which would be the kicking off point for the landings in Gallipoli. The harbour and roadsteads at Mudros, the main collection point for the invasion on the island of Lemnos, was, by then, totally filled with shipping. Harry's flotilla accordingly headed on for the island of Skyros, the alternative rendezvous point.

For some days the force – naval and military – remained on this delightful Greek island – all day the sun shown down from a bright blue sky. The whole island seemed to be made from great blocks of irregular white marble, piling up on small mountains, up to 2–3,000 feet high. These were all covered over with masses of lilac, sage and purple thyme. The shepherds and villagers of the island carried on as they always did, ignoring the sudden arrival on their island of all these fair-haired, blue-eyed and impossibly young men. Harry found himself wondering whether they had acted in precisely the same way two millenia before, when Leander had passed by with another invasion force.

Two days before the force was due to move out, Harry was approached by a Petty Officer.

"I'm sorry, Sir, but could you please come to the division

lines. I'm afraid that Lieutenant Brooke is dying."

Harry hurried on to the ship's cutter, reached the shore and raced up to where Brooke's tent had been, though it appeared that by then he had been transferred to a hospital ship. Several people were gathered round.

"He died a few hours ago, Harry," said an acquaintance. "After all that romanticising, he never got to witness the glory of war, which he so wanted."

"My God – what poetry he would have written if he had had that experience," added another fresh-faced, incredibly young subaltern.

The poet had died of a mosquito bite on his lips. It was as if Hector had slipped on a banana skin and infected his little finger, or Achilles had died of a bowel infection. They buried him that night under a few olive trees, and Harry helped carry his body slowly and carefully up the hill that evening.

Later that same night, back on board, writing to his mother, Harry referred to the difficulties in getting the coffin up the narrow mountain path.

"Mother, you would wonder at what a beautiful spot it was where we buried poor Rupert. It was at the top of a little stony hill surrounded by weeping olive trees, with the wonderful scent of Greek flowering sage, thyme and spring flowers. It was a beautiful moonlit evening. The path up was very narrow, and it was tricky going, carrying the coffin. It took us over an hour to go just the one mile. A party of the others had gone ahead to dig the grave. We simply laid him in it, covered it with the marble stones strewn all around, and piled up on top of it all the flowers we could find. We then returned down the same narrow path, by which time it was completely dark, as the moon had gone behind clouds."

In the same letter Harry referred to the young subaltern's remark as to the sort of poetry Rupert might have written had he finally got to war.

"Mother," he wrote, *"the lad was right in a way, Rupert did so want to experience the camaraderie and energy of shared action. But who is to say how it would have affected his poetry. Already you can see how the young poets, who are actually now beginning to experience the horrors of trench warfare, are starting to change their views and style. Poor Rupert,*

missing the actual experience, means I think that he is always going to be misunderstood by later generations. Here, mother, is one of his last lines, in case you haven't seen it before."

> "These, laid the world away;
> Poured out the red sweet wine of youth;
> Gave up the years to be of worth and joy,
> And that unhoped serene that men call age;
> And those who would have been their sons,
> Their immortality."

What Harry did not know was that on a piece of cardboard, pinned to the back of the simple little wooden cross that they had stuck at the head of the grave, the division's Greek interpreter had written in Greek, in pencil, the words -

"Here lies a servant of God – Sub-lieutenant in the English Navy – who died for the deliverance of Constantinople from the Turks."

Two days later the Royal Naval Division embarked to join the Anzacs for the Gallipoli landings.

CHAPTER 12

Guests at the Avakians

Karekin, stood in the bedroom and adjusted his tie carefully in the mirror. He indicated to Armineh that she should wait a moment, before she bustled down to see to the family breakfast.

"My dear, yesterday, Mr. Levonian – do you remember him, a textile merchant with business mainly in Germany and Vienna – offered me his seat in the tram going up from the bridge. He said he was just about to get off at the next stop. I couldn't refuse obviously, although for heaven's sake he's almost as old as I am. Anyway, he never did get off at the next stop, but after a few general words about the difficult situation in the business world, he began talking about his son George. It seems that George has managed to get deferment for one reason or another, and has started working with his father."

"Karekin – for heaven's sake, do keep to the point of whatever it is you are trying to say. I haven't got all day." Armineh, tapped her foot impatiently, and waited with her hand still on the doorknob.

"Ah – er – well, yes, at first I really wasn't clear at all what he was talking about – what with all the usual clanging and clattering of the tram. Ridiculous, I must be getting past it, as I should have realised at once. Anyway – Armineh, don't get impatient – suddenly it dawned on me that he was talking about our Sima. I have no idea why it got into his mind at such a critical time, but he seems to be interested in a merger of our two merchant houses."

Karekin finished fiddling with his tie, now perfectly knotted, and turned quickly to face Armineh to stop her interrupting again.

"Look – sooner or later, Armineh my dear, this war is going to come to an end. Undoubtedly, he is right to believe that there will be room for expansion into Western Europe. Our cotton crop has not been affected in any way. So, with me fully committed in Great Britain, and he covering Germany and central Europe, we could do very well in a postwar world. Armineh, I don't suppose life is going to be all that different in 1916 than it is today, if the war ends by then of course"

"Karekin," said Armineh, whose mind was fairly distracted and who had only been half listening to Karekin's rather hesitant delivery – in particular she had, most surprisingly, missed the reference to Sima – "I've had enough. I can't believe that you are asking me advice about a purely business matter. You know very well you'll do exactly as you want in that area. Now, unless there is something else that you don't seem to be able to get round to, I am going down. Please hurry yourself, it's getting late."

"Armineh – some patience please my love. The question on which I need your advice is as to whether you think Sima is ready to consider the question of marriage."

Armineh, who was just about to leave, stopped, took her hands away from the door handle and stared, suddenly paying close attention.

"Of course she is ready to consider marriage – she's 19 and most girls of her age are already married and with child. She's always been a great help to me, and I'll miss her, particularly as Olga is so useless these days in the house – but it's quite certainly time she was settled. Have we met this young man?"

"I don't think so, but we are certainly going to meet him tomorrow, as I ended up inviting the family to tea," Karekin admitted rather sheepishly.

"Karekin – are you mad – you've lost your head. Now he tells me," expostulated Armineh glaring at him and stamping her foot in irritation. "I'll simply never manage. You know very well how bad the situation is for entertaining. Really Karekin, how could you – it's going to be quite impossible – totally out of the question," said Armineh, as she stormed out, leaving the door ajar.

"There'll be four of them – the parents, the young man, and a younger sister," called out Karekin to the departing back of his wife. He grinned with satisfaction, being relieved that she had taken it so well. After over 20 years of marriage it was crystal clear to him that Armineh was already working out how she was going to cope. He was also certain that she would. The only thing he would have dreaded was silence, after he had blurted out the invitation for the next day.

Armineh, irritated as she was by having something like this thrust on her so suddenly, nevertheless knew perfectly well that she would manage. She could hardly not, after all the hints she had been passing to Karekin that he start bestirring himself where Sima was concerned. Her mind raced ahead as to how she would plan tomorrow's entertaining. All thoughts of the war, the rumours of a possible Anglo-French attack on Constantinople itself, the awful news from Van, passed right out of her mind – not that such thoughts much occupied her, anyway. What was important was this – the first direct approach to be made on behalf of her first-born daughter. Oh yes! She would certainly do it right. Mentally rolling up her sleeves, she bustled downstairs for the daily tussle to get her delicate son to eat something before school.

Breakfasts at the Avakians remained noisy and full of life, as always – but there was increasingly an undercurrent of tension, noticeable in all of them with the exception of little Seta. Although Haik had discovered that other boys at the school were also being accompanied to school by elder brothers or servants, this had not lessened the element of shame for him. Sima seemed sad and subdued, whilst Olga always appeared to be in a state of febrile excitement, quite incapable of sitting for long at the table.

Nerissa, calmer and more reflective than the others, was sensitive to all the conflicting feelings around her, and she was the only one aware of the reasons for Olga's animation. But Nerissa didn't realise that the fears and anxieties swirling around them in the city were having their effect on each one of them.

On an intellectual level, the Avakian family chatted on incessantly and with spirit, but except for Karekin himself, without any real fear for themselves. Above all, Armineh herself bustled about fulfilling the age-old role of making sure that the everyday practical details of life were sorted out. By competently dealing with these, and despite all the problems outside her control, she gave the five children, and to some extent her husband, a firm anchor from which to contemplate the world's follies.

As Karekin came down to his glass of tea with lemon, Sima rose and said to Haik, "Come along young man, time for school." Haik, having avoided most of the food thrust at him by Armineh, and looking paler and more fragile every day, jumped up, hugged his father cheek to cheek as Karekin sat down, and went out. Karekin looked round at the rest of his children – Olga, Nerissa and little Seta.

"'Tomorrow, my dears, some friends of mine will be coming to tea after church. I don't think you've met them – the Levonians – they live in Bebek."

"Gosh! That's quite far out, Baba," said Nerissa – "a long way for them to come."

"Yes, well, there'll be four of them – Hovannes and Yvonne

Levonian, with their son George, and a younger sister whose name I don't know – nor actually even how old she is."

"Father", Olga looked directly at her father, "how old, then, is this son – George?"

"Well, I believe that he's about 24. Anyway, I want you all to be well-behaved and careful. They are fairly old-fashioned, and we mustn't shock them – and that applies just as much to you Seta, my girl."

Seta looked up and grinned at everyone, undisturbed by her father's comment, and happy to be taken notice of.

Karekin rose – his breakfast these days was short and sharp – he couldn't wait to get back to the city, in order to hear all the latest conjectures flying around the coffee houses and the bazaar. For his family's sake, he knew he had to be ready for any eventuality, and to be alert to all the political possibilities. The three girls jumped up and kissed their father, who took his hat and coat and walked out.

"Seta, sweetheart, go and help Marie in the kitchen." Seta grumbled, but got up and went out. As soon as she had gone, Olga turned to Armineh and Nerissa, with shining eyes.

"Mother, I know something's going on – Father wouldn't comment about an ordinary tea-party. It's Sima isn't it. Nerissa, can you believe it, these Levonians are coming to inspect our Sima, and with a view," she giggled, "to matrimony, my dear." Olga wriggled with glee and laughed out loud.

"Oh no!" wailed Nerissa, "it's disgusting, like a cattle market. Mother how can Baba even contemplate putting one of his daughters through something like that – I can't bear the thought – poor Sima."

Armineh, impatiently sipped her coffee, as Olga looked on with a mischievous grin.

"Nerissa – it's not like that at all. How do you think that Sima or any of you are going to meet pleasant young men, if we don't arrange meetings like this. But above all my dear – how could you imagine for one moment that your father would be party to a cattle market as you put it. No one, but no one, is ever going to make one of my daughters marry anyone whom they do not choose themselves – for heaven's sake, Nerissa – least of all your father. This is simply an occasion for two young people to meet – neither of them need take the matter a single step further. Nerissa, how could you ever think for a moment of coercion where your father is concerned – you know his principles and his love for you all."

"Oh mama don't get upset," said Nerissa, "of course I know that Baba wouldn't ever force any of us to do anything against our wishes. On the other hand, his idea of what is best for us may not be the same as ours. Love is not the issue here – mama. I have no doubts about Baba's love for all of us, of course. However, that is not necessarily the same as trusting his judgement of what is right for us."

"Mother," suddenly Olga intervened, "when did you come to love father. You had only just met him once before when you married him, or so you told us. He was at least 15 years older than you – you yourself were scarcely much older than Nerissa here."

"Girls, life was very different in those days. Whilst I had brothers, and was aware of young men – I never met anyone outside the family. Life at home was constrained. There was no school. I never left the home except to go to Church. We never contradicted our parents, and frankly had few thoughts that weren't planted there by them. To be honest, I couldn't wait to get away and have my own home. I was ready to fall in love with the first young man to whom I was introduced. I was in addition used to doing what my parents wanted, unlike you lot."

"Yes, but when did real love arise," insisted Olga. "Was it on the very first night?"

Nerissa blushed deeply and looked away, although she was just as keenly interested in her mother's answer.

"Olga, my dear, I was only sixteen. Most of my real education came after I got married. I learnt more from your father in our first year together than in all my years of childhood …"

"Yes. Mother, but you haven't answered Olga, what about love?"

"What about passion?" Olga added.

Armineh sipped her coffee and reflected. She was 38, and beginning to get dumpy. Her husband had taught her to read and write. He had been gentle with her always, though he insisted on having his way in most matters. He relied on her to manage his home and daily life for him, which she did well and efficiently – and he was now 52 years-old! She realised that she could not even recall very clearly that first night, in which Olga was so interested, and which caused Nerissa to blush. She could recall clearly and with a sense of warm contentment that very morning's act of love. However, she knew that that was not what her daughter's wanted to know about.

Her relationship with Karekin – that was what they were after for reasons of their own. 'Contentment', certainly – 'Affection', oh God yes – but 'Love' …? Armineh gently put down her cup and rose as the two girls waited, watching her carefully for the different answers they each wanted for themselves.

"Come along girls – you'll both be late." Armineh walked out – slowly and calmly, to check on the kitchen, get Seta ready for school, and make plans for tomorrow's tea party.

There was a clear ritual that Karekin followed in welcoming formal guests in the afternoon to his house in Makrikoy. Finding out the time of the train they would be taking, he would walk down to the Cobancesme station. There, he would make sure that both Abdul and Mustapha were free with their arrabas. He would more often than not take Haik with him, but the girls and Armineh would always remain at home. So it was on the occasion of the visit by the Levonians.

Hovannes Levonian was a fairly typical Ottoman Armenian business man – corpulent and with a gold chain across a wide expanse of stomach. He wheezed and grunted as he got out of his first-class carriage, turning to help down his wife – Yvonne. With his sharp and curious eyes, Haik picked them out at once.

Yvonne Levonian was a thin, somewhat brittle lady, who had the habit of bursting into rather poor French, at every possible opportunity – no one knew quite why. Following her out of the carriage came a serious-looking young man – beginning already to become portly – sporting the usual Enver-style moustache, and certainly looking older than the alleged 23 or 24 years of age. In his turn, he was followed by a pert young girl, with long fair hair and a bright grin.

"Karekin, my friend, meet my wife Yvonne. My dear, this is Karekin Avakian, of whom you have heard so much."

"*Enchanté – enchanté*," said Yvonne, extending her hand, as if she expected it to be taken and kissed. Karekin smiled and took it into his own hand, for just the right amount of time, but making no attempt to bend down to kiss it.

Hovannes introduced his two children. "My son, George, and my daughter, Tamara," Karekin then introduced Haik, who was wearing long trousers for the occasion and who dutifully shook hands with everyone. They all strolled out of the station, and clambered into the two waiting carriages – the three parents in the bigger one, and Haik and his two guests in the other. George and Tamara sat in the comfortable carriage seats facing forward, whilst Haik had to sit opposite them, in the rather uncomfortable single seat facing backwards. He stared at Tamara, who stared back at him, swinging her legs beneath layers of Alice-in-Wonderland skirts. Although she was physically smaller than Haik, at 13 or so – Haik couldn't tell – she looked a good deal more mature. Whilst Haik was thin, with his huge brown eyes dominating his face, Tamara was plump with full thick lips.

Tea parties of this kind, in these years in Constantinople, tended to follow a fairly standard ritual. First, after the preliminary introductions, the guests would be seated in the main sitting room with all members of both families sitting in a semi-circle round the fireplace. However, this would be without the presence of the girl whom everyone had come to meet – and this was the one part of the ritual which was always the same. The inference made by the hostess, and graciously acknowledged, would be that she was out preparing the tea – although everyone knew perfectly well that the tea had been prepared by the servants long before.

Talk would be general, and would avoid politics or anything contentious. However, in this respect, in the present political situation, with the war and the rumors of a direct attack on the City by the Allies, Hovannes and Karekin were soon locked in a fairly heavy discussion on the subject. Armineh and Yvonne talked rather desultorily about the cost of vegetables, listening half-heartedly to their husbands. George said nothing. Haik, Tamara and little Seta fidgeted, whilst Nerissa and Olga, knowing that they were not supposed to say anything unless directly addressed, chafed under what seemed to them to be an impossible restraint to which they were not accustomed.

"Karekin, my friend, what about the situation in Van? It's time we stood up for our rights. The day of the Ottomans is over – this is a hopeless ramshackle empire, and the best thing would be for either the Germans to take over, if they win the war, or for the Anglo-French to do so if they win. Then we can have, as well as an independent Armenia, an independent Kurdistan, an independent Lazistan, an enlarged Greek state, and a Turkish Anatolian state. That's the way we can all become modern and westernised."

"And what will happen to Constantinople, with all your separate little nation-states. They'll all end up squabbling about it. For, Hovannes, it is this city and the Straits that is important to the world – not what is going on in the mountains of Anatolia or in the valleys of the Caucasus."

"Karekin, for heaven's sake – look what happened under the unspeakable Abdul Hamid. At least if we all had our separate states, no one would end up being oppressed by their own government."

"Don't you believe it, my friend. Exclusive one-nation states can be just as oppressive as any empire – in fact more so very often, as they consider themselves to have a legitimacy that the old multi-racial empires didn't possess."

"Come, come, Karekin, let's have done with the decadent and ramshackle old Ottomans once and for all."

So the conversation swung back and forth, with the corpulent Hovannes taking a more and more anti-Ottoman line, and Karekin mildly reproving him.

"In the end, Hovannes, this empire, however ramshackle, has

been home to at least twenty different peoples and languages, at least five major religions, a whole raft of cultures and has kept a tolerable peace between them all for centuries. Do you really believe that the nation-states that might follow would be more tolerant of each other?"

The moment would, of course, then come, when the hostess would rise, excuse herself, and say she was going to arrange the tea – an unnecessary pretence – but there it is, it was the custom! Armineh rose and went out, returning almost at once, to be followed, in theory, by a discreet and demure Sima.

Sima, however, in true Avakian style, was in no way discreet or demure. She came in ahead of the trolley with a plate of cakes, and with none of those downcast eyes called for by the script for these occasions. Seta giggled at Marie, but was immediately silenced by a sharp look from Karekin. Sima, meanwhile, looked long and hard at George and his two parents, and went forward sociably to shake their hands. Karekin smiled to himself, saying nothing; Hovannes was slightly put out, but rallied; Armineh noticed nothing; and Haik looked on with pride at his statuesque and dignified elder sister, who had effortlessly taken centre stage without having said a word.

After a notional cup of tea and a cake, the young ones, if there were any, would be excused. So on this occasion Haik, Tamara and Seta got up and left. Nerissa, of course, now 16, had to stay with the grown-ups although she would have much preferred to leave. Seta led Haik and Tamara into the large garden, at the back, but then excused herself as she had to go and help in the kitchen, where Marie was on her own. Haik was appalled at being left alone with this girl who looked at him appraisingly under thick eyebrows. He had no idea what he was supposed to say, and she didn't appear to be listening to anything he was mumbling anyway. He looked at the garden with its dense orchard of apricot and peach trees at the far end, then turned to look at his companion.

Haik saw a young girl, fashionably over-dressed, with several skirts that came down below the knees. He saw long dark hair, strong eyebrows and thick wet lips and the usual large brown eyes. Tamara, for her part, saw a boy, who looked younger than his 12 years, had pale delicate white features with a sharp pointed nose, unruly long hair, and big, bright inquisitive eyes – the whole having a somewhat feminine aspect.

"Come," she said taking him by the hand, "let's explore your orchard."

She led him down to the far end, as if it were her garden, and not his. Haik was somewhat bewildered, but was glad for the way she had taken charge, relieving him from the obligation to initiate conversation. Wandering amongst the trees, he was aware that they could not be seen from the house. Haik pondered the fact that they had nothing much to say to each other, whilst he simply didn't have the social graces to make small talk.

Tamara stopped, and began kicking idly at some dead branches on the grass. Haik leaned against an apricot tree and watched, fascinated, though uneasy, at the first young girl of approximately his own age that he had ever encountered alone. Tamara came up and facing him put her hands on either side of his face on the tree trunk, then she leant forward and touched his lips with her own. Neither of them really knew what they were doing – certainly Haik didn't, though he felt that the moment was important in some way. He was surprised to find that the sensation, though surprising, was very pleasant. Tamara pulled back and their eyes met. She smiled.

Haik could only stare and wonder, but the more anxious he became, the more her confidence grew. Once again she leant forward, and once again her thick lips pressed against his thinner ones. She held them there for several seconds – no more than the lips touching. Haik felt himself holding his breath and an unaccustomed erection rising, but he kept his arms firmly pressed back against the tree trunk. Unlike their first touch, their eyes were wide open as they looked at each other. The moment stretched into eternity.

"Haik – Tamara – where are you, come and join us," a voice called out from the house. Haik shuddered, full of an inexplicable guilt. "We must go," and ran up the garden. Tamara stepped back, and walked calmly after him.

At the top end of the garden, Sima and George were standing awkwardly, waiting for Haik and Tamara to accompany them for a walk in the garden. The walk had been arranged inside, and expecting that Haik and Tamara would already be there, there had been a moment of uncertainty when they walked out of the doors to find the garden empty.

As she waited, Sima reflected on the young man standing by her side. She saw a man of about 24 – though he looked older. He was already turning to plumpness, with smooth, well-groomed skin and a round baby-face. On his part, George saw a very proud, stiff and statuesque young woman, with the great Avakian eyes, but rather too talkative and direct for his taste. The irony was that whereas Haik and Tamara had been left free to roam as they wished in the garden, getting up to any mischief they liked – Sima and George had to be strictly chaperoned. Not all the social customs of the time made sense.

Both Tamara and Haik were well aware of what was expected of them. Sima walked ahead with George, doing most of the talking, whilst Haik and Tamara, silently walked behind with their own thoughts, as they all slowly paced round the lovely garden.

George and Sima made polite small talk without communicating very much to each other. In an odd way, Haik and Tamara were communicating much more with each other without saying a word. Haik, who had already experienced nocturnal emissions, was nevertheless an innocent sexually. He had become erect immediately Tamara's lips had lingered on the second occasion, and he had felt both excited and guilty. Tamara on the other hand, had experienced exactly the sort of thrill that she expected, and there was no confusion in her mind at all.

And so the four of them walked sedately round the garden, and through the orchard with George and Sima commenting on the flowers, Haik glancing anxiously at Tamara, reddening at the thought of her lips and Tamara, walking demurely alongside.

That night Karekin knocked at the door of his eldest

daughter's room, and walked in.

"Well Sima, what did you think of the young man?"

"Oh Baba, I don't think I could ever come to feel anything for him. There's no arrangement or proposal is there?"

"No, no, my darling, the important thing is to be clear right from the start so no one gets any wrong ideas. Don't worry, mother will see that it's all sorted out without any hurt feelings tomorrow."

The next day however was the 24th April – the day the Ittihad government was expecting the allied invasion, and also the day when it decided to begin the showdown with the minority in its midst ...

CHAPTER 13

The 24th April dawns

It was clear to the authorities both in Constantinople, and for that matter even in Berlin, that having been defeated for the first time in a century, by the Turks of all people, the proud British Navy was going to attempt a landing of the allied armies somewhere along the Dardanelles, most probably on the Gallipoli peninsula. The Turkish High Command didn't really need any agents sending radio messages from Egypt, to be aware of the approximate landing place. Even the date was fairly obvious, as more and more shipping gathered in and around the islands of the Aegean.

The British plan was that the elite 29th Division would land at the tip of the Peninsula on five separate beaches, in and around Cape Hellas, which was flanked by the old Ottoman Castle on the one side, and a modern fort on the other. From the start it was a death trap, unless the Navy could successfully intervene. The small French contingent would make some feint landings on the Asian side. The Anzac, backed by the small Royal Naval Division, to whom Harry's ship was assigned, would land further north at the narrow waist of the peninsula.

The landing was fixed for the 23rd April. The armada grew larger every day, with all types of ships, in varying condition, crowded into the narrow harbours and deep blue bays of Mudros and Skyros and other islands. Then, just as the moment was about to arrive, a fierce, but typically short-lived, Mediterranean storm blew up, and the landings were postponed. The German military agent infiltrated into Alexandria in Egypt could not have reported this decision, as by then the British HQ was no longer there, but on board the Queen Elizabeth, already in the Aegean. Nevertheless, the delay simply increased the readiness of the Turks. Their military dispositions were already in place in the peninsula. Anticipating the arrival of the invasion force on the coast, the 24th April was the day chosen to deal with the minorities in the interior.

It was the morning of the 24th April. Several days had passed since that dreamy tea party at Tokatlians, when Olga had sat lost in a romantic reverie, staring into the eyes of Selim, oblivious to the strains of music from the little orchestra. Over the next few days, Selim and Olga had continued to speak to each other at least once or twice each school day. All shyness and restraint between them had vanished. Olga spoke to Selim with a straightforward honesty, which, though disconcerting, he nevertheless found thrilling, as he came to enter into a new level of understanding of the workings of her mind. Although not nearly so articulate, Selim bestowed on Olga an intimacy and warmth that she had never experienced from any other person outside her family.

Her father had left home particularly early this morning. Olga walked slowly down to the Cobancesme station, past the open fields of the Vali Effendi racecourse, over the railway lines and into the little station. Although her thoughts were entirely on the coming meeting with Selim, she was not entirely unconscious of the excited buzz of conversation swirling around her as she waited for the train. Small groups of businessmen, split by ethnicity into Jewish, Greek or Armenians, stood huddled together on the platform, in a way that would not have happened only a few days before. Snatches of conversation could be heard.

"Do you know whether they have landed yet or not?"

"I heard the booms of big naval guns last night coming from the Sea of Marmara. The British Navy must have broken through, and I am afraid there will be a bombardment of the City this afternoon."

"Have you heard that Enver and Talaat have fallen out, and that Talaat has left for Germany together with Liman von Sanders, who has been recalled to Berlin."

"I have it absolutely on the surest authority that the Greeks have declared war and are marching on the City to join an English force which has landed only 50 miles away in Thrace."

The voices and rumours, most of them well wide of the mark, swirled around her, but the feeling of fear and uncertainty was palpable, like a cloud of gas drifting from group to group, enveloping her in a subtle, but unmistakable, way. There was a sense that the whole of society was on the verge of a collective breakdown. Where did they stand in relation to the government? These were all family men, going to work as a matter of routine, trying to keep the unfamiliar at bay, in a situation which was desperately fluid.

These were also deeply confused men. Despite the failures of the Ittihad government, there always remained a residual loyalty to the old Empire, in which they had all lived for generations. There was no historical imperative making it inevitable that the Empire would end in a maelstrom of ethnic hatred, but rather the actions of men that would determine what happened.

Olga was only taking in any of this turmoil around her subconsciously. Her thoughts were totally on the coming day at Robert College, and the delicious knowledge that she would be seeing Selim – and seeing him alone. Selim had made friends with the old caretaker in charge of the boiler room – Olga had no idea how, though she suspected the handing over of baksheesh. Over the past two days the old man had placed a couple of wooden chairs for them by the side of the enormous old boiler that provided heating for the buildings in the winter.

Twice now, Olga and Selim had sat on these two chairs, whilst the old man bustled about amongst the pipes in the dark depths of the basement room. A wonderful old man with a kindly creased face, a fez always on his head, and wearing old-fashioned baggy trousers, he was prepared to provide the chairs, but not to leave them alone. The chairs were placed close enough for them to touch hands for the 15 minutes or so that they could afford to be together. Somehow it had not crossed their minds to draw the chairs closer than where old Mustafa had carefully placed them.

How could Olga possibly take any notice of what was going on around her, when she felt sure that as well as having the joy of witnessing his love for her in his eyes, their lips were surely going to touch today for the first time. So she stood and waited for the train and smiled to herself.

However, on reaching the College, it was simply impossible to ignore the sense of foreboding amongst her particular friends and the other girls. Once again she caught snatches of conversation as the girls talked with each other.

"My father said that the English and French landed today in the Gallipoli peninsula," said Angelina, her Greek friend. "But he says that it is quite untrue that Greece has declared war and is joining in the attack on the city."

"I heard that the old Sultan has called for a Jihad, but that Enver is opposing the idea, and a good thing too."

"My father's shop, which is just below our flat in Beyoglu was attacked this morning and the windows broken."

This last comment from another Greek girl, was dropped like a stone into the pool of anxious girls, causing an immediate, apprehensive, ripple of silence. Even at 17, the girls were well aware of the difference between the ritualised violence of armies manoevring hither and thither in remote places, and the immediate uncontrolled violence of the mob.

"I must say, however," said the same girl after a pregnant pause, "the Police were there, for once, within minutes and they got rid of the small crowd immediately."

A discordant voice called out from the back -

"You're all disloyal parasites. By God, you're all revelling in the difficulties we're facing. You'd love to have the bloody Greek army at our gates wouldn't you? Then you would treat with them, and join them, and betray this country which has nurtured you for centuries."

This comment was followed by nods and vocal agreement by one section of the group of girls, and murmurings of dissent by another group. Racial tensions, dormant, and usually well below the surface in this great polyglot city, were clearly rising to the top as the city waited breathlessly for news of the foreign invasion, and this was reflected here in the small world of the College.

Olga looked over to where a much noisier group of boys were shouting and gesticulating at each other. She could not see Selim. There was a fairly significant racial gender difference at the college. Amongst the boys, in the separate building they occupied, there was a majority of Turkish students, reflecting the fact that liberal Turkish parents were ready to send their sons to the progressive American college; in the girls' building, there were far less ethnic Turks, as that liberal attitude did not extend to their daughters. Accordingly, amongst the girls, there was a higher proportion of Greeks, Armenians and Jews.

The tension in the college grounds was conspicuous. A group of young men called out, taunting the girls, something unheard of in normal times. Olga, was not oblivious to the sense of menace in the air, becoming increasingly nervous and emotional, she tried to keep in her mind the coming lunchtime rendezvous with Selim in Mustafa's boiler room. Just before going in to the second morning class, she saw a young Greek student, with a bleeding nose and bruised face, being led away by a group of his friends.

The class was already smaller than usual – some of the students had already gone home or been fetched. Olga could only think of the moment she would be within Selim's presence. The interminable hours did at last pass, and then without looking left or right, she hurried through the corridors, into the courtyard and down the stairs leading to the basement room.

Like everyone else that morning, Selim had been caught up

in the rumours of a landing by the enemy in or near the Straits. He possessed the ability to compartmentalise his feelings more easily than Olga, so he was able to put his whole mind to the political situation, and forget his emotions where Olga was concerned. Accordingly he entered wholeheartedly into the debate amongst his classmates. There had always been a much greater racial tension and division amongst the boys at the college than amongst the girls – and accordingly, Selim was discussing the events almost entirely with his Turkish friends. Once again they gave voice to conflicting rumours.

"My father said that the Russians had landed at the Black Sea entrance to the Bosporus."

"The Greek army has entered Adrianople, and there has been a terrible massacre of Muslims. The great mosque has been burned down."

"Did you hear that the French have landed at Bursa?"

Selim smiled at the last one – how did the speaker imagine for a moment that the French had got through the Dardanelles, when the British had failed so signally a few weeks before. Selim had not forgotten Olga and the coming lunchtime rendezvous, and was well aware of the deeper issues and dangers involved. He was simply gripped by the thrill and knowledge of great events happening around him, as were most of the other young men.

Before going into the second morning class, a fight had broken out between a Turkish student and a Greek. They were separated before any great harm came to either of them, although the Greek boy's face was bloody and he was led away. Selim reflected that these were two young men who disliked each other anyway – there was some rumour about them both paying attention to the same Jewish girl – and the political tension had simply exacerbated a personal rancour and resort to blows they had probably wanted to exchange long before.

Despite this, Selim was looking forward to this his third short meeting with Olga. What neither he nor Olga were aware of, was that their interest in each other had not gone unnoticed by some, at least, of their fellow-students, although nothing had actually been said.

Selim hurried out after class, avoiding any further discussions, which were growing uglier by the minute, as the young men began to mirror, in microcosm, all the worries and problems of the adult world outside. He raced into the courtyard and down the stairs and called out to Mustapha as he arrived.

Mustapha was a calming influence. He knew that Olga was a *giavour*, but this had made it easier for him to accept Selim's tips, as he expected no better from infidel girls. He salved his conscience, which had indeed given him a few moments guilt, by making sure that he always remained within sight and earshot of the young pair, but Mustapha was totally unaware of the wider political events unfolding around them. Selim waited.

"Oh Selim, Selim" cried Olga as she ran into the room.

Selim grasped her hand. Even now, despite all the emotional turmoil, their upbringing and training made it impossible for them to clasp one another. It was not Mustapha's presence, it was simply a cultural impossibility at that stage. Both of them were aching for physical contact, but, in its absence, everything had to pass between them through their interlocked hands and their eyes.

"Selim, my soul, what is happening, what is going on, where are we going? It's all so awful – some of these girls seem to hate me. Oh Selim, it's so wonderful to see you, but what are we to do – Selim, what are we to do?" Olga gasped out her words disjointedly. For the first time in their short relationship, she was afraid and confused.

"Sit down here Olga, my love – calm yourself, my loved one. The world is certainly turning upside down, but it shouldn't affect us, Olga. Oh! Olga, please don't cry. Who cares about the other girls or what people say – it will all pass – it will all pass. Today the Germans – tomorrow the British – it will all pass."

Olga felt her heart bursting with an emotion that she had never felt before. She knew that what she was doing and feeling was not only rash, but also positively dangerous. For the first time in eight weeks she felt the cold touch of fear – not fear for herself – but fear for the love that she felt for this man. Selim did not have the same feeling of fear at all. Whether it was the gender difference, or the fact that, as a member of the majority group, he had never experienced the insecurity endemic in minority status, would be difficult to judge. Either way, where previously Olga had always been the stronger in their relationship, her fear now gave him more strength.

There was a short moment of silence between them as they stood facing each other, but then Olga turned away. She could bear it no longer.

"Selim – we have to part for the moment. I don't know what's going to happen, but oh Selim, – oh Selim, I love you – I love you," she cried out for the first time, through tears of joy and fear.

Selim's mouth went dry as he stepped forward. He grasped Olga for a brief, fleeting moment round the waist as she looked up at him. Their lips touched for just a moment – just a touch – then Olga ran up the stairs, as Mustapha coughed loudly in the darkness behind them.

Upstairs in the courtyard, the atmosphere had turned more ugly. Rumours of arrests and worse were running round amongst the students. Something the two halves of Robert College – the Mens department and the Girls School – had not witnessed before, was happening, and the student body was fracturing into its ethnic subdivisions. Already the place was thinning out – but it was the minorities that had been hurrying home, whilst the young Turkish men and women in their separate groups, stood about discussing the situation loudly and aggressively. The boys, in particular, were all goading each other on into more and more extreme positions. It was into this whirlpool of young, undirected, passions that Olga suddenly emerged from the stairs leading down to Mustapha's basement.

"What were you doing down there, hanum," called out Leila, whose envious personal feelings about Olga and her relationship with the popular Selim, could at last be given free rein, masked behind a political passion that had suddenly become acceptable.

"*Giavour* – why are you still hanging about – don't you know all your infidel friends have all gone home ready to welcome our enemies," called out another one of the group of girls still milling about in the courtyard, and now pressing forward.

"You and your lot are all parasites waiting for the Empire to fall – you can't wait for the enemy to get here, and then you'll spit on us," shrieked Leila, working herself up to answering yells from the other girls, who crowded up to Olga as she tried to walk away.

Olga had no fear of the young men – she knew absolutely and for certain that they might jeer, but under no circumstances would they touch her, not one of them. But the girls were a different matter. For these Turkish girls, Olga was a scheming slut of the worst kind, who had contrived to ensnare one of their own boys. Little had Olga realised that while she had been able to keep her relationship with Selim hidden from her parents, this had not been the case in the closed, gossipy world of the college. Furthermore, they all put the worst and most lurid construction on it.

Olga was a spirited, lively girl, who could stand up for herself in most matters, but the threatening atmosphere in which she now found herself was tipping her into a state of extreme distress. Her lips quivered as she tried to elbow her way through the girls taunting her and pushing her from side to side. They were not consciously mean, these girls – they, too, without realising it, were being affected by the strains their parents were feeling, as the war which had seemed so far away, suddenly appeared almost at their doorstep.

No one was really ever going to hurt Olga physically – there were enough level-headed students around to ensure that there would be no real violence, so it was unfortunate that Olga finally gave way to an outpouring of sobs and tears of frustration and anguish just at the moment Selim appeared in the doorway at the head of the stairs. He couldn't see much – all he took in was the sight of Olga standing sobbing in the middle of a crowd of girls, most of whom were in any case now pulling back, suddenly appalled at their own behaviour. The sight of the girl in tears of distress had brought most of them back to their senses. But this was not clear to Selim.

"Olga, Olga," shouted Selim and began running toward her without thinking. Several young men, good friends of Selim, grabbed him and held him tight.

"Yok, Yok," they gently chided him, and without any rancour, but nevertheless holding his struggling form tight to make sure he didn't get himself into any real trouble by having a go at any of the girls.

Olga looked up at his cry, but through her tears saw only that Selim was struggling and being restrained by some of the other young men. She looked round at everyone staring at her, and then with a strangled cry, she turned and ran blindly out of the school gates.

CHAPTER 14

Karekin

That very same morning Karekin had arisen early.

"My soul," he said, as Armineh bustled about behind him, "You must be careful. The town is in a very excited state; rumour is that the Allies were supposed to be landing somewhere along the coast yesterday. There have been crowds in the streets, and yesterday I saw that some Greek and Armenian shops had their windows smashed. However the police were out in force for once."

"Karekin, what does it all mean? Are we going to have a pogrom or killings in the streets?"

"No, no my love, fortunately the presence of the German and Austrian legations are probably a guarantee that even this ridiculous government is not going to let the mob get out of hand. But that won't prevent individual anti-Christian violence by hoodlums. I do think that you and the girls must be careful. We must all keep a low profile in these circumstances."

"Karekin, my darling, leave me to manage the house and the children – you be careful yourself. Keep away from those politician friends of yours – the deputies – and try to come back early if you must go to work today. Karekin, are we going to be affected by the invasion?"

"My soul – if the British do break through to Bolis, our whole world will change for ever – of that I have no doubt at all. The opening of the Dardanelles and then the Bosporus, to Russian shipping, and the ensuing likely collapse of the Ittihad party and the Committee of Union and Progress will bring us all to a situation with no obvious end. Anything could happen and we must be prepared for all eventualities."

"But we've had rumours and crises like this before. Look – why didn't they appear yesterday? They were supposed to be landing on the 23rd , weren't they? Perhaps it's all just idle chatter. We've heard it all before."

"Armineh, my dear, a British landing of some sort, somewhere within 50 miles of Constantinople will happen. Everyone knows about it – it's no secret. Ever since the British Navy failed to break through to the Marmara, there's been no attempt by them to hide the fact that they are preparing for a major invasion."

Breakfast that morning at the Avakians had been as lively as ever, but surprisingly there had been little discussion about the war.

"Sima, my dear," said Armineh – "I think it would be a nice gesture if you called on Yvonne Levonian this morning. Take her a bunch of those lovely spring flowers that have just come out in the orchard. Don't worry, George and his father will be out at work. Your father has plans for a possible merger or association with Hovannes' business after the war ends, and it would be a nice way of keeping friendly relations between us, quite apart from the fact that it would be a really kind gesture on your part."

"Mama, that's fine – I'll go straight after breakfast, as I really must be back to pick up Haik these days. Honestly – that woman though – it's such a bore having to speak French half the time whenever she gets it into her head to switch. She really is a bit silly! Does anyone want anything by the way, whilst I'm in town?"

"For heavens sake, Haik, eat something" snapped Armineh. "No dear, we're well stocked, but I'll check with Marie. Oh! Olga, are you off? Can't you wait for Sima, and then you can go in together."

"No, I'm sorry Sima, but I really mustn't be late today – we have a test in the morning. Bye everyone – see you all this afternoon." Olga had risen and had rushed out, grabbing her bag from the table in the hallway.

"Listen, Mama," Sima interrupted as her mother began to protest, "Olga's right, I have to wait for Haik anyway. Look I'll go and pick some flowers now. Tell Marie to prepare some nice wrapping paper, and then I'll go on to the station after leaving Haik at school. Nerissa can come with us if she doesn't mind waiting a few minutes."

Olga had left the house first, but very soon after, Karekin strode out, immaculate as always, in his grey suit. Nerissa, with her hated dowdy round school hat in her hand, and a smart leather bag, waited for Sima and Haik. Finally came Sima, ready to go, clutching a glorious bunch of Spring flowers, and Haik with his scratched old satchel.

Karekin arrived at his office in the city, determined to try to get some business dealt with for once. He felt that he had had enough of political alarms and turmoil, as day after day had passed with excited café talk between his friends and business acquaintances, to the exclusion of almost everything else. The news from Van seemed to have disappeared from the papers, and his friends – the Armenian deputies in the Parliament – had given no hint of any impending trouble. Karekin sighed and considered the good sense of his wife's comments that morning – it was certainly a time for a low profile.

The young men who had been his assistants had departed – one to the army, the other to who knew where. Karekin had had to employ two elderly and somewhat tremulous clerks, one Jewish and the other a Turk, to do some desultory typing and deal with enquiries in the outer office. Karekin was working at his desk, still fairly early in the morning, when there was a knock at his door.

"*Effendi*," said the old clerk "there is a policeman at the door asking to see you."

"Well – show him in, show him in," Karekin rose to his feet.

An elderly Turkish gendarme from the local police station, whom Karekin recognised, came diffidently into the office, and bowing respectfully, offered Karekin a sealed note.

"*Effendi* – Karekin bey – I have been instructed to ask you to come down to the station please, to answer some important and necessary questions that have arisen."

"What! Right now?"

"*Effendi* – yes please. I understand the matter is urgent, and my commander has asked me to impress this upon you. It will only take a few minutes. Perhaps you could accompany me."

Karekin was not completely surprised. These summonses were happening more often, and he didn't suspect any deeper motivation. The natural politeness of the policemen was normal. Karekin nodded, and picked up his hat, but left his stick. He gave some minor instructions to his two clerks, and left the office – the elderly policeman politely making way for him at the door.

On the way to the local station, through the busy and crowded streets, the gendarme kept politely a step or two behind Karekin, perhaps out of respect for his privacy, but perhaps also because he didn't want to be questioned. Karekin noticed the restlessness and excitement of the crowds on the pavements. But this was not very different to what had been going on around him for days. He raised his hat to the occasional business acquaintance. It was all perfectly normal.

On arrival at the station, the elderly gendarme disappeared. Karekin was asked by the Clerk at the desk to go in, and he was conducted by another policeman into a large bare room at the back of the station. This room was like a large white-washed hall with a few tables and chairs scattered about, and with only two or three windows high up in the walls. Already seated at the tables, looking puzzled and disconsolate, were a group of about seven other gentlemen, amongst whom he suddenly picked out his old friend Doctor Aram Manuelian.

Karekin felt the first little butterfly feeling of uncertainty, but went forward smiling.

"Aram, my old friend," he walked forward, as the door shut behind him, "Whatever are you doing here – and what the blazes is going on anyway?"

"Karekin, I really have no idea, and neither have any of these others," said Aram gesturing to the others in the room. "All I can say is that we are all Armenians, but there seems to be no rhyme or reason why we should be here at all. We now have in this room a doctor- myself, two lawyers, a journalist, and now you, a prominent business man."

At this comment, everyone suddenly started talking together at the same time. This chatter continued unabated for some moments, until the door opened again, and the local commissioner entered with three other people, who were ushered into the room.

"Gentlemen I have to inform you that you are all under arrest," the commissioner stated, looking at none of them directly. Karekin recognised the man who had called regularly at his office, year after year, during the time of the Bairam festival, to extend the compliments of the local Police force, and to collect the charitable contribution that would then be offered by Karekin for the local police fund. His bland announcement was met by a babel of comments, objections and questions, from the eight people now in the room. The commissioner raised his hand and called out – again looking no one in the eye,

"I can tell you nothing except to inform you that last night Talaat Bey, from the Interior Ministry, has ordered the arrest of Armenian leaders suspected of having extreme nationalist sentiments, and of aiding the Allied war effort."

Amidst an ever-increasing tide of objections and cries, he turned and walked out – the gendarmes closing the door behind him, and they heard for the first time the ominous turning of the key.

Karekin sank into one of the chairs and ignoring the noise around him, he began to reflect, though his thoughts did not get him far, except to increase the creeping unease in his stomach.

As the morning progressed, more and more people were ushered into the room – all as bewildered and annoyed as those already present. There was something particularly odd going on. It wasn't until fairly late in the morning that four of the Armenian Parliamentary deputies were brought in, and by then there were about 50 people in the room, which was becoming crowded. The odd thing was that this was not just a group of politically motivated people. There were now scholars, musicians, a large group of lawyers, a couple of doctors and even some clergymen, none of whom, by any stretch of the imagination, could be said to have any possible connection with the political events surrounding the city at the moment.

This was more than a round-up of what might be termed 'the politicals'. It constituted a microcosm of the prominent men of the whole Armenian community. This was 1915 – none of these men had as yet had any experience of the new vicious tyranny that could emanate from governments claiming to act on behalf of a unified tribal people. There had of course been plenty of random cruelties in the old Ottoman system. But this was different, and Karekin could feel it in his bones, even if the others couldn't.

By midday, the group had become too large to be accomodated in the hall and they were all led out to the courtyard in the centre of the station. Once in the courtyard – it was a fine fresh morning – yet more people began arriving. One of these, a certain Doctor Allavertian, was known by Karekin to be a well-known member of the Ittihad party itself. He had raised considerable funds for the CUP, and was supposed to be well in with Enver and Talaat – indeed to be one of their friends.

"Dickran, whatever is going on," asked Karekin, when he had the chance to get to his side.

"Oh God! I don't know, I don't know," wailed the doctor. "I said to the Commissioner when I arrived that I would be grateful if he could ask the questions to which he wanted the answers as soon as possible, I told him that I had to get back to my office quickly. But he merely smiled and said 'soon, soon' and left me. I just can't understand it."

"But, Dickran, don't you realise that we are under arrest – this is not a matter of answering some questions. That was just an excuse – it's all much more serious."

"Nonsense, Karekin, and I would ask you not to say these things out loud – bad for morale you know. It's all a mistake – someone is carrying out orders that have not been issued as precisely as they should have been. They are acting over-zealously and perhaps too literally. I've asked the Commissioner here to send a message to Talaat."

"Dickran, Dickran – what's the matter with you – can't you see what is happening?"

"Oh tush, Karekin, leave me alone – you're bats. We are at the start of the 20th century for god's sake – this is not the days of some crazed medieval Sultan." With that parting shot he walked away, unwilling to continue a conversation he was finding distasteful.

Karekin shrugged, but now began thinking of how he could get a message to Armineh to tell her what was happening. He could see the signs of something a lot more sinister than Dr. Allavertian would allow. His friend Aram, though equally at a loss, was beginning also to see a pattern as more and more people were herded into the courtyard. The mood however was still, for the moment, anxious and troubled rather than frightened and panicky. There were even jokes, as people assured each other that somehow, somewhere, the whole thing was a mistake.

In the age-old Ottoman style, there was the usual inefficiency with people coming and going in and out of the courtyard without too much supervision. Several of the people had been accompanied by sons or servants who had entered, but were then required to leave by the guards now permanently stationed round the walls. Names would be ticked off by the clerk at the door – and those not on his list would be asked to leave. Karekin sidled up to the doorway set in the wall leading back to the main station, and waited for his opportunity as midday passed. There was, by now, less movement in and out of the courtyard, and the numbers of people milling about had already risen to over one hundred and fifty. Suddenly there was a sort of gasp from those standing near the door as, ushered into the courtyard was the familiar figure of Father Komitas – the acclaimed musician and moderniser of the Armenian liturgical Mass, who had given such a commanding performance at the concert given before Talaat only three weeks ago. He was looking as bewildered as everyone else on their arrival.

Accompanying him was a young man – clearly a student and registered at the Harbiye in his cadets uniform – and also clearly an Armenian. He was holding the cleric and steadying him as he was obviously distressed and finding it difficult to walk. Karekin recognised that the arrest of this man confirmed his burgeoning suspicions, as in no way could Father Komitas be described as any sort of political risk. This was a man who had studied in Germany, and whose life and passion was ancient music. What was happening was something totally new and very dangerous.

Karekin edged up to the young man, who had now let go of Komitas, as the clerk ticked his name off the list. Father Komitas himself moved on into the courtyard to join the other two clerics already there.

"Young man – my name is Karekin Avakian." He then gave the man his address in Makrikoy. "I desperately need to get a message to my wife telling her what has happened. I know it is a lot to ask, but would it be at all possible for you to do this for me."

Karekin then felt in his pocket and produced a silver Lira and proffered it as delicately as possible. The young man looked at him and glanced quickly at the clerk, who was still checking his list. He shook his head at the proferred coin, and smiled.

"Sir – it's very tricky in the city at the moment, but I will certainly do my best to try to get to Makrikoy, though to be honest, I have no idea what is going on either."

"Never mind that – just let them know where I am at the moment. I am really most grateful to you."

The young man then went over and kissed the good Father, and turned and walked out, nodding at Karekin as he went past, reiterating with his eyes that he would not forget.

The arrival of Father Komitas, for some reason raised the spirits of the group. Komitas now radiated optimism, claiming like Allavertian that the whole thing had to be some sort of administrative error, and would be sorted out one way or another soon. There was the approaching Allied intervention on the one side, and there were the foreign ambassadors still in Constantinople on the other. Karekin was not so sure, but wisely he said nothing, as morale was indeed important. Some elderly men were clearly frightened, depressed and close to tears.

It was in this way that the greater part of Constantinople's prominent Armenian citizens were rounded up during the course of that day. These were not just the politicals, but a whole cross-section of a community, under arrest, not for any specific misdemeanor, but simply because they were Armenian. Gathered in three separate police stations, they numbered almost four hundred men. Meanwhile, an enemy army was approaching scarcely 100 miles away.

CHAPTER 15

Sima

After Olga and Karekin had left the house that morning, Sima and Haik had walked down the hill together as usual, save that they were accompanied on this occasion by Nerissa. Once Sima had left Haik at the school gates, she walked on down to the little station of Cobancesme with Nerissa, who did not have to be in school for another hour. Nerissa proposed keeping Sima company while she waited for the next train. There was no one waiting on the platform, the station being almost empty. The gates were open as they walked round, crossed the line and into the little hall to buy a return ticket to town for Sima. The sun was up in a beautifully clear blue sky. Sima felt good and was glad of the calm presence of Nerissa, as they sat on the bench by the station.

"Nerissa, I'm confused about the way things turned out when I was introduced to George Levonian. I know I have no particularly warm feelings for him, and Baba has said that we don't have to take the matter any further, but surely, I ought to feel more thrilled by the fact that someone has shown some interest in me as a woman, shouldn't I?"

"Sima, my love, you're not 'thrilled' as you say, because, in truth, it was not that sort of interest that was being shown. This was a social occasion only – neither of you had the slightest chance to explore any possible deeper feelings – and so you felt no thrill. It would in a sense be sort of sad if you did."

"Nerissa, my soul, you're really rather wise for your age – where do you get it from," asked Sima, not thinking for a moment that she was being patronising. "What do you think of this way of getting married, after social occasions of this sort?"

"I don't know. My first reaction is to condemn it entirely. Honestly, how can people think of it as a business transaction – when you are put into the position of making a commitment to live with another person for the rest of your natural life. What a decision! – it's frighteningly vital that you get it right isn't it. So how can you leave it to be manipulated by someone else – however much they love you."

"But Nerissa, what other way is there? Would it be likely to be any more successful if we chose ourselves – based on what? It would, I suppose, have to be purely physical magnetism towards another human. What would that be founded on? Conversations hurriedly held in school or university corridors, rendezvous in crowded coffee houses, clandestine unsatisfactory meetings, perhaps, like those novels you're forever reading. Would it be any better? Mother and Father's marriage seems to be fine enough isn't it, and they had only met once before they married."

Nerissa didn't answer. She thought of Olga and Selim, and wondered whether Sima had any idea of Olga having the sort of relationship to which she was referring. Nerissa thought back to that tea party at Tokatlians.

'Unsatisfactory clandestine meeting' – was that a fair description of that long dreamy afternoon, and that look in the eyes of her sister and the young man as they discreetly held hands under the table and stared at each other? This was certainly not, she supposed, anything that Karekin and Armineh had experienced in their younger days On the other hand, was it, even remotely, a reasonable basis for a life-long marriage? Even she, who was normally so self-possessed and clear in her opinions, felt confused.

The whistle of the local train sounded from down the line, and the girls stood up. Not a word had been said about the war, largely because here on this little suburban station in the middle of a glorious spring morning, there appeared to be nothing to disturb the peace – an exquisite moment of calm.

Sima kissed Nerissa, who turned to trudge back to school, whilst Sima settled down in her corner seat, clutching her bunch of flowers. She sat back to enjoy the short journey to the city, the day was really so perfect.

The moment Sima arrived at Sirkeci station, however, the whole atmosphere of the day changed for her. The crowds appeared at first sight to be the same as usual, with a stream of people strolling down from the station to the Galata Bridge. Here the scene also seemed to be normal. The trams clattering each way across the bridge, the carriages waiting along the pavements to pick up the passengers from the ferries, the ferries themselves hooting and pushing in and out – getting eventually to the jetties under the bridge, dropping off and picking up passengers.

Despite this, there was an unusual undercurrent, which the more sensitive Nerissa would have noticed at once. Clutching her flowers, Sima threaded her way alongside the trams to the Galata bridge, down the steps to the quays, stepping on to the right ferry. The ferry departed, chugging up the Bosporus, swinging from the European shore to the Asian and back again. The ferry station for Bebek, the home of the Levonians, was not far down the straits. Soon Sima stepped out onto the landing stage, and made her way up to the Levonian house. She had been given clear directions how to get there, and on such a lovely morning, there was no need for a carriage.

On arrival, Sima was shown into an ornate, baroque sitting room with imitation gold-legged Louis Quinze chairs, where Yvonne Levonian was regally ensconsed. Yvonne graciously, if casually, accepted the simple spring flowers, which suddenly looked a bit bedraggled next to the great blossoms of hothouse concoctions gracing every corner of the room.

"*Enchanté, ma cherie,*" said Yvonne. "*Assayez-vous, s'il vous plait.*" The '*tu*' originally utilised by the brittle Yvonne in Makrikoy, suddenly becoming 'vous' here in sophisticated Bebek, thought Sima. Having had the thought, Sima then immediately felt guilty, and wondered if she was not being unfair.

After some banal exchanges of compliments in French, Sima , anxious not to spend the entire morning in her stilted and indifferent French, changed to Armenian and launched into a description of the unusual atmosphere in the city. Yvonne was not unsympathetic. Even to her shallow mind, centred, as it was, round her house and her social pretensions, there had come a realisation that some sort of crisis more serious than the previous vague talk of a war far away, was at hand. The decision, taken that morning by Hovannes, that young Tamara was not to go to school, had come to her as a greater surprise than all the newspaper reports read out to her, which had gone in one ear and out the other.

Once her usual attempts at speaking only in very formal French was overcome, conversation with Yvonne was not too difficult. Sima only needed to sit back and let her prattle on about the many friends and recent social occasions she had attended, expressing some surprise that Sima had not been present at one or the other.

It was in the middle of all this chatter that the unusual sound of a telephone came through the open door. The Levonians, like several households in Bebek, possessed a private telephone. There were still none in Makrikoy. Within a few moments, the young Tamara came in, looking prettier and more natural – Sima thought – than when she had come formally dressed and made up to the tea party at Makrikoy.

"Mama, that was father. He and George are coming home right away. There's a lot of trouble in town. He says that there's nothing to worry about, but it appears there have been a few arrests, and there is a mob throwing stones and getting excited in the Grande Rue de Pera. Tokatlians' windows have been broken. He says that we must put up the shutters. He'll be back soon."

"*Mais c'est affreux – qu'est que se passe?*" wailed Yvonne, reverting to her execrable French. "Why the panic? Tokatlian's windows get broken regularly don't they? I wonder they ever bother to repair them. Oh my dear, don't go."

But Sima, recognising a crisis, jumped up, assured Yvonne that she would be quite all right, kissed Tamara on the cheek, and hurried out after suitable goodbyes. She walked briskly down to the Bebek landing stage.

Here, all still seemed to be as it was in the morning. As always, there was hardly a moment needed to wait as the next boat came up and pulled alongside. Out went the board plank, unnecessary really as the deck came right up to the landing jetty without any gap. On pressed everyone who had been waiting. At this stage of the journey, with only a few stops before the Galata terminus, there were no seats left. Sima stood watching as the ferry weaved near the battleships in the harbour, crossed once to Asia and recrossed, before approaching the bridge.

Once here, however, all had changed. Sima looked at the bridge above. This was filled with a large mob of excited and gesticulating men, who were milling about and totally blocking the road. The jetties below the bridge were also full of people. There was nowhere for them to go, as, such was the crowd already on the bridge, most of the passengers coming off the ferries could not get up the stairs. Several ferries, unable to dock, were milling about, turning their engines on and off, unable to get in to discharge their own passengers. In all the shouting and excitement, Sima could not hear what the mob was yelling.

Suddenly, in the midst of all the noise, there came the unmistakable, loud foghorn blast of one of the two great battleships in the Straits. Like almost everyone else, Sima turned, and saw the *Goeben* and the *Breslau* – oh dear, she thought, what were they now called, *Sultan Selim* or something – belching out great spurts of smoke from their funnels. Even as she looked, the majestic *Goeben* which must have been raising steam for some time, began slowly to move forward turning heavily on its axis, until it had completed a total 180 degree turn. The battleships began steaming south towards the sea of Marmara and the Dardanelles. It was a majestic sight, and Sima was rivetted by its metallic grandeur. However the whole manoevre had taken well over half an hour, and meanwhile here she was still stuck on the ferry-boat, admittedly with hundreds of others in the same predicament.

As Sima stood waiting for someone somewhere to do something, she suddenly remembered for the first time that there was going to be no way that she was now going to be able to get back to pick up Haik from school. However, there was nothing at all that she could do about it. Whilst she felt a bit guilty that she had not thought of it before, she dismissed the worry. After all, nothing had happened for days since Karekin had first insisted on Haik being picked up from school, and surely he would make his own way home, once he realised that she was not coming.

By now, it had become clear that the demonstration involved only a purely Turkish gutter mob. They were yelling the usual stuff about *giavours*, Greek pigs, Armenian parasites and Jewish scum. Sima did not feel any personal fear. Quite apart from the fact that the passions were not at this stage directed against individuals, there was a certainty in that old Ottoman world, shortly due to pass away for ever, that a woman, whatever her race or religion, if dressed discreetly and demurely, would not be touched in public. Meanwhile, time was getting on, and here she was still stuck on the ferry trying to get onto the bridge.

"Well, Madam, what a mess – I'm afraid we're still going to be stuck here for another hour or so, before we are likely to be able to get off the boat and away."

Sima looked up in surprise to the tall man standing by her side, leaning on the rails. The unusual circumstances in which they both found themselves had obviously given him the courage to speak to her – something which in the normal course of events would have been impossible. Sima saw a rather long angular young man, tall, rangy and rather dour in looks, who stared back at her unabashed by her metaphorically raised eyebrows.

"Hello. My name is Garen. I'm afraid that you are going to have to be patient for a little while longer." He then smiled at her for the first time. Sima, though taken aback, felt the fellow-feeling of shared discomfort, and knowing now that the young man was an Armenian asked –

"What's going on, Sir – do you know?"

"Well I'm not sure, but there are three main rumours. One is that there has been an enemy landing somewhere in the Dardanelles. The second is that Greece has declared war on the Empire, and that the Greek army is at this very moment advancing on the city. The third rumour is that some prominent Armenians are being arrested in the city. I have no idea if any of these rumours are anywhere near the truth. As to what the crowd up there are demonstrating about – again I'm not entirely sure. However on this last point I can give you a fairly good guess. Some of them are just plain frightened, most of them are just a troublemaking, unwashed rabble, and some, only a very few actually, genuinely have some sort of a grudge against the Christian millet. My own good mother got worried about my father, who came into town this morning to see the doctor, and I have been deputed to come and bring him home at once, whether he's managed to see him yet, or not."

"And where is home," asked Sima, increasingly at ease with this unusual conversation.

"Buyukdere – right up near the entrance to the Black Sea. I can at least confirm that the rumours about the Russians landing up at the top end of the Bosporus there are groundless – that is if you had any such idea at all," he grinned at her.

"Sir, I had no such thought in my head – though I suppose it might have made sense," Sima smiled back, and then finally introduced herself. They shook hands warmly, exchanging names and addresses.

It was certainly much less than an hour before the arrival, at last, of police reinforcements. Then with yells, whistles and a bit of pushing and shoving, the mob began to thin out. All the people still on the wharves were able to climb up the stairs and go on their way, whilst those ferries which had been waiting , were able to move in and discharge their passengers.

Sima said goodbye to Garen, and began to make her way back up to the station. A train was already waiting. She climbed in and sat down thankfully, having been on her feet in the boat now for almost two hours. Her mind turned back to Makrikoy, and she hoped that Haik had already reached home. She determined, nevertheless, to pass by his school on the way back to make sure.

The train arrived at Cobancesme station. This was a station where in order to get off the platform on the downside, you had to cross over to the other platform and go out through the little booking hall. Sima, still not hurrying, or aware of any problems, crossed over the footbridge, and was just coming out of the ticket hall into the dusty entrance to the station, when she saw a very flustered looking Armineh just alighting from a gharry. Armineh came hurrying up to Sima who was standing, mouth agape, wondering what was going on.

CHAPTER 16

Vahan in Makrikoy

This same morning of the 24th April Vahan was due to go to his weekly singing classes with Father Komitas, which he enjoyed so much, and for which he did not want to be late. Father Komitas gave music lessons not only in the Armenian church liturgy which he had already done so much to modernise, but also, much to the disgust of the traditionalist clergy, in secular classical music. These lessons were a collective affair, usually with at least twelve pupils. That morning Vahan had received a letter from Caesaria from his mother, Mariam, which jolted him out of his carefree student life, and which with the remainder of this day's events was to change his life for ever.

He was, of course, perfectly well aware of the tensions in the city, and knew of the rumours of the allied landings due to take place somewhere on the Gallipoli peninsula. However, he had not been following the growing concerns of the Armenian community as to the events in Van, and the implacable movement by the Ittihad government towards a 'final solution' in the Armenian highlands. Life was really too good and too exciting for him to allow these external political events to have made a diference to his way of life. So it was that he read the letter from his mother with ever-increasing dismay and incomprehension.

"*My dear son,*

May God bless you, and may you walk with Christ beside you all the days of your life. I kiss your brow and pray for you every day. God be praised, we are now all well. But I must inform you of the shock which we suffered recently. A week ago a police officer came to our house and told us that he wanted to see your father. Garabed was at home, as it happened, and as we knew the policeman, who had come to our house on previous festival occasions collecting for the station, we had no hesitation in summoning your father. When Garabed came down, the policeman simply said touching his forehead in the usual way -

'Garabed effendi, the Chief Commissioner of Police has asked me to request you to accompany me to the station as he wishes to ask you some questions.'

This Commissioner was a man, Vahan, my son, who had eaten at our house. Your father, not suspecting anything untoward went with him straightaway.

You may remember that in the year before you were born, we had trouble under the old Hamidian regime, and it was known then that your father's house was a refuge which would have been stoutly defended with firearms if it had been attacked by the mobs. It seems that the authoirities had not forgotten this in all these years. For some reason they are now looking for any firearms that the Armenian population might still have.

But, my boy, there were no firearms left in the house at all. Garabed had handed all of them in at the start of the war, when the order was first given that all firearms were to be brought to the police station. We did have an old Mauser, but your brother Raffi had thrown that away.

I am sorry to have to tell you that your respected father was roughly interrogated, and was beaten several times throughout the day. It seems that they did not believe him when he assured them that there were no more guns in the house. They hit the soles of his feet repeatedly with an iron bar, and kicked his face with their boots. He fainted twice as far as he could remember - but on his revival they kept on at him again and again most of the day. I must say, my son, I had heard of such things being done at the police station to rogues and thieves, but somehow the reality of it had never struck me before, and I never thought it could happen to us.

Your father was returned early in the evening, like a piece of luggage or furniture hanging over the back of a donkey. This was an animal that belonged to a local Turkish carpenter who knew your father and who happened to be passing when father was dumped outside the police station. My darling boy, I worked for almost a week to restore his ravaged face and to get his swollen feet well enough to walk on. You wouldn't believe the state he was in when he was returned. I had a hard time calming your brother down. But you know your father, he is getting better fast and has become impatient already to get back to work. I suspect he will go back tomorrow regardless of what I say. I have found the time to write to you. Father ordered me very strictly that I was not to worry you about what has happened, so please don't write to him about any of this, but both I and Raffi thought you should know.

I pray to God to keep you safe and in good health, my child.
Your loving mother."

Vahan felt a surge of anger. He knew that this outrage must clearly have been carried out by men who had come to his father's house many times on official business. Hospitality had always been offered to them, when they called. But he also recalled that he had been told in an earlier letter that the old Ottoman Commissioner of Police had been replaced by another of those hard-faced nationalistic members of the Ittihad party some months ago. They were in any case no doubt carrying out orders emanating from Constantinople.

He wondered how his emotionally more volatile younger brother Raffi was coping with the clearly deteriorating situation in the interior. For the first time he felt the political situation affecting him personally and directly. However, with the thought that there was nothing he could do about it for the moment, he put on his Harbiye uniform, and after breakfast with the still silent Christina and the now also more subdued Marisa, he went out to walk to the house of Father Komitas where the classes were due to take place.

On his arrival at the house which was in a narrow street in the Beyoglu district, he found a scene of some turmoil and confusion. Most of the other students had already arrived and were milling about in the small hall at the foot of the stairs. Sitting in an upright seat by the front door, looking a little uncomfortable, was an elderly police officer. Father Komitas himself was standing on the bottom stair expostulating with one of the students – Kegham.

"What's going on?" Vahan asked one of the other young men.

"Look, this police chap has just arrived and asked the Reverend Father to accompany him to the police station as the Police Commssioner wants to ask him a few questions. You know how jumpy everybody is these days. He says that they'll only need him for about five minutes. But you know Kegham - he has got excited and is telling the good Father not to go."

"Hi, Vahan, we need your good sense - tell Kegham to calm down," called out another of the students.

Vahan suddenly thought of his mother's letter that morning, and felt a surge of fear. To everyone's astonishment he remarked:

"I agree with Kegham. There's no need to go. They can either ask him the questions here, or issue a proper official request for him to attend at the station which everyone can see and check."

This caused yet another uproar. This, however, was dealt with when Father Komitas himself, already dressed in his long black clerical gown, finally raised his hand.

"My children, I am going with this officer. We don't need any trouble. I am not going to change my habits of a lifetime now. Vahan, my son, if the authorities want to ask me some questions why shouldn't I go and help them - I have nothing to hide."

Kegham, still holding on to the Father's black sleeves, spoke urgently.

"Don't go, don't go. At least if you do, let me come with you."

This was met by a chorus of approval from all the waiting students.

Father Komitas looked round. The policeman still sat quietly and diffidently on the chair by the front door. The pupils milled about getting more excited - in particular because Vahan, always considered the sensible and calm one amongst them had so surprisingly backed up the Bruiser's excited objections. It was the good Father's own inclination, now clear in his mind, to accompany the policeman to answer whatever questions that might be put to him. But he knew that he had to calm everybody down, and this could certainly best be done by taking one of them with him. However, there was no way he was going to let the emotional Kegham accompany him.

"Very well, Vahan if you don't mind, I would be happy if you would accompany me with this officer," indicating the unhappy police officer who now rose from his seat. "Gentlemen," he turned and smiled at everyone - "although he said only five minutes, we all know how long these formalities can take, when dealing with officials - so I am afraid this morning's class must be abandoned. Come Vahan, let's go."

Then, smiling all round at his pupils, and gesticulating at the gendarme to go ahead, he walked out, with Vahan in some confusion trailing alongside. Vahan had called out in support of Kegham largely as a result of his mother's letter, but he had no real anxiety for Father Komitas. What might happen in provincial Caesaria could not happen in sophisticated Constantinople. Furthermore, he also felt a little proud that Father Komitas, whom he admired so much, had chosen him out of all the others to accompany him.

However, once at the station - everything began to turn into the surreal Kafkaesque nightmare which had already overwhelmed Karekin Avakian. Vahan stood by the side of Father Komitas, both of them becoming more and more bewildered. Komitas was a man who could not cope with hard or rude words. So when the desk Sergeant brusquely ordered them to go through to the courtyard, without answering any questions and without the usual politeness, the Father's steps faltered. Vahan accordingly linked his arm with the priest to give him support, and they walked through to the courtyard at the back of the station. Here, as they arrived, Vahan gave the Father's name to the clerk at the door.

Vahan heard a sort of gasp from those nearest the door as he and Komitas walked in and people recognised the priest. There appeared to be a crowd of about a hundred or more men - all Armenians - milling about in the courtyard. Vahan recognised one or two, such as the well-known parliamentary deputies. As it happened by then there were some clergymen there also, and Father Komitas walked across to them and began conversing earnestly. Vahan stood at the door uncertain what to do next. It was then that a tall distinguished-looking gentleman in a grey suit came up to him and introduced himself as Karekin Avakian.

"I know that you don't know me and I'm sorry to have to request a favour from you, but as you can see I can do nothing here myself. I must get a message through to my wife as to what has happened. It is a lot to ask, but could you possibly get the information to her."

At this point he fumbled in his pockets, and muttering something about expenses, produced a coin. Vahan, still with his eyes on Father Komitas, shook his head declining the tentatively offered coin. However, reflecting that the singing class had been abandoned and that he was free all day, he answered:-

"Sir, I will of course do my best. I will certainly get a mesage to your family one way or another. Could you give me your address."

Karekin was ready and gave him a card showing his private address. Vahan took this and said again that he would do his best. He then strode forward, embraced Komitas warmly and left the courtyard, smiling and nodding at the grey-suited man indicating again that he would not forget.

Vahan was not insensitive, but Makrikoy was fairly far, and it was not certain that he would have gone personally. If, for instance, one of his many friends had perhaps accosted him at that moment in the street, or if he had found any other matter with which he might have had to deal, he would not have gone himself. Of course he would always have done something - but that could have been simply to send a messenger with a scribbled note. As it was, with nothing much else to do now that the class had been cancelled, he wandered down towards the bridge, deciding as he went through the narrow streets to go to the station and take the next train himself. The tense atmosphere in the city was getting on his nerves, and the thought of a stroll in the leafy suburbs of Makrikoy had its attraction. The collection of over a hundred prominent Armenians in that police station courtyard had still not penetrated into the forefront of his thoughts. He had still not seen any sinister connection, despite his mother's letter.

When he got to the bottom of the Pera hill, he saw that quite a crowd was gathered on both the bridge itself and on either side. This consisted of the usual odiferous riff-raff yelling about *giavours* although Vahan was surprised that the emphasis seemed to be particularly against Armenians on this occasion. "Shoot them all" rang out the cry from the crowd and although Vahan did not fully realise it at the time, it was clear that news of the arrests was beginning to seep out.

The crowds were not too dense as the police reinforcements had just arrived. Vahan slipped through and walked up to the Sirkeci station. He noticed that some ferries were milling about below the bridge trying to discharge their passengers, who were only just beginning to trickle off up the stairs leading from the jetties.

Vahan had been to Makrikoy before, to the racecourse, but he had no idea where the address given to him by this Mr. Avakian was. Accordingly, when he got to the little station he felt it essential to get a gharry, and a carriage was in fact waiting in the dusty station courtyard when he arrived. He gave the driver the address, and the old man replied: -

"Ah, yes - the Avakian house " and named his price for the round trip. Vahan climbed in and they trotted up past the fields bordering the Vali Effendi racecourse.

Vahan breathed in deeply enjoying the green fields and the fresh air, and even the horsey smell of the carriage. They soon passed the fields and almost immediately stopped outside a substantial house - having the usual blank wall with few windows looking onto the street. There were long walls on either side of the entrance, so it was clear that there were large grounds behind. Vahan, not expecting to be more than a few minutes told the driver to wait and knocked at the door.

Meanwhile the fleeing Olga had caught one of the last trams to get across the Galata Bridge before the crowds gathered blocking the bridge. She, of course, noticed nothing through her tears. She had stopped running almost immediately after leaving the college - girls did not run through the streets of Constantinople, however distressed. She kept shaking her head, trying to clear the fears and impressions that were running though her imagination. She was oblivious to all the tension in the streets; everything centred round her own feelings. She walked on automatically.

As she sat in the tram, and later on in the train, she became more and more distressed. She had no idea that the young men forcibly restraining Selim were his friends, anxious that he should not get himself into real trouble in his anger, by lifting a hand against any of the girls tormenting the unhappy Olga. It seemed to Olga as if he was being attacked because of his friendship with her. Furthermore, although she had been blithely carrying on over the past eight weeks without a thought for the possible consequences, nevertheless at a subliminal level she knew that at the very least she had been deceiving her parents. Her supreme self-confidence had for the first time just been shattered, and she now swung to the opposite extreme of despair, and a feeling that she was being punished for the relationship.

The fraught political atmosphere in the city, and the inevitable fears for the future that now lay in the hearts of most residents as a result of the arrival of an enemy invading army, was totally banished from her thoughts. She could only see everything in terms of Selim and herself, and of their love for each other.

So, on her arrival at the Cobancesme station, seeing that no gharry was currently waiting outside the station, she immediately made the decision to walk home. She knew she would not have the patience to wait for one of the carriages to turn up. She crossed the lines and began hurrying up the hill a little further on from the racecourse to get home as fast as possible. She was not exactly running, but was walking very fast, and in her distress she found she could not stop crying, although by now, on one level, she was beginning to get impatient with herself.

When in her anxious emotional state the distinctive yellow silk scarf she often wore slipped off her shoulders, she never noticed the loss. If she had only turned round at that point, she might have seen the two rough looking louts, who had been trailing behind her all the way from the station, pick up the scarf where it had fallen on the road. She might then have turned back and retrieved it from them. But that light kiss, which she knew was going to come, the spitefulness of the girls, the sight of Selim struggling in the grip of some bullies as she thought, and that last heart-rending cry of "Olga" as she ran away - were all churning around in her head, driving everything else from her mind. So it was that a chain of events began with the otherwise totally irrelevent dropping of a yellow scarf.

She tried to collect herself when she reached the door of the house. She pulled the bell knob and wondered suddenly and with more rising feelings of panic what she was going to say to her mother. She need not have worried. The door opened, and for the first and probably only time that day everything went right. Instead of Marie at the door or one of the kitchen maids, there stood Armineh. Armineh knew at once, within a second, what this tear-stained girl standing fearfully at the door needed. None of her clever intellectual daughters, nor her strong upright husband would have known what to do or say. Armineh simply and instinctively opened her arms wide in the sort of gesture that mothers have used over the centuries, and with a great heaving sob Olga threw herself into those arms in a way which she hadn't done for years.

"Oh mother, mother" cried Olga as she was quickly drawn in to the house and then into the sitting-room. Marie who had heard the sobs came out and closed the front door, and the door to the sitting-room, leaving mother and daughter alone. At last Olga began pouring it all out - her love for a young fellow-student at the College - the meeting at Tokatlian's with Nerissa present - the taunts and threats this morning - and finally a somewhat exaggerated version of the young man in question being attacked by the other boys, an incident which she had been continuously building up in her mind out of all proportion the whole morning.

Armineh, continuing to hold Olga tight as they sat together on the sofa, was more and more confused. The name 'Selim' had not as yet been mentioned, and so, seeing little to worry about, she remained fairly calm. In any event it was clear to her that for the moment she did not need to say anything, but only continued to stroke Olga's beautiful hair, as she sank down with her head in Armineh's capacious lap. She simply murmured sweet nothings as Olga went on and on pouring out things she had kept bottled up for weeks. Armineh sat quietly, thinking hard, but she had still not cottoned on to the real problem.

As nothing but encouragement seemed to be coming from her mother, Olga began feeling better and better, as her rambling discourse went on. After about fifteen minutes of this, the front door bell rang again. The door was opened and the welcome tones of Nerissa rang out from the hall -

"Mama, Mama, I'm home"

The sitting-room door opened, and Nerissa walked in, throwing her dowdy round school hat onto the chair in the Hall.

"Mama, we've been let out early, as there is trouble and demonstrations in the city, and even here. Oh! Olga! What are you doing home."

"Nerissa, come and sit down" said Armineh, as Olga finally lifted herself and sat up, dabbing at her eyes with the lace handkerchief always kept up her sleeve. In true Olga fashion she had already convinced herself that all was now well, and that her problem had somehow miraculously disappeared.

"Oh, Nerissa come and give me a kiss", she gestured gaily and sat upright. "I've been telling mother about the tea-party we went to at Tokatlian's, and all about my feelings. She's been so understanding. It's been an enormous relief to get it all off my chest."

Nerissa stood totally amazed. She loved her sister and had a great faith in her mother, and it simply did not cross her mind that there might be any misunderstanding between mother and daughter. She rushed forward, hugged the two of them, now sitting up next to each other.

"You mean Mama now knows all about you and Selim - oh I'm so glad my darlings."

The confusion in Armineh's mind suddenly and sharply cleared with a snap.

"Selim. Selim. What's this about Selim?"

At exactly the same instant, both Olga and Nerissa realised that Armineh had had no idea that Olga had been talking about a young Turkish boy, and not some Greek or Armenian Romeo. There was a dreadful silence. Then Olga jumped up and ran out of the room upstairs to her bedroom. There were no more tears - the whole emotional merry-go-round had gone on too long. Nerissa was about to follow her, when Armineh, in a voice Nerissa had rarely heard, ordered her to sit down.

"Now, Nerissa, I want no lies or half-truths, no little fibs, no attempts to hide anything. I want the whole story. Who is this young man for whom Olga appears to have lost both her heart and her head?""

"Oh mother, honestly, I don't really know too much, believe me. All I know about him is that he studies at Robert College, and is the son of a doctor, who I think is employed at the German Hospital. I did go to tea with them at Tokatlian's a few days ago - you remember - to be a companion for Olga, and he seemed a nice boy. But oh! Mama, you should have seen them - they are truly in love"

"Love - tush!" snorted Armineh, as she began to contemplate with some trepidation the awful and tricky explanations with which she was going to have to cope, when Karekin got back in the evening. "What do they know about love - the ninnies. How old is this boy, Nerissa?"

"I think he's about nineteen - certainly not more than twenty.

Oh, mother, what is Baba going to say."

"Your father is not going to say anything, as he is not going to know about it for the moment. He has enough problems on his mind without having to worry about his daughter's stupidities. Nerissa, my dear, can't you see the impossibility of the situation. I'm really surprised at you. Haven't you thought for a moment how unhappy this is going to make your sister sooner or later. This whole nonsense would have been out of the question even during normal times, but now with all this tension it's ... Nerissa really!"

"Oh! Mother, of course I saw the problem very well, and I always have, even before I met the young man. But, Mama, how could I have put it to Olga. You know she thinks of me as still a little girl. Then when I first met him I could say nothing. Mama you haven't seen them together - I've never seen Olga so sincere and genuinely involved. It's something beautiful, but you wouldn't be able to see it I suppose."

Armineh sighed, and looked sadly at Nerissa, who had the grace to blush deeply and look away totally ashamed at her insensitive comment. It suddenly struck Armineh that she had not spoken in any serious and meaningful way to Nerissa for a long time, and that this had been her own fault. However, she mentally braced herself. She was not going to be distracted at this stage with a long heart-to-heart with Nerissa, which she realised she should have dealt with long ago. She now had to face up to a showdown with Olga. It was going to be very uncomfortable, there would be an excess of emotion and tears. However, it was better by far to deal with it, here and now before Karekin got home and matters inevitably became more complicated one way or another.

She went to the bottom of the stairs and called up loudly and firmly, trying to keep any anxiety or anger out of her voice :-

"Olga, my daughter, you must come down, and you must come down now. You know we have to talk."

The door to Olga's room opened, and she came down the stairs, pale and anxious, but with all the evidence of the recent tears washed away, her hair brushed, and with two high spots of colour on her cheeks. Nerissa came out of the sitting-room, unsure whether her mother wanted her to stay or not. Armineh's calm nearly wavered when she saw the stubborn determination on Olga's face. Armineh's emotions were now in turmoil. On the one hand she itched to be able to get angry and lay down the law to her silly daughter, on the other hand she knew she had to remain calm.

"Olga, my love, it is vital that there are no lies or any hidden agenda between us now. Please tell me again what you ..."

Then, at this point there was a knocking at the front door - clearly a stranger who as so often happened hadn't seen the bell-knob. All three glanced at the little window by the door which looked out at the street, and saw outside old Abdul sitting in his gharry, obviously waiting for whoever was knocking.

Nerissa hurried forward to open the door. Standing somewhat anxiously in the door, dressed in the uniform of the Harbiye military college, with his cap in his hand, stood the young man who had smiled at her in Tokatlian's - could it only be a few short days ago. A moment of silence stretched out as the three women stared at the stranger, and he with a shy smile looked back.

"I am very sorry to disturb you like this, unannounced. My name is Vahan Asadourian. I have come on behalf of Mister Karekin Avakian - I trust that I am at the house of the Avakians."

Vahan continued to stand at the door. He, of course, had not in any way recognised Nerissa, the eye contact at Tokatlian's had been so fleeting, and it had not for him been such a memorable afternoon as it had been for her. Armineh, whose mind had been entirely on the problem posed by Olga's infatuation, turned sharply at the mention of Karekin's name and came forward.

"What are you thinking about Nerissa, standing there staring like a silly goose. Come in, my boy, come in. Yes, we are indeed the Avakians. This young lady staring is my daughter Nerissa, and my daughter Olga." She waved back vaguely towards Olga still standing on the stairs.

Vahan came into the hall, and wondered where to start. Largely as a result of his mother's letter which he had received earlier that morning, he was aware, more than many others that day, of the increasingly dangerous situation.

"Madame Avakian, I am afraid I have some bad news."

"Oh my God, my God - Karekin - his heart."

"No, no," said Vahan quickly. "He's in good health so far as I could see. However, I am sorry to have to tell you that he has been arrested this morning, and he's currently in the main prison in Beyoglu."

"Arrested!", all three women burst out together.

"Yes. I don't know the circumstances in which he himself was taken. I myself had gone this morning to Father Komitas for one of his group music lessons. When I arrived, I found that he had been invited to go down to the police station to answer some questions. I went down with him, and when we arrived we found that there were about a hundred Armenian gentlemen there all in the same predicament, all under arrest without any idea why. Whilst there, I was approached by your husband, Madame, who asked me to do him the favour of coming to tell you what had happened. He gave me this address."

"Oh my God - why? What's it all about? He has always been very particular about paying his taxes - it can't be that. What's going on? Oh Karekin, Karekin!. You said there were others there - who were they? " Armineh spoke disjointedly as she tried to grasp what was being reported to her.

Vahan felt distressed that he was unable to give any real comfort or any hard information to these three women. He had never been able to fashion meaningless purely comforting words.

"I can tell you nothing for sure, Madame, but my opinion is that it's political I saw two of the deputies there, and the rest also appeared to me to be men of some importance in the community. There was, unquestionably an official list, from which names were being ticked off."

"I must go to him - I must go at once," Armineh's practical mind already beginning to plan what she was going to do.

"Madame, I must warn you that there is a lot of tension in the City. It isn't entirely clear at the moment whether the British have landed or not, or indeed whether there's been any Greek or

Russian involvement as well. The streets are full, and there are the usual mindless mobs milling about and shouting anti-Greek and anti-Armenian slogans."

"Thank you, young man. Olga, I suggest you go up and have a rest, you look all done in. Nerissa, this gentleman - Mr. Asadourian isn't it? - has come all the way from the city to give us this news; the least you can do is to close your mouth - it's been wide open now for at least a whole minute. Please arrange for a coffee and some refreshment to be served to him at once."

Vahan began demurring, but Nerissa had already hurried out to the kitchen. Armineh meanwhile grabbed her coat, stuck a sensible hat on her head, and said to Vahan -

"Mr. Asadourian, I wonder if I could call on you for one more favour to the Avakian family. May I take your carriage outside to go now to the station."

"Madame, of course. Indeed I'd have walked up anyway if I had known the way. Please take it - I'll go and tell the driver."

"No need, no need. It's old Abdul, I'll deal with it. Mr. Asadourian I don't know how to thank you for all the trouble you have taken. I hope we will meet again in happier circumstances, but meanwhile do please sit down - please".

Armineh bustled out of the front door with her mind now cleared of all the domestic problems and firmly fixed on the new situation facing her husband. She firmly stuck a pin into her hat, as she clambered into the gharry. Abdul didn't seem to be the slightest bit surprised, and immediately roused the dozing horse and started trotting down to the station.

CHAPTER 17

Armineh and Sima

As Armineh settled back in the carriage and began the drive down to the station, she started calmly to work out what she was going to do. There was a ritual for this sort of emergency, which womenfolk through the ages had learned to cope with; the way that wives and mothers have had to act over the centuries when armies roamed over the land, or when there was civil strife or government oppression. Difficult to define, but unmistakable. She checked in her bag to make sure that she had the key to Karekin's office safe, his official papers, her own nufus, and a roll of low denomination currency notes – the basic requirement for the purchase of 'baksheesh'. The road, as always at midday, was deserted save for two rough looking youths chewing stalks as they lounged on the grass, just on the other side of the fence, and stared at the carriage as it drove past.

On arrival at the station, she clambered out, handing Abdul some money.

"Madame Avakian hanum," Abdul waved aside the coins. "I have already been paid by the young gentleman for the round trip".

Armineh nodded, putting the coins back in her bag. This was honesty of the old school to which she was well accustomed, and she made no effort to insult his honesty, by pressing him to take the coins. As she hurried into the station, she suddenly saw Sima coming out – obviously returning from her trip to the Levonians. Armineh had lost all sense of time, and it didn't register how late Sima was in getting back, nor the thought that she hadn't been in time to pick up Haik. She made up her mind immediately.

"Sima, my darling, well met. Look, we have a crisis. Father has been arrested. I don't know why exactly, but I will have to go and find him. Can you come with me – two heads are better than one in these circumstances?"

Sima turned back without a word, assuming that by now Haik had already returned home, and went with her mother to get the train back into the city. On the way, Armineh explained as much as she could of the circumstances, becoming ever more fearful as she did so. This sort of police tyranny, although rumoured to be prevalent in the provinces, did not take place in Constantinople – particularly against well known and respectable gentlemen. She could not imagine what was happening, though it must in some way be connected to the invasion fever. But why should that affect Karekin?

On their arrival in the city, they went first to the office, where the old clerk recently taken on by Karekin was still sitting at his desk, staring into space with bewilderment. Armineh hurried in, as the clerk rose and bowed to the wife of his employer. Armineh didn't mean to be rude, but her mind was now racing ahead of her body. She hurried into Karekin's back office, indicating to Sima to shut the door. Opening the safe, she extracted the little velvet bag of gold coins kept there for emergencies, ignoring everything else. She counted out the coins which amounted to about forty, and popped the bag into her own handbag.

Then, they hurried out, nodding again to the clerk, but making sure not to enter into any conversation with him, though it was clear that he was bursting to know what was going on. Their first object was the main Beyoglu police station. Armineh, whose mind was now firmly on what she was about, had not noticed the menacing crowds still milling about, although the police were out in force. The police station itself was totally quiet, and for a moment Armineh wondered if she had come to the wrong place.

"I would like to see my husband – Karekin Avakian – who was detained here earlier this morning," she said to the desk sergeant. The officer rummaged about with some papers on his desk.

"I am sorry Hanum, but I appear to have no record of this name in the list of people currently at this station."

His eye lit on the straight-backed and striking Sima standing behind Armineh and staring at him. He grinned at her somewhat sheepishly, and she smiled back although she was now in a state of nervous exhaustion. The sergeant fidgeted as Armineh also said nothing but stared somewhat belligerently at him, willing him to say more.

"Dear ladies, we no longer have any detainees of any kind at this station. It is however true that more than one hundred men were arrested this morning from this area. About half have been sent to the Yedikule Police station, which has a large gaol, and from where, so I understand, they'll eventually be going to the Sarayburnu boat station to be deported to the interior. The other larger group has gone direct to Haydar Pasha station, where they will be boarding a train this very evening for the interior."

"But why – what's the charge?" asked Armineh.

"Madam, I don't know but I suppose wartime espionage may cover it. Either way they are destined for internal exile. Now, ladies I must ask you to leave. There is no way that I can help further, as I have no record as to who went where."

Armineh and Sima walked out and stood on the pavement uncertain what to do next. Sima, unaccustomed to such emotional crises, found herself unable to think clearly. The effect on Armineh, however, was just the opposite – whilst obviously on edge, she was now thinking very clearly.

"Sima, my dear, we have to assume that what the policeman said was accurate – his words are all we have to go on. Those who were sent to the Yedikule local prison are going to spend the night there before going on to Sarayburnu – but those sent direct to Haydar Pasha may be leaving tonight. It's no use trying to find out who was sent where. We must be off to Haydar Pasha now, and see if Karekin is in that group – we can always try Yedikule later if he's not there."

Taking the tunel back down to the Galata bridge, they had no difficulty boarding a ferry taking them across the Bosporus to the landing for Haydar Pasha station. This ferry passes Leander's Tower, and this particular trip gives probably the best view of the great Constantinople skyline – but neither woman was in the mood to stare and marvel. Sima sat with silent tears running down her cheeks – not just of sorrow, but also compounded of sheer exhaustion, physical and emotional. Armineh just stared ahead, with pursed lips, trying to work out what she was going to do when they arrived.

On their arrival they saw that the station was brightly lit and was full of soldiers and policemen. A flight of white marble steps swept up from the open area between the ferry station and the grand façade of the railway station. The main entrance was blocked off and no civilians were being allowed in without showing valid tickets for trains departing that evening. Armineh thought fast. Trying to get past the surly-looking guards was obviously going to be a waste of time. Even if she could persuade them to go and get an officer, it would waste hours and might still not succeed. It was late afternoon already and now getting darker. She turned on her heel, and went quickly to a ticket booth that was at the side of the station. There was no one waiting there, and she went up and asked for two single tickets to Eskishehir. She cheerfully paid for first class, as she realised that for her and Sima to produce cheaper class tickets on this line would undoubtedly look suspicious.

Back at the front entrance, she and Sima worked their way to the front of the queue waiting to get into the station. After a careful scrutiny of their papers, and tickets, they were let into the main hall. Here, there was no usual hustle and bustle of milling crowds. Instead there were a large number of fully armed soldiers standing guard. Over in the far corner of the hall, outside the station restaurant, was a particularly large group of soldiers preventing any entry. Inside, a group of respectable looking gentlemen could be seen through the windows behind the pillars standing about or sitting at the tables. Armineh, holding Sima firmly by the arm, manoevred herself closer, but she could not spy Karekin through the windows.

Clearly, getting inside the restaurant just by asking was going to be quite impossible. The last scheduled train of the whole day was due to leave in about an hour, and Armineh reckoned that once this train left, the station would be cleared of everyone. She turned and facing away from the guards, she whispered to the white-faced Sima.

"My darllng, take this bag of coins and slip it into your bag, then move across a little and stand with me near to that young officer over there. You must be brave, and pretend to faint or feel the heat or something. Just close your eyes, drop down and let me do the talking. If you do manage to get inside, try to see your father, and if you do, give him the bag. Just do your best. If you find out he is there, but you can't get to him, give it to anyone to pass on to him – I can see from here they are all respectable and upstanding men."

Sima, whose heart was bursting with anxiety for her father

and a deep fear, did as Armineh had directed. They stood for a moment together, then Sima gave a strangled cry, closed her eyes and fainted into her mother's arms. It required scarcely any acting on her part, as she was both physically and emotionally exhausted.

It worked. The young officer came forward

"What's the matter Madam?"

"Oh, officer, we are waiting for the next train. There's nowhere to sit, and my daughter here is not well. Can she go in and have a glass of water and sit down just for a few minutes. I'll stay out here," she added as she saw him hesitate. Sima opened her eyes and began to try to struggle up, as Armineh produced her tickets.

"Perhaps this soldier can go in with her," she indicated the young soldier who had come up with the officer – "I'm sure he can make certain that all will be well, and he can escort her back here."

Saying this, she produced two notes – both generous, but carefully graded in her mind. The officer had already half made up his mind to let them in, and he took the notes, pocketing the bigger one, and giving the smaller to the young soldier standing alongside. Sima, now recovered, but still looking very white, was permitted to lean on the soldier, and the two of them walked through the glass doors and into the *fin-de-siecle* dining room.

Here, milling about amongst the dark mahogany tables, potted plants and dusty chandeliers, the cream of the Armenian community of the city was standing or sitting about in varying attitudes, from boredom to near panic. Sima and the soldier went to get a glass of water from the bar, which was doing a roaring trade. Sima's eyes roamed round the room anxiously, as the young soldier sat her at a table near the door – the occupants hastily being waved away. Sima was the only female in the room, and she had no idea what to do next.

As it happened, Doctor Manuelian was wandering about and was the first to spot her. He had the sense not to call out, but immediately went to fetch Karekin, who fortunately was indeed in this group. Sitting in the far corner he had not seen Sima's arrival. Aram warned Karekin that Sima was here, but that she was accompanied by a soldier, and that it was clear that she was here under some sort of false pretences.

Karekin strolled over, and then saw her, sitting white-faced, and with a tearful expression. His heart turned over at the thought of his daughter in such surroundings, and he had to make a real effort not to run across and comfort her, as she was clearly distressed and close to tears.

They sauntered over, planning how they would tackle the situation. Aram came first, making clear with his eyes to Sima that she should not show any sign of recognition. He ordered up two 'rakis', and offered one to the soldier, with whom he began an animated discussion about a recent wrestling match which, against all the odds, had gone against the favourite. Karekin moved and stood behind Sima's chair, touching the back of her hair with his chest, but making no other sign. Sima whispered to him -

"Oh Baba – we've only got a minute or two. I am dropping this little bag under the chair. It has gold coins in it for you – you are going to need them. Oh baba, baba, what is going to happen."

"My soul, it's in the lap of the gods – I don't know. Tell everyone that I love them all, and don't weep my love, don't weep."

"Baba, mother is outside. When I leave, go to the window so she can see you; but don't wave, don't make any sign. We are supposed to be travellers on our way to Eskishehir on the next train."

Even in that dire and critical moment, Karekin grinned to himself at the thought of Armineh's deception. Having finished the glass of raki, the young soldier bestirred himself and got up, asking Sima if she was feeling better. Sima, through the tears she could barely restrain, smiled at him and said she was. She then rose and walked out through the glass doors with the young soldier behind, but not before seeing out of the corner of her eye, her father bending down and picking up the little velvet bag.

For twenty minutes Armineh stood beyond the line of soldiers as if waiting for the next train, glancing every few minutes at the figure of Karekin in the window. For his part, Karekin stood there staring at her fixedly without moving. She and Sima clearly had to leave before the last train was called, to avoid any suspicions. Armineh took one last look at the man she had married, knowing that it was most unlikely that she would ever see him again. He raised one arm, and held it palm forward by his ear in salutation, as she and Sima turned to make their way out of the station to return home.

CHAPTER 18

Raffi, and the arrest of Garabed

The situation in the rest of the Empire on that morning of the 24th April was not that much different to that in the city. Caesaria was no exception.

Although he would never have admitted it to anyone, even to himself, Raffi missed Vahan after his departure to Constantinople more than he ever imagined he would. Raffi was now 16, and had already accompanied his father Garabed several times on trips to the highlands of Eastern Anatolia to meet and consult with the families weaving carpets on commission. He was physically the stronger of the two brothers, and his personality was certainly more adventurous and emotional. However, his elder brother's good sense and unflappability had helped Raffi in many a scrap. It was Vahan who had often stood between Raffi and their father, when he displayed his rather hasty and alarming temper.

Raffi and Vahan had slept together in the same room ever since Raffi could remember, and Raffi had in fact absorbed most of his opinions and ideas through Vahan. Although like normal siblings, they also continually disagreed and argued about almost every conceivable subject.

Once war had been declared in November 1914, Raffi

realised that his own dreams of going to the University at Stamboul were unlikely to come to anything, unless the war was soon over. So a slight touch of envy had crept into his reflections, whenever his thoughts turned to Vahan.

Raffi had been deeply shocked at the sight of his father when he had been brought home on the back of the carpenter's donkey from the Police station, two weeks before. It was not just the trauma of seeing his father's condition, there was also an odd feeling of shame and fear at the thought that this figure of authority, whom he had looked up to all his life, was as vulnerable as he was himself. When Garabed had not returned immediately from the police station, Raffi had had the presence of mind to find and throw away the old Mauser pistol left over from the 1895 troubles.

After his return, Garabed had recovered quickly from the beatings. He had in fact been going back into work for the last few days, despite all the efforts of his wife to dissuade him.

Apart from the extraordinary violence meted out to Garabed, there had so far been no other open attacks on the Armenian minority in the town. By the 24th April the siege of Van had been going on for almost two weeks, together with the slow advance of the Imperial Russian army towards that town. Neither of these had as yet resulted in any street violence or demonstrations. Somehow, as the Ottomans had after all been fighting the Russians in the remote mountains of Eastern Anatolia for centuries, the current Ittihad leaders looked on that front with some equanimity. It was the arrival of a Western army within striking distance of their ancient capital, which triggered the paranoia, which was to lead to the terrible events of the next few months.

On this morning, bright and sunny everywhere in the Empire, except ironically on the shores bordering the Aegean Sea, Garabed had decided to stay at home and rest. Raffi and his father were sitting together at breakfast, just before Raffi was due to go to school. Once again a policeman came to the house, and being known to the maid, was immediately let into the breakfast room. Raffi's mother – Mariam – hastened in as soon as she heard that a policeman had again arrived.

"Garabed *effendi*, I have been asked to come and request you to attend at the police station this morning, in order for you to deal with some official business in your capacity as Mukhtar of the district."

"Baba, baba – don't go – let them deal with the business with you here," cried out Raffi, whilst his mother remained standing quite still, covering her face with her hands.

Garabed looked at the policeman, who stood diffidently to one side. Raffi, getting more and more excited and emotional shouted again, -

"Baba, you don't have to go – we'll deal with it together," and he jumped up with clenched fists, tipping over his chair.

It was fairly clear that Garabed was going to comply with the polite request of the policeman, but this outburst from Raffi, and the implication that he might easily knock the policeman down, decided him. After all, he had little choice. He had no idea of what was happening on this day all over the Empire, and at this stage, all he could think of was shielding his family.

He rose from the table, put on his hat and coat, kissed his wife and strode out with the policeman following politely behind. For a short time there was a silence in the breakfast room. Raffi simply could not credit that his father, this strong-willed big man of whom he was both in awe and a little afraid, had meekly gone to the police station, when he had had such a terrible experience only ten or so days before.

"Mother! Mother! Why didn't father object more strongly? Mama what will happen if they beat him again? I can't bear it. We must do something. Why did he go so meekly?"

"My son, my son, calm down. Getting excited isn't going to help your father. I think he knows, and I too believe, that there is no question of a repetition of what happened a couple of weeks ago. Several Turkish business acquaintances of your father, old and respected Ottoman families, raised the matter with the Governor. There will be no repetition, believe me. However, as to why he has been asked to report again, I just don't know. Tensions are running high, ever since the Van situation broke out. If I was to have to give you a reason, I suspect that they are going to go for another forced loan from the Christian community."

"If they beat father again – I'll – I'll kill them," yelled Raffi, who had scarcely taken in a word of what his mother had said, while jumping up and down, unable to keep still.

"Raffi, you must calm down. The situation in the town is very difficult. I want you to finish your breakfast, and then go up to the bazaar and see if you can find out anything. First, my soul, you must look at me and promise, promise faithfully, that you will avoid speaking to anyone that you don't know and not endanger yourself in any way. Don't go to school today, but come straight back to me."

"I promise, mother," Raffi was suddenly sobered by his mother's calm but beseeching tone of voice.

Wolfing down the remainder of his breakfast, Raffi left the house and walked through the narrow streets, eventually coming out into the square in front of the main Armenian Church of St. Gregory. To one side of this was the Kapali Charshi – the covered bazaar – in which most of the merchants were Greeks or Armenians. Raffi went in and was immediately met with an uproar of shouting and noise, quite unlike the usual hustle and bustle of the market. He did not have to speak to anyone – the gist of what was happening soon became clear to him. It appeared that that morning there had been arrests of about a hundred of the more prominent Armenians from all over town. He gathered that most arrests took the form of polite requests to come to the station to answer some questions, although it also appeared that some had been more violent.

Raffi went from group to group gleaning all the information that he could, and eventually came across Ismet, his father's Turkish foreman. Ismet looked at him sadly.

"Ah, Raffi, I'm sorry but I've just found out that Garabed *effendi* is one of those who have been arrested. He, together with the others, have been taken to the Town Hall, where they're all gathered at the moment in the gardens. I am sorry that I haven't got any more hard information – but, my boy, I believe that they're going to be sent out of the town into exile."

"But Ismet, why? ... and where to, where to?"

"My boy, I've no idea. All I know is that bad things are happening, things that I never expected to see in all my days. Please tell your mother Mariam Hanum to be very careful. She can call on my help at any time. I'll surely try to keep the business going until, ishallah, Garabed *effendi* returns."

Raffi touched his forehead and bowed and was about to race home when he recalled his promise to his mother to remain calm. Instead, he sauntered out, hands in pockets, and strolled back.

On his arrival he found the house in an uproar. His old grandmother was roaring at his elder sisters. It appeared that the Turkish wet-nurse, recently taken on to look after the newborn baby of one of his married sisters, had suddenly, in some fear, given notice that morning, and had fled from her house not even waiting for the balance of her wages.

Raffi took his mother aside and told her all that he had discovered. Mariam stared at him as despair flooded over her. A beating could always in the last resort be dealt with, but this was something new and sinister, and she had had no previous experience of how to deal with it. However, one thing was clear – it was still April, and here on the Anatolian plateau it could get cold again, very suddenly. She took Raffi by the hand and led him into her bedroom. There, bending down, she pulled out from under the bed, the heavy old strongbox. Raffi moved to help, but was waved aside.

Taking out a key from her belt, she opened the box. Inside were the deeds of the house and other properties, together with various documents that Raffi could not distinguish, some baptismal and other certificates, and finally in the corner some paper money and a bag of gold coins. Ignoring the paper money, Mariam took the bag of coins and pouring them out on the bed picked out most of them, amounting to about thirty, and handed them to Raffi. Then going to the large wardrobe in the corner of the room, she lifted out the warm sheepskin coat that Garabed used to take with him on his trips into the highlands, and handed that too to Raffi.

"Now Raffi, take these coins – hide them carefully – also take this coat, and give them all to your father, if you can get to see him. Raffi, make sure that he takes them all. He'll make a fuss about the coat, I know him, but say I insist. Once done, hurry home. Don't loiter on the way back. I know by experience that the mob will soon be out on the streets, excited by these events and looking for trouble."

She looked carefully at him, and then suddenly put out her hand.

"My son – give me that cross you're wearing round your neck."

Raffi pulled it over his head and handed it to her without a word. Then taking the coins and the coat he hurried out. Once again, heeding his mother's words, he sauntered through the streets, though he badly wanted to run. He draped the coat over his shoulders, and put the coins in his pockets.

When he reached the square in front of the Town Hall, Raffi saw a large detachment of gendarmes who were guarding the steps up to the entrance of the building. Standing on the steps, there were several Armenian women milling about trying unsuccessfully to get some information from the officer standing behind the guards. Raffi could see that they were not getting far and so strolled round to the road leading away from the square alongside the gardens of the building. Here, looking through the high iron railings, he saw several well-dressed men, walking amongst the trees. Now out of sight of the guards at the front, round the corner, Raffi pressed his face up to the bars and waited. Shortly, three of the men came past, talking animatedly, and Raffi called out to them.

"Gentlemen, please can I talk to you."

They wandered over.

"What do you want, my boy? You know you'd better go away, it's not safe here."

"Please sir – do you know my father – Garabed Asadourian – a big man? Do you know if he is here?"

"Asadour *effendi* – yes, yes, he is here somewhere,"

"Could you please, sir, ask him to come here. Tell him his son is waiting."

"Why certainly. You must be his son – Raffi isn't it. Look, wait here, but stand away from the railings until he comes – it will be safer for you," saying which, the man turned away and, joining the others, they walked back towards the Town Hall building, which could just be seen through the trees.

Raffi moved away to the other side of the street, and leaned against the wall. His heart began beating fast. He had not been frightened before, but now that he was about to face his father, childish anxieties began to rise, anxieties which till now had been contained by the sheer rush of adrenalin.

"Raffi, my soul," came a quiet voice.

"Oh Baba, Baba," cried Raffi, racing forward and clasping his father's outstretched hands through the railings.

"My son, my son, calmly, calmly. You must be strong for your mother's and sisters' sakes. No tears now – nothing has happened yet – all may be well."

He smiled at his second son. But Raffi was no longer a child; he knew that death was probably just round the corner, and that his father was trying to comfort him. However, he gulped down the tears that had been threatening to flow, and pushed the coat through the railings.

"Look, for heaven's sake it's hot, I don't need this".

"Baba, mother said I was to insist that you take it, she knew that you would probably refuse, but it's still only April, and heaven knows where you'll be at night."

Garabed grinned.

"Well, we must do as your mother commands."

He took the coat, shook it out, and then draped it over his own shoulders.

Raffi then handed him the thirty gold coins. Garabed took them and looked down thoughtfully at the coins in his hand. There was a moment of silence. He carefully counted out five of them, slipping them into the pocket of the coat now draped over his shoulders. He then took another hold of Raffi's hand and gave him back the other twenty-five.

"Raffi, take these back to your mother. You'll all need them more than I will."

The inference was very clear. Garabed knew it, although he did not at this moment realise that Raffi, also understood. Although no one could be sure what was going to happen, but one way or another, the likelihood was high that within a few days, Garabed would be dead. Raffi had no idea what to do or say. All his life he had looked to his father for comfort. He had no experience of giving it back. He knew only two things for certain – firstly that he must follow his mother's wishes and insist on his father taking all the coins, and secondly, that he must not under any circumstances give way to any tears.

"No, Baba, I can't. Mother said I must make sure you took them all." Raffi hesitated, even in this terrible moment, he reflected that he had never before had the courage to contradict his father.

Garabed looked at his son, and a short moment passed as they looked into each other's eyes. Then in a stern hard tone, and gathering together all the moral authority he could muster.

"Raffi, you will do as I say, and you'll do it now and without any question. Take these coins home and leave straight away, right now. Tell your mother not to despair, and remember, remember that I love you all."

Garabed dropped the coins into Raffi's hand, which he had been holding with his other hand all this time, and then without another look at him, without a kiss, without a sign, he turned on his heels and walked away through the trees. He never gave a single backward glance, but simply walked straight out of sight.

With the departure of his father, probably forever, Raffi could no longer control his emotions. He walked to the other side of the street, leant against the old stone wall, and gave way to floods of tears. Unlike his more contained brother, Vahan, Raffi had always found release by letting his tears flow easily; on this occasion, his body was racked with sobs, but the tears gave him no release at all.

Eventually he gathered himself together sufficiently to walk back through the streets, with the 25 gold coins clutched in his sweaty hands, thrust deep into his pockets.

CHAPTER 19

Van. The last effort

By this time, the rebellion in Van was almost into its third week. Halil Bey, and his demoralised Turkish regular troops and gendarmes, were becoming increasingly frustrated at their inability to dislodge the 1,500 or so Armenian irregulars, holding on in their square mile of fortified enclave. Meanwhile, General Yudenich and the Russian army was somewhat ponderously approaching Van from the north. Turkish families in the smarter suburbs were beginning to pack their belongings and drift away out of the town, many in boats crossing the lake to the northern and western shore.

Halil Bey decided to mount one final offensive in an attempt to crush the rising before the arrival of the Russians. The large mob of Kurdish irregulars, originally operating with him, had long since deserted. They clearly preferred to terrorise and loot the defenceless villagers in the countryside, rather than to serve under old Halil, with all the inevitable discipline of a regular force. He was aware of the poor morale of his remaining 6,000 men, and realised that his only hope of containing the Russian advance was to clear the enclave, so as to turn the town into a proper defensive bastion.

Halil slowly built up an attacking force of about 4,000 men behind the entrenchments, facing and surrounding the Armenian defensive perimeter. Unlike the smart new Turkish officers of the nationalist Ittihad party, old Halil Bey did not despise his Anatolian peasant troops, and made sure that there would be adequate medical support for the offensive. Accordingly, Dr. Nazım and his medical team, were ordered forward into the front lines facing the makeshift barricades and demolished houses, at the perimeter.

The final push, destined to be the last major attempt to crush the little force desperately defending Van's Armenian quarter, opened a day or two before the 24th April. The strength of Turkish military arms had always lain in their capacity for dogged defence, rather than in their offensive ability. Accordingly, like almost all the major offensives of the Great War, this small, lesser-known one, also failed. Like all the combatants on both sides, the ordinary young men carrying out their orders did not lack courage, but they died in their hundreds against the implacable might of the machines facing them, as thousands did on other fronts.

On the other side of the barricades, similar young men, anxious for their families, defending their own homes, fought back tenaciously, unable to retreat anywhere even if they wanted to. The cleared ground around the perimeter became filled with the dead and the dying. By the morning of the 24th April, the repeated attempts to break into the enclave had finally been given up, and both sides took a breather.

Within the American Mission compound, Dr. Ussher had been continuing his medical work, careful, as he had been from the start, not to let any armed men into the main hospital grounds, even though the hospital was still being shelled from the Castle Rock. He prayed ever more fervently with his small group of Protestant converts, and he continued to avoid any political attitude to the conflict going on around him.

However, on this morning of the 24th April, Clarence Ussher went down to the church hall where the Armenians had set up a temporary hospital for their own wounded. He saw the piles of dead and dying in the no-mans-land between the barricaded stone houses of the perimeter, and the surrounding Turkish entrenchments. He noted also, with some horror, the hovering vultures, and the moans of the badly wounded unable to crawl forward or back.

Dr. Ussher hurried back to his office. Sitting at his desk in the gloom of his cool, windowless office, he hastily composed the following letter to Djevdet Bey, whom he imagined was still in charge of the operations round the enclave :-

'Your Excellency, having seen the awful slaughter of many young men on both sides, and the plight of the wounded in no-man's-land between the forces, I would like to take this opportunity respectfully to suggest a twelve-hour ceasefire to enable both sides to bury their dead and tend to the badly wounded. I am sure I can prevail on the Armenian leaders here to agree to such a proposal, and to allow your men to remove their dead and wounded. Perhaps you could signify your agreement by giving your answer to these proposals with any alternative suggestions you might have, to this messenger, whom I will instruct to remain at the Italian consulate to receive your reply. I remain, with the greatest respect, your humble servant."

After signing this note, Dr. Ussher called for nurse Alicia, and handed her the note -

"Alicia, could you give this note to the good lady who has been carrying letters to the Italian consulate for me. She must stay there until she receives a reply from Djevdet Bey, which she should bring back to me."

Alicia was not one of the small handful of converts to Protestantism from her own traditional Gregorian faith. She looked carefully at the doctor, whom she deeply admired, without saying a word. She wondered if the man knew that three of these elderly ladies had already died in this regular exchange of messages, that had been passing back and forth throughout the siege. Had he simply chosen to ignore the deaths in the interest of, for him, the greater good of God's work, or was he simply totally unaware. She would never know.

"Yes, very well Doctor. I'll deal with it." She took the sealed letter and hurried out to seek out Nevart, who had already delivered four messages across the lines since she had first arrived to work at the mission.

"Nevart, mother, I have another letter which Dr. Ussher says is very important for you to deliver as usual to the Italian Consulate. After delivering it you must wait at the consulate, inside if the Signore will allow, for a reply. You see that Dr. Ussher has marked 'Urgent' on the envelope, so you must wait for the runner to return with Djevdet Bey's reply before returning yourself. Be careful, make sure that you hold the white flag up high all the time. You must go now while there is a lull in the fighting."

She kissed old Nevart's creased brow, and handed her the stick with the bedraggled white flag of truce.

Nevart touched the ground and lifted her hand to her brow and crossed herself, took the flag and the letter, and walked out of the compound and along the now quiet cobbled streets to the spot between the demolished stone houses, where she had set out on previous occasions.

This was a sector of the line commanded by one of the revolutionary nationalist leaders thrown up by the conflict. This youth was impossibly young, fair-haired and blue-eyed, with that look of fanatical zeal in his smiling eyes that left little room for ordinary human compassion. His name was Aris, and he had already, on two previous occasions, shown impatience at Nevart's simple, old-fashioned, blessing whenever she went past him.

He stared dumbly at her as she came up to warn him that she was going into no-mans-land with a flag of truce to deliver a message to the other side. His face was set hard, his body dirty and tired after two days unceasing fighting.

"May Our Lord Jesus Christ protect you," Nevart tentatively raised her hand to bestow a blessing, and her lips to offer a kiss. Aris stood there staring at her, making it clear that he did not welcome the superstitious gesture, nor did he want a kiss. Nevart, confused and hurt stumbled away. She lifted the flag high as she had been taught, waited a few seconds so that it could be seen by both sides, and then walked between the rubble of the demolished houses and into the cleared area between the two forces.

Right opposite her, and sheltered behind another stone house on the other side of the no-mans-land, stood Dr. Nazim Kemal, temporarily unoccupied since the offensive had petered out. Exhausted after two days of non-stop work, when he had spent hour after hour patching up horrific wounds, removing embedded bullets, cutting off shattered limbs, until he was acting on autopilot. Despite all that labour, he remained sharp and alert. Even in these difficult circumstances, he had already managed to have a shave that morning, much to the amazement of the men around him.

Nazim was profoundly aware of the badly wounded and dying men still lying about, unable to crawl or move between the Armenian barricades and the Turkish entrenchments. He contemplated the possibility of going out protected by a Red Crescent banner. However, he then wondered whether it should not after all be a Red Cross banner. His mind went round and round on the point. After all, was this a regular battle; the men on the other side were irregular guerillas were they not, would they respect such rules of war? He stood there in a state of uncertainty, wondering what to do, considering all the various options. He simply could not make up his mind, whilst the increasingly demoralised men around him lounged about, smoked, and were clearly losing what little discipline they had ever had.

Nazim was the first to see the white flag waving on the makeshift stick and moving out between the two crumbling houses in front of him. The men beside him stared with tired and lack-lustre eyes, as a small old woman, dressed all in black, but without any veil, shuffled out of the gap between the two buildings and began advancing across the dusty corridor between the two lines. The old lady gingerly stepped round the dead bodies in her path. She had just about reached half-way, when Nazim saw one of the Turkish soldiers, lying with a leg almost off and dangling uselessly, and with dried blood all over his face, raise his hand to the old woman as she passed and call out in a harsh strangulated cry -

"Mamma! Oh my god, Mamma! Mamma!"

Nazim watched and saw the old lady start and look down. She dropped the white flag, bent down and took the man's head into her arms, for what purpose Nizam could not immediately tell – for just then a shot rang out from the Turkish lines and the old lady staggered forward and dropped to her knees, blood spurting from her side. As she fell she cradled the young soldier's head and then sat up holding his head in her lap. Another shot rang out from the Turkish lines kicking up dust at her feet.

Nazim, forgetting all his cool, all his rational thoughtful consideration before action, all that carefully cultivated overlay of city civilisation, sprang out of his position shouting, "Cease fire – cease fire you louts," to the men around him, and raced over the dusty uneven ground. There, alone between the two lines, Nevart was rocking back and forth, blood pouring out of her side, with a trickle now from her mouth. She sat there, cradling the young Turkish soldier's head in her lap, stroking his brow and his black hair, and crooning an old Turkish lullaby.

Nazim, after all the carefully considered thoughts about what type of identification he should show, had come running out without even an armband. As he ran up to the pair, he was already fumbling for the dressings and antiseptics, which he had instinctively grabbed before rushing out. As he arrived a shot rang out, this time from the Armenian side. Nazim stood clutching his breast as blood spurted out. Nevart, for the first time looked up. Nazim and Nevart stared into each other's eyes for a split second – an eternal moment – and then Nazim died, fatally shot through the heart, by the guilt-ridden Aris, who had spurned Nevart's blessing, who had seen everything, and who had inevitably misunderstood everything.

Immediately, the whole sector became a maelstrom of shots as both sides began blazing away at each other. In the middle of it all, Nevart continued to rock back and forth cradling the dying soldier, her own strength slowly ebbing away. Finally, in the midst of a fusillade of shots, Nevart, who, somehow had not been touched any further by all these flying bullets, bent down and kissed the lips of the son she had never had –

"May your Allah receive you into your heaven, my son," murmured Nevart as she slumped forward, dead, across the breast of the unknown young Turkish soldier.

"Mother, oh mother," groaned the young man, as with the ghost of a smile on his face, he too finally expired.

The aimless shooting went on in this sector for several more hours, as the message, carefully composed by Clarence Ussher to

Djevdet Bey, now torn and blood-spattered, fluttered away in the wind.

Later, in the course of clearing up the Doctor's effects, his orderly discovered the last letter written by Nazim to his son Selim, which he had not had time to send. This was sent on to the family in Constantinople with his other personal effects and together with a letter of commendation from Halil Bay himself. The letter to Selim read –
'My incomparable son,
I am writing to you from my camp bed on the shores of the lovely Lake Van. The nights here are bright and clear and fresh, though still very cold. When the moon is full and high, the lack of any artificial light makes the visibility crystal clear, and you can almost see across the lake to the high mountains on the other side.
I have been moved up to the front with the whole of my medical team, as Halil Bey is proposing to mount a full-scale major offensive to clear the town of the rebels, before the projected arrival of the small Russian force currently advancing towards us.
My son, I have had a lot of time on my hands which I have spent thinking about our lives, the Empire, and what it all means. War often consists of days of intense and terrible activity with not a moment in which to catch your breath. These, however, are interspersed with long periods of utter boredom, when there is nothing to do but think about one's loved ones and write letters like this one.
I remain rather sad at the way the Armenians here have treacherously risen against the Empire at this moment of crisis in our history. However I am not perhaps quite so incensed as I had been earlier when I first arrived here. The intensity with which they are defending the perimeter of the town does indicate at least a certainty of their moral position, which I had not expected. I have also now heard terrible reports of the weaknesses and cruelties of the Ittihad Governor here, one Djevdet Bey.
Part of the problem, I believe, is the rise amongst them over the last 30 years of 'nationalist' ideals. The belief these nationalists have, is that a 'people', however you define it, should act together to have a one-nation 'state'. I am sorry to add that I can sense that it is growing now amongst the Turks and Kurds of Anatolia. It is precisely what I object to in the

current Ittihad government – the urge to create a single exclusive and intolerant nation-state.

But, my son, it is not preordained or unstoppable. It is possible, my boy, to love one's own religion, one's own language and literature, the ethnic food you have eaten all your life, the dancing and the music and the theatre you have enjoyed, yet still be content to be part of a country that has no particular connection to these things, or which carefully takes no part in trying to regularise or influence them.

Ah well!

My darling boy – I know that you have been brought up with truth, and that your heart is strong, and your convictions firm and honourable. Always consider all sides of any position on which you are obliged to make a stand, but act decisively once your mind is made up. Look after your mother and your young sister in case any accident may befall me. You will recall the details of the savings box in my study of which I told you before leaving.

However, I believe that a fully equipped regular regiment with its own medical facilities is moving up to Bitlis shortly, in view of the imminent arrival of the Russians. Should this rumour – it's incredible isn't it how rumours fly around during wartime – be true, I should be due to return to Stamboul soon, as my detachment will no longer be needed.

My respectful embraces to your mother,
Your ever-loving father – Nazim

CHAPTER 20

Haik

Haik's school was not let out early that day. The age of the boys at this school was significantly lower than the school Nerissa attended further away in the little town. Accordingly, the staff, were anxious not to let the boys out early. They decided that it was necessary to keep them in a little longer, in order to give plenty of time for those who might be coming to pick them up, to get there.

So, Haik was a little surprised when he got to the school gates and found that Sima was not there waiting for him. He sat with some of his friends on the grass beside the dusty track leading to the school from the road. Eventually, as time passed, the others were either picked up or themselves drifted off to go home. Haik, in the end, found himself alone, throwing stones at the posts of the fence on the other side of the track.

"Hello, Haik, what are you still doing here," one of the teachers asked as he passed out of the school gates on his way home, "Are you all right?"

"Yes, sir, I'm waiting for my sister who is coming to pick me up. I'll go on home if she doesn't come soon."

"Well, don't wait too long – it's a funny day with a lot of excitement and trouble around. She might be delayed in the city, you know."

The sun was hot, but it was a beautiful fresh clear day as Haik sat throwing stones and thinking of nothing at all. Finally, he decided that he had better get on home. If Sima came to find him gone and the school empty, she would know that he had returned on his own. After all, he had been walking home by himself now for well over a year, before his father's recent decision insisting he be picked up. He hoisted his worn-out old satchel, hitched up his trousers, and sauntered along to the road, and began the walk up the hill.

He was about half-way up the slope, having already passed the racecourse, when he first noticed the two rough-looking men staring at him as he walked up the deserted road, swinging his satchel. One was wearing baggy trousers with a dirty green shirt, the other with an equally dirty old-fashioned red blouse. Turks? Albanians? Gypsies? Haik had no sure idea, and indeed never found out.

The boys at the school had no really clear idea of what was going on. They were conscious of the raised temperature around them, and both Haik and his friends were aware of their parents generalised fear. Accordingly, as he had never seen this couple of toughs before, Haik instinctively avoided any eye contact and trudged on though no longer swinging his satchel with quite the same abandon. All might have been well, if he had not glanced over as he passed, and saw one of the louts sniffing at a distinctive delicate yellow silk scarf. Haik stopped, turned and stared. He immediately recognised it as belonging to Olga; there simply could not be another like it.

"Hey!" he shouted, pointing, "that belongs to my sister. Where did you get hold of it?"

"Does it indeed – squirt," jeered one of the youths languidly and, even to Haik's unpractised ears, clearly not a city accent. He grinned at Haik and waved the scarf like a red rag to a bull.

Haik, surrounded by a houseful of loving sensitive women, had led a very sheltered life. The only violence he had ever experienced was the rough and tumble of boys of his own age at school. He therefore failed to recognise the menacing danger in the eyes of the two men.

"If it belongs to your dear sister – why don't you come and take it. I'm sure she'll be overjoyed," the other sneered with words considerably stronger and dirtier. Haik failed to understand the menace in their words, or he might have been warned, and gone on his way.

Instead, he came over and clambered over the wooden fence and onto the grass verge running alongside the road, where the two youths lay lounging, laughing at him. Haik walked up to them and held his hand out for the scarf.

"And what are you going to give us in exchange," said green-shirt with a new and even more dangerous glint in his eye, as he stared up at the pale and delicate Haik.

"Look – this scarf belongs to my sister, and I haven't anything to give you anyway. She must've dropped it on her way home. I bet you found it on the road."

"Well – I'll tell you what – you give us your nice clean shirt and pants in exchange and we'll give you the scarf – that's a fair exchange," red-blouse answered, grinning.

Haik stared at them both. He hesitated, not entirely sure what to do – anything might have happened, even now he might have walked away unscathed. What, however, finally took place was that Haik lost his patience. Thin and smooth-featured though he was, nevertheless Haik had all the Avakian spirit, plus the healthy energy of any 12 year-old boy. What he lacked, however, was any sense of self-preservation or avoidance of danger – a danger he did not recognise in any case.

The physical aggressiveness of the two youths was fairly clear to Haik, but what he failed to see was the sexually-charged, sadistic menace in their jibes, as he had no comparable experience with which to judge. The scarf was now lying on the grass in front of greenshirt. Haik bent down and grabbed the scarf, then straightened and turned to walk away.

Like a flash both youths were up, and to Haik's genuine surprise, he was grabbed by red-blouse from behind and his arms pinioned to his side, whilst greenshirt came in front of him and punched him several times in the face and in his stomach. Haik began struggling and yelling, out of a mixture of both fear and anger.

"Shut your gob, you little pig," whispered red-blouse with his stinking breath right into Haik's ear. It was unlikely that Haik would have stopped yelling, except that greenshirt then gave him a really vicious punch right across his mouth. Haik's nose now began to bleed, together with his cut lip. Even this might not have stopped Haik's spirited yells, if greenshirt had not produced a long knife from the depths of his filthy trousers and held it firmly to Haik's throat. This, even Haik could understand. Two things then happened – firstly he stopped wriggling or making any noise, and secondly real fear as he had never felt it before gripped his guts, and a trickle of urine involuntarily escaped into his pants.

Tears now began to flow, but without any sobs – tears of fear and frustration. Blood was streaming from his nose and mouth, and his huge eyes for the first time searched the face of his tormentors. What he saw gave him no comfort – green-shirt had a vicious grin and a look in his eyes, which Haik was unable to read.

"This is one of those damned *giavour* kids from the school in that town down below – I'm sure." Red-blouse was still holding Haik tight, whilst green-shirt held the knife steadily at Haik's throat.

" Yeah – you're bloody right – and you know what, they've all been shouting in the city that all *giavours* are traitors, and should be slaughtered like the pigs they are."

"So, how are we going to make sure that he's a damned *giavour*."

"Well, we'll soon be able to tell, won't we," greenshirt laughed and with one hand still on the knife, he fumbled at the buttons of Haik's trousers with the other and yanked them down. They both looked down as the pants fell to the ground, then both laughed –

"There, you see, I knew he was a filthy Christian pig."

"Not a pig – he's a sow – let's show him."

Even now, even at this late stage, it could have ended with just a scare for Haik – a loss perhaps of shoes, shirt, trousers and dignity. But for the first time Haik realised what they had been doing; they had pulled down his pants to see if he was circumcised or not, and therefore if he was a Muslim or not. The knife, as it happens, had also gone back into greenshirt's baggy pocket, and unfortunately Haik's courage returned.

Haik had no idea what greenshirt had meant by his last remark. With the disappearance of the knife, he found the courage to start yelling again and struggling to get out of redblouse's grip. He was yelling and sobbing at the same time, and it was this that finally tipped the balance of violence from thoughtless aggression to a perverted, lustful and sadistic attack.

These youths had spent the whole morning milling around with the mob in the city; listening as adults denigrated and cursed the members of this boy's race and religion. The crucial moment had come when these different people became totally dehumanised in their eyes. In these situations, sooner or later, the gutter is persuaded to stop thinking of the denigrated minority as humans. And here they were, holding a young *giavour* boy totally at their mercy.

Suddenly, Haik found himself thrown down onto the grass, his face thrust into the earth, his shoes and pants pulled right off and his shirt torn from his back. Then Haik felt his genitals pulled and pinched, and felt one of the youths falling down on top of him. Something was happening to him that was causing a terrible pain. He lifted his head, kicked his feet, which connected violently with the youth on top of him and at least relieved the pain. He let out one enormous cry of 'help', before his face was again thrust down into the earth. He began suffocating, and again greenshirt fell down heavily onto his back. Once again the knife was out, held against his cheek and a complete terror gripped him. He heard the sinister voice of red-blouse whispering unintelligible words into his ear as he almost passed out.

Back in the compound of Robert College, shortly after Olga had run out of the school gates, Selim was released by his friends.

"Don't go after her, my friend," Nurhan counseled, "she's already left, and consider, at this moment it might be too much for her if you were to chase after her."

Selim, whose body was quivering with repressed emotion, shook himself free. However he did not run anywhere. The young men, friends and others, stood back, watching him carefully, some with sympathy. The girls looked away and one by one hurried off, many in shame at what they had done, but some in exultation. Selim smiled at his particular friend Nurhan, and the others around him.

"Thank you," he said quietly, but without really meaning it. "Hopefully I'll see you all tomorrow." He went in, collected his things and walked calmly out of the College gates.

Once outside, however, he began hurrying down to the Galata bridge. He knew that Olga would be making for Sirkeci station and the train home to Makrikoy. By the time he got to the bridge, it had already filled up with the crowds that were preventing Sima from disembarking from her ferry.

Almost at once, Selim made the mistake of trying to push his way through the crowds. His emotional state prevented him from considering the situation logically. Had he waited, even for a moment, he would have seen the impossibility of trying to push his way through, in which case he might have thought of other ways of getting across to the Stamboul side. As it was, he plunged impetuously into the milling crowds without thinking.

The shouts of *"giavours* to the gallows!" and "Death to the traitorous pigs" and "Down with the British dogs" and so on – the usual mindless yells of the gutter – passed right over his head as he struggled to get through. But the more he pushed, the tighter he became wedged. Eventually it got to the point that he could go neither forward or back. He roared with sheer animal frustration, as he remained stuck in the middle of the senseless crowd. No one took the slightest notice of him, because of course everyone else was also shouting.

Whereas Olga's tram had been one of the last to get through, and climb up on the other side, Selim, who had walked down from the College, got there in the middle of the demonstration. Nevertheless, police reinforcements eventually arrived, and slowly the crowd began dispersing, with every passing minute, agony for Selim.

As the crowd thinned, Selim finally pushed and shoved his way across the bridge, and walked up to the Sirkeci station. No train was in, and he had to wait in increasing frustration and impatience on the platform, by which time he had been joined by many others, waiting for the next train.

When Selim got to the Cobancesme station, he jumped out. He knew exactly where the Avakian house was. In all the conversations that he and Olga had had together, she had spoken at length about her house and the daily walk down to the station. As he left the little dusty square beside the station he saw a dumpy middle-aged lady getting out of a carriage, but he was far too nervous and excited to contemplate sitting in a carriage for ten idle minutes while it would slowly wind its way up the hill. In any case the horse looked as if it was on its last legs. Selim crossed the railway line and began walking rapidly up the road beside the Vali Effendi racecourse.

He was about halfway up, with the racecourse left behind on the right, and a field beyond a low wooden fence on the left, when he heard the piercing scream of what sounded like a young boy, crying for help. Ahead and in the field to the left, there appeared to be a boy, almost naked, being set upon by two rough men, both of whom Selim immediately recognised as thugs from the city slums. In other circumstances, Selim might have acted a little less precipitously, though he would never have just ignored it. However, in his fraught emotional state, he did not hesitate for a second – taking the fence at a running jump he charged up to the little group shouting unintelligibly. The youth who had been on top of the young boy rolled off and began fumbling at his dirty baggy trousers as he stood up. The other lout who had been kneeling by the boy's face also jumped up, and Selim saw for the first time a wicked looking knife in his hand.

Selim had had no more direct experience of street violence than Haik, but he was eight or more years older, and he lived in the city and was much more streetwise. Above all he was in a rage – a generalised inchoate anger at everything, and this gave him a momentary advantage over the two ruffians. Had he stopped to remonstrate with them, he would probably have lost the initiative. As it was, with fists flailing, he knocked down the green-shirted man who was still fumbling with his trouser belt. Then he turned to face the man in the red blouse who had an inane and vacuous grin on his face, and who was circling round with his knife, ready to lunge.

The young boy on the floor, clearly traumatised, had lifted his head from the grass, and was trying to sit up, his face a mass of blood, and taking great heaving gulps of air. Selim jumped at the red-bloused man and they rolled onto the grass. For a moment all seemed well as Selim ended up on top, but then Selim felt the cold steel of the knife bite into his side. He jumped up and felt his bleeding hip, and then he sensed rather than saw the green-shirted tough circling round to his back, as the man with the knife began to get up, ready to strike again.

Meanwhile, back at the Avakian house, after Armineh had left in Vahan's carriage, Vahan had settled in the sitting room, no longer in a hurry to leave this charming house. Olga, though still distraught and red-eyed from weeping, had not gone to her bedroom as had been suggested, but sat on the other couch waiting for Nerissa to return with the coffee. Vahan felt surprisingly at ease, and did not attempt any small talk with the startlingly beautiful Olga. She only had thoughts of that last desperate view of Selim, apparently being man-handled by a group of College bullies. They sat silently, but comfortably, waiting for Nerissa.

Nerissa, who had finally come to her senses, returned very quickly with strong sweet Turkish coffee, and some 'courabides' biscuits, which Vahan politely declined.

"Where are you from Mister Asadourian?" Nerissa asked, as she sat down next to Olga,

"Caesaria – but I have been living in Constantinople now for over eight months," Vahan replied with some pride. "I'm studying music and drama at the Stamboul University, although as you can see, I'm also enrolled at the Harbiye military academy."

"And what of your family, Mister Asadourian?"

"Well … er … by the way, my name, Miss Avakian, is Vahan – er, do you think you could call me that?" Vahan glanced at Olga who, truth to tell, was not paying much attention.

Nerissa did not blush – she was not that kind of girl. She simply looked at Vahan, speaking without any hesitation.

"Why, yes, Vahan it will be – and my name is Nerissa."

At this, Vahan rose and came over to where the two girls were sitting together and extended his hand somewhat formally. They shook hands with Vahan still standing.

"I have a brother about your age Nerissa – Raffi – and three elder sisters back in Caesaria."

Who knows how long this ever so delightful and totally unrevealing conversation might have meandered on, if Olga had not at that moment got up to hide some more involuntary tears welling up and said, again extending her hand -   "Oh, goodbye, Mister Asadourian – I'm sorry, Vahan, of course – if you'll excuse me I'm exhausted for various reasons. I'm going up to have a lie-down. Please do feel free to remain and finish your coffee."

It was a decisive moment. It had only been about 15 minutes or so since Armineh had left. Vahan could see that Olga meant what she said, and that there was no objection to his staying and chatting with Nerissa – an increasingly pleasurable experience for him. Nerissa said nothing and Vahan was tempted. But after shaking hands again with Olga, he finally turned, smiled and shook hands with Nerissa, indicating that he would be on his way. She accompanied him to the front door. He waved again and turned and started walking briskly down the hill back to the station.

He had just reached the point where he could see the start of the racecourse below when he saw the fight going on down to his right. He could see the two Turkish youths, a young man standing in a posture of defence but holding his side, which was bleeding profusely, and a young boy who was almost naked, with blood running from his mouth and nose, struggling to rise from the grass. The boy was being ignored, whilst the two toughs were circling round the bleeding young man each holding knives in their hands. The young man was shouting something at the top of his voice, but he could not distinguish the words.

Vahan, too, was unused to violence, but his own experience in provincial Caesaria had taught him to differentiate between poor peasants dressed roughly because they couldn't afford better, and city ruffians. He too did not hesitate, but began racing down the road shouting out at the top of his voice – "Stop, stop, police, stand back, stop …" He had immediately realised that he would be unable to reach the fight before the knives could do further irreparable damage, and hence his instinctive decision to try and advertise his impending arrival.

Everyone looked up at the approaching figure of Vahan hurtling down the road. What gave Vahan the brilliant idea of using the word 'Police' in all his shouting and gesticulating he never knew, but it was enough. The arrival of reinforcements, and the use of the magic word decided the two thugs, first green-shirt, and then red-blouse to take to their heels and run down the road, into the racecourse, and away.

Selim, still bleeding from his right side, but now pressing his left hand over the wound in an attempt to staunch the flow, sat down heavily on the grass. Haik, who in his earlier terror when pressed face down into the earth had again wet himself, now knelt, looking first at the bleeding Selim, and then at the panting Vahan, as he climbed over the fence and finally arrived at the scene.

"What's going on, what's going on?" panted Vahan as he ran up drawing great gulps of breath.

"Heaven knows, *effendi*," said Selim, "All I know is that this young lad was being attacked when I arrived and tried to intervene."

Haik, meanwhile, now for the first time aware and ashamed of his near nakedness, scrabbled about in the grass for his torn pants and shoes, both of which had also been wrenched from him. He began to tremble in reaction to the fear which had devastated him. He imagined he could still feel the hard touch of the wicked knife on his cheek. There were no more sobs, the tears had dried up, but he could not control his trembling.

The two young men, however, understood at once what had either happened or was about to happen, and despite Selim's bleeding side, where the knife had clearly penetrated between the ribs, they both instinctively thought first of the young boy's distress. Vahan went to pick up one of the shoes and brought it back to Haik, who was in the act of pulling on his torn pants. Selim, releasing for a moment his grip on his own wound, fitted the other shoe as tenderly as he could on Haik's other foot. Both Selim and Vahan were by now quite aware that Haik, uncircumcised, was a Christian. It made not a whit of difference to either of them. They were careful not to question him, or at this stage even to offer support by touching him. They had no idea how far the assault had gone.

It was as Haik finally struggled up, with a tentative smile at the two young men, that Selim saw and recognised for the first time lying abandoned under where Haik had lain, the yellow scarf. He gasped as all the memories of the day came flooding back. Vahan, who also saw it, but without any recognition, did not hesitate. Once he saw Haik's pained and shy smile, he bent down and grabbed the scarf, tearing it down the middle. He tied the two parts together. He then picked up Haik's shirt, still lying torn on the ground and stuffing it over Selim's wound he then bound the scarf very tightly round Selim's waist to hold it in place and to stem the flow of blood.

Selim thanked him with his eyes, but his mind was on the scarf.

"Where did you get this, lad" he addressed Haik and indicated the yellow scarf, as Vahan tied it tight.

"It belongs to my sister" said Haik eventually, somewhat hoarsely, speaking for the first time. "These two men were trying to make off with it, when I tried to take it back."

The two young men stared at Haik, wondering at the foolhardiness, and sheer stupidity of this frail boy in risking himself for a mere scarf.

Haik's nose and mouth were still bleeding as he stood there in his torn pants and muddy shoes and bare chest. Selim was swaying with weakness as blood still seeped through the shirt. Vahan too stood still, stunned, knowing that he ought to be doing something, but also himself now suffering from the reaction of all that adrenalin draining away. It was Haik who broke the moment of silence.

"My parents' home is just up the road. My name is Haik Avakian – do you think, sir, we could go there now. I'm sure that my mother will look after this gentleman."

Neither man had the energy nor the wish at this stage to question what appeared to be an extraordinary coincidence. With both Vahan, and now Haik, supporting the ever-weaker Selim, they clambered back over the fence and shuffled slowly up the road. Eventually they reached and knocked on the Avakian front door, the door which Vahan had left only a few short minutes previously.

CHAPTER 21

The last hours of the 24th April

After the departure of Vahan, Olga had finally gone up to rest, while Nerissa moped about downstairs. Following all the emotion of Olga's confession to Armineh, and the devastating news of her father's arrest, Nerissa suddenly felt the need to think of calmer things. Her thoughts turned to her younger siblings. So far as the rest of the family were concerned, she had been the one who had always been made responsible for seeing to both Haik and little Seta. Seta, she knew, was being collected from school for her weekly piano lessons with the elderly Madame Chatelle. This would last for the rest of the afternoon, as she always took her tea there as well. However, she was just beginning to wonder what had happened to Haik, when the doorbell rang. This must be him, she thought, as strangers usually missed the dratted doorbell, hidden as it was behind the overgrown ivy.

Nerissa ran to the door, opened it, and met there a scene she would never forget – a sight which was instrumental in thrusting her into adulthood. Standing there, clearly short of breath and not gabbling away immediately as usual, she saw her young brother with his nose freely bleeding, dressed only in torn pants and shoes, his chest bare and dirty and with his mouth covered in dried blood. Partly leaning against him was an incredibly pale Selim, clutching his side, with Olga's distinctive yellow scarf tied round his waist, and with blood seeping between his fingers. Taking almost the whole of Selim's weight on the other side, was the same young man – Vahan – who had left the house only about 15 minutes previously.

For once Nerissa did not just stand there with an open mouth. She immediately beckoned them in, and yelled out – something she never normally did – for Marie and Olga. She then took Haik's free hand and gently drew him in. At the tender touch of his beloved sister, Haik at last, and for the first time, burst into entirely childish sobs – no longer the sobbing of anger and fear, but the despairing cries of a child, needing feminine comfort.

Nerissa could see at once that Selim's physical condition was much worse than that of Haik, but she felt instinctively that Haik's hurt, whatever it was, was ultimately more serious. She held him tight, as the other two entered behind him. Marie, who had bustled in from the kitchen on hearing Nerissa's shout, took one look at Selim and ran back to collect what was needed. Olga, bleary-eyed, arrived at the top of the stairs, took one look at the melodramatic scene in the hall, and almost fainted there and then, unable to make any sense of what she was seeing. However, when it came to the crunch, Olga had more than enough of Armineh's practical good sense and indomitable will to rise to the occasion. Quickly fully alert, she ran down the stairs, and like the other women asked no questions, but took the weight of Selim from Vahan, and led him to the chaise-longue in the sitting-room and got him to lie down. Selim himself by now was dizzy and almost on the point of fainting from loss of blood, incapable of saying or feeling anything other than the pain in his side.

Marie came bustling in with a bowl of steaming hot water, some sort of bottle of bright purple antiseptic, and a roll of linen dressing. Nerissa held on tightly to the now quietly crying Haik who had buried his face in her breasts, while Vahan stood panting and getting his breath back.

"Miss Olga," Marie explained, when she saw that Olga was not going to relinquish her position by the side of the wounded young man, "You must wash the wound carefully all round – then you must make sure that this antiseptic goes all over the area, and that some of it goes well into the wound. It will sting and he will shout, but you've got to make sure it goes right in. Don't worry, my dear, he's in no real danger – he'll do fine – the only danger is that the wound gets infected, and that must be prevented above all."

Olga nodded, and delicately undoing and removing the scarf and Haik's shirt now entirely soaked in blood, she began, efficiently, and with a surprising calmness, working as Marie had directed. Without any hint of embarrassment or uncertainty, she lifted Selim's shirt and pushed down the top of his trousers to reveal the full extent of the wound – her mind totally on the purely nursing task required.

Meanwhile Haik had finally cried his fill. Some brightness had come back into his previously dulled eyes, and Nerissa decided that it was time he was cleaned up, and whispering in his ear, she persuaded him up the stairs to the bathroom. Marie moved to follow, but before she started up, Vahan suddenly bestirred himself and came over signalling her to wait a moment. Marie duly waited looking steadily at the anxious brown eyes of this stranger. Vahan was deeply embarrassed, but he felt it to be absolutely vital that the situation concerning Haik should be made clear. He believed that some attempt must immediately be made, before any major emotional damage had time to sink in, to find out exactly how far events had gone before Selim had turned up.

He outlined the facts as he knew them and which had been quietly confirmed by Selim, making certain that Marie understood that one of the toughs appeared to have been on top of the half-naked Haik when Selim had arrived. Marie nodded – she was well versed in the ways of the world – particularly the Turkish world.

"Madam," said Vahan who was not quite sure of the position Marie had in the household, "I do believe that you should try to find out the basic facts now, so that you can inform his mother and father when they return, without involving him directly. Er ... Madam ... I hope that you will be careful, and er ... also not involve Miss Nerissa at this stage ... I mean ...," and Vahan finally dried up at seeing Marie's penetrating stare.

"My dear sir," Marie haughtily replied, "I have nursed these children for 20 years, do you think I don't know my job. Really!" and she marched upstairs. Vahan reddened even more than before, and withdrew, wondering if he had gone too far.

Marie arrived in Haik's bedroom with yet another bowl of hot water. He was sitting up on his bed, shoulders still drooping, but his eyes more alive. Nerissa, no doubt cleverer than almost everyone else in the family, was not, after all, as practical. She was simply sitting on the bed, holding him tight, without doing anything about the still bleeding nose or the cut lips.

"Now then, Miss Nerissa, run along and help your sister downstairs. We need to get this young man tidied up, and, my dear, you're a little in the way here."

Nerissa nodded, gave Haik a tender kiss and went out. Haik

at the touch of the kiss, was almost about to start crying again, but was stopped by his old Nurse's stern look.

"Now Haik," Marie carefully wiped away the blood from his nose and mouth, "this is not too bad a cut – go and change into these pyjamas, hold your head right back putting this cotton wool to your nose, and then have a good wash all over and come back here."

Marie knew that Haik had to be left alone to change – the latent shame in his semi-nakedness being fairly clear to her experienced eyes.

Haik returned in about five minutes in his pyjamas, cleaned up at least to the somewhat half-hearted point natural to a 12 year-old boy. The nose bleed had at last stopped, and the cut lips, now washed clean, did not look at all bad. Above all the eyes had brightened even further, and there was a new alertness in the way he was holding himself.

"Haik, you better get into bed and have a rest."

"But I'm not at all sleepy Marie, and I want to know what the others are doing."

"I know, dear, but it's all been a bit of a shock and you need the rest. Don't bother to try to sleep, you can read until Mummy comes back. Would you like to tell me now what happened?"

Haik told Marie about the walk back from school, the two youths lounging on the grass, Olga's yellow scarf, their sudden attack as he tried to take the scarf, the knife, their inspection as to whether he was circumcised or not, his torn shirt and the assault, all without any embarrassment – after all Marie had bathed and dressed him as long as he could remember, until the last few years.

Marie listened, then chose her words carefully.

"Did you feel any bad pain down below when you were thrown to the floor."

"Well, yes, I did feel a sudden pain starting, Marie, but it was then that I kicked out and yelled at the top of my voice. The pain stopped, and never came back again, as it was just about then that the first gentleman came running up after he heard me shout."

Marie registered these facts carefully, ready to be able to pass them on to Armineh when she returned, and otherwise sighed in relief at Haik's words, spoken totally innocently and without any guilty or self-conscious reserve. She knew that it was now a matter that Karekin was going to have to deal with on his return that night. Indeed Marie had always felt that Karekin had been neglectful of his son's education in this field, even though she knew it was nothing to do with her.

"Call me, my love, if you need anything."

When she got downstairs, she found Selim still lying stretched out on the chaise-longue, with Olga still kneeling alongside putting the final touches to the new clean dressing round his waist and tightly bound over the wound. Nerissa had obviously been helping to tighten the dressing, and was standing behind Olga waiting with scissors to cut the end of the linen. The bleeding had stopped. Vahan was still standing and dumbly looking on, none of them saying anything. Marie went over to him.

"It's all right, sir, the other gentleman seems to have caught the situation just in time, thank God. No permanent damage seems to have been done, and I don't think it will haunt his memories. Either way, it is a matter for his parents now when they get back this evening."

Vahan nodded and smiled at her, probably the first smile that had crossed his face that whole day. With that, Marie left the room, saying that she would be back shortly with some coffee and biscuits.

Selim was already recovering, and some colour had returned to his face under Olga's careful ministrations. Having worked almost like a professional nurse ever since Marie had gone upstairs, she suddenly became aware of Selim's body – bared to the chest, and with his trousers right down to the hips. She also became conscious that her fingers had worked over this male body. Their eyes met, both of them aware of the swiftly changed mood that had all at once arisen between them all over again.

Olga stood back indicating to Nerissa to finish the work by

pulling up Selim's trousers and pushing his shirt back. She felt faint again all of a sudden, and turned away, different, though welcome, emotions flooding over her. It was clear that Selim was not going to be able to move for some time, and so the four young people settled themselves in the sofas and chairs round the chaise-longue, as Marie came in with a tray of coffee and some welcome food.

Somehow the drama, which in one way or another they had all just been through, had removed most of the normal social constraints between them. The girls, aged 16 and nearly 18, and the young men – 19 and 20 – at last drew a sort of collective breath and settled down to a semblance of normality. Vahan and Selim, already experiencing a bond, having shared and overcome danger together, at last introduced themselves and their background to each other. The whole coincidence of events unraveled, even including a guess at the hitherto unexplained failure of Sima to turn up at Haik's school.

It was clear that Selim could not leave for at least another hour or two while he recovered his strength. None of them were in a mood for inconsequential chit-chat. It was Selim, who, now hearing for the first time of the arrest of Olga's father that morning, raised the issue behind all the current problems of the multi-racial Ottoman Empire. He turned to Vahan and commented -

"Here I am amongst an Armenian family for the first time in my life, although I have always lived next to Greek or Armenian neighbours. What an experience! Tell me Vahan, my friend, do you feel more Armenian, more Christian or more Ottoman."

"I feel all three," replied Vahan. "Your identity isn't exclusively, or even mainly, one thing or another. Your identity comprises all your many different affiliations, your varied interests, your cultural activities, even the type of food you eat – indeed you're a mixture of many elements, all of which make up your own unique identity."

"That's fine as far as it goes, but – what about 'deep down inside you', isn't there some deeper inner allegiance that is more 'you' than anything else in your make up."

"No Selim, I don't really think so. This is the mistake that the new Ittihad party is making here and now. They're trying to suggest that no aspect of identity is more important than that of being a member of a particular nationality, one that they are currently trying to create in the place of the multi-national one we have at the moment. It is a narrow, exclusive and prejudiced attitude of mind that reduces all the rich varied aspects of a person's identity to one simple and overriding affiliation – your race – often expressed violently and in anger. In the end it is a recipe for massacres and oppression, which I fervently hope the coming 20th-century is going to reject."

"Come, my friend, I do agree that of course my identity is unique and is what prevents me from being the same as anybody else. However, surely, I have one or two overriding allegiances or convictions that are so much more important than most of the others that they might legitimately be called my principle identifying factors. After all, my heavy stubble I have so much difficulty shaving is clearly part of my identity, and actually quite important to me at the moment, but it can't compare with my identity as a Muslim or my allegiance as a Turk. I do believe that these two allegiances – Muslim and Turk are more significant than my identity as a middle class Ottoman, which is, of course, one that I would share with you for instance ... Basically, what I am saying is that you can rank all these allegiances in a sort of order of importance."

"Well, perhaps, but think a bit. Things change – one day your being a Muslim is the most important of your identities, but the next day it might be your education in a liberal American college that becomes the most important factor. Above all Selim, my friend, your identity is likely to change as you grow, and as society itself changes. Yesterday, if asked, you might have answered proudly – 'My identity? Why, I am an Ottoman citizen.' Today, or at least very soon, you might say with as much certainty, 'My identity? I'm a modern Turk'. Tomorrow, if the nation-state wobbles, you might just as surely say 'I'm a Muslim'. It's all relative to the times, and there is no deeper 'you' at all."

"Very well, Vahan, but taking your point to its extremes,

aren't you in danger of losing any sense of identity at all. We all need to belong somewhere."

"Look, it's part of my own identity that this conversation is taking place in Turkish, a language not naturally my mother tongue. It's a language which I, and my family, probably speak better than millions of Anatolian peasants, but if I had only a narrow version of my own identity – only as an Armenian say – I might resent it. However, I don't. The language I speak reflects only a part of my identity. In the last resort, for me, being Armenian or a nominal Christian does not override everything else."

Vahan continued, attempting to lighten the discussion -

"Selim, my friend, believe me, you and I understand each other better and have a closer identity than you and Nasreddin Hodja could ever have, if you could possibly meet him. That, in its way, is another facet of your identity, which your identity as a Turk does not override."

Selim laughed out loud at the thought of actually meeting the legendary old Turkish figure of fun, the Hodja on his peasant donkey. This, however, suddenly gave him some more twinges of pain reminding him of the wound in his side. He was no longer thinking so clearly, though he was certain that he was right.

"Vahan, in the end why do you think that the one-people nation-states in the west have become so much more successful than our own ramshackle Empire, It is because they are one people, speaking one language exclusively, and not an amalgam of many. That's what we now need here."

"Don't be fooled! Don't be fooled! The danger of the coming nation-state espoused by the CUP and the Ittihad party to which you are looking forward so much, is that they will be insisting on a one and only overriding aspect of identity – nationalist and tribal. That is not the secret of the success of the Western states. On the contrary, it has been one of their failures over many centuries. The Spanish monarchy couldn't abide the different identity of the old Moorish and Jewish elements in their midst, and thus impoverished their own society immeasurably, by oppressing and eventually deporting them. Louis XIV couldn't tolerate the different identity of the Huguenots, so he threw them out to the great detriment of France in the long run. Even the tolerant British for centuries required a conformity in religion as proof of loyalty to the overriding requirement of the national identity."

Nerissa had been listening to all this in rapt attention, after she had come down. Olga had not said a word, being content to sit on the sofa next to Selim holding his hand tight, and feeling his body close to her own. At this point, brought up in a household where the girls did not just stay silent and listen to males sounding off, Nerissa interrupted.

"Good heavens! – you're both beginning to lecture each other. In all this question of identity neither of you have referred to your identity as a male, which after all gives you an affiliation – I think that's the word you used – with half the human race. I have a female identity, which Selim, is surely just as important as my being an Armenian. In the hammams the most important identity factor between us all gossiping and using the baths, is being female."

"Well, I don't know," Olga responded, "I only know that my own identity has changed over the last eight weeks."

"Oh Olga," said Nerissa impatiently, "can't you ever think of anything but your own feelings. We are discussing something serious here."

Selim looked down at Olga at his side, and winced as he moved slightly closer to her on the sofa, while Vahan looked on vacantly.

"Hang on Nerissa – let's hear what Miss Olga has to say."

"Come, come, Vahan, surely 'Olga' by now."

"I'm sorry, 'Olga' of course," replied Vahan with a smile.

"Well, what I suppose I meant was that had you asked me a mere eight weeks ago where my main allegiances lay, I would have said – I am an Armenian, and a Christian, and above all a member of a closed family unit, and that my principle 'deep down inside' identity was as an Avakian daughter. Now, eight weeks later, I am not so sure anymore – my sense of my own identity has suddenly become bound up with the identity of someone else."

Selim squeezed her hand hard, but couldn't squeeze his body any closer due to the fact that his wounded side, already pressed too close, was giving him a fair amount of pain.

By now all four of them were thoroughly engrossed and excited by the discussion. Vahan was enjoying immensely a fascinating argument with a man for whom he was beginning to feel a great affection. Nerissa, because she had never felt so accepted before in what she thought of as a grown-up exchange of views. Selim, by the continuing throb of the wound in his side, but more by the whole atmosphere of friendship and affection which boded so well, or so he thought, for his love. Olga, by the simple proximity of the young man by her side whom she imagined that she might have lost for ever only a few hours previously.

Time was getting on, and it was clear that Armineh would not be returning for some time. Nerissa suddenly spoke in some distress -

"Oh, Olga, I forgot mother, and probably Sima too, if they met at the station. What can be happening?"

The mention of the arrest, and the departure of Armineh to find her husband, brought all four of them back to the present. Nerissa, recalled that Haik had surely now been left upstairs on his own long enough. Olga began worrying about what was to happen to Selim. But it was Vahan who then rose and asked Olga how he could arrange for a carriage to the station, as clearly Selim ought not to walk back. A servant was duly dispatched to go down and come back with one of the gharries.

The doorbell rang again. Nerissa, knowing it must be a member of the family in view of the overgrown ivy, ran to the door.

"Hello everyone – it's me, it's me," called out a breathless Seta as she ran in, not even acknowledging Nerissa, who slipped outside and waved a thank-you at Madame Chatelle's maid hurrying away down the hill. Seta stopped at the sight of the two young men, but showed no shyness.

"Hello, I'm Seta – who are you?" holding out her hand and not listening to anyone's reply.

"Where's Haik? Did you all hear that great foghorn of the big ship in the harbour this morning? We saw it from the windows, out in the sea. Where's Mummy? Madame Chantelle was all excited today – it must be her birthday or something."

This was not by any means all that she said, but by now the party was breaking up.

Selim and Vahan eventually departed on the carriage when it arrived, with Selim leaning heavily on Vahan. Arriving in the City, Vahan saw Selim into a carriage prior to trudging home himself to his lodgings in the now much quieter streets. Selim trundled home, unaware of the telegram awaiting him informing him of his father's death that morning. Vahan, too, walked home, equally unaware of the letter winging its way to him from his brother as to his own father's arrest and disappearance from home, that very same day.

It was the last hours of the 24th April. The City brooded, as the great western armada finally began arriving at the fatal entrance of the Dardanelles.

CHAPTER 22

Harry at Gallipoli

General Hamilton, the British Commander in Chief was no mere "donkey commanding lions." He was a kindly intellectual gentleman of impeccable breeding and manners, a poet manqué, with a lyrical turn of phrase, very popular wth all the troops, but unfortunately overly concerned with hurting anybody's feelings. Whilst capable of commanding a division or even perhaps an army corps, he was simply not ruthless enough to take command of a whole army. From the very start, although he saw clearly the administrative errors and weaknesses of the plan of campaign, he had been unable to stand up to Kitchener and Churchill, two far more forceful characters. Accordingly, he failed to insist on those matters of detail, which bored his two superiors, but which he knew were vitally necessary if the botched up operation, had any hope of succeeding.

There was never any question about General Hamilton's bravery. He was, without doubt, a lively and curious man with an optimistic character of great charm – careful always, as far as he could be, for the welfare of the men under his command. But temperamentally, he was the wrong commander in the wrong place at the wrong time.

> "'Good morning, good morning,' the General said
> when we met him last week on the line.
> Now – the soldiers he smiled at are most of 'em dead,
> And we're cursing his staff for incompetent swine.
> 'He's a cheery old card' grunted Harry to Jack,
> As they slogged up the hill with rifle and pack.....
> But he did for them both, by his plan of attack."

The contrast with Mustafa Kemal, the Turkish General in command of the defences of Gallipoli, was enormous. Inevitably, Turkish accounts of the Gallipoli operations have concentrated on the part he played in the defence. But this is, for once, a justified piece of hagiography. General Liman von Sanders, the German military advisor was certainly present, and did a lot to evaluate and distinguish the feints from the genuine landings in the early stages, but in the end it was the dogged defence of the high ground – the spine that ran down the centre of the peninsula – by the patient Anatolian peasant-soldiers, inspired by the direct and personal leadership of Kemal, that 'did for' Harry and Jack and the entire allied operation.

He turned up everywhere, inspiring his troops with sheer guts and decisiveness, leading them forward, from the front, to the sound of the guns wherever they might be. On one occasion, he came across a body of men fleeing from the enemy and shouted out –

"Why are you running away?"

"Sir, the enemy," they replied.

"Where?"

"Over there, over there," they called out, pointing to one of the hills behind them, up to which a British contingent had finally clambered.

"You can't run away from the enemy, men, sooner or later you'll get shot in the back that way," said Kemal.

"Sir, we have no ammunition left," they replied standing about disconsolately.

"Look, you have your bayonets. Fix your bayonets now, and then turn openly and lie down behind this ridge facing the enemy."

Whether this did the trick, or if there was some other reason, the enemy certainly stopped advancing as the Turkish soldiers dropped to the ground and appeared to be taking aim. Kemal, himself, immediately rode back and ordered up some reinforcements and spare ammunition.

Back on the other side of the lines, the ship on which Harry was stationed lay close in to the shore as the infantry debouched onto the beaches.

"Harry," said the commanding officer of the ship, "I want you to go ahead with the second wave. I believe the preparations for the wounded have been totally inadequate. The chief RAMC officer here told me yesterday of the ridiculously small number of casualties they are expecting. I blew up, as you can imagine – it seems to me that there is no real provision for taking off the wounded. We could help out a bit, with some first aid. I'll send Seamen Jim Conrad, and Jack Jones with you – they're good strong lads. We are not leaving till tomorrow morning, and we could help out by taking off a few of the wounded, if there are any with whom the RAMC can't cope. But look Harry, whatever the situation, I want you back by daybreak as we must leave by 0700 hours."

So, an hour or two after nightfall Harry landed at Geba Tepe in the dark, and in a miserable sleeting rain. With the two seamen, Jim and Jack, they packed into a lighter, already full to bursting with the Australians, who while quieter than usual, seemed in fairly good spirits. As they drew nearer to the shore, bullets and shrapnel were splashing into the water, and some thunking into the boats.

"Hey, mate, how far are we from the shore," asked one of the soldiers.

"I'm not at all sure," Harry replied, "but it was deep enough here for the ship to come quite far in. I doubt if it's much more than about ten minutes." He was trying to sound as off-hand as possible, though he was in a fair state of panic himself inside, much more so than when on board. Somehow the solidity of all that iron on even a small ship seemed so much safer than the feeling of having his body so exposed in the lighter.

"I bloody well hope so – I'm getting fucking sea-sick, much worse than when we were at sea. Oh, bloody hell! – I'm going to throw up."

"Hey, Jacko, if you're going to be sick come here and stick your face over the side, bullets or not," called out another.

"Don't be daft. I can't bloody well move. Oh God I can't keep it down."

"Look, put your head up and look at the stars, and take deep breaths."

Harry watched as Jacko lifted his head – but at the first breath, down came his head again and Harry heard the splash of the sour vomit falling into the scuppers of the boat, as some of the others tried to edge away from the unfortunate man.

"Christ, you fucking old gumsucker – for god's sake belt up and save your breath. You'll be all right lad – just think of how wonderful that hard solid ground is going to feel once we arrive," called out the old Sergeant at the front of the tossing boat.

Harry looked round at all these young men, apart from him and the sergeant, none much more than nineteen; excited, deadly frightened, but still grinning, carefully hiding their real fears from their companions.

Once the boat crunched onto the sand, they jumped out into a scene of indescribable confusion, which had clearly been going on all day. On the narrow strip of sandy and stony beach, at the foot of the hills, which rose ridge after ridge above them, men were moving about in all directions. Troops jumping out of boats, troops marching west, troops marching east; mules and horses – some stationary with their heads drooping, some carrying stores to god knows where; water barrels dumped haphazardly; and, above all, stretcher bearers coming down the cliffs with wounded and dying men.

The next day on the ship, as it ploughed its way back to Egypt, Harry sat down and wrote to his mother –

"Before half an hour was over, after I landed, my work began, and after that I never had a moment. It went on till about three in the morning. One wounded and dying man following on after the other. Poor fellows, with wounds of all kinds, all disfigured and caked with blood and dirt; some of them totally unrecognisable, with their features blown away. But, mother, what's wrong with me – within minutes, in the midst of all this suffering and death, I found that I was ceasing to feel the terror and horror of the situation at all. Sights that ordinarily would have upset me to the point of vomiting, seemed to pass over me without any feeling at all. Have I lost my sensitivity for pain and suffering in others – I just don't know. I closed the eyes of one young lad, he couldn't have been much more than eighteen, who had been moaning for his mother for two hours. I did it almost absentmindedly when he died, whilst I was bandaging up someone else.

Mother, dear, it was bitterly cold all night, but one of the desparately few ambulance men around, made and lit a fire. There was still the sound of sniper shots coming from the hills above us, but even this sound died out as the night wore on. At about four in the morning, the noise started all over again. Mother, can you believe it, but we suddenly found ourselves being shelled by the Goeben, *which had crept up during the night and began lobbing shells at us from the other side of the peninsula, anchored as she was safely in the Straits. I thought of the Report I had written, and the dramatic sight of the* Goeben *on that very first day of the war, whilst I stood on the bridge of the* Indefatigable, *and saw the great ship slowly slipping away from us in the dusk. Now here she was again, hurling shells at us. At times I fancied that she was aiming at me personally*

The confusion remained incredible. I imagine Dad knows all about this aspect of warfare. Eventually saying goodbye to the Ambulance lads, we followed the stretcher bearers still working their way down to the beaches, which were again being raked by rifle fire from the heights above. Jack and I helped to put some final wounded into our pinnace which was waiting, and we set off for the ship. Jim was no longer with us. Shrapnel fire from the Goeben *had done for him, as he had been coming down with the stretcher bearers some minutes before us. Love Harry"*

Looking over the cliffs onto the other side of the artificial line separating these two bodies of men, there was the same fear, the same adrenalin working, but not quite the same mess or confusion. As the line solidified during the night and the next day, Kemal Pasha set up his headquarters right on the front line, and issued the following order of the day -

> "Every soldier who fights here with me must realise that he is honour bound not to retreat one step. Let me remind you all that if you want to have a rest, this may result in our whole nation having no rest for the rest of time. I am sure that all our comrades agree on this, and that you will show no signs of fatigue until the enemy is finally hurled into the sea."

This was the authentic voice of the new Turkey Kemal was later to create. It wasn't as lyrical or as articulate as Hamilton's exhortations, but it had a harder, more direct, edge.

And so it was that yet another Great War stalemate began. After some six months, out of about one million men drawn in to the conflict in the Gallipoli peninsula on both sides, about a half became casualties of one sort or another. Of this half million, about a quarter were dead.

The effect of the whole campaign from a military point of view was negligible – it had no effect, one way or another, on all the other campaigns being fought throughout the Ottoman Empire. But, politically, the operation was undoubtedly instrumental in triggering the first of the many attempted ethnic cleansings which so disfigured the rest of the 20th century.

CHAPTER 23

Garabed's escape

The next day after Raffi had seen his father, and given him the coins, Raffi went out again to see if the arrested men herded into the Town Hall gardens were still there. The place was empty, and after peering through the railings for a time, he turned away. The news of the landings at Gallipoli the previous evening had been filtering through all morning on the telegraph line. The town criers had been calling out what facts were available. Fearful for his father, Raffi walked back through the narrow streets, avoiding any eye contact with other men, all of whom appeared preoccupied and nervous. Raffi hadn't dared make any enquiries at the town hall as to the whereabouts of the arrested men. He returned home to his grieving mother without being able to hold out any hope.

In fact, that very morning, early, before dawn broke, four decrepit old lorries had arrived at the town hall. The whole group, including doctors, lawyers, business-men and some district heads, had been herded into the back, where there was only standing room. There were very few lorries in Caesaria, and certainly no motorcars, except that belonging to the Governor. Somehow, this particular group had been considered important enough to warrant the use of these rare vehicles, which had been provided by the military.

The government had recently released criminals from the prisons, and the whole countryside around Caesaria was to become a killing ground for people about to be deported and made to walk from the town. This was the policy of 'ethnic cleansing', now in the process of being planned in Constantinople by Talaat and the others. But for this group, the leaders of the community, the first of these deportations, there were lorries! The significant difference between this and all later mass deportations, was that sitting in the front of each lorry alongside the driver were two or three armed Turkish soldiers. There were several other soldiers also, standing with the arrested men in the back.

There were some petrol cans slung along the sides, but nevertheless, Garabed knew that the lorries were only going a short distance, after which they would drop their human cargo and turn back.

Everything that was happening was an entirely new experience for these men. There was no precedent, no point of reference, which they could grasp onto, in order to inform them how they should act. Between them, they had a wealth of experience in managing the affairs of their local communities and churches. They were used to acting in committees or on the boards of their business enterprises. But the latent violence and intimidation in their present treatment, had sapped their collective will.

These were strong and successful men – not one of whom would have hesitated if one of their children had been threatened; natural leaders of their community, facing only a few slovenly guards with obsolete rifles; by now fully cognizant of the danger of their situation, yet they took no action at all.

The lorries trundled on over rough roads winding up and through the wild mountains and mainly bare countryside. Little was said by the men squeezed together, standing and swaying as the trucks jolted about. Garabed reflected that he had perhaps made a mistake in not taking all the gold coins. He had been under the impression that he was not going to survive beyond that night, and that in any case, any coins he might have on him would surely have been quickly stolen. However, surprisingly, none of the deportees had even been searched, and many of them had managed to retain some cash.

As they passed through the poor impoverished villages, those with some money purchased bread and other provisions which the villagers offered whenever the lorries stopped. No arrangements for food seemed to have been made by the authorities, and even the guards, with no officer amongst them, were without food and had little idea of what was to happen.

Eventually the group came to a halt in a narrow valley, with bare moss-covered hills, rocky and strewn with boulders, on either side. Running down the middle was a little stream – but even here, so far from anywhere, the countryside was ugly, with rubbish and the bones of dead animals alongside the stream. In the middle of the valley there was a small *khan* – a local wayside inn – a ramshackle building with some rooms for travellers and a large kitchen with trestle tables and rickety chairs. This was a barren desolate spot, and had clearly been chosen to be the first night's stop as it was well away from any inhabited area. Standing in the dusty area in front of this unprepossessing building were eight or nine high-sided carts. The oxen intended to pull the carts were grazing on the sparse grass nearby.

Everyone peeled out of the lorries, and some of the prisoners wandered into the *khan* to purchase food, encouraged by the guards who now produced several bags of unleavened bread, which were stowed in the back of the carts. They distributed the loaves. There was little sign, at this stage, of any racial tension between the prisoners and these local soldiers. This was early days, before the grim machinery of the deportations had been devised and implemented. The prisoners shared their purchases of boiled eggs, onions, olives and cheese with each other, and with the guards who had accompanied them from Caesaria.

It was still light when the starting handles of the lorries were turned with some effort, and they reversed and drove off back to the town. At almost the same moment a further cart, holding a dozen smartly uniformed soldiers, appeared over the hill behind them and drew up in front of the *khan* alongside the other carts. The men all piled out of the cart and formed rank. Garabed saw that they were a detachment of gendarmes and were led by a hard-faced officer – an Enver look-alike with the unmistakable stamp of an Ittihad supporter. The atmosphere darkened immediately.

A few bedraggled tents had been in the back of the carts when they had arrived. Some of the prisoners now set about, somewhat inefficiently, putting them up in the grass around the *khan*. It was not a particularly cold night, although at this altitude anyone without a good coat would have been in real difficulty. Garabed chose to sleep outside, wrapped up in his good sheepskin for which he blessed his wife. Before settling down, he smoked a cigarette with an old acquaintance.

"Garabed, agha, what in heaven's name is really going on. Are we facing some sort of pogrom like 20 years ago?"

"My dear Levon, I've no idea, but I fear the worst. We seem to be a very carefully chosen group – don't you see that? This is not just a round-up of *giavours* to satisfy the gutter instincts of the mob, but a carefully selected list prepared by some bureaucrat. I believe it presages a campaign of some sort or another against the whole community."

"Nonsense, Garabed, the regime isn't clear-minded or efficient enough."

"Levon, it might not be clear-minded, but it's certainly efficient enough. Think about it! In the old days of Abdul the damned, there would have been screaming and shouts and yells – there would have been no lorries or carts laid on – there would have been no food of any kind – there would of course have been bullying and blood-lust and death, but not for god's sake this awful cold Prussian efficiency. I fear that we could be facing imminent executions at any point, somewhere remote on the way, – maybe even here. I may of course be quite wrong."

"But look, Garabed, why would they go to all this trouble, for heaven's sake, when they could simply have had us all shot in the town hall gardens yesterday?"

"Because, Levon, they still have European allies and they daren't risk the adverse publicity. Quite apart from the unrest that would be aroused in the Armenian population if there were open shootings in the town, it is likely that there would be a few influential Turks of the old school who would object and report to Constantinople."

"Well, even if you're right about that – why are they doing it? What's the point of this carefully drawn-up list you're talking about?"

"First, Levon, they get rid of the natural leaders of the community. Most of the young men are gone already, either in the army or in labour battalions. They can then deal with the old men, the women and the children as they want."

"My God, Garabed. Aren't you being over pessimistic?

Nothing like this has ever happened before. Go to sleep, my friend, you'll feel better in the morning."

Once wrapped up and alone, Garabed began considering his position further. On the one hand, although he was not an intimate friend of any of the others, he knew most of them, and they knew him. He felt the warm camaraderie of men sharing the same discomfort and danger. Being part of a group meant the occasional laughter and joke, the occasional breaking into song even in the midst of fear, at least easier to bear in being shared.

On the other hand, Garabed was one of the few prisoners who was aware of the changed political situation within the empire. This awareness was as a result of the beating that he alone, apparently, had suffered two weeks before at the police station. He recognised a sinister under-current, camouflaged by the basically indifferent attitude of the Anatolian peasant soldiers guarding them, but which was not manifest in the new guards who had just arrived, or in their officer. In the last few weeks, officials had become curt and evasive, answering questions with hooded eyes that did not look at you. Garabed knew that this was not just some war-time emergency measure. Death was present, group or no group.

The choice was clear. Did he stay with the group, sharing its fate, one way or another, or did he try to make it on his own? If escape was to take place at all, it had to be done this very night. It was a pure question of survival. Would survival be more likely if he struck out now on his own into unknown territory in a wild countryside, or if he stayed instead with the group being led like sheep to God knows what fate?

He did not know where he was, he had no food apart from that one loaf of bread, which the guards had handed out. Maybe he was abandoning his one chance of survival by leaving this guarded group. He lay awake, turning it all over in his mind. In the end it all came down to the fact that by slipping away, if he could, he would at least be taking his fate back into his own hands.

Gathering up his coat quietly and wrapping it round the loaf, he began crawling slowly along, avoiding the tent pegs and the sleeping bodies. He had noted the exact position of the two guards on night watch. Both were dozing and he knew that he must get away before they got up to awake the next two for the second watch.

"Good-bye Garabed – good luck – may God be with you," whispered one of the sleeping bodies as he slithered past. An elderly voice, Garabed never knew who it was or what became of him. Slowly and stealthily he drew away from the light of the two fires burning away near the two guards.

Once out of sight and across the stream, Garabed rose, stretched and began striding away up the hillside northwards. He reckoned that this would be in the opposite direction to that taken by the group, which would presumably be going to the south towards the Arab provinces – if it was going to go anywhere at all. He planned to be several miles away, well into the hills, long before the camp rose in the morning.

He stumbled on, heading northwards guided by the stars. As the sun rose the next morning, he found himself in the middle of mossy, rocky hills with no sign of cultivation or any life anywhere. Garabed, a leader of the Armenian community in the city, a father of six children, a respected merchant dressed in a dark town suit already crumpled and totally unsuitable for the countryside, found himself in the middle of the Anatolian wilderness, alone, afraid, unable to return to his home, and presumably some sort of outlaw. All this enormous change in his life had happened in just a mere forty-eight hours. For the moment, putting all thoughts of his family and former life out of his mind, he strode on.

Two days later, his eldest son – Vahan – received the news of the arrest and immediate deportation. The news arrived in the form of a letter written to him by his brother Raffi –

My dear brother,

I know that mother wrote to you a week or so ago about the awful experience our father had to go through at the Police station. I was so mad, Vahan, when I saw father slung across the back of that bloody donkey, like a sack of grain, I simply couldn't keep still. Once we had got father inside I left him to our mother's and sister's capable hands, and went running out into the countryside. I didn't care; if I had been accosted by anyone, I would have gladly fought him, I was so charged up.

I am afraid, Vahan, that this is not the end. Yesterday something terrible happened and we are all afraid that it is only the beginning. Father was arrested and taken to the Town Hall. Mother gave me some money to take to him once we got over the initial shock and knew where he was. There were about eighty other Armenians arrested with him. I saw them all milling about in the town hall gardens. Vahan, I was scared stiff – the news of the allied landings only arrived later, but the general feeling in the town was awful. The news of the Van rebellion, and the killings in the East, are all over the town and we all move about with a very low profile.

I went again to the town hall this morning, but they had already been taken away. Oh, Vahan, father made it clear that he didn't expect to survive. I knew that I ought not to let him see me cry, but I couldn't help it. He held my hand tight, and looked hard into my eyes, and then spoke quite sharply, telling me to go home and look after his wife and daughters. He would not even lean forward to kiss me through the railings – I couldn't bear it.

We keep hearing terrible rumours of what is being prepared for the Armenian community here. My dear brother – if it is at all possible, could you send urgently to our mother a copy of your commission in the Harbiye Military academy. I am not certain, but I feel that now most of the leaders of our community have gone, the authorities are planning something awful for the women and children left behind. I believe it may be very helpful to mother if she can show that her eldest son is an officer in the Ottoman army – even if only a student. Please don't worry if what I ask is impossible – I just don't know. Vahan, look after yourself.

Your loving brother.

CHAPTER 24

Karekin's escape

Karekin remained at the window of the station restaurant for several minutes staring at the spot where Armineh had been standing, long after she and Sima had departed. Although few of the group had any real idea what all this was about, Karekin himself didn't rate his chances of survival very high. Slowly, after the last scheduled train of the day left, the station emptied until there were not even any railway employees present. In the concourse, groups of soldiers stood about bored and disconsolate, whilst in the restaurant, general conversation had dried up as people waited for something to happen.

In due course, after it had grown dark outside, the special train ordered by the government finally arrived.

There was the usual whistling and shouting as the prisoners were shepherded out, counted, and ordered into the coaches. No one had any idea what was happening, nor was there any order as to how the prisoners sat themselves in the various coaches. Even the officers in charge seemed unclear about what was going on. The world had not previously witnessed the spectacle of trains filled with scared and bewildered humanity, and no one, neither guards nor victims, were sure how to react.

The coaches themselves, were of perfectly good quality, with standard second class seating throughout. The doors from the corridors into the compartments were all open. An order was given that all doors must remain open at all times. Three or four armed guards were allocated to each coach, sitting at each end and patrolling up and down the corridor at regular intervals. Otherwise, the prisoners were free to sit wherever they wanted, and to talk amongst themselves. Some bread was distributed. Many of the group had purchased cheese, olives and fruit in the station restaurant, all of which was shared in each compartment. There were those among them who were resigned, those who were in a state of denial that there was any real danger, those who were calm, and those who were in a state of complete fear and panic.

Karekin noted that only a couple of officers boarded the train. Both were in the front coach. The rest of the officers and remaining soldiers lined up on the platform waiting for the train to leave. Eventually, to the accompaniment of whistles and yells, the train let off steam and began pulling away. The officers left on the platform saluted.

"My, my," muttered Aram to Karekin with a wry smile "what an honour".

"Morituri te salutant," murmured Karekin, getting his quote totally the wrong way round.

Karekin and Aram had managed to get a compartment to themselves and were able to lie down, sleeping on an off during the night. The train steamed along – stopping every so often for no apparent reason in the middle of nowhere, then setting off again. Within an hour or two of leaving the lights of Haydar Pasha station behind, most of the passengers were sound asleep, exhausted from the physical and mental strain they had been under for over 12 hours.

During the course of the next day the train trundled on, passing through Eskishehir and turning south to take the line which would eventually lead to Eregli, and the as yet unfinished tunnels through the Taurus mountains. It appeared that their eventual destination was to be the Vilayet of Aleppo in the Arab province of Syria. As a group they had, however, become too shattered to care.

"Karekin, what is this all about?" asked Aram Manuelian.

"My dear Aram, I've no idea, but I suppose it's all tied up somehow with the allied invasion in the Dardanelles. Unfortunately, I can see some logic in why this particular group of people have been picked out. You can see that they haven't just arrested the 'politicals' – the deputies or the journalists or the activist lawyers. It isn't therefore just a round-up of what the government might regard as the troublemakers. It includes all the leading elements of the community, religious, artistic and social as well as political."

"Well, Karekin, that means – doesn't it – that it is not simply a 'security' issue in the face of an enemy invasion, but an attack on the whole Armenian community."

"I'm afraid that is exactly what I do think. What we have to face up to right now, in this incredibly slow train, is whether they intend to shoot us all somewhere, or whether they genuinely intend to send us to Aleppo."

"My dear Karekin, what the blazes would they do with us all once we got to Aleppo anyway? Are they going to put us in some sort of camp – I doubt it? That would mean having to feed us and provide some sort of shelter. No, no this train has to be emptied soon after Eregli, whatever their present intentions, because the tunnels through the Taurus are not completed yet. So once there, we will have to walk or ride. At that moment, my friend, there will be a story of a breakout, or of marauding Kurdish brigands, any old story, and the entire group will disappear – murdered – and the authorities will wring their hands and talk about the impossible conditions in the interior."

"Well if that's the case, Aram, why don't we just try to get out of the window next time the train stops."

"Sheer inertia, and the fear of the unknown, Karekin. At the moment we still remain in touch, however tenuously, with civilisation and the way of life we've always known. This is a train, it's fairly comfortable, the soldiers belong to our government, and we can't believe in our hearts that it has changed so drastically. Above all, we have the companionship of over a hundred others around us. Out there, we would be in the middle of practically a desert, on our own, and with no experience at all of how to survive. So, we sit where we are, heading for god knows what, but afraid to do something about it."

"Yes, I understand. But we're free agents, we can surely think it out, one way or another," Karekin mused.

Night came again – more dry bread was distributed, and the passengers settled down for a second night as the train trundled on through the desolate Anatolian countryside. Eventually, early in the morning as the sun was rising, the train arrived with much stopping and starting, shunting and hooting into a goods yard alongside the main station of Konya. Konya, a larger town than

Caesaria, was the capital of the Vilayet of the same name.

Karekin woke with a start – it was about six o'clock in the morning. Checking that there was no guard in the corridor outside the compartment, he opened the window and leaned out, taking a deep breath of the cold fresh air with great satisfaction.

"For God's sake, shut the window, it's freezing cold out there,"

snapped Aram, turning to find a better place to put his sleepy head, and stretching his legs out.

Karekin grunted and continued to look out. Directly in front of him. on the other side of the railway line, was a platform, clearly not intended for the travelling public, but for some sort of freight handling. Over to his left was a marshalling yard with several lines of trucks, either waiting for despatch, or just standing waiting to be unloaded. In the middle of the platform were some railway employees, dressed in brown overalls, ready for track maintenance work.

Seeing Karekin leaning out of the window, one of them – a young man scarcely more than a teenager, jumped down from the platform and sauntered over.

"Hello, *effendi*, this is unusual, to have a passenger train stopping in this goods yard."

Karekin, recognising at once by his accent that he was probably Armenian, switched to Armenian and gave a short account of what seemed to be happening.

"*Effendi*, there are no guards here on this side of the train – you must get away. We have been hearing all day of arrests and deportation orders all over Eastern Anatolia. Your lives will be in danger if you continue to stay on this train."

Just then, there was a whistle and a small engine came into sight pulling several flat trucks, loaded with tools and sleepers and rail lines, together with some high-sided closed trucks.

"That's our work train," the young man pointed. "Good luck, *effendi*, my name is Aram," saying which he saluted and ran across the line in front of the advancing train to join the others on the platform. The train now pulled up, with the closed high-sided trucks standing between the deportation train and the platform.

Karekin did not hesitate. Whatever it was that triggered his decision he would never know. Perhaps the bright morning and fresh air, in contrast to the stuffy atmosphere of the train; perhaps the fact that the railway workers name happened to be Aram. He never worked it out, he simply acted.

"Wake up Aram, wake up" he whispered, shaking the dozing doctor violently but quietly.

"What is it, what is it?"

"Quick, Aram, now's our chance – probably our last one. We've got to get away. Both of us are agile and fairly thin, we can easily get over the window and jump or fall out. There is a train right alongside, we can only be seen by anyone looking out of the windows on this side, unlikely whilst the train is next door. Come on, come on."

Karekin began pulling himself up onto the lowered window, squeezing through and ready to drop out on the other side.

"I don't know, Karekin, I don't know," wailed Aram in a state of frightened indecision, although now fully awake.

"For God's sake, Aram, the worst that could happen at this stage is that we'll get a very painful beating if we're caught. Look, I am going – are you coming."

"Yes, Karekin, yes – go – go!" and Aram jumped up, and with a quick look at the still empty corridor, clambered onto the window as Karekin dropped down to the ground between the two stationary steaming trains.

They both stood there, crouching and panting, not so much with exertion, but from the rush of adrenalin. Then running between the trains, bent almost double to avoid being seen from any windows, they sprinted along until they passed the last coach. Then they both stood up and trying to act nonchalant, they began walking slowly across the rail tracks to the left, towards the marshalling yard. They felt that by walking slowly they might be taken for native inhabitants. This was ridiculous if they'd thought about it; no one in his right mind would have assumed that two middle-aged gentlemen, fully dressed in smart city business suits, even if now soiled and crumpled, belonged there. Fortunately for them, they were not spotted before they reached the first of the waiting goods trains. They ran up and down between the trucks trying out the great metal doors. Most of these were locked, or already wide open, showing empty holds.

Eventually they found one that was closed, but not yet locked. With some effort they managed to pull the door open enough, allowing them to squeeze inside. They found they were sharing the freight car with a cargo of hazelnuts. The space was filled almost to the top, and already the action of pulling open the door had dislodged the cargo and many nuts had trickled down into the grooves of the sliding door. They hauled themselves up and in, and then spent the next five minutes straining and pulling to close the door, dislodging the nuts, which split and cracked as the door slid over them. They never managed to close the door completely, as each effort caused yet more nuts to slither down and into the grooves. Then they burrowed into the pile of nuts at the far end of the truck – dislodging yet more.

Back on the deportation train, the open window and the empty compartment had been discovered. When a count of numbers was made, the discrepancy was found and a detail of soldiers was deputed to make a search of the station precincts. Like many railway premises in Anatolia, the station area was surrounded by a high wall and barbed wire fencing. There were several gates and entrances, but these were usually manned during the day.

Aram and Karekin heard the soldiers calling out to each other when they finally arrived at the several freight trains waiting in the marshalling yard. With pounding hearts, and unable to say anything, Karekin heard them moving down between the freight cars, trying each door, looking inside those that were unlocked and that could be opened. Eventually one of the soldiers arrived at the hazelnut car. Grunting with effort he tried to open up the door, which not being completely shut was clearly not locked. Trying to slide the door open over all the dislodged nuts, he found it was completely wedged. Karekin, out of pure nervousness, began chewing a previously cracked nut. The guard continued to strain at the door. He then stopped and called out to his mates –

"This one is either locked or rusted, so there can't be anyone in there," and he moved on to the next car.

The search went on all over the station for about another hour, and Aram and Karekin could hear the officers yelling and cursing at their men. At about 8.00 in the morning, as the sun rose higher, they heard the shriek of the train's whistle. Then they heard the welcome sound of the pounding of the rails as the deportation train pulled out of the station, with its load of passengers either on their way to safety in Aleppo, or to their doom somewhere before.

The two friends now had to decide what to do. Their quick look at the area had already revealed that the station yard was surrounded by walls and fences, and that they would not be able to walk out during daylight. Yet whatever happened, they would have to open the truck door sooner or later. They scrambled out of the pile of nuts slowly, trying hard not to dislodge too many more. Then, using only their pens and their fingers, they started to prize away the nuts stuck in the grooves. By midday, they were able to move the door sufficiently to allow them to squeeze out whenever they needed to. But they had nowhere to go, with the goods yard buzzing with employees going about their business. As it was, they had to take the risk and slip out into the space between the trains, when the call of nature made it necessary.

With no food, they munched away at the hazelnuts and waited.

Suddenly in the late afternoon, after boredom had driven them both to distraction, they felt the jolt of an engine being connected to the head of their train. Karekin got ready to jump out, almost in relief, but Aram put his hand on his arm –

"Karekin, my soul, don't move. This is one certain way out of the yard. It's only a goods train, it will travel very slowly. We'll jump out once we're free of the station."

Karekin nodded, and they waited tensely.

Karekin kept cracking the nuts and nervously chewing.

Within minutes the coaches shuddered, jolted back and forth, and then began slowly trundling out of the station – through the great gates, and into the outskirts of the town. The hazelnuts were thrown about haphazardly all over the car. The two friends stood and slithered about as the train jerked and stopped and started again.

Eventually with continual shrieks and whistles, the train began running alongside a beaten dusty path, with houses and sheds on the other side, moving very slowly as there were no fences or any other safety devices preventing pedestrians moving across the rails. Karekin stood by the door with Aram behind him, waiting for a moment when nobody would be around – although such a moment was likely to be very short-lived. Suddenly it came –

"Now, Aram, now," he cried and jumped out – followed immediately by his friend. They sprinted across the path the moment they landed, and melted away into a narrow street between some houses, not knowing where they were or what they were going to do. They stood panting a moment, leaning against a wall. They had escaped but now found themselves in the middle of a hostile world, where they would appear to be outlaws of some kind. The train moved on and out of sight round a corner. They grinned nervously at each other, catching their breath.

CHAPTER 25

Mikael and his father

It was a fine warm day on the 25th April, when Mikael Sarafian stood on the Galata Bridge leaning on the iron railings and staring down at the ferries, hooting and tooting and pushing their way up to and away from the quayside. It was already almost six months since the empire had entered so pointlessly into the great European war in the winter of 1914. The war had already changed Mikael's life as drastically as it had changed that of so many others.

Mikael was a tall, thin young man, aged about 24. Sporting the standard black moustache of Ottoman young men of the period, he had flashing black eyes and straight dark hair and a superiority of expression that marked him more as a Turk, than an Armenian.

Gazing over the railings, he was reflecting on how he had joined up in the Ottoman army in November, 1914. The revolution of 1908, which he, like most of the minorities, had originally welcomed, was supposed to have established the principle of equality before the law. This decreed, among other matters, that Christians of the Empire, should be entitled to serve in the military, as well as Muslims. Reciprocally, the Muslims were supposed to pay the special tax, previously levied on the Christian millet, in lieu of military service.

Mikael, from a poor family and unable to get any deferment, had been one of the first of the Armenian youths to become a private in a Stambouli army unit training outside the city. As he stood on the bridge, he recalled the conversation with his father, Avedis, on the day he registered at the government office in the suburb of Makrikoy, where the family lived.

"My son," his father had said, "you know my views. I stand totally against all these changes that are being forced on the dynasty. It is simply not the way that the Empire has thrived over the centuries. We were always prepared to pay the exemption tax instead of the right to bear arms – why change now?"

"But father, only by enforcing absolute equality before the law will the Empire stand any chance of survival. After all, you wouldn't suggest returning to the 'devshirme' system of taking the first-born sons from Christian families and forcing them to become janisseries, just because it worked so well years and years ago. "

"Come, come – don't be sarcastic with me, son, I'm not arguing against any change. I'm simply pointing out that not everything taken from Western European practices is inevitably correct in all circumstances. Above all, I don't believe that the Army will treat Armenian and Greek recruits in the same way as it treats Arabs and Turks. Decrees, my boy, don't change people's basic attitudes that easily."

"Father, you're just plain wrong. The right and duty of all citizens to bear arms is a fundamental principle for any nation. That's what being a citizen is all about ultimately."

"Yes, yes, my boy, that is indeed what we are all being taught by the West. My country, right or wrong they exclaim from the rooftops! All that matters to them, son, is their nation's capacity to impose its will on other nations, by force if necessary. Oh dear, don't mind me, my son, go and fight for the Padishah if you want to."

"Father, it's not just a matter of 'want to' – I have to, in these days of conscription."

Mikael watched as two ferries almost collided as their respective Captains tried to nose each other out for the next space on the quayside. He reflected that four months in a Turkish regiment had shown that his father had after all been right. Mikael hadn't experienced any overt racism from the other soldiers, most of whom were from Stamboul, in any case, and used to the rich racial mixture of the city. However, the attitude of the officers, carefully secular though they were now trying to be, was different. The Armenian and Greek soldiers were inevitably given the more menial and less military tasks, and Mikael had in fact been fortunate to escape being sent to the interior in the labour battalions to repair roads.

After the many months of training, Mikael's unit was ready to be assigned to a front, and there had been much speculation among the soldiers whether this would be against the British in the Sinai, or the Russians in the Caucasus. It was on the 18th April that he had received a message that the duty officer wished to speak to him immediately. He had hurried off to the office of the young lieutenant, currently the duty adjutant. Mikael had saluted and standing at attention waited for the officer to speak.

"Private Sarafian, I must tell you that this morning we received a note from your mother informing us that your father is dangerously ill, and unlikely to survive for more than a few days. Under the circumstances, soldier, I am issuing you with a week's pass to go home. I trust all will be well. May Allah protect you and your family."

With that, Mikael had saluted and turned away. He had packed his very meagre belongings and hurried home. The Sarafians lived in a modest, ramshackle, terraced house in the middle of the small township of Makrikoy. Mikael, in his ill-fitting uniform of a private in the Ottoman army, was entitled to free railway travel, and had no difficulty in getting home, despite the fact that he had hardly a piastre on him. Alighting at the main Makrikoy station in the middle of the little town, He had walked quickly through the quiet dusty streets. At first, Mikael recalled, he had scarcely comprehended the lieutenant's words, and acted like an automaton. But the closer he got to home, the more anxious and upset he had become.

On reaching home, after embracing his mother at the door, Mikael had raced upstairs, his mother having indicated with a nod that his father was in their bedroom. Avedis lay propped up in bed. He was unshaven and looked pale and sickly.

The bedroom, at the back of the small house, was dark and had a faint smell of mothballs, which had never changed for as long as Mikael could remember. There was a large, heavy, dark mahogany wardrobe, which took up the whole of one wall of the room. Mikael recalled that all the linen of the house would emerge from this wardrobe. Always locked, it held all the secrets of the household, the family savings and all their more important possessions.

The small window on the other wall looked out onto the back alley and was always shuttered. On the wall behind the bed hung old sepia photographs, heavily touched up, of the four parents of Mikael's father and mother. Mikael had never known these venerable looking people – his grandparents – except through these old highly posed photographs. Finally, against the fourth wall there was an old French dressing table, probably the only valuable piece in the whole house, which had a cracked and discoloured mirror with two swinging side panels which had always fascinated him as a child.

"Baba, Baba, what's the matter" stuttered Mikael, running

forward to his father's side as his mother stood at the door looking on.

"My son, my son, welcome," whispered Avedis as Mikael embraced his father.

Michael, remembering this scene as he continued to stare over the water at the bridge, recalled with a deep sense of guilt that even in that sad and emotional moment, he had recoiled from the musty 'old man' smell of his father, which seemed to be much worse than usual. Mikael, gulping down the wonderful fresh air of this April morning, tried to recollect that peculiar smell – a mixture of bad breath, mint juleps, old man's body odour, and death. He could not do so.

"Father, what's wrong?" he asked, drawing back from that first embrace.

"My son, it's a mixture of old age, and something going wrong with my breathing."

"But Baba, come, come, you're not even 60 yet. What does the Doctor say?" Mikael, turned to his mother as he spoke.

Vartuhi had looked hard at him, no sign of any tears or any other emotion in her eyes, but said nothing and turned away.

"My boy, the doctor says it's TB. I just don't know. All I know is that I have difficulty breathing and I cough all night. Come, sit down and let's talk. I've missed our discussions together."

All week, after returning from the army, Mikael spent his days sitting next to his father, by the side of the bed, in the dark and enclosed environment of the bedroom. In the afternoons, his young brother and 15 year-old sister would return from school and come to join him. Mikael would leave for an hour or two and talk to his mother. Mikael always thought of his mother as a dry and dissatisfied woman, with thin disapproving lips and an unhappy disposition. Avedis, on the other hand, was an expansive, jolly man, filled with bonhomie and confidence. When guests had come to the house, he was always the life and soul of the party.

After an hour or two of desultory conversation with his mother, Mikael would return to his father's bedroom. His sister and young brother would leave, and Mikael would spend the rest of the evening chatting and playing interminable games of backgammon with his father. To his surprise, Vartuhi would not join them. He had been aware that she had made up a bed for herself in the small attic room many years ago, but had been under the impression that she had returned to the parental bedroom.

Avedis was clearly getting weaker by the day, but was hanging on, and he had remained interested throughout in what was going on in the wider world. In fact it was on this 25th April that he had asked Mikael to go into the city and purchase the latest newspapers – Turkish as well as Armenian.

The British had landed in the Gallipoli peninsula that morning. There were rumours that the Russians were going to invade from the north, and perhaps that the Greek army was also approaching. The Greeks in the city were in a state of excitement. The Turks were anxious and angry. The Jews were worried for the long-term future of the Empire, which had sheltered them for so long. The Armenians were in a state of total confusion, caused largely by the arrests of the day before. Mikael had arrived in the city just as the news of the arrest of over four hundred prominent Armenians the day before had become common knowledge. It appeared clear that they had either been deported to the interior, or had been liquidated in some way.

Mikael, who had now been staring at the busy shipping for over half an hour, at last sighed and turned away. He hurried across the bridge and turned to go down to the Armenian Patriarchate compound. There, he prayed for a few minutes in the church, and then went round to the office to ask if there was a priest available to accompany him home for a final visit and blessing for his father, who was not expected to survive for more than a day or two. He was told that no Priest was immediately available, as too many had been called out to minister to and give comfort to families distraught at the loss of their men. However, the staff on duty told him that if he left his address, and the return fare, a priest would follow as soon as possible, the next morning.

When Mikael got home that evening, he reported all the news to Avedis.

"Father, the really devastating news is the arrest of over four hundred of our people. It is clear that they were arrested simply because they were Armenians. Even our gentle Father Komitas was among those deported. This is pure racial persecution isn't it? We have to stand up for ourselves – honestly it makes me hopping mad."

"I'm sorry, my son, truly sorry," whispered the ever weaker Avedis, but whose eyes remained as bright as ever. "This sounds like state repression of the worst kind. Even that awful idiot Abdul Hamid never acted like this. He simply manipulated the mob, and then withdrew the police for a few days, whilst they rampaged. I fear, my son, I really fear for the future of our community."

At this point, the sheer effort of speaking, gave rise to a fit of coughing from Avedis, and a hug, and a 'hush, hush' from Mikael. There was silence for a time before Mikael spoke.

"Father, I heard that my army unit has already left for Gallipoli – I will have to go soon. My leave runs out in a day or two."

Avedis had given no reply to this, but had sunk back onto the pillows, already exhausted by the few words he had already spoken.

The next day in the morning a priest arrived. On entering, he blessed the house, and extended the blessing to Vartuhi, who knelt and kissed his hand as he came in. The Sarafians were all firm and devout believers. Mikael himself came down, crossed himself at the sight of the priest and also knelt and kissed the priest's ring. He then hurried the priest upstairs to the bedroom. Vartuhi did not follow.

"My name is Father Haroutiune" the priest said to Avedis, who had struggled to sit up a little in his bed. Mikael's sister, who had stayed at home that morning, plumped up the pillows and held her father up as the priest took out his oil, put the sign of the cross on Avedis' forehead, and began reciting prayers in a quiet sing-song voice. Eventually he gave the final blessing to all in the room. Mikael brought forward a chair, and the priest sat down by the bedside and stretched out to hold Avedis' hand.

There was then a long period of silence. Eventually his father had turned his increasingly feverish eyes on the old priest, and making an effort to speak in a whisper.

"Father, my son is a conscript in the army. His unit has been sent to the new Gallipoli front. Armenians are being arrested and deported all over the Empire for no other reason save that they are Armenian."

At this point he began coughing and gasping for air. Everyone in the room urged him to stop talking, but he raised his hand making it clear that what he had to say was important to him.

"You know, Father, I've always been a believer. I've also always supported the Ottoman state. I have never had any patience with the nationalist revolutionaries. But, Father, where the state has deliberately turned against a part of their own people, do those people still have a moral duty to support that state?"

"Render unto Caesar that which is Caesar's and unto God that which is God's," Haroutiune intoned a little sadly. "That is the Christian teaching, my son. The Muslims of course say that it's one and the same. The head of their state, the Sultan, is for them the same person as the head of their religion, the Caliph."

The three Sarafians stared at him uncomprehendingly. Haroutiune sighed, belatedly realising that here was a family not in the slightest bit interested in the theological difference between the Christian and Muslim attitude towards duty to the state. He paused and thought for a moment before starting to speak again. Everyone in the room at that moment, waited breathlessly to hear what the Father would say next. He cleared his throat nervously.

"Avedis *effendi*, a month ago my answer to your question would have been that loyalty to the state that has nurtured you as best it could was all-important. However, the reports that I have been getting from the interior, the deportations that have begun all over the empire and which we have seen even here, the terror that is being turned against our people by the state itself, has, I now feel, unquestionably changed the moral position. Your son must, of course, act according to his own conscience. However, I do now believe that the moral authority of a state, which is openly picking out our young men to be sent to the most dangerous sectors of the fronts, or to labour battalions in the interior like convicts, has been compromised. I fear that the deportation of whole families, whole villages, to God knows where, Avedis *effendi*, is the beginning of a great evil the like of which has never been seen before."

There was a long pause – a moment of silence that hung heavily in the air between them all. Then Father Haroutiune stood up, raised his hand high above the bed to make the sign of the cross, and spoke in a loud and firm voice.

"Whatever may befall … May the blessing of God almighty, the love of his son Jesus Christ, and the spirit of the Holy Ghost be with you all in this room, now and for evermore and to the end of time."

Mikael, whose head had been bowed, looked up and saw the little priest immediately bend down and kiss his father on the forehead. The priest then turned and walked out of the bedroom accompanied by his sister, Nairi.

Mikael remained in the room all day, rejoined by Nairi, once the priest had left. His father clearly began sinking, as the afternoon went on, and his breath became more and more laboured. In the evening, Avedis, in a hoarse whisper, spoke his last words to them both, sitting by the bed on either side, whilst Vartuhi stood silently in the doorway,

"Mikael, my soul, I have thought hard about what I am going to say. I've thought of all the possible consequences. My advice to you is not to rejoin your unit. Don't go back, Mikael, my son, don't go back. My son … my son …"

He then looked up at Vartuhi, standing in the doorway. They stared at each other for a moment of eternity. Avedis then closed his eyes and was dead within minutes.

On the death of his father that April, Mikael had inevitably been involved in all the details of arranging for the funeral. He was already two or three days overdue from the expiry date of the pass issued by his superior officer. Mikael did not worry too much about this. It was clear to him that he had to fulfil his duty to his family, and see to his father being honourably buried, before any duty he might have to the state. He knew that he would be in trouble when he finally did return. A good Muslim would appreciate the requirement of seeing to a proper burial as a sound reason for being a few days late in getting back to his unit.

Father Haroutiune had agreed to conduct the service, and Avedis was to be buried in the cemetery at Sisli. Mikael, Nairi and Vartuhi set off early in the morning; Mikael's younger brother – Mardiros – was left with a neighbour at Vartuhi's insistence. Mikael, in an emotional state himself, simply could not understand his mother's attitude to the death of her husband. She shed no tears and seemed perpetually distracted.

At the little church in the cemetery, the service was duly conducted by Father Haroutiune. There were only about thirty people present – friends of Avedis, some cousins and other relatives whom Mikael scarcely knew. The ancient rituals of the Armenian Orthodox burial service droned on, beautified by the music of Father Komitas. Mikael felt the usual prickle of tears and a welling of emotion as the liquid notes of the "Sourp, Sourp" rose from the voices of the small choir. It was at that moment that there was a slight disturbance, as three more people entered at the back of the little chapel. Mikael, intent on his memories of his father did not look back. However, he saw his mother Vartuhi, standing alongside him, glance back. For the first time since he had returned from the army as his father lay dying, he saw that she was distressed. She sat down on the hard pew, as everyone remained standing and as the music soared.

Mikael sat down beside her and took her hand.

"Mama, Mama – cry – cry." He mumbled. She looked at him and then away, pale and trembling. Nairi on the other side also then sat and took Vartuhi's other hand, while, for the first time, some tears appeared in Vartuhi's eyes.

Father Haroutiune finished a short homily and blessed the coffin. The bearers moved up solemnly and bore it out down the aisle to the graveyard led by the priest. As was the custom, Mikael, walking alone, went immediately after the coffin followed at a short distance by Vartuhi and Nairi. As he got to the door, Mikael heard a short cry, and a gasp from the small congregation behind him.

He turned. Vartuhi was standing stock still, her face flushed, staring at a woman, considerably younger than herself, who was standing at the back holding the hands of two small boys. Mikael, stopped and looked at his mother, who was standing breathing hard. Nairi, looking even more distressed than before, was grasping Vartuhi tightly round her waist. There was a moment of silence. Meanwhile, the coffin bearers, with Father Haroutiune ahead of them, were walking on through the cemetery, having noticed nothing.

"I am going home," hissed Vartuhi, handing Mikael a brown envelope for delivery to the priest and the small choir. Then, without another word, pulling herself roughly away from Nairi, who desperately tried to hold on to her, she strode past Mikael and down the path out of the cemetery without once looking back. Mikael, in a turmoil of emotion and total confusion could only stand and stare, as Nairi, and the rest of the congregation behind him, waited for him to move on.

Mikael hurried after the coffin in a daze, followed by Nairi and the rest of the congregation, catching up with the cortege at the open grave, which was waiting for them. The bearers laid the coffin in the grave, Father Haroutiune gave the final words and the blessing, and the waiting grave-diggers began filling it in.

Everyone moved up to shake hands with Mikael and Nairi, and at that point Mikael saw the young woman, at whom his mother had been staring, begin to walk away holding the hand of each boy on either side. Making his excuses to those who had not yet come forward to offer their condolences, Mikael hurried after the trio as they walked towards the gates of the cemetery. He walked briskly past them, and then turned and faced them in such a way that they simply could not walk on. The trio stopped and stared at him.

"Madame", Mikael started, "my name is Mikael Safarian. I am the eldest son of Avedis Safarian, whose funeral has just taken place in there … May I thank you for attending my father's funeral, and ask you how you and he are related." Mikael then extended his hand towards the woman.

The woman ignored the proffered hand and said nothing, but continued to gaze down at the ground gripping hard onto the hands of the two boys who were both staring up uncomprehendingly at Mikael.

Mikael was totally thrown by this. He had no idea what to do. There was a long moment of silence as the young woman refused to reply or even look up. Mikael tried to catch the young woman's eyes to no avail. There appeared to be a deadlock, but then Mikael squatted on his haunches, bringing himself down to the level of the two boys. He faced the elder of the two, and smiled.

"Hello! My name is Mikael. What's yours? How old are you?"

For a moment Mikael thought that it was not going to work – but then the boy piped up, pulling himself away from his mother's grip.

"My name's Mardik, and I'm seven years-old".

Still the woman said nothing, staring at the ground. Mikael turned to the other younger boy.

"And you, my lad?"

The other boy, taking courage from the fact that his elder brother had pulled away from his mother, looking at with curiosity at Mikael.

"My name is Ardem, and I'm already five years-old. I'll be six soon. What are you doing at my daddy's funeral. Are you his brother?"

Mikael stood staring, saying nothing, upon which the eldest, Mardik, not to be outdone by his brother said, " Well, you must be my uncle then."

The young woman grabbed at the two boys, saying not a word and began dragging them off. But Mikael was having none of it. He stood firmly in their path making it quite clear that he would not allow her to leave. He saw the other mourners walking away from the grave in the distance, and Nairi slowly making her way towards him through the cypress trees.

Mardik, who had clearly had enough of being held by his mother, again wriggled free of her grasp, and looked at Mikael, to whom he had obviously taken a liking.

"Why did that old woman you were with spit at me, sir?"

Mikael was again only able to stare in confusion. Nairi approached, curiosity overcoming all her other conflicting emotions. Mikael had turned again to the woman –

"This is my sister Nairi. Could you please, Madam, now give me an answer. You must surely see that neither I nor my sister can leave here without knowing who you are."

"Mikael, my dear brother, what do you … "

"Nairi, quiet! Madam, please …"

At last the young woman turned and, sitting down heavily on the grass alongside the stone path just inside the gates, she indicated to her two boys that they could go and play.

"But, Mardik, don't go out of the gates, and always keep an eye on Ardem. Don't pick any flowers anywhere, and stay in sight."

The boys ran off, glad to be off the leash.

"My name is Katya," the young woman said. Mikael recognised a fairly heavy Russian accent – or could it have been Greek – in the Turkish words.

"I can't say anything to you to make this any easier for you, so I will say it simply and directly. Your father and I have lived together off and on for many years. The two boys are your half-brothers. Oh my God, my God, we should never have come, we should have kept away, I didn't mean … ," and she burst into tears.

Mikael, although something close to the truth had already started to occur to him, nevertheless, was stunned into silence. As the weeping continued, Nairi spoke.

"But, how is that possible? I've scarcely ever known my father to be away for any length of time. At most, he was away for a day or two every so often when he had to stay in town for work."

"Yes ... well," mumbled the fair-haired Katya almost under her breath. "We live in Yedikule, in a tiny house near the station. On days when your father stayed in the city, he would stay with us. As you know, Yedikule is only a few stops away from Makrikoy. My boys knew that their father had to stay away at nights and could only be with us occasionally. Mardik has recently been getting curious, as he sees how other families live. I've been begging your father to clear up the position one way or another for some time – but you know Avedis – oh my God ...so charming, easy-going and such fun, but never decisive."

At this point Katya began quietly sobbing again, hiding her face from Mikael.

"But, my mother ..." Mikael asked.

"Well, she knew all about us of course," Katya wiped away her tears. "She came once to my house. She stood at the door, and we stared at each other for what seemed like an eternity. I knew at once who she was. My boys were much younger, and they came and stood beside me holding my skirts. Your mother stared at the boys and then, without a word said by either of us, she turned and walked away. I never saw her again until this morning. However, Avedis told me that on that very day she had moved her bed, and that they never slept together again."

Nairi got up and moved away. She joined the two small boys who had been playing with stones, and squatted beside them. Mikael watched her talking quietly with them, while he sat, absolutely shattered, by the side of this young woman, probably only some four or five years older than himself.

In between the long silences between them, he ascertained that Katya's parents were originally from the Crimea, and that she was in fact half Greek and half Russian. He must have sat there some time before he came to realise that he was suffering from emotional trauma, and that his mind had completely blanked out. He rose and as they parted, she gave him her address. She and the two boys hurried away as if they were being chased.

As he and Nairi took the train back home from Sirkeci station, he found that despite the revelation, he was unable to change his feelings towards his mother. During the whole of the previous six or seven years, he had condemned his mother for her bitter and acerbic attitude towards his jolly father, for whom he had great affection. Suddenly, the reasons behind his mother's feelings had been thrust brutally upon him. He was unable to feel in his heart the sense of betrayal that his mother must have felt. All he had room for in his heart was his father's friendly, open-hearted attitude to life as against what he saw as his mother's repressed and disapproving character.

Neither Vartuhi nor Nairi said anything to Mikael about his continued failure after that day to report back for duty. Day after day passed, and Mikael stayed on in the ramshackle old house. He would take his seven year-old brother Mardiros to school in the morning, and then take the train up to town to work in the great covered bazaar with a Turkish friend from school, who had purchased deferment, and was currently working for his father at their shop. Mikael received no pay and did not ask for any. In his mind, he kept thinking that he would have to make a decision and rejoin his unit, now in Gallipoli.

Twice he went to consult Father Haroutiune about the discovery of his father's secret life. On the second of these occasions, he had referred to his inability to feel for his mother, or wholeheartedly to condemn his father. Haroutiune had replied –

"My son, you don't have to condemn your father in order to feel sympathy for your mother. Avedis undoubtedly sinned, but he seems to have tried to keep his original family together as best he could. Your mother could not forgive him, and that was her prerogative, I suppose. However, in repressing her natural instincts for the sake of her three children, she became bitter and destroyed herself emotionally."

"I don't know what to do, Father. I've become a deserter, and I wander about all day without purpose. I can't get the thought of those two little boys, my half-brothers, out of my head. Oh God! I'm so mixed up, I'm not even ... What shall I do?"

"Mikael – you have their address – why don't you go and see

them? They're only children. It might do you good. Above all, my son, try to make an effort to understand and comfort your mother."

Fateful words. Mikael felt lighter and more at ease with himself after this conversation. The very next day, on his way up to town, he suddenly took it into his head to alight at Yedikule, as the train pulled into the station. He began wandering around the back streets of the poor working-class area near the old fortress, looking for Katya's house.

He had just turned into the little street that he was looking for, when in the road right in front of him he ran into a patrol of three burly policemen. None of them recognised him as a resident of the area, and they immediately demanded to see his papers, surrounding him and making it impossible for him to flee. Mikael at first bluffed and said he hadn't got them on him – already an offence. Holding him, however, they took his wallet. Inside was all Mikael's papers, which confirmed his name and his religion. Also with the papers, was the military pass which confirmed that he was in the army, and that he had leave of absence only until the 27th April, which was already weeks before.

"*Giavour!*" the burliest of the policemen had spat out, after studying the papers and noting the name. "You're a bloody deserter. You're under arrest."

Then with a mighty blow he struck Mikael across the face, as the other two held him, followed by a great punch in the stomach. Mikael was dragged off to the dreaded Yedikule police station, retching from the blow to the stomach, and with a cut lip and bleeding nose.

CHAPTER 26

Garabed in flight

Garabed spent his first morning, after fleeing from the group, trying to get as far as possible from the spot where he had left the other deportees and their guards. He kept as high up the hillsides as possible, avoiding the occasional villages he now began passing. The scene was desolate, endless hills covered with green scrubby moss-like grasses, dotted with rocks and stones.

This was an area where large flocks of sheep were wandering, tended by a shepherd, usually helped by a boy and a dog. Garabed gave them a wide berth. Whenever he saw a flock ahead, he stopped and watched carefully to see which way they were headed, and then strode in another direction; sometimes, after seeing a flock moving straight across his path, he stopped and rested until the way was clear once again.

As the sun came up and it got warmer, Garabed looked about him for a spot to lie down and sleep. He realised that it might be better to sleep during the day, while it was warm, and walk at night during the cold. In this treeless landscape, shelter, if only from prying eyes, was difficult to find. He was now in an area where there were several tiny streams, running down the hillsides. He could not be sure that they were not polluted further up, but he had no choice and knelt and drank whenever he had the chance.

Eventually, amidst all the rocks lying about, he came across a spot where several were clustered close to each other. Here he found a position where he could lie down and not be seen by anyone, unless they came up close. Garabed blessed his wife for her foresight in sending his warm coat, wrapped himself up and tried to sleep.

For the first time, his thoughts caught up with him. The desolation of the countryside brought home forcibly the desolation of his own thoughts. He was a man who rarely spent time worrying or analysing his feelings. However, here was a situation the like of which he had never experienced. What was happening to his family? How had his life changed so completely in such a short time? Were others, like him, wandering lost in this desolation? His stomach rumbled with hunger. He had no answer to any of his reflections, and eventually drifted into a deep sleep.

He woke just as dusk was falling, and the chill of the night was beginning. He carefully and slowly chewed at the loaf, eating about half. His clothes, now in a state that would have brought tears to the eyes of Mariam, were sufficiently soiled and crumpled to appear somewhat less conspicuous in this remote countryside. However, he knew that he would have to try and get a change of clothes soon. Even with his sheepskin coat he was still far too conspicuous.

Garabed rose, splashed his face in a stream and walked on, guided by the stars in the mercifully clear night. He passed more and more villages as the area began to become more cultivated. There were no lights or fires to be seen in the darkness, and he was often only alerted to the fact that he was approaching a habitation by the barking of dogs. He would at once stop and walk away, attempting to skirt round the farm or hamlet as far as possible to quieten the dogs.

By now he was getting more and more hungry, but the risk of trying to get into a henhouse and steal some eggs, if there were any to be had, was too great. Every farm and village had dogs, who started barking the moment he got near. Garabed felt that the time had come at last when he should attempt to make some human contact. His one asset was the precious five gold coins in the pockets of his sheepskin coat. However he could not be sure if a coin of such value would be acceptable here in the countryside. Furthermore, if offered, it would certainly arouse suspicion, and could alert the authorities.

Garabed was getting increasingly tired from lack of food and the exertion of walking over rough ground. He stopped well before dawn was breaking and ate the last of his bread. With no idea where he was, he lay down to sleep, just where he was, on the bare grass of a hillside.

The sun was already quite high when he next awoke to the

sound of cow's bells. Garabed struggled up, immediately alert. He was on a gentle slope, lying on the coarse grass with rocks sticking out of the ground wherever he looked. At the bottom of the hill were a few rough houses – one could not call it a village. Coming up an uneven path, that lead past where he had been sleeping, was a young boy, with a small dog running alongside, driving about five meagre cows up the hillside.

Garabed rose, picked up his coat, and draped it round his shoulders. He tried to compose his features into a friendly smile. He realised, however, that with four days of stubble, and his extraordinary clothes, he would look very alarming to the young lad. Kurd? Turkish? Or even possibly Armenian? He could not tell. The cows came wandering on up the gentle slope, but the boy had stopped on seeing Garabed rise. He called to his dog to come to stand by him. The call was in Turkish, but this of course didn't mean anything.

Garabed moved forward – smiling – and talked in Turkish, the only language that he knew anyway.

"Good morning, young man. I've lost my way. Could you tell me where I am."

"*Effendi*, our village is called ...," and the boy mumbled something rather quickly, which Garabed did not catch, and which, on reflection, probably wouldn't have meant anything to him anyway. At least he had made contact, and whilst the boy remained suspicious and alert, somehow the fact that this apparition had spoken, in a language he understood, had reassured him.

"Do you know the name of the nearest town?" asked Garabed hopefully.

"I don't know," said the boy, "do you mean ..." and he came out with another name which sounded like 'kutchuk bagh', and which again meant absolutely nothing to the well-travelled Garabed. Garabed thought to himself that it was probably simply the next village down the valley. Garabed changed his strategy.

"Perhaps you could tell me whether your father is at home, so that I can speak to him and ask him my way."

"*Effendi*, I'm sorry but my father is away in the army. He is a corporal," the boy answered, proudly straightening up. "My mother told me that he's serving in a group that is defending the big city."

"You mean Stamboul"

The boy looked at him after this comment, blankly. Garabed again changed tack –

"Young man, could I speak to your mother? Which house is yours? What is your name?"

Garabed knew that here in the countryside, women, Muslim as well as Christian, were unveiled, worked alongside their men, and were ready to speak to a stranger even if their husbands were not present. The boy hesitated, but eventually pointed to one of the four houses at the bottom of the hillside.

"That's my mother's house. My name is Achmet. I must go now, *effendi*."

Saying which, he whistled at his dog and ran off after the cows, still plodding slowly up the hillside, waving back at Garabed as he ran. Garabed wished that he had some sweets or a small coin to give the lad, but he had nothing. He nodded at the wave, and began walking down the path to the house the boy had pointed out.

As always, dogs started barking as Garabed approached the hamlet. He walked into the beaten earth courtyard of the dwelling that the boy had indicated. Fortunately this was the first house at the bottom of the path, so he had no need to pass the others. The path ended at the houses, and there was no road or track of any kind between the farms. However each farm had a rough wooden fence around it, and one of them even had a gate. Garabed saw that after the furthermost building another track started and continued down the valley.

No dogs barked as he approached the faded and rather worn out front door, the top half of which was open. He coughed as loudly as he could, and then knocked at the closed half of the door. He could hear a baby crying inside, but his knocking aroused no further reaction. Somewhat non-plussed, Garabed stood considering. He considered that these were people who probably had little experience of the 'knock' as a request for entry. They probably just walked in and out of each other's houses, which usually had only one other room.

Garabed called out loudly,

"Hanum – I'm sorry to disturb you."

He then stepped well back from the door and out into the yard. A strong-looking and weathered woman appeared at the door with a baby on one arm; a small girl, sucking her thumb, clinging to the woman's long multi-coloured skirts, could just be seen peering at him over the top of the half-door. On seeing Garabed, the woman raised her free arm and put it across her face covering her mouth and the lower half of her face below the eyes. She did not however appear alarmed, much to Garabed's relief.

"Hanum, I must apologise for disturbing you. May Allah protect you and your family. Your son – Achmet – directed me to your house. I have lost my way. Could you tell me the name of the nearest town?"

"I suppose you mean Malatya" replied the woman. "It's about a days walk from here."

Garabed could now see into the house as the woman swung open the bottom half of the door. It was stone built, and as was familiar to Garabed from his travels, it consisted of one large room with a fireplace at one end, with a small fire at present burning in it. There was a door at the other end leading into a small, second room. The floor was the standard cool mud floor, hard and clean. There were iron pots hanging from the walls, together with a couple of faded carpets. There was little furniture, save a roughly made table, several solid, wooden chests, and a wooden crib with soft, clearly new, straw, but no linen of any kind. The baby was wearing a long white smock, like a nightgown, but nothing else.

There was a rich variety of smells coming from the dwelling, ranging from the faint smell of a baby's urine and excrement, to the musty smell of a rich, bulghur porridge with spices. Garabed's mouth watered, but he realised that a gold coin here would be quite useless.

"Which is the way to the town, hanum?" asked Garabed.

The woman pointed to the track going down the valley at the other end of the little hamlet.

"It's that way. When you get to the end of the track and the stream it follows, you will come to the river – just follow that, as it goes all the way to Malatya."

Garabed considered how best to proceed as his stomach rumbled. Anything was of some value to these people. Slipping off his sheepskin coat, he took off the smart jacket of his dark suit. He offered this to the woman who was still standing at the open door.

"Hanum, please take this jacket. Your husband might like it when he returns from the army."

She stared at him, but did not take the proffered jacket. Garabed continued somewhat desperately,

"I am hungry, and have a whole day's walk ahead of me before I can reach Malatya – can you give me some food?"

This the woman understood at once. She motioned to Garabed to squat where he was. She then disappeared into the house. Shortly after, she re-appeared, still carrying the baby, and with the little girl still clinging to her skirts. In her free hand she had a bowl of the bulghur porridge, out of which stuck an old, and not too clean, wooden spoon.

Garabed did not rise from his cross-legged position on the ground, and indeed this was clearly what the woman expected. She came forward and handed the bowl to Garabed. He took it in both his hands and raised it to his forehead in thanks. He then began eating it quickly, nodding at the jacket which he had left draped on the swinging half-door. The woman still did not take it, but left Garabed to eat and went inside again, whilst at long last the little girl left her mother's skirts and stood just inside the door, sucking her thumb, and staring with huge eyes at the strange man greedily wolfing down porridge.

Garabed had just finished when the woman re-appeared. The baby had at last been put down. She had in her hands two large onions and a rough loaf of bread. Garabed now gently rose, leaving the bowl on the floor and salaamed. Silently she handed the food to him, and then for the first time stepped back and picked up the dusty jacket, smelling it. She smiled. Garabed smiled back and bowed deeply.

"May Allah, the all-merciful, protect you and your family and bring your husband back home to you soon, safe and sound."

"Inshallah," replied the woman.

Garabed slipped the food into the capacious pockets of the sheepskin coat, then turned and walked out of the yard. The dogs immediately began their cacophany, but Garabed ignored them and strode on and away, following the track down the valley, as the woman had indicated. The moment he reached the point where the stream he had been following down the hillside reached the river, he immediately recognised the river as the one he used to follow on his trips to the home of Sarkis, the son of Shahan, whose family made such beautiful carpets.

"Yes!" thought Garabed, almost shouting out the word aloud in glee and triumph. "That's where I'll go – it's obvious. My god, it's a good thing I came in this direction. I'll certainly be safe with them for a while."

Armed with that thought, and with hot food in his belly, and some reserves in his pockets, Garabed's confidence began to return, for the first time since the arrest. He took a long drink at the stream before it reached the river, and strode out with purpose and renewed hope.

By the time Garabed finally arrived in Malatya, the town was in turmoil. There had always been a large Armenian community here. Once again, however, there were no longer any young men in evidence. The arrests and exile of the leaders of the community had already taken place, while the younger men were away either in the army or in labour battalions. Accordingly, the general population was helpless and unprotected, facing hatred and a murderous official policy.

The town of Malatya had been designated by Talaat as one of the main gathering points for the Armenian deportees driven out from the interior further west. Already people were arriving and assembling in the rocky fields outside the town, where a ramshackle shanty town of tents, broken down old carts and makeshift shacks, was growing.

Garabed eventually managed to exchange one of his gold coins with a local money-changer, and found a cheap *khan* in which to stay whilst he worked out his best course of action. He was aware that already there was an increasing lawlessness in the countryside outside the main towns. Kurdish tribesmen, encouraged by the clear signals from the central authorities that they would not be punished, were regularly attacking the slow-moving lines of Armenian refugees, as they were forced out of their homes. Turkish criminals had also been released from the prisons, and they, too, were roaming the districts around the towns, terrorising the helpless deportees.

Garabed later reflected that it might just be possible to suggest that Talaat and the others may not have realised that, once started, lawlessness to this extent would be impossible to contain. However, reports of the unfolding catastrophe were being sent by the few conscientious Ottoman officials who were still in place. This was also confirmed by the few European consulates that were still operating. All the reports were studiously ignored by the new masters in Istanbul. The scum of town and country, deliberately freed by the government from their normal restraints, was beginning to attack and pillage even those Armenians who were not yet on the roads.

Garabed stayed in Malatya for a week or more before he decided to make his move and attempt to get to Sarkis' farm, some days ride from Malatya in the mountains to the east. He needed to be armed, but it had to be unobtrusive. Pistols would be hard to obtain, and dangerous if he was stopped by soldiers. Furthermore, ammunition would be impossible to find outside the city. In the end, he opted for a long wicked-looking knife. He did not expect to have to use it, but he hoped that the sight of it, coupled with his determination, might deter someone bent on violence. He did not imagine for a moment that it could prevent any gang attack, if he ever had to face that.

He had got rid of the remainder of his clothes, except of course the wonderful sheepskin coat. So now, blending much better into the local colour, he at last set off up the hills. Instead of wearing a fez, associated as it was more with the towns, he had decided to wear a very simple turban wrapped round his head, a headgear still regularly worn in the remoter rural areas. This advertised to the world that here was a pious Muslim walking home. Of course it would not suffice if there was a direct confrontation, but it might just prevent such a confrontation taking place.

Moving slowly but steadily, avoiding any contact with any other person as much as possible, Garabed took several days, travelling continuously uphill, to get to the area where Sarkis Shahanian had his farmstead. This was an area with which he was familiar as a result of the many trips he had made both alone, and latterly with Raffi.

All along the way, Garabed passed burning farms, corpses and old men, women and children, looking lost and helpless – most of them obviously already at the end of their capacity to survive. There were too many such sad sights for Garabed to take in, so he steeled himself and kept walking on. It was ironic that, not speaking Armenian, apart from a few phrases, Garabed didn't even understand the few pleading words that were uttered by one or two of these dazed people as he passed.

Garabed pressed on, now becoming anxious, with his food provisions beginning to run low. It was now well into June, and whilst the nights were still fairly cool, he had been able to sleep outdoors without too much discomfort. On the last day, he pushed on as fast as he could in order to get to Sarkis' farm before nightfall. He was relieved to see that he was passing houses and farms that he recognised and which did not appear to have been touched. But he noted that the doors were bolted, and that several of the farmers, who appeared to be Turks were standing at their gates, with their sons alongside, holding rifles ostentatiously at the ready.

Garabed hurried on as the sun began to disappear under the horizon. Everything seemed quiet as he approached the farmhouse of Sarkis. Further down the valley – quite a distance away – Garabed could just make out a group of men, some on foot and some on horseback, who appeared to have surrounded a farmhouse and were milling about, yelling and gesticulating. Garabed could not hear the shouts, but he did suddenly hear the slight popping sound of gunshots. He hurried up the track, once again and stopped dead.

There in front of him, with the doors and windows smashed and hanging loose, but otherwise not too badly damaged, stood Sarkis' neat farmhouse. The outhouses, the stables and the henhouse were all burnt out and were still faintly smouldering, but the stone house itself seemed fairly intact. Garabed ran forward with his heart pounding. What met his eyes as he approached was more horrific than he could ever have imagined.

Hanging from the eaves of the roof, just by the space, which had been the front door, swaying gently in the breeze, swung the body of Sarkis. Blood, now dried up, had flowed from a deep gash in his side. His face was battered, his eyes open and staring, and his tongue hung out, purple and bloated.

Garabed sank to his knees, for just a moment, from the shock of the sight. He quickly looked about him, but there was no one near. He put his hands on the floor in front of him, and knelt like a dog, with his head drooping, for a few seconds retching, though he was not actually sick. He knelt like this for several seconds, and then for the first time became conscious of a low moaning coming from inside the farmhouse. He arose and went tentatively into the main room of the dwelling. At this point, as his eye took in the scene inside, he did become violently sick. His whole stomach heaved and he had to run outside again as his vomit spewed out of him.

Eventually, pale and exhausted, and lifting his rough pullover over his nose, he went back into the room. In front of the fireplace, lying face up on the stone floor, with her clothes torn almost all off, her legs wide apart, lay Adrineh. Blood and semen was seeping from the bruised and battered area between her legs. She was clearly unable to move, and it was from her lips that the low animal noises that Garabed had heard outside were coming.

To one side of her lay the bodies of the two little girls, covered with flies, with their legs and arms hacked off and quite dead. In a state of shock, Garabed next heard a movement from the small bedroom. He staggered over and went in – the door having been torn from its hinges. In the room the sight was even more horrific. Spread-eagled across the bed were the two older girls – Anna and her younger sister. Both appeared to have been violently raped, probably by several people, like their mother outside. Anna's lips were moving but no sound was coming from her. Her younger sister was already dead. In the far corner was the younger of the two boys whose body was covered with sword or knife cuts, also clearly dead. Next to him, whimpering with fear and shock, with huge staring eyes, huddled the eleven-year older boy, his naked body a mass of stripes and weals.

For what seemed to be an age, Garabed stood totally still unable to act, his mind refusing to accept what he was seeing. The flies and the stench finally brought him to his senses. He had to act. He first made sure that the younger boy and girl were both dead. He then stepped up to the eleven-year-old lad and took his hand. The boy screamed and shrank back. Garabed stopped and backed off. He turned back, and taking Anna in his arms he lifted her, taking her out into the yard and laying her down near the well.

Then he returned, picked up the little bodies of the two girls by Adrineh's side and took them into the bedroom. He tried once more to coax the boy, who again shrank from him in terror. Overcoming any scruples, knowing he had to get the boy out of the room, now with four dead bodies in it, Garabed suddenly grabbed him, put one hand over his mouth to stifle the screams, and bore him struggling and kicking out of the room and outside, leaning him against the wall of the house. Finally he went back in to deal with Adrineh.

This was much more difficult, but he had to get her out of the charnel house which the building had become. He could not lift her properly, every movement caused her to cry out in pain. Eventually he half carried and half dragged her out of the house. He lay her down next to Anna, who was still lying muttering to herself. Garabed could do nothing about the boy, whose name he could not even remember. But he could try to do something for the two women. Fortunately, the pail and the pulley, above the well in the yard, had not been destroyed along with everything else. He drew some water, and came and knelt by Adrineh, murmuring words of comfort, but not sure whether she heard them or not.

He looked at her, and did not know how to start. To use her own clothes – what was left of them – was impossible. He went back into the house, but the place was gutted and there were no clothes or linen anywhere. Swallowing down all his horrified instincts, he took out his knife and went back into the room now holding four dead children. With his eyes almost shut, he cut away the cleanest strips of the children's clothes he could find. He then hurried out, his gorge rising again.

Working carefully and as gently as he could, he dipped the strips of cloth into the water and gently wiped away all the blood and filth in and around Adrineh's genital area, and then turned to do the same for Anna. He kept drawing up more clean water, always giving each of them a sip or two before continuing the cleaning process. The water at last revived Adrineh, who nodded at Garabed in a sign of recognition. Anna, however, was completely traumatised.

All this time, the boy stared at Garabed saying nothing, lying naked against the wall. Every time Garabed moved towards him with the pail of clean water, the boy shrieked and drew back in terror. Garabed had no idea how to get round this, so gave up and concentrated on the two women. It was already beginning to get darker, when Adrineh at last lifted herself up, at least sufficiently to lean back against the low stone wall of the well. The full realisation of Garabed's presence came upon her suddenly, and to his relief this brought back some sense of modesty, and she wrapped her torn and bedraggled clothes around her legs.

"Garabed agha?" she said, looking directly at his face for the first time.

"Adrineh, hanum, yes it is I."

"Where is Sarkis, sir?"

"Madam Adrineh, you must be prepared for the worst."

"I know, Garabed *effendi*, my Sarkis must be dead. Oh my God, my two little ones too – my two little ones – oh God my two little ones." She brought her hands up to her face, and at last, to Garabed's relief, she began sobbing deeply.

Garabed had no idea how to proceed. It was clear that she was still not aware of the other deaths. He decided that it would be best if she now started dealing with the situation directly. He pointed to Anna and the boy, still huddled up against the wall. Adrineh looked round and stopped sobbing. She staggered upright and shuffled over to Anna, keeping her legs apart in an odd crab-like movement. She fell alongside the girl and took her head in her arms and began rocking back and forward murmuring words Garabed could not follow. Garabed tried to adjust what was left of Anna's clothes, but Adrineh waved him aside. Then she looked up.

"Garabed *effendi* – could you please fetch some clothes – they will be in the big wooden chest in the back bedroom."

"Adrineh, hanum, there is nothing at all left in the house – no clothes no linen nothing."

There was a long silence in which the only sound was Anna's unintelligible muttering. Then Adrineh spoke.

"Garabed, *effendi*, would you please go and ask Nefise Hanum to come. She is the wife of our neighbour Mustapha Mahmud. Their farm is the first house as you go down the hill."

Garabed hesitated.

"But they are Turks. Will they help you? Are there no Armenians nearby."

"Please, Sir, do as I ask. I know what I would do for her, and what she would do for me."

Garabed looked about at the devastation around him and nodded. Once he saw that Adrineh was again involved in crooning to Anna, he took out his knife and moved quietly to the front door. He was just able to reach up to the rope from which Sarkis was hanging. At full stretch he sawed away at the rope and held tightly onto Sarkis' body. Eventually the rope gave way, and Garabed gently put the body of Sarkis down – all the time conscious of the young boy's eyes staring at him as he worked.

Once completed, he raced off down the hill to deal with Adrineh's request, with a guilty feeling of momentary relief to escape the horror, if only for a short time.

When he approached the first farmhouse on the way down the hill, he saw a man standing at his door with an old but serviceable looking rifle held up in his arms. Beside him stood a boy of about 12 years-old, holding an old hunting rifle. Both looked very grim. Garabed slowed down, made sure that they could see his hands were empty, and walked up to the fence and called out to the two who were staring back at him -

"My name, sirs, is Garabed Asadourian. I am a friend of Sarkis, son of Shahan. There has been a terrible tragedy at their farm. Adrineh, his wife, has been -er -er – molested, but she is still alive. She's asked if Nefise Hanum will come to her. There is no more immediate danger, as there are no intruders left."

Garabed gabbled all this out in a breathless rush. Before he had finished, a large well-bosomed lady, dressed in several layers of black skirt, pushed past the man, and ignoring him, the boy, and Garabed, began hurrying up the hillside – taking no notice of the restraining hand which the man had extended as she swept past him. He shrugged.

`"Burhan, my son, go with your mother and follow any instructions she may give you."

As the boy ran off after his mother, the man turned to Garabed.

"Yes, I have heard of you from my friend Sarkis. You are the merchant from Kayseri who buys his carpets. My name is Mustapha Mahmud. I must remain here, there are small children inside. But please know that my house is your house. What has happened to the Shahan family?"

Garabed, still catching his breath told him of the death of Sarkis, and a short description of everything else he had seen. Mustapha, a grizzled weather-beaten man, whose age Garabed could not judge, hung his head during Garabed's recital then raised his hands palms up to heaven and cried out some words to Allah in a dialect Garabed could not follow. Then he turned back to Garabed.

"I saw these men passing my house earlier. They were led by an official from the town, and I was relieved that there were even two soldiers with him. However, most of the rest were a drunken mob of Kurds. I am ashamed to say that there were also many Turks – scum from the town. You know, *effendi*, that a decree has been issued that all Armenians were to leave the area to go to the Vilayet of Syria."

Mustapha paused, and Garabed could see that he was clearly in some distress.

"Oh, my God, my God – I advised my friend Sarkis to stay put for the moment and see what might happen. What have we done, what have we done. I should have realised that the official from the town was one of those godless Ittihad devils."

He sank to his knees – but then jumped up immediately as Garabed, too, turned and saw the boy running back down the hill. Garabed noticed Mustapha hastily arranging his features so as not to alarm his son.

"What is it Burhan – what is it?"

"Oh Baba – it's terrible. My friend Ara won't talk to me. He is lying there naked, and when I went up to him he screamed and turned his face away. Mother says I am to bring some of my clothes for him, and also some of Hikmet's dresses. She also wanted some of that soap you made recently – oh, and something else – oh yes, a cup."

"Quickly then Burhan my boy, bring everything out here, and we'll make a bundle."

Mustapha nodded at Garabed and went into the house, leaving Garabed standing outside. Garabed had deliberately not returned to the stricken farmhouse straight away with the boy, in order to give Adrineh and Nefise some time together to work out what should be done, without any male presence. However, when Burhan came out from the house staggering under an armful of clothes, Garabed took some of the clothes from Burhan, and the soap and a cup from Mustapha, which he wrapped up with the clothes. He then turned to the weather-beaten man.

"Mustapha, *effendi*, I salute you. May your Allah reward you for all your kindness, and for the risk I know you are taking in helping your neighbour."

Garabed then bowed and touched the floor at the man's feet, then straightened up and touched his forehead. He did not, however continue with the sign of the cross on his chest. Then he turned and hurried off after Burhan, who had already begun climbing up the path to the Shahanian house.

CHAPTER 27

The Avakians without Karekin

Even though neither Robert College nor the attached Girl's school closed its doors during the whole period from the outbreak of the Great War, there was no way that Olga was going to go back. It was not that she had been intimidated by her experience on that dramatic day of the 24th April. Once Selim had appeared at Makrikoy and she knew that nothing had happened to him, she was ready to take on the whole faculty if necessary. It was simply that she felt that in that one single day, she had outgrown any desire to remain a student at that institution.

This feeling was of course partly induced by the arrest and deportation of her father. Karekin, had he been present, would undoubtedly have urged Olga to continue her studies. Armineh, however, gave her no such encouragement. Indeed she welcomed Olga's decision not to go back. In Armineh's opinion, everything was in favour of Olga staying at home for a bit. Armineh was not devious, but it did cross her mind that a separation from Selim, for a time, might also be useful.

On that day, when she and Sima had finally got back home from Haydar Pasha station, Armineh had been totally incapable of taking on board any more problems that afflicted the family. In fact, the whole family, physically and emotionally exhausted, had collapsed into bed at the same time as little Seta, much to her surprise.

The next morning, Armineh had to face all the vital matters that had arisen the previous day. First, and probably the most difficult for her to deal with, was the issue of the assault on Haik. Marie was waiting at the bottom of the stairs and accosted Armineh before breakfast, and before the others came down.

"Madam Armineh, I am most sorry to hear the terrible news of the arrest of Karekin *effendi*. I understood from Miss Sima that you were able to see him and say goodbye. I will pray to the Virgin Mary every night for his safe return. But Madam, something else happened yesterday which you have to deal with immediately."

"Oh Marie – I do know about Olga's unfortunate infatuation with a Turkish lad. Come, it's not all that difficult – she is not a complete fool. We'll sort out something."

"No, Madam, I am referring to Haik."

"Haik! Heavens, woman, what are you talking about? What's happened? He seemed fine to me, fast asleep, when I popped in last night."

Marie carefully explained exactly what had occurred: Haik having to return home on his own after school – Olga's lost scarf – the assault – the arrival on the scene of Olga's boyfriend Selim, and then Vahan. Both of them were experienced women and Marie made it clear that she had tried to ascertain what exactly had taken place. Armineh sighed. She knew that she was going to have to cope with everything: the house, the business, the children's education, everything, but this particular problem should have been Karekin's task. The chances were she would only make things worse by talking to the boy.

"Marie, is he all right for the moment?"

"Madam, I believe so. But you know Haik. He is so naïve and trusting that he doesn't realise at the moment what those two young men were threatening to do. But what about later? I am sure you know, that, even though he is only 12, he has reached puberty. He is at a very sensitive stage, and this is an experience which must be explained and exorcised from his mind."

"Oh Marie, you've been reading too many popular books on

this new-fangled psycho-what's-it rubbish coming out of Germany or Vienna. Typical German tosh! Forget it – he's a healthy boy. Let's just thank God that nothing happened. Too much talk can only do harm, especially if it comes from me."

In one corner of her mind, Armineh knew that Karekin would have taken Haik into his full confidence and would not have let it go undiscussed. But already, only 24 hours after his departure, she was badly in need of her husband. She could cope with nearly anything, but on this one matter, she felt paralyzed. She was trying to convince herself that it was right to do nothing

"Marie, thank you, I think we'll take the whole matter slowly. We'll wait and see. I may try to have a word with him sometime, but he is unlikely to be any more forthcoming with me than he was with you. I believe it will go from his mind soon."

Marie looked hard at Armineh, then nodded and turned back to the kitchen.

Nerissa had been the first down after that, and Armineh quickly got out of her the full details of everything that had happened whilst she and Sima had been gone looking for Karekin. Armineh probed gently, but it was clear that Nerissa hadn't appreciated the possibility of what might have taken place during Haik's assault. In the midst of all her other problems, Armineh finally put the matter out of her mind. Once out of her own mind it went out of the forefront of everybody's, including Haik'.

Unfortunately – Germanic tosh or not – it began to figure in Haik's dreams, and inexplicably to him, began to coincide with his 'nocturnal wet dreams'.

In explaining to her mother everything that had happened, Nerissa showed a new, more unromantic appreciation of Selim as a person, and a more mature awareness of his relationship with Olga. Armineh turned almost thankfully to the problems of her daughters and away from the experience of her only son

"Nerissa, my soul, I accept your appraisal of this young man. How can I be indifferent, after all, towards a man who may have saved my only son's life. Olga is a silly goose, but I never feared for a moment that she would ever fall for a bad or vicious man.

But Nerissa, my dear, we don't live on an island; love isn't enough in these troubled times."

"Oh mother – I've already said I am sorry for what I said yesterday. I understand the situation perfectly well, and I daresay that Selim does too. Neither of them are going to act precipitately. I feel sure that you can rely on that."

Sima was the next one down. That long hour or two in Haydar Pasha station had brought home to her, more forcibly than to her brother or sisters, the possibility that she might never see her father ever again. Her eyes were red with weeping all night.

After the others had come down, they had a somewhat subdued breakfast. Marie took Seta off to school. Immediately after she left, for the first time ever, an Avakian breakfast conclave took place without the all-powerful presence of Karekin. It had been remarkably efficient. It was as if the removal of the patriarch of the family had brought out the competence of the women. Some of the decisions taken on this very first morning, after his disappearance, lasted for the whole of the next year. Armineh was the first to speak.

"With your father away, children, I must go to the office, if not daily, at least once or twice a week, to see to his investments and other business interests. I think Sima, you must accompany me so that you can pick up the threads. Eventually I'll expect you to deal with most of the routine matters there."

"But mother, what about my taking Haik to school and back," said Sima, who had not yet got over her feeling of guilt over her failure, the previous day, to arrive in time.

"Mama," Haik pleaded, his bloody lip and nose having almost cleared up overnight. "Yesterday was a one-off. I know I shouldn't have tried to get that scarf of Olga's back. I'm sure, Mama, that I'll be fine now. You must trust me to be more careful."

There was a deep silence as all the women reflected, then everyone began talking at once. Armineh held up her hand and eventually, reluctantly, there was a silence again. Armineh regarded her son, who was not only eager, but in whose eyes she saw, for the first time, an anger at what was happening around him.

"Yes, Haik, I agree with you, but we will all have to take more responsibility for each other now. From now on I want you to be responsible for taking Seta to school, even though this means that you'll get to school yourself earlier and will have to wait. I'll instruct Seta's teacher that she must be kept at school till you arrive to pick her up in the afternoon. Remember, Haik, you will be responsible not just for yourself, but for your little sister as well."

Haik's eyes shone with pride, and he nodded.

Olga then stated firmly that she was not proposing to go back to the college. Even at that early stage, at that first morning's meeting, she indicated that she would be trying to get work at one or other of the city's hospitals. She went on to say to her somewhat startled family,

"Don't stare at me like that. You saw how well I coped yesterday with Selim's wounds. It's work I think I could do well, and would enjoy doing, if people will let me.

"But Olga, hospital work isn't all tending the wounds of romantic young men. There is filth and excrement to clear up and potties to empty and heavy lifting," Nerissa pointed out.

"Nerissa – you have never ever considered that I might have any common sense. For God's sake – sorry mother I know I'm not putting this well but I have to say it – for once have some confidence in me as a person, instead of forever laughing at me."

The blood rushed to Nerissa's head and she went a deep red. This was the second time within 24 hours that she had been guilty of intellectual arrogance.

"Oh my darling Olga, I'm so sorry, I'm so sorry."

Nerissa rose, took a step towards Olga, dropped to her knees by her chair and buried her head in Olga's lap. At this turn of events, Olga suddenly laughed out loud – the first laugh in the house in what seemed like days – patted Nerissa on the head, and, still giggling, shooed her off. Nerissa and Haik then got ready to go out to school. In the midst of all the drama, and the devastation of their father's arrest, somehow, carrying on everyday routine seemed to be the best way of coping.

Armineh made no comment on Olga's declaration. Like Nerissa, she doubted that Olga would have the resolution to go through with this current obsession. Although Nerissa was now careful not to say so to anyone, this was surely, she felt, just another bit of Olga whimsy.

As it happened, however, within a few weeks of that morning's discussion, Olga had indeed found a job. She deliberately avoided going to the highly prestigious and efficient Armenian Hospital – Sourp Pirgitch – and had instead picked on the Turkish military hospital in Uskudar, even though that entailed a much longer daily journey. Her interview with the administrator of the nursing staff, had been a great success. She was already learning how to temper her outgoing nature and superficial charm into something more sincere and mature. She arranged to do shift work, so she could stay in the hospital for four or five days at a time, and then return, for her days off, to Makrikoy.

Of all the children, it was Nerissa, who had the most difficulty in adjusting to the changes wrought by the arrest and disappearance of Karekin. The English High School for Girls had finally closed down for the duration of the war, and without Karekin's guidance and encouragement, Nerissa had no idea what to do when she finished at the local school in that difficult summer. She ended up by giving English lessons to the sons and daughters of well-off Makrikoy families, Turkish and Greek as well as Armenian, and this had helped to bring in yet more welcome ready income to the family. The proximity of an English-speaking army, within a hundred miles, stimulated the wealthier residents of Makrikoy, most of whom already had a smattering of French, to tackle this new language.

And so the family struggled on reasonably comfortably. Sima began going regularly into Karekin's office in the city. Whilst there was not much to do, she was able to keep up the correspondence with agents and old customers. This at least maintained the belief that the business was still alive. At the same time, Olga brought in a small income from her job as a nurse, and eventually even Nerissa was bringing in some money.

About two months after that terrible day of the 24th April, Armineh received an unsigned postcard – postmarked from Konya – with the single word "GABRIMGOR" written on it in Latin capital letters. It was this unsigned postcard with its single word – "I am living" – which gave the whole family an enormous boost and will to carry on.

It arrived at just the right moment. For over a month, Armineh had driven the family. She had encouraged Olga in carrying through with a project for the first time. She had taken Sima to Karekin's office, dealt with the departure of the old Turkish clerk, whom she could not afford to pay anymore, and instructed Sima in the basic tasks. She had dealt with all the rest of the family problems. But at the end of the month, as the little practical matters began falling into place, and she began to have some spare time on her hands for the first time, despair began to eat into her heart. Nothing had been heard from any of the deportees, and several more arrests in the city had aggravated the situation. Rumours went round from one family to another, but there were no real hard facts. Then out of the blue came the postcard. Suddenly it all became worthwhile, and Armineh bounced back, redoubling her efforts.

The first thing that the two friends Karekin and Aram had done after jumping out of the train, reaching the shelter of the houses, and collecting their breath, was to wander down to the clothing bazaar of the town, still open in the late afternoon. The town of Konya was fairly well known to both of them from previous visits. They had no difficulty in finding their way to the bazaar.

There, as hurriedly as possible, they bought thick, rough pullovers, strong and equally rough trousers and some local shoes. Fortunately Aram had a little small cash on him, which they were able to use. At the same time Karekin, wandering round the market, found a money changer and managed to change a couple of the gold coins at his little desk. This was a simple old wooden table covered with many different currencies, and scales for weighing gold and silver. The grizzled old man sitting at the desk had looked sharply up at him when offered the two heavy coins, but, making a substantial profit, he said nothing. Finally they also purchased a cheap leather suitcase.

Leaving the bazaar as quickly as possible, as their city clothes, however creased and shabby, were already attracting some attention, they found a sheltered spot between high blank walls down a side alley. Whilst Karekin mounted guard, Aram changed into the shabby, ill-fitting, newly purchased clothes. Aram then took up the look-out position, while Karekin changed. They then stuffed their city clothes into the case. Feeling much less conspicuous, they walked out of the alley and wandered down to the old square of the food vendors. With night falling, and hour by hour feeling more confident and anonymous, they sat on the rickety bench of a kebabji and ate a couple of the surprisingly tasty shish-kebabs.

"My God, Aram," said Karekin, with meat juice running down his face, "What an enormous difference some decent hot food makes to the way we feel about the world."

Aram edged along the bench towards the little charcoal grill on which the kebabs were cooking, and warmed his hands.

"You're right Karekin – but I'll tell you what, I'm beginning to get a bit of a reaction. Look, I'm shivering and feeling cold. It's all been too exciting – and we're not out of the woods yet. It's going to get cold tonight and where the hell are we going to stay."

As it happened both of them knew that there was a small Armenian community in the town, most of whom lived together in one of the suburbs, which had even become known locally as Ermeni-mahallesi.

"We certainly won't be able to find anything tonight," reasoned Karekin, "but I suggest we walk out of town in the direction of the Armenian quarter, and see what we can find tomorrow."

The two men were replete with bread and kebab. They were enjoying the feeling of wellbeing, resulting from the meal they had just eaten in the friendly noisy atmosphere of the dimly-lit eating areas in the square. They were still euphoric from the adrenalin rush of their escape, as they walked through the suburbs and into the farming area outside the town. Here they eventually came across an old ruined barn, not too far from the road, where they fell fast asleep.

The following morning, once again nervous as they considered their next step, they walked over to the small Armenian quarter. Sitting in a miniature coffee-house, smoking a narghileh, and speaking as little as possible, to hide their distinctive Stambouli accents, they sipped their coffees and began enquiring as to possible lodgings. Someone told them of some lodgings with a young Armenian couple, who owned a modest house nearby. A friendly woman, who was just about to go to work, came to the door, agreed to take them on immediately, on payment of a good deposit. She explained that she and her husband ran a little sweet shop in the centre of the town. They had no children, and she said that she worked with her husband, but had stayed at home later that morning to complete some domestic tasks.

For several days, Karekin and Aram hardly stirred from the house, feeling somehow more nervous now that they were more settled, than they had been when they were on the run. Eventually, they had to think of the future, and how best to survive the situation. In any case, they soon became bored of their interminable games of tavloo, in which millions were won and lost each day.

The situation in Konya was somewhat unusual at this time. The then Governor of Konya – Djelal Bey – was still the old Ottoman appointee. He had little sympathy for Talaat and the Ittihad gang in Istanbul. He was not a liberal, and not even particularly sympathetic to the Armenians, who were in any case only a very small minority here, being far less numerous than the Greeks in the town. Nevertheless, he had ignored, and continued to ignore the spate of vicious decrees and widespread deportation orders emanating from Talaat's ministry, which required all people of Armenian origin to leave Anatolia and move to one of the Arab vilayets.

Karekin very quickly became aware, even at that early stage in the unfolding catastrophe, that the severity of enforcement of these deportation orders varied from vilayet to vilayet, according to the disposition of the Governor. The general pattern was that the further east in Anatolia, the more severe were the effects of the decrees. In the eastern-most vilayets, bordering on, or close to, the Russian frontier, where the Armenian rural population was at its densest, long lines of women, children and old men, had trudged through the countryside in the general direction of Aleppo. Set upon by released criminals, Kurdish tribesmen and Turkish riff-raff, including some soldiers, large numbers of them were dying on the roads. The women were being raped and the children abused. Those that were managing to struggle through, out of Anatolia, were then dying, in their thousands, of starvation in the Syrian desert.

During these early days, as Karekin was coming to terms with his situation, he had plenty of time to watch, listen and reflect on what was happening in the Empire. It became clear to him that the whole terrible catastrophe had been carefully stage-managed. It was not unfolding as a spontaneous massacre taking place due to chaotic conditions in the countryside. It had begun all over the Empire with that carefully considered list of the leaders or potential leaders of the community, arrested and removed, as had indeed been his own experience. The young men were mostly in the army or in the carefully policed labour battalions. With the leaders arrested or killed, and the young men disarmed and out of the way, the stage was thus set for the removal of the whole general population, in the clear knowledge that, in the prevailing conditions, most would perish on the way.

Karekin and Aram survived those first months due entirely to the invaluable gold coins that Armineh and Sima had brought to Haydar Pasha station at such risk to themselves. Once settled in their lodgings, and ready at last to venture out, Karekin began looking about town for some opening. Eventually his natural entrepreneurial instincts led him to use a good part of the coins to buy up the stock and town shop of a dealer in that thin diaphanous material from which the better-class yashmaks were made.

At some time during those first two months Karekin, fearful of giving himself away, or endangering his family, nevertheless contrived to send an unsigned postcard to Armineh – the postcard which had given such comfort at home, and which had been so instrumental in helping to keep up their spirits in their own efforts at survival.

Once he had purchased the shop, Karekin threw himself whole-heartedly into improving the layout, and using his natural talents to make the decoration and atmosphere of the shop welcoming. Having only ever been a doctor all his life, Aram found himself working enthusiastically in this new trade, and getting considerable pleasure out of it, despite the occasional panics when police or others asked too many questions. With Aram helping in the shop, and with their unfailing courtesy to all, they had not only kept going, but were indeed doing quite well. In the course of time, with a bit of bribery, and using some connections they had made, they both got false papers – though they retained their identity as Armenians.

They soon fell into a steady routine. The friends would leave early in the morning. On the way into town, they would pass the local villagers bringing their produce into town to sell in the open food markets. The shop itself opened early in the morning, and would remain open all day until the bazaar closed in the early evening. Lunch would be provided by the itinerant vendors who went round all the stalls and shops, and would be eaten at the back of the shop. The two friends would then walk home at night to their lodgings, where their evening meal would be taken with the young couple.

Most mornings towards the end of this period, they began passing on their way into town, a bright young lad, pushing an enormous wheelbarrow filled with fruit of one kind or another. They even began buying fruit from him for their lunch, as it was so obvious that his fruit was fresh and carefully chosen. Karekin reckoned that despite the rough Turkish clothes, the man was Armenian, but the youth, when asked, said his name was

Soliman. Karekin and Aram began arguing about it, and as always with them it ended up in a bet.

"You wait and see" said Karekin, "if we see him again tomorrow, I'll prove he's Armenian."

"All right. I currently owe you five million seven hundred thousand. Double or quits – but you only get the one chance."

"Done!"

The next day – as it happened, the last day of tranquillity in Konya – they again accosted the young Soliman. They stopped him, and Aram chose a couple of peaches and some grapes. Karekin waved the lad on after the transaction was completed. After a couple of seconds he shouted out at him in great alarm in Armenian –

"Deghas, deghas, shood- shood – vazeh."

There was no hesitation or sign of any kind from Soliman, who clearly did not seem to have understood a word and who plodded doggedly on. Aram burst out laughing – saying,

"My boy, my boy, run – run away fast." Oh! Karekin you're priceless. Anyway my good fellow that makes us even."

Still roaring with laughter Aram, followed by a sulky Karekin, overtook the boy, clapping him on the back and asking him where in town he usually set up his wares, in case they wanted more fruit.

However, as the summer was just beginning to fade, the even tenor of their fugitive life was about to disintegrate.

As the weeks had passed, the Armenian population in Konya had continued to hang on, keeping a low profile, but unharmed. But Konya was not Constantinople or Smyrna. Sooner or later Talaat and his cronies were bound to step in and enforce their policy. It was only in Smyrna, or Bolis itself, that the old Ottoman ruling class, backed by the presence of foreign ambassadors, was strong enough to object successfully to Ittihad pressure. As the summer of 1915 began to turn to autumn, the moment finally came, when orders for the dismissal of Djelal Bey arrived from Istanbul. His replacement was to be an Ittihad appointee – yet another 'one-language, one-folk, one-culture' nation-state fanatic. It was clear that, shortly, a man impatient to have done with Ottoman diversity, would arrive in Konya.

That evening, as the posters announcing the deportation orders went back up on the public notice boards, the mood in the town began to change. Karekin and Aram, all bets forgotten, began to discuss their next move.

CHAPTER 28

Raffi faces life and death

It was still early in May in Caesaria and the days were getting perceptibly warmer. Almost two weeks had passed since the arrest and deportation of Garabed, together with most of the other leaders of the local Armenian community.

Cries of "*Giavour asiliyor – giavour asiliyor,*" "an infidel is to be hanged," rang out in the meat market, as Raffi stood waiting to be served in the butcher's shop.

Since that terrible moment when his father returned the coins into his reluctant hand, then turned and left without a further word, Raffi and the whole family had had to come to terms with the knowledge that they would very probably never see him again. Raffi had increasingly taken on the role of his father as a support to his mother and the other women in the household. Thus it was that on this particular morning, he had come out to the market to buy some fresh meat – a task formerly carried out by Garabed, as he returned from work in the evenings.

"An infidel is to be hanged ... Quick – quick – let's go."

Raffi found himself pulled along helplessly as everyone in the shop, and it seemed like almost everyone in the whole market, began running excitedly to the nearby main square in front of the town hall. There, pressed in by the crowd all around him, unable to get away, Raffi watched as he saw his gym teacher from school being frogmarched down the road between two policemen. He was swinging his arms vigorously in the characteristic manner that he had, and which the boys used to cruelly imitate in happier times.

Raffi's immediate neighbour in the crowd – who was to his surprise a fairly well-dressed man – laughed and dug Raffi in the ribs saying,

"See, the *giavour* pig – swinging his arms like a soldier. Doesn't he know that he is going to be hanged. They won't be swinging like that when he's swinging from the gibbet – the bastard."

Raffi had aged by years in the weeks since his father's disappearance, and he had no difficulty in stifling the tears that might have raised suspicions in the crowd.

"Yes, yes, amazing ..." he muttered.

A great roar arose as the man's body was raised, kicking and swinging, and with the noose tight round his rather scraggy neck. The gym teacher was still swinging and jerking there, when only a minute or two later, Raffi saw his headmaster escorted down the road in the same way – with a policeman on either side. Raffi had always been particularly fond of this man, whose name was Vahan, like his brother's. The headmaster was young for the seniority of his post. He was an inspiring teacher who had a way of rousing enthusiasm in his boys.

Raffi found that he could not prevent his body trembling. He looked down and to the side. He was not tall, and had no difficulty in shrinking down behind the men in front of him. He knew that he had to hide his feelings and not attract attention to himself, but he could not stop trembling, and he was beginning to feel dizzy and hot. Fortunately, no one seemed to notice his distress, and Raffi kept his gaze firmly on the ground. He simply had to stand there, unable to move to either side, parroting the cries of '*giavours*' and 'Christian dogs' whenever his neighbours said anything to him.

Eventually, as those at the front kept up their hate-filled chorus, the edges of the crowd began to drift away and the crush eased. Raffi was free to move. He looked up for the first time since his first sight of Vahan, the headmaster, being led down the road. At that moment, he almost fainted away, for there, swaying in the breeze, swollen tongues purple and hanging out of their mouths, eyes staring and bloodshot, were the six principal teachers from his school. For a moment he almost vomited, then turned and hurried home forgetting all about the meat.

At the sight of his mother, when she opened the front door, he burst into paroxysms of tears.

Very shortly after this incident, the deportation orders from Talaat's ministry in Istanbul, were posted all over town, and reinforced by the town criers calling out in all districts. All Armenians were to leave town within a week. There was to be no selling of any goods, no drawing of any money – everyone simply had to leave and make their way to the Arab vilayets. Supposedly there were to be guards posted along the way.

The only exceptions at this stage, were to be families of officers serving in the Turkish army, and those few who could show that they were Catholics or Protestants, rather than Orthodox. However, even this latter exception lasted only a week, as soon as it became clear to the Ittihad leaders in Stamboul that their Austrian and German allies were not, after all, going to raise anything more than a formal protest.

Raffi had written many weeks before to Vahan, asking him to send some evidence as to his officer status. Vahan had immediately contacted his superior officer at the Harbiye military academy. An upright old Ottoman official, he had promptly furnished a stamped and signed copy of Vahan's commission. Sensing the possible importance of this document for his family back in Caesaria, Vahan had written to Raffi immediately, confirming that he had passed on the document to a trustworthy Turkish merchant, who had known and done business with Garabed, and who was travelling to Caesaria within days.

Raffi received the document within a day or two of the public hangings in the town square.

The emptying of the Armenian quarters now began. Raffi had already purchased a large tent and a couple of donkeys ready for the journey. The streets of the Armenian quarters were filled with Turks looking for a bargain, knocking at doors and asking people if they had anything to sell, despite the formal government ban. People were parting with valuable heirlooms and all their furniture for a pittance.

Raffi was in a state of panic-stricken indecision. Everything happening around him seemed so utterly arbitrary – so completely tyrannical and lawless – that he did not know what would happen when the local commissioner finally arrived at their house. After all, in the last resort, Vahan's commission was only a piece of paper. There was nothing he could do if it wasn't accepted. Meanwhile, he would have lost his chance to sell some of the contents of the house. Suddenly those 25 gold coins which Garabed had returned into Raffi's care, became vital to the chances of survival of the family.

Too soon, the day came when their little street was ready to be emptied. Accompanied by some local policemen who knew the district, the local commissioner came down their little cul-de-sac. Almost everyone was ready, and began moving out. Raffi watched from the door as he saw his neighbours leaving. Like all his neighbours, he knew the dangers; they had all heard the rumours of the killings in the countryside outside the towns. Nevertheless, neither he nor his neighbours, were aware that not one Armenian from this street would survive the killing fields which stretched all the way to the Syrian deserts, where almost all of those who made it that far, would die of starvation.

Raffi knew everyone in the street. In one of the first houses, Raffi watched as the elderly father of a family with many children remonstrated in vain with the commissioner, having established that he had two sons who were serving with labour battalions of the army.

In the last house before that of the Asadourians, the family was ready, as they all were, but they asked to be exempted at least for some time. It appeared that their old grandmother could not walk at all – indeed could not be moved from her bed. They had no cart to carry her. Raffi watched as the old man explained all this to the commissioner. It was to no avail. In the end they were forced out, and the whole family trudged away, leaving their sick grandmother in bed in the house. They left some food and water by her bedside, and left the main door open. Raffi watched as they walked away, eyes downcast, saying nothing to anyone. In his own state of anxiety, he forgot almost immediately the plight of the old woman left behind.

At last, the police group came to the Asadourian house at the end of the street. Raffi had prepared the tent and all the other items on the backs of the two donkeys, which were still inside the courtyard standing patiently and fully loaded by the side of the old well. He now stood, trembling with anticipation at the door, with his mother a step or two behind him, as the commissioner approached.

"Come, come, you must leave now – everyone in the house must be gone today." The official had repeated these words all day to a series of desperate and confused people.

"Commissioner bey, my brother is an officer in the Ottoman army," Raffi answered, as confidently as he could manage. He handed over the Harbiye Commission. The official turned to the local policeman standing beside him.

"Whose house is this?"

"It belonged, *effendi,* to one Garabed Asadourian, who has already been deported."

"Well – did he have an elder son or not,"- and the Commissioner looked at the document in his hand – "called Vahan?"

"Yes, your Honour," said the policeman.

There was a long pregnant silence as everyone waited for the commissioner's verdict. Law, such as it was, had broken down completely; anything could have happened at that moment. Even at that moment of stomach-churning panic, Raffi reflected in a corner of his mind that this was the true definition of tyranny – the totally arbitrary nature of a society, where a decision of life or death, could depend on the whim of a single unaccountable person.

The moment stretched out, as Raffi waited. Then the official took a piece of chalk and wrote in large letters on the front door – 'Zabit ailesi' – 'officer's house.'

Without a further word he turned, and he and the other policemen walked out of the now totally empty street. Raffi, whose nerves were stretched to the limit, almost fainted, as his mother came forward and held him tight.

Three days later, a Turkish old lady who lived on the next street, and who knew Mariam and her daughters, came knocking on the door, and asked to speak to her.

"Mariam hanum, I have just heard some weak shouting and crying coming from the last house in this street. I went in, the door was open, and lying there was the old lady crying, abandoned and unable to move. What shall we do?"

Mariam said nothing but immediately called out to Raffi, who was listening in the corridor behind her, as the old lady walked away muttering to herself.

"Raffi, listen, did you hear that? I had no idea. You must go right away and bring her here."

"Mother, my soul, mother, listen – we have grandma already in bed here. We have sisters and a baby. Also, your old bedridden aunt will come when she hears that we've been exempted. How can we look after anyone else?"

"Raffi, please, we must. Neither of us is going to be able to sleep if we don't act"

Raffi felt guilty that he had forgotten the plight of this old woman in all the worry, and he left immediately. Taking one of the donkeys he went into town. Here he eventually traced Hassan the local garbage collector, who had his own donkey. He persuaded him to come back with him to the little street, and they both went into the empty house, and found the old lady.

The woman was lying on her bed, covered with her own dirt and urine, abandoned, weeping softly and unable to move. Working together they lifted her, carried her to the street, and put her on the back of Raffi's donkey. They brought her back to the house, where they lifted her into the bathroom, under Mariam's direction. Hassan left, refusing any bakhsheesh, but instead giving a deep bow to Mariam. Without any embarrassment, Raffi helped his mother carefully wash the old woman, and took her to a bed.

The house now held six women, including two helpless old ladies who had to be fed, bathed and changed. In the midst of it all, half-boy half-man, the hapless 16 year-old Raffi, had to do all the lifting and carrying. Fortunately he found himself too busy to think too much. Meanwhile, the whole of the rest of their little street now stood completely forlorn and empty.

As the weeks passed, two further old women were brought round to the Asadourian house on the back of Raffi's donkeys. Within a few weeks of the day that the little street had been emptied, there were eight women living in the house: Mariam, Raffi's two elder sisters, probably widowed by now, the two bedridden grandmothers, and the two newcomers.

The whole of the Armenian quarter around them had become a ghost town. The streets were quiet and empty, and the atmosphere was eerie and oppressive. One or two displaced Turkish families, from the areas currently occupied by the Russians, had moved into a couple of the empty houses, but the majority lay quiet and abandoned. Indeed the whole town was subdued. Most of the remaining Turks found, to their surprise, that the forced departure of the hated Armenian minority was not, after all, as welcome to them as they had imagined.

The government was now calling up the 17 year-olds for military service. It had therefore become dangerous for Raffi to wander the streets. Whilst there were still a few Armenian families left in the town, none of these were young able-bodied males.

If Raffi had not found himself doing all the heavy work involved in taking care of the three bedridden old ladies, he might have become depressed and bored, and started taking risks. Of course Mariam and his sisters did most of the pure nursing work, but it was Raffi who had to carry them to the toilet and turn them over in their beds. Mariam had paid heavily to get some false papers for Raffi, which gave his name as Soliman, his religion as Muslim and his age as sixteen.

Raffi's grandmother, his father's mother, was sinking the fastest. Her condition had been deteriorating from the moment her son Garabed had been arrested, and it was fairly clear that she was going to die soon. She was a particularly pious old lady, who had been with her husband on a pilgrimage to Jerusalem many years before and while there, she had purchased a specially blessed and holy burial shroud. This garment was a beautiful white linen cloth, embroidered with angels and crosses, resplendent with the whole paraphernalia of Christian iconography. Raffi had often seen her take it out of the wooden chest, hang it up and contemplate it with great satisfaction.

The day eventually came when Mariam and Raffi sat by her bedside as she slowly slipped away.

"I will be buried in my shroud, won't I," she whispered to Mariam.

"Yes, yes, I promise, mother. Don't be anxious."

Raffi said nothing, but continued to hold his grandmother's withered old hand, as with a sigh the old lady finally expired. There was no priest left in the town so far as Mariam knew, and the Armenian churches were all closed and boarded up. Mariam and Raffi sat together whilst the others in the house came, kissed the old lady and left. Eventually Mariam rose, called her daughters, and as Raffi looked on they bathed the body and brought out the burial shroud and began putting her in it.

"Mother, for heaven's sake it's far too dangerous," said Raffi urgently. "How can we take her down to the cemetery in this climate, with that garment calling out our race and religion to all the world. You know how it is in the town at the moment."

"My son, my son, it was her last wish – I promised, I promised. I'll suffer years of guilt if I don't fulfil it now."

"But mother, it's just superstition – what does it matter what she's buried in?"

"Please, son, I'll find a blanket to wrap round her whilst you take her down – but you must remove it before you bury her. Raffi, don't shake your head like that. I know it's not a religious duty – but I couldn't live with the thought that we didn't do our best. It was such a source of pride for her."

Racing through Raffi's mind was the thought – 'for god's sake she's dead, nothing can affect her now,' but what he actually said was

"Very well mama, get her ready, I'll do it this evening."

Raffi was impatient at what he considered to be religious

nonsense. He had been much influenced by Vahan's secular view of life and that religion was 'women's business'. However, it would never have crossed his mind for a moment to consider converting to Islam, as some others had done to save themselves. Even though he basically believed that both religions were a "load of old superstitious rubbish", he could not see that it could therefore make no difference at all if he paid lip service to one rather than the other. Vahan would have tried to analyse the paradox, but Raffi just took his feelings for granted.

So that afternoon, Raffi went on one of his rare trips into town to seek the help of old Hassan, the local rubbish collector who had always been a friend of the family. There were no Armenian males left in the town to whom Raffi could turn for help, at least as far as he knew. Hassan blinked and hesitated when Raffi explained the task he required, but he did not refuse. Hiding their spades in bags, they carried the old lady's body, wrapped in the blanket, laid her across the donkey and set off.

The gates of the Armenian cemetery were open, but Hassan drew the line at going inside. He and Raffi began digging a grave just outside in the grass by the gates. They had not gone far when an army officer came by on a horse. Leaning down he said to Hassan, whom he recognised,

"*Giavour* or Islam?"

Hassan was tongue-tied and speechless, but Raffi quickly answered in his place –

"We don't know, sir, as we found her already dead in one of the empty Armenian houses."

"Well, take her down to the Muslim cemetery just in case," suggested the officer. He then lit a cigarette and trotted off. Hassan stared at Raffi, and there was a long moment of silence between them.

"Hassan, I can't do it – I simply can't."

"Oh for God's sake, Raffi, what does it matter where she's buried? Her own God will no doubt claim her. Come on, that man is a fellow who could easily come back to check on what we're doing."

"I can't do it, I can't. Mother will collapse with the shock."

"Look, I have every respect, as you know, for Mariam hanum – but just don't tell her. I can't take the risk, if he comes back and takes a look under the blanket and sees the shroud, we're in for it – you're dead, and I'll be badly beaten."

Raffi was momentarily lost, not knowing what to do. But he was growing up fast. He grabbed one of the spades.

"Hassan, my good friend, start walking the donkey and the old lady away towards the Muslim cemetery as you are supposed to do. Go in a circle. I'll finish the grave here. When you get back it'll only take a moment to tip her in and bury her."

It was of course a totally unnecessary risk. Neither of them could have explained why they persevered. However, when Hassan did as suggested and returned, it did indeed take only a moment to bury the old lady. Raffi pulled away the blanket, as the first clods of earth were hastily piled back onto the resplendent shroud.

When in due course he recounted these events to Mariam, Raffi somewhat mischievously paused at the point that they had been ordered to bury the body in the Muslim cemetery. Mariam paled and almost fainted. Raffi knew, then, that he had been right to take the risk, seeing his mother's face clear, as he hastily proceeded with his narrative.

It was not long after this incident that the police arrived at the house. One of the new neighbours, a displaced Turkish family who had moved in from Russian-occupied Erzurum, had seen Raffi on the roof and denounced him to the police.

Quite by chance, that same morning a Turkish family, the wife, sisters and elder daughter of a certain Major Suleyman – an old acquaintance of Garabed – had come visiting Mariam and her two daughters, whom they knew well. They were all sitting in his sisters' reception room taking coffee, when there was a knock at the front door.

Raffi never answered the door, but would make himself scarce whenever there was a unexpected knock. The policemen explained to Mariam, who had hastily covered her face with a yashmak, that they had been informed that there was a young man in the house. Mariam spoke loudly to make sure that Raffi could hear.

"Yes, it's true. My second son was here recently. However he demanded money from me, and when I told him that I didn't have any – he hit me here and ran away. I haven't seen him since."

"Madam, we intend to search the house. Please stand aside."

Raffi had long since slipped through into the private women's area of the large house. He walked into his sister's room. The Turkish ladies all began hastily drawing down their veils, looking at Raffi curiously. Raffi immediately faced the wall so as not to look at them. Under his breath, he told his sister, Sira, what was happening. She bundled Raffi into the next room as the Turkish women looked on excitedly. Shortly after this the police appeared outside the door to the area that would normally be 'haram' – forbidden – for any honest Muslim.

"Madam," the senior policeman addressed his remarks to Mariam, who was still with them, "we have to search the whole house."

"But officer, we have the family of Major Suleyman here visiting my daughter. They are inside, unveiled."

"Madame. Certainly, of course we cannot go in while they are unveiled. However, please ask them to veil themselves and then come through to the other part of the house where we have already looked."

Mariam knocked at the door, not knowing that Raffi was inside, and told Sira what was to happen. The ladies quietly donned their veils, while Sira went hastily to the next room where she bought out a feradjeh, and some ladies shoes, and quickly dressed Raffi in the loose gown and veil, whilst the ladies of the Major's household, now fully veiled, waited to be escorted out. Sira then opened the door, and she and the ladies walked out – each lady carefully looking down at the floor as they passed. However, the policemen too avoided looking at the ladies as they passed, trained as they were by years of culture and custom. They were already uncomfortable enough in that part of the house which would normally be 'haram' for any strange males. Raffi, in a state of terror and scarcely able to walk, shuffled past the policemen with downcast eyes as Sira waited behind to show the policemen round.

The lovely ladies of Major Suleyman's family said not a word, neither then nor later when they left the house. When it was the policemen's turn to leave, they told Mariam,

"We know full well that your second son is somewhere around. We'll be calling again we can assure you."

That night Raffi packed a small bag and took out his false papers. He kissed his mother passionately and said his farewells to everyone. Mariam's men would finally now all be gone. She took out the gold coins, now down to 15, and wrapping them up in a cloth gave them to him with her blessing. Raffi, with deep pride in his heart, mixed with the pain of parting, carefully counted out five, as his father had done, and returned the rest to her.

Raffi left early in the morning while it was still dark. He spent the whole morning in the dusty square, where the carriages and lorries set off for other towns, watching out all the time for police presence, and waiting for his chance to board.

CHAPTER 29

Garabed drives on

When Garabed arrived back up the hill at the ruined farmstead of the dead Sarkis, accompanied by Burhan, the 12 year-old son of Mustapha, the situation had not greatly changed. Adrineh was now looking somewhat less dishevelled. Both she and Nefise Hanum were gathered round the still recumbent figure of Anna. Neither woman appeared to have made any attempt as yet to comfort or deal with the problem of the naked Ara, who was still crouched up against the old wall of the farmhouse.

Burhan handed over the women's clothes to his mother. Garabed carefully looked away after nodding at the two women, and moved over to stand near the boy, wondering whether he could try once again to get through to him. Dusk was falling and Garabed felt that the first priority, if he couldn't do anything about the boy, was to start a fire somewhere. It was clear that no one was going to go back into the slaughter house that the farmhouse had become, and so, with Burhan's help in bringing twigs and then some wood, he prepared and lit a fire in the yard.

The flames immediately began to add a touch of warmth to the scene, as the dark began cutting out the sight of the devastation around. Continuing to ignore the two women still fussing around Anna, Garabed motioned to Burhan to fetch the pottery cup. Garabed filled it from the well and then went over to Ara, who had been watching all the activity around him, but clearly without much awareness of what was happening. He crouched beside the boy and tried to hold the cup up to his lips. But Ara, though now no longer screaming, turned his head away and squeezed up in a foetal position against the wall.

Garabed, in some irritation, backed away. At this point, Burhan, who had been watching this latest attempt to get through to Ara, came and took the cup. Burhan walked over and, for the first time, a tiny flicker of recognition came into the dulled eyes of the young boy.

Burhan held forward the cup, not pushing it demandingly towards the lips as Garabed had done, but offering it to be taken by the hand.

"Ara, my friend Ara, please drink some water."

For the first time Ara did not shrink back, but took the cup from Burhan's hand and began drinking. Once started, he asked for the cup to be refilled and drank and drank, as Burhan ran happily back and forth to the well.

Garabed did not take in the joy of the young Turkish boy, whose face was suffused with pure delight at succeeding, where an adult had failed. Burhan watched with satisfaction as his friend became increasingly aware of his surroundings, and within a few further moments, Ara took up the clothes Burhan had left by his side. Standing up, he began to dress himself.

It was a warm evening, and Garabed asked Burhan to go down to his father and bring back a spade. Nothing had been left intact in the Shahanian farm, and there were no tools anywhere. While Burhan was away, Garabed carried out the bodies of the four children, and lay them down side by side on the grass outside the courtyard. As he did this, Nefise looked across every so often in sorrow and sympathy, but Adrineh looked away continuing to ministrate to Anna. She could cry no more.

Garabed tried to be as discreet as possible, dragging the body of Sarkis across the courtyard to be laid alongside the children. When Burhan returned with the spade Garabed started digging. The bodies were buried in two shallow graves, Sarkis in one, and the four children together in the other. Anna had by now been washed and dressed by the two women, and Nefise persuaded Adrineh to come and stand by the mounds, as with arms outstretched and palms up to heaven in the fashion both of the Muslims and the Christians of the area. Garabed mumbled some words which at least sounded like prayers. To everyone's relief, Adrineh began crying again, but now softly and copiously, whilst Nefise hugged her close.

Gathering together the remaining clothes, Nefise squeezed the hand of the still weeping Adrineh and bowed to Garabed saying -

"May Allah preserve you, sir."

Garabed raised his hand to his forehead and bowed in his turn without saying another word. Burhan and Nefise returned home, taking the remaining clothes and the spade, but leaving the cup. Garabed tried to wrap his sheepskin coat round Ara, but the boy flinched away from his touch, clearly he could not accept the presence or touch of an adult male. Adrineh and Anna huddled together and fell asleep by the fire.

Though completely exhausted, Garabed could not sleep. He stared at the flickering flames, every so often throwing some more wood on the fire. What was he going to do now, where was he going to go? Suddenly, from being an active strong middle-aged man on the run with good prospects for survival, he had become saddled with a whole family: a woman who had just been raped, and who had lost her husband and four of her children; a totally traumatised young girl; a young boy, fearful, and who looked on him with suspicion. Whilst there were many possible courses of action open to him, one was quite impossible – there was no way he could now abandon them.

Garabed looked round, and there, wide-awake and staring at him with the intensity of madness, he caught the eye of Ara, lying nearby. Garabed shuddered a little, turned on his side, and eventually dropped off into a troubled sleep in the early hours of the morning.

The next morning, with no food available and just some water, Garabed had to start making some decisions. Adrineh clearly looked to him, as she would have done to her husband. It was impossible to stay – sooner or later, the authorities from the village below would catch up with them. Questions would be asked as to why Sarkis, or whoever was at the farm, had not left with the other deportees, but where were they to go, and how?

Garabed finally decided. He strode down to Mustapha's farm in the hope of catching him before he started work in the fields.

"Mustapha, *effendi*, I will have to leave today, and I must take Sarkis' remaining family with me."

"You are right, Garabed bey. It is not safe for you to remain here. I have spoken with my wife, and we are prepared to take in the boy Ara. We don't require him to take up Islam, but we will want to have him circumcised, both for his and our own protection. It has already been decreed that anyone harbouring Armenians will be punished."

"I will put it to Adrineh hanum. I thank you, but I don't believe that she will want to break up what remains of the family. May I propose that Adrineh formally gives you all her husband's farm. If you have some paper – any paper will do – I will write out a formal gift and get her to put her mark. Perhaps in return you might be in a position to let us have two of your donkeys."

Garabed knew it was not a fair exchange. After all, once they had left, Mustapha could have walked up and simply taken the land. However, it might be of help to Mustapha in the future to have some evidence of formal ownership, and he agreed. Garabed then produced one of the invaluable gold coins, deciding to keep the already changed notes. He handed the coin to Mustapha saying –

"Mustapha *effendi*, I would request you to load one of the donkeys with any spare rice or provisions you can manage. Perhaps your son, may Allah be with him always, could walk them up the hill. We will be leaving as soon as possible, but will be going on up the hills and away from the valley."

Mustapha took the gold and nodded. The two men looked at each other for a long moment, and then without a further word, Garabed turned and walked back up the hill.

When Burhan arrived later that morning, Adrineh and Garabed put her silent and distracted daughter astride one of the donkeys. The other donkey was laden with a bag of rice, a pan, a bag of onions and two squawking hens tied by their legs.

Burhan tried to embrace Ara, but stopped as soon as he felt Ara flinch. He salaamed Garabed and stood watching as the little party trudged away. Garabed led the laden donkey in front, followed by Ara walking firmly alongside his sister, making sure that she did not fall. Adrineh brought up the rear.

Garabed had decided to make for Diyarbekir and Mardin, which were on the way to Aleppo, but to keep away from the recognised roads and tracks. On the first night, he discovered that the admirable Mustapha had hidden at the bottom of the bag of onions an old but usable pistol, with some ammunition. Not much use against a band of determined men, but maybe enough to ward off the individual robber.

Day after day passed as the little party walked on, avoiding any towns or villages, and, indeed, any human habitation at all, as far as possible. Garabed moved along in a sort of daze, but he knew the country and managed, almost absent-mindedly, to avoid the bands of Kurds and lawless men roaming the countryside and looking for giavours to rob and murder. They had been travelling for about two weeks, when Garabed became aware that they were now coming out of the bare mountainous terrain, and that there were more and more villages to be avoided. He began to see the occasional camel, and the days were getting warmer.

One night, Garabed awoke in the early hours of the morning and lay staring at the stars above him. He became aware of the sound of very soft weeping. He turned quietly onto his side and looked at the form of Adrineh lying beside him. Garabed pushed off his sheepskin coat. There was no analysis, no thought process, he moved over and wrapped his arms round the silently weeping woman. Adrineh herself responded immediately, though her weeping continued. Her arms came up to envelop him. Garabed moved gently across her and their lips sought each others with tenderness, but without a sound.

Garabed fumbled with his trousers, whilst Adrineh did the same with her rough and tattered skirts. Silently, and scarcely moving at all, Garabed and Adrineh made love, not mechanically, but with a desperation that had little to do with affection.

As they continued, during the day, to move down from the Anatolian plateau towards the Syrian desert, their nightly encounters became more and more passionate. They were still very cautious as they travelled, with their eyes peeled for strangers and possible robbers, yet they scarcely said a word to each other during the day, and certainly there was no acknowledgement of their night-time trysts. The physical comfort they gave each other in the middle of the nights, was a simple gift after the rigours of the days.

It was probably about five days later that the daily rhythm of their travels came to an abrupt end. Garabed's increasing eagerness to find relief in Adrineh's arms had, by now, inspired him with greater confidence. The coupling had become more passionate and less silent. So it was that on this occasion, in the midst of his passion, Garabed felt a sudden presence, a warning, a sixth sense of danger. He stopped and looked up. Staring down at him with mad, inflamed eyes, stood Ara. Held in his hand was the long knife originally bought by Garabed in Malatya. Adrineh was still wriggling below him, but she quickly sensed that Garabed had become suddenly still, and although she had no idea what was happening, she opened her eyes and looked up at Garabed, who was staring up at something behind her.

The tableau of this threesome – with Ara glaring at Garabed in a tremor of rage, with Garabed breaking away gently from

Adrineh but keeping his eyes warily on Ara, and with Adrineh just staring up at Garabed – held for a long, impossible moment. Then with an almost insane scream, Ara lifted the knife and shouting incoherently –

"turk – kurd – beast – murderer" he struck down at Garabed with all his boyish force.

Garabed had had sufficient time not to be taken totally off guard. His arms were still around Adrineh. With all his considerable strength, he rolled the two of them away as the knife came down, but he felt it slice through his arm. With all passion spent, and now free of Adrineh, he jumped up, blood pouring from his arm.

Ara screamed again, dropped the knife and turned and ran off into the night. Anna, who had woken and seen all, was gibbering and muttering, but for the first time there was some reaction in her eyes. Even in that dramatic moment, as Garabed sat heavily down on the ground holding his bleeding arm, the thought came to him that Anna had either gone completely insane, or she had been jolted out of the dazed trauma of the last few weeks.

"Garabed, Garabed," said Adrineh, addressing him familiarly for the very first time in their relationship, "What happened? What happened? Your arm is bleeding – come let me see it – what happened – was that Ara? Oh my God what happened, where has he gone?"

"Adrineh, my love," Garabed responded with affection to her first words of intimacy, "Ara must have woken up and was watching us. I suppose you must know how much your son knows about the facts of life. In any event, what he saw tonight must have brought his mind back to … Well you know … and how could he tell the difference?"

Garbed stopped and then called out, "Ouch – that hurt," as Adrineh poured some precious cold water over the wound and tied a rag tight above the wound to stop the flow of blood.

It was pitch black, and there was no question of anyone going to look for Ara before morning. Anna, still muttering, moved over to cling fiercely to Adrineh. This was the first positive emotion that Garabed and Adrineh had seen, since that terrible day. Adrineh held her tight, and they all sat quietly together as they waited for the sun to rise from the east. Garabed felt that he received more affection from Adrineh during these few hours, as they sat together waiting for the sun to rise, than in all the passion of the previous nights.

At first light, Garabed rose, splashed his face, took up his knife, and with one of the donkeys, set off to look for Ara. They were in a fairly populated area, and before leaving, he carefully took out the old pistol, loaded it and handed it to Adrineh.

"My darling, you know how to use this I'm sure. If anyone approaches point it and first fire away if they look like molesting you. Ara looked as if he would run for ever and only stop when he became completely exhausted – so it might be some time before I get back. But don't worry, I'll find him. I'll find him, I promise you."

This was a countryside of scrub and low hills, interspersed with cultivated fields that were surrounded by small boundary stones. There were no woods, but only the occasional single tree and no bushes at all, so there was no cover anywhere. Garabed walked round the campsite in ever increasing circles until he was fairly sure which way the boy had run. He then set off in that direction.

He was surprised and worried by how far the boy appeared to have gone. It was two hours or more before he finally saw the huddled form of the young boy, fast asleep, nestled up against a solitary rock. Garabed stopped, leaving the donkey, and considered the best approach to the problem, without alarming the boy unnecessarily. He slowly shook the boy by the shoulder.

"Ara, my son, Ara, my soul, my son Ara."

The boy still half asleep stretched up his hands as Garabed, straining with the effort, picked up the boy in his arms.

"Father, father," Ara cried and clung on tightly to Garabed, laying his head on to his shoulder, with his cheek firmly against Garabed's.

Garabed walked slowly back to where he had left the two women, followed docilely by the donkey. He held Ara tightly in his arms, without the slightest intention of putting him onto the back of the donkey, brought along specifically for that purpose. The boy was heavy, and the wound in his arm began bleeding again. But short of food though he was, exhausted, desperate and short of sleep, Garabed never faltered, never once contemplated removing the boy from the position he had adopted but weaved his way back, feeling a sense of triumph that he had not felt for weeks.

There was less than a kilometre left to go when, in the clear morning air, two gunshots rang out ahead of him.

CHAPTER 30

Selim and the Arab dimension

After the funeral service for his father, Selim decided, without much hesitation, that he could not return to Robert College to resume his studies.

Although he had never been very close to his father, his death had inevitably come as a shock, and he felt that he needed to make some sort of a clean break with his past. He had known his father, Nazim, as an educated, honourable and dignified man, always carefully correct in his dealings with everyone. However, Nazim had always kept him at arm's length, believing, somewhat like Colonel Bridgeman, Harry's father, that sons should not be shown too much overt affection by their fathers. Unlike his mother, Selim felt no bitterness towards the men who had caused his father's death, but they had inevitably become the enemy, and this in turn coloured his thoughts of Olga. Finally, like all the young men in these years, Selim felt the need to be part of the unfolding historical drama surrounding him. He could no longer remain a student.

He wrote a short note to Olga letting her know that he had decided to abandon the College and was considering joining the army.

Despite his mother's appeals, Selim soon went round to the local Army Board. He handed back his deferment papers, and asked to be taken into the army immediately on active service. Like Vahan, Selim had been seconded to the Harbiye officers' training establishment. He had been attending regularly there, and the Army took the line that he was, to all intents and purposes, fully trained. Selim expected to be sent to the Gallipoli front. He was therefore surprised and excited to hear that he was to be posted to Damascus, where he was to join one of the three Arab divisions stationed in Syria.

Before leaving, Selim wrote another short letter to Olga. She had answered his earlier letter very shortly telling him that she too was not going back to College. The death of Nazim at the hands of Armenian revolutionaries, and the arrest and deportation of Karekin at the hands of the state, had left them both anxious not to upset their respective mothers further. By a sort of mutual agreement, without actually communicating with each other directly, they had taken the decision not to meet. So, apart from simply telling Olga that he had been posted to Damascus, Selim made no further attempt at contact, and left from Haydar Pasha station in a state of excitement and anticipation.

The railway tunnels through the Taurus Mountains were still not completed – so Selim alighted at Belemlik, like everyone else, and travelled on, across the mountain passes to the end of the line on the other side, and then on by troop train to Damascus.

The triumvirate who ran the CUP and the Ittihad party consisted of Talaat, the sinister Minister of the Interior, Enver Pasha, the flamboyant Minister of War, and Djemal Pasha, once military governor of Istanbul, but now in charge of the whole Arab front. Just as Enver fancied himself as a great general, so Djemal Pasha also believed himself to be a great leader of men. Enver's absolutely disastrous campaign against the Russians at the start of the war, was mirrored in the south, when Djemal took command of the Ottoman Fourth Army and made a wild stab at crossing the Sinai desert to take the Suez Canal. He had been decisively defeated by the British in Egypt. Since that defeat, Djemal had settled in Damascus and had ruled, as Governor of

Greater Syria, the whole of the Arab vilayets of the Ottoman Empire, almost as a private fiefdom.

Once he had arrived in Damascus, Selim reported first, as ordered, direct to Djemal Pasha. Djemal was a large jolly man, the son of a respected army officer. Due to his large, corpulent frame he was known – to his great secret pleasure – as 'Buyuk Djemal'. He was a clever and ruthless man in his forties, and had been an early adherent to the Ittihad and a member of the CUP. Djemal, however, had been partly educated in Paris, and of all the Ittihad leaders he was the only one committed to the continuation of the multi-cultural aspect of the Ottoman Empire.

Within a few days of Selim's arrival, and his first interview with Djemal, he had been appointed to one of the three Arab divisions stationed in Damascus. His official position, for which he had the acting rank of Captain, was as a liaison officer between the division and the headquarters of Djemal himself. His job was to represent his commanding officer at headquarters, and to transmit any orders from Djemal back to the division.

Selim soon became aware of the simmering tension in the city. The attempts by a cabal of young English officers, in Cairo, to rouse the Arabic-speaking population of the Empire against the Ottomans, was well known to the astute Djemal and his staff. Secret societies, all with innumerable different proposals for the political future of the Arabs, abounded in the town. Djemal was aware of all of them, and periodically engineered a crack-down whenever they appeared to be getting out of hand.

Slowly, officer by officer and without any great publicity, Arab officers in the Fourth Army, together with many ordinary Arab soldiers, were being transferred to the killing grounds of the Gallipoli campaign. They were being replaced in Syria by Turkish officers. Selim had been a replacement for an Arab officer who went to Gallipoli and who, as Selim later discovered, died in the trenches like so many others.

The official motivation for this slow and steady draining of the Arabs from the army facing the British in the Levant, was based on the clear and reasonable belief that in Gallipoli, less than a hundred miles from Constantinople, the Ottoman Empire was fighting for its life. Here in Syria the battle was far less decisive, and so it was a valid military requirement that troops should be transferred to the area with greater military priority. However, Selim also saw that it was helpful to Djemal that most of the officers so removed, were often those active in the secret societies milling about amongst the Syrian elite.

Selim soon settled down in the town and started work with his unit and the HQ staff. A quick learner, he soon mastered vernacular Arabic and came to enjoy the café life of the town and the continual restless talk of the future for the Arabs within the empire. One day Djemal asked to see him in his office. Saluting, and standing to attention, he was offered him a chair.

"Selim, my boy, how do you like Damascus?" asked Djemal jovially

"Sir, I find it fascinating."

"And your work here?"

"Equally so, sir," replied Selim rather stiffly.

"Well now Selim. I want you to know that I have today arranged for your immediate commanding officer – Colonel Al-Hussein – to take over a post under General Mustapha Kemal in Gallipoli. He will be leaving shortly. Your new Commander will be arriving within a week, and as he is from Istanbul you will have that in common. I want you to help him to settle in quickly on his arrival."

"Certainly sir," replied Selim.

"Selim, my lad, I knew your father quite well in the days when I was military governor of the city. I was very sorry to hear of his death at Van. I remember him as a great supporter of the Ottoman imperial ideal – I'm sure you discussed these matters together. Where do you stand in our great debate. Please do speak frankly – we are all soldiers here, not politicians."

"Well, sir, my father and I did disagree at times on these matters. He was, as you say, a believer in Ottomanism – and I understand that in his younger days as a student, he was a member of that group who called themselves the Young Ottomans – you know, in Abdul Hamid's time. I, myself, however, have always believed that our nation should base itself on its Turkish national identity, rather than on any spurious imperial mission."

"And what about here – the Arabs? What about Islam and the Holy Places which we have guarded for so long? What about the Caliphate?" replied Djemal, leaning forward, watching for Selim's reaction.

"I don't know, sir, I really don't know. After only a few weeks here, I do see that they can't govern themselves – we are a necessary governing force in that sense. But, sir, isn't all this Caliph business really nonsense, to us?"

"Hmm – maybe," said Djemal, fiddling with a pencil on his desk. "Leaving aside the Arabs then, what about all the various Christian sects living amongst us for centuries – the Orthodox, the Jacobites, the Armenians – what's to happen to all them?"

"Well, sir, the problem does go much deeper than, perhaps, I first thought."

"Now listen, Selim. I believe you attended for some years at Robert College. You must have met many races there, and you must have met Armenians. I believe your father – who put on that great concert, last April wasn't it – or March? – had many Armenian friends."

Selim's interest quickened, but he remained silent waiting for what was coming – probably the real reason he had been summoned here.

"Look, I have said all this to you, because I need to know whether the death of your father at Van means that you can't deal with Armenians anymore. I want you to undertake, for me, a somewhat delicate task. But I wouldn't want you to do it, if it would be objectionable to you in any way."

"No sir, although I have to admit I now think of them as the 'enemy', but I have no prejudice against them – on the contrary," replied Selim.

"Right. Here in town, I have been approached by the Dashnaks – you may have heard of them, they're an Armenian political society, which I might add, I believe to have terrorist connections."

"Yes, sir, I'm well aware of them."

"Well, I've agreed to meet them and see what they want, and I want you to arrange it. I'll give you an address, and I want you to meet their representatives and bring them to see me here, in this office, as discreetly as possible. Can you do this for me – it's got to remain a tight secret of course."

"Certainly, sir."

"You have, I suppose, heard of the deportations and killings going on amongst the Armenian population in Eastern Anatolia. Many are being driven towards us in Aleppo, and I believe people are dying in their thousands."

"Only by rumour, sir," replied Selim, "Nothing like this seems to be happening in Istanbul."

"No, well ... well yes ... it's all very difficult. Stamboul is, of course, different. Thank you Lieutenant, you may go now. I'll be in touch with you later with details about the arrangements I want you to supervise."

Over the next few weeks after this conversation, Selim had collected two well-dressed and middle-aged Armenian business men three times from a nondescript address in the bazaar – clearly used only as a meeting place. He had then escorted them through the sentries and directly to the inner office of Djemal pasha. Selim never discovered exactly what was discussed between Djemal and these representatives of the Armenian Revolutionary Federation, a legitimate Armenian political party for some, but a treasonable terrorist organisation for others. Either way, Selim understood that Djemal was sticking his head out on this, one way or another.

Selim came to have considerable respect for Djemal as a man of great intelligence. He recognised that Djemal, like Selim's own father, was an Ottomanist at heart. Selim, in many further conversations, could see that Djemal looked at all the wonderful diversity of the peoples of the Empire, and didn't want to lose it. It was the old argument going on, round and round, as to the future of the region.

As the meetings grew longer, Djemal became less open with Selim, who felt he was now being kept at arm's length by his superior. Eventually, after a few more weeks, Selim heard that he had been promoted to full Captain on the recommendation of Djemal, and been posted to the garrison at Baghdad, facing the advancing British Indian army, moving slowly up the Tigris from their outpost in Basra.

Within days of his arrival at Baghdad, Selim was sent to his new unit, several miles away down the Tigris. This was part of the stand taken by the Turkish forces against the Indo-British army, commanded by General Townshend, which was advancing very slowly up the river heading for Baghdad. General Townshend had arrived at Basra, starting this advance in that same ill-fated month of April, which had also seen the landings at Gallipoli.

The Ottomans had been unable to do anything about the initial British landing. They had only a few weak Arab units there, operating at the end of a long and tortuous supply line. However, as Townshend's troops were brought up, until they were only some 50 miles south of Baghdad, his supply lines became longer and equally tortuous. Meanwhile the supply lines for the Turkish forces were becoming easier, and correspondingly shorter.

Selim joined an Arab unit, officered entirely by Turks, and found himself overseeing a slow retreat, as the British were drawn further and further away from Basra. Selim was in the middle of a countryside of swamps and deserts, without roads of any kind. Everything – men and materials, arms and even basic food – had to move up and down the meandering and shallow River Tigris. The conditions were terrible. There were maddening and sickening swarms of flies and mosquitoes. Pestilence and fever was in the air, and the climate was hot, sticky and lethal for the Turks, used to the more equable north. The Arab soldiers were immune, but on the one side the British were losing more men to disease than to any military action, and, on the other, the city-bred Turkish officers, were also succumbing.

Fighting was continuous, and Selim was always in the forefront. So it was that while commanding a Company holding back a British patrol, sent forward in advance of the main army,

Selim received a bad wound in the lower part of his arm. After the skirmish died down, he retired and had the wound roughly patched up at the main camp. There were no sedatives of any kind, and after drinking a half bottle of raki, he went to his tent to rest.

The next morning Selim awoke, with his face swollen and unable to open his eyes, and with a raging fever. Delirious and often unconscious, death in these circumstances tended to follow within days. His arm was infected and would need medical attention, and was poisoning his system. As the British were advancing more slowly each day, Selim had to be immediately evacuated back to Baghdad. There, in the still incredibly primitive conditions of the makeshift military hospital, Selim, was operated on. His increasingly gangrenous arm was cut off just below the elbow.

More dead than alive, it was decided he should be sent back to Constantinople. Once there, if he survived the journey, he could be treated at the military hospital at Uskudar.

So it was that in the company of a coach-load of other wounded and dying officers, Selim was transported across the whole of Anatolia, with his badly treated arm continuing to fester. In reality, he was being sent to die at the hospital at Scutari, where Florence Nightingale had first done so much to raise the vocation of nursing as a respectable profession.

CHAPTER 31

Harry and the Arab Bureau

The ship on which Harry had been serving, had made several further journeys to and from the Gallipoli staging areas, escorting supply vessels on their way out to the peninsula, and then hospital ships returning, loaded and crowded with the wounded..

Sooner or later, it was almost inevitable that Harry, a bright and knowledgeable regular officer who had already worked for several months in the Admiralty, would be transferred back to an Intelligence job. Despite his request to be left on active service, he found himself working at the Administrative Naval headquarters in Alexandria, a building situated near the Montazeh Palace at the far end of the corniche tramline.

Harry had only been stationed there for a few weeks, when he first met a young Polish deserter from the German navy, who was being employed by the Navy as a general translator. They met in the staff canteen, where the young man had approached Harry, as he sat alone, and asked to share his table. He introduced himself as André Tarkowski. Harry, looking up, saw a strikingly handsome young man with rather hard glittering eyes offset by a warm and charming smile, and as it later turned out a wealth of lively and interesting conversation.

Harry smiled, and indicating the empty seat said,

"Harry Bridgeman – Intelligence."

Then as he picked up his knife and fork to continue eating, a memory stirred, and he looked up.

"Hang on – weren't you a Radio Officer on the *Goeben*?"

André looked very startled, and glanced away for a moment. He dropped his fork with something of a clatter and bent down and fumbled for rather a long time picking it up. When he rose, his smile was firmly back in place.

"Why yes, certainly, I was indeed on the *Goeben* at the beginning of the war – I suppose you must have seen my file. As a Polish patriot, I found myself in a bit of a difficult moral dilemma. I felt unable to support the German Empire. I left the ship – well, look not to put any gloss on it, I deserted whilst I was on leave in Constantinople. I eventually made my way here, where I offered my services to the allies. So, here I am."

Harry reflected for a moment on the opinion given by the military attaché in the British embassy in Constantinople, who had interviewed this man. He recalled how the attaché's report had given a completely different slant on the reasons for Andre's desertion.

"Well! Well! What a coincidence! I was on the *Indefatigable*, you know, on the day before war began between England and Germany, when we passed the *Goeben* and the *Breslau* going in the opposite direction."

"I can't believe it," said André, "Good heavens, I remember it so well. What a dramatic moment! But how did you know that I was the Radio Officer on board that ship."

This time it was Harry's turn to hesitate before replying. He realised that he could not make any reference to the Report he had seen.

"Well, old man, as you are aware, I have indeed been looking through the files of our employees here, and I noticed yours – well, you know because of the fact that you had been on the *Goeben*."

As the days passed, both of them, being single, of the same age and without connections, became good, if not particularly intimate, friends. Harry had always been rather shy and diffident in his relationships with others. He was basically lazy when it came to personal contacts, and his friends tended to be those who were prepared to make the effort to keep in touch with him. André appeared to be such a person, an extrovert ready to make all the necessary effort to sustain the relationship on his own. He had a fund of interesting stories, and Harry was fascinated by the confident cosmopolitanism that seemed to surround him. There was always an exciting, almost sexual, tension whenever André was present, but he never forgot the comments made about his character in the Report. So, he kept a discrete distance between them, which André was always striving to overcome. This reserve was both natural to Harry's character and, in the circumstances, a necessary protection in their relationship.

Harry made no effort to try to find out more about André, but in due course André himself told him about a recent personal tragedy in his life. He explained that while hiding in Constantinople and waiting for the Embassy to issue travel documents for him, he had fallen deeply in love with a Greek girl. Harry, who remembered all the details of the Report, said nothing, but he was relieved when André openly and, without guile, talked about this aspect of his life.

"Elena and I – oh sorry, yes, that was her name – got the necessary travel documents, and as this was just before the outbreak of war, we managed to make it here to Egypt. Ah! Harry, what a wonderful period for me that turned out to be. Here we were living just for each other. An idyllic moment in the midst of terrible events."

"Gosh!" Harry replied, all his rather boyish naïve romanticism aroused. "What an experience – and what happened?"

"Terrible, Harry, terrible. I'd been working late at the Navy Office, and I came back soon after midnight to our little flat. When I got in, Elena was fast asleep, or so I thought. However, I sensed that something was wrong, and when I came to try and wake her, I coundn't tell whether she was dead or totally unconscious."

Harry stared at him.

"I immediately contacted a Doctor I knew who lived close by – a Swiss, Doctor Gurstein. The doctor rushed round as I was so distraught. He said that she had had a massive heart attack. At least she hadn't suffered, as it must have happened in her sleep. God, Harry, you can imagine how devastated I was. Thousands are dying daily in this awful war – but one death, like this, inevitably affects you more than a thousand others."

André buried his head in his hands, as Harry clumsily tried to comfort him by patting him on the back. But there was something – something about this event – which troubled Harry. He could not put his finger on it, but in due course he made a point of looking up and seeing the death certificate. He then felt ashamed, blaming his suspicions on the wartime atmosphere, as it all seemed quite clear. The certificate referred clearly to a coronary attack, and was duly signed by a registered practitioner – a Doctor Gurstein – who appeared to have lived in Alexandria for some years.

Harry watched and wondered as the horrific death toll of the Gallipoli campaign got worse and worse. Nothing that was tried ever seemed to go right. Harry recalled all those eager young Australians on the landing craft with him, on that April day earlier in the year. He wondered how many of them were still alive.

It was well into the winter of the year 1915 that the Gallipoli campaign was eventually wound up. By dint of a brilliant strategy, almost a quarter of a million Allied soldiers were evacuated in the very face of the enemy, and hardly a single life was lost. It was the only moment of glory in the whole mishandled campaign. Harry had long since lost any illusions of the glory of war, but he was thrilled by the sheer military brilliance of this event.

A group of young Englishmen, imbued with romantic ideas about Arab sheiks riding through the desert in flowing robes, were at that time organised in what was known as the 'Arab Bureau' in Cairo. They were obsessed with trying to engineer an Arab Revolt against the Ottomans. Their chosen method was to act through Sheriff Hussein of the Hejaz, the Ottoman-appointed nominee ruler of that province, which included the two Muslim holy cities of Mecca and Medina.

The Ottoman governor who would be in the firing line of such an outbreak, would be Djemal Pasha – the governor of Greater Syria, and of all the Arab provinces of the Empire. As it would be the Navy's task to give whatever logistical support would be necessary, if such a revolt could be instigated, Harry was instructed to begin a concentrated research study into the character of this man, known to be one of the three principle leaders of the Ittihad. Harry also began a consideration, on behalf of Naval Intelligence, of the whole Arab situation within the empire.

Harry had had the same basic educational background as these young officers of the Arab Bureau. They were all products of the English upper-middle class educational system – Oxbridge and ex-public school boys, with a strictly classical education. However, Harry was somewhat different. It was not just that he had become disillusioned by his experiences at Gallipoli. The adolescent conflict with his father, and his rebellion against the attempt to push him into the army, already separated him from his class peers. Above all, the fact that he had studied science, rather than the classics, also gave him a dissimilar outlook from those eager young officers of the Bureau.

Harry found himself questioning the romantic visions of these young men. As he researched their position more thoroughly, he saw that what real strength there was amongst the Arabs, lay in the great Arab towns of the fertile crescent – not with these flamboyant ideas of the hard-riding Bedouin tribes of Arabia. He could also see that when it came to the crunch, an intelligent Arab, from these great cities, would in the last resort, tolerate a foreign Muslim Imperial ruler, however decrepit and moribund, above a foreign Christian one.

It was in the middle of all this ferment of ideas and proposals passing between the young Oxbridge officers of the Arab Bureau in Cairo, and the more careful Naval Intelligence Services in Alexandria, that Harry was informed that a representative in Cairo of the Armenian Revolutionary Federation – the Dashnak party – had contacted the High Commission with an extraordinary proposal emanating directly from Djemal Pasha himself.

By this time, it was known that Harry had become the Navy's expert on the person of Djemal Pasha and the Arab dimension of the Empire. He was accordingly invited to go to Cairo to be at the meeting with the Armenians – together with Army Intelligence, officers from the Arab Bureau, and other experts on the question of the future of the Ottoman Empire.

On the day of the meeting, Harry took the tram along the corniche to the railway station and then the three-hour train journey, through the lush Egyptian delta, to Cairo. He stared out of the windows, which were always kept spotlessly clean, despite the soot and smoke of the engine. The train passed by the ancient panorama of the fellahin working in the fields, unchanged for centuries, with their patient camels and donkeys plodding round and round the picturesque water-wheels, tended by a small boy with a stick. A few looked up as the train passed. 'What great War?' they might well have asked.

A most extraordinary meeting then took place in a room at the British High Commission. There were several young English officers, all ready to carve up the Ottoman Empire in their own image. Lord Kitchener's current favourite and representative – Sir Mark Sykes – was present. Then there was, in addition, a young official representing the Foreign Office, three young officers – classical scholars from the Arab Bureau, two Army intelligence officers. and Harry.

Harry knew he would have to give a written report of the proceedings to his superiors, on his return. Never comfortable with speaking extemporaneously in public, it was his usual practice to jot down the entirety of his personal impressions of what occurred in his notebooks, like a diary entry, and use these notes to compile a report. Like so many Englishmen in his time and class he was more articulate on paper than in speech. On his return to Alexandria later in the day, he referred to his notes, which formed the basis of his report:

> "I went straight from the station, with its usual bustle and pandemonium to the High Commission building. Somewhat surprisingly, it was not particularly well guarded, and I was directed, without much interrogation, to a large boardroom. This looked out on the gardens of the compound, and was cool and shaded by blinds. There were electric fans in the ceiling and a wonderful mahogany table in the middle of the room.
>
> There were several people in the room already when I arrived. I remember in particular the three young men from the Arab Bureau – an Oxford Archaeologist, Philip Graves a journalist from the Times, and another young officer – Thomas Lawrence. However the most important person there was Sir Mark Sykes – a Tory MP – who was probably the oldest person there, but was not much more than 35. While he is a good and amusing talker – he has an easy and fluent turn of phrase that I envy – he tends to hold very strong opinions, and is impatient of any opposition. He is a committed Roman Catholic, a convert, and I believe that that factor is an important part of his make-up.
>
> After introductions and some general discussions between us, two Armenians were brought into the room,

and given seats at the end of the table. One was a young man – a hostile, dark-haired individual who introduced himself as Aris, from the city of Van. Throughout the whole of the proceedings, he looked as if he was about to explode. The other, the only man present who was over 40 years-old, was a tired-looking, grey-haired merchant who introduced himself as Sarkis Papasian. It was he who opened the discussion, informing us he had been told, in great secrecy, by party members in Damascus, that Djemal Pasha had indicated a willingness to overthrow the current government, if he could count on the support of the Allies.

"How did you get this information," asked one of the officers. It was the young Aris who replied, speaking rather brusquely,

"I was present at one of the last discussions between my party's leaders in Damascus, and Djemal himself. We were regularly taken to see him in his private office by a Turkish officer, a member of his staff."

"It appears," continued Sarkis, "that Djemal wishes to distance himself from the terrible massacres and deportations of Armenians currently taking place in Anatolia and is prepared to act to save those surviving Armenians, still in the area, if he can get allied support."

One of the Arab Bureau's delegates shook his head, and looking directly at the Sarkis.

"So, why should we be that interested in saving Armenians. Djemal's got it all wrong if he thinks that is a priority in Allied thinking. In fact, it is providing amazingly good propaganda for us against the Central Powers."

I have to say that while I did tend to agree with what the young man said, it wasn't very tactful in the circumstances. I felt rather uncomfortable. As it was, after this comment, the scowling Aris jumped up and was about to say something when Sarkis pulled him down and muttered something to him in Armenian. I've learnt a few words of Armenian while in Alex, and all he said was – "my boy, sit down and keep calm".

The old man then continued, "Look, I believe that the same suggestions proposed by Djemal have been passed on to the Russian foreign ministry, and Sazonov has already indicated that the Russian government are interested. Djemal has proposed, with allied help to march on Constantinople, depose the Sultan and the current government, and set up a new regime."

The young foreign office official, who to my mind had been looking more and more ill at ease, nodded his head at this.

"Yes I can confirm that we have indeed heard something along these lines from the Russians. The proposal seems to be to create a new Empire, including a Turkish Anatolia, a greater Syria, an autonomous Christian Armenia, and a Kurdistan, all under a new Imperial dynasty – I suspect probably Djemal himself."

At this point, Sykes, making sure that he had everyone's attention by rapping on the table, started speaking for the first time. "Our political masters would not agree. Our friends, the French, will insist on taking most of Syria, and I am already in negotiation with Monsieur Picot on that. Also, frankly, we have our own eyes on Mesopotamia at the very least. Forget Djemal's proposals – we can finish off the Ottomans without his help."

Sykes then stood up and surveyed us all as if he was going to give a speech in the House of Commons. Totally ignoring the two Armenians, sitting somewhat disconsolately at the other end of the table, he announced, as indeed I'm sure he will report later in writing to Kitchener, and as I have carefully noted, word for word –

"Never mind all the natives, Armenians, Jacobites, Maronites, whatever. This ramshackle middle-eastern Empire must cease to be. Smyrna can become Greek, Adalia – Italian, Cilicia and Syria – French, Filistine and Mesopotamia – British, and everything else can go to the Russians – yes even including Constantinople itself. Gentlemen, I shall sing a Te Deum in Constantinople in the

Santa Sophia, and a Nunc Dimittis in Jerusalem in the mosque of Omar. We'll even be prepared to sing it in Polish or Armenian or Welsh, in honour of those gallant little nations, bless their bleeding hearts."

I have to say that I was frankly surprised. It was not the lack of empathy or the hard-edged rudeness that struck me. It was the fact that it was so unnecessary. Surely, simple silence would have sufficed. However, perhaps I'm wrong, and it might indeed be kinder to be clear about our own priorities right from the start. In any event, I looked around and it didn't seem to have worried any of the others round the table, who smiled, but did have the grace not to look at the two strangers at the end of the table.

Aris stood up, fists clenched and eyes smouldering, but once again the elderly Sarkis was too fast for him. He too stood, and holding Aris by the arm tightly, in order to make sure that he said nothing, turned and said to everyone in the room –

"Gentlemen – we have carried out our task – no doubt you will have your own ways of communicating with Djemal Pasha if you want to. For us, the priority was to prevent the murderous and genocidal death of our people in central and eastern Anatolia. I see that, sadly, your priorities are different. But gentlemen, bear in mind that you have not as yet conquered the lands you are busy dividing up amongst yourselves. You may well, in your internal intrigues and conspiracies with the French, be storing up great problems for the future in this vital area. Beware, gentlemen, beware of the quagmire you may be creating for future generations to deal with."

I expected the young Aris to make some more remarks, but the two Armenians then left without another word. I returned on the 7.00 pm train."

Harry did not record that after the Armenians left, Sykes and the young men of the Arab Bureau spent the next hour discussing and dismissing the Djemal proposals. This was followed by a further happy and stimulating hour, which they spent drawing lines across the map of the Ottoman Empire, as their young fancies and romantic ideals led them. For all of them, including Harry, this land was a blank playground for their romantic and heroic impulses, not a place where people had lived and died for centuries.

Harry knew that he should keep these notes safe, and he put them in a small file in the bottom drawer of his desk, after preparing and submitting his official typed copy marked 'Secret and Confidential' to his superiors.

It was about a week later that he came into his office to find André waiting to see him, as he often did these days. He had been sitting at his desk in his chair as Harry walked in. André rose immediately with a ready grin and started his usual friendly chat.

That afternoon, when Harry was looking through the Djemal papers, he imagined that they were no longer in the order that he had left them. This worried him, but then he decided it must be his own memory at fault. He arranged to have them burnt.

CHAPTER 32

Mikael and Olga

The police station in Yedikule was at the southern edge of Stamboul, right up against the great Theodosian walls of the city as they came down to the Marmara Sea. Mikael, held firmly between two burly policemen, was dragged, rather than walked into the station, still retching and with his lips and nose bleeding.

"Name," rapped out the sergeant at the desk.

Mikael did not reply, but looked up at the officer with the dark look that was his unfortunate trademark.

"His name, sergeant, is Mikael Sarafian, and he's a fucking *giavour* deserter," said the policeman, putting the papers down on the desk, and indicating the out-of-date pass.

"Put the bastard in the cells," said the sergeant dismissively.

"One of the public ..."

"No," interrupted the sergeant, looking meaningfully at the three policemen, "in one of the single ones down below."

Mikael was taken down to the basement. He was thrust into a dismal dungeon, stone-walled, without any window, and a single, dim electric light swinging from the damp roof. There, almost absent-mindedly, he was punched, thrown to the floor and kicked as a matter of course, rather than viciously. He lay there, spitting blood and thinking – 'well I suppose it could have been worse – I'm in for it when I get back to the army'. He lay there imagining the more formal punishment that would be awaiting him when he was returned to his unit.

However that night, the desk sergeant accompanied by a couple of guards, came into the cell, where Mikael sat on the bench, propped up against the wall – the only item of furniture. Then, without a word, Mikael was systematically beaten for half an hour. Dragged up from the bench, he was repeatedly punched in the face and stomach until he collapsed on the floor. There, he was struck over and over again with the sergeant's thick cane, while the two guards kicked him continuously as he lay curled up on the floor, trying hopelessly to protect his genitals. The men never said a word, and the only sound was Mikael's screams. However, the screams soon became moans. Mikael did not have a very compact body and, mercifully, he finally passed out. He did not recover consciousness until long after the three men had left the cell.

Mikael was left bleeding and alone in the dimly lit cell for over 24 hours, without food or water, lying in his own urine. Early the next morning, having been reported to his regiment, three soldiers accompanied by a young lieutenant, came down to the cell to take him back to the unit headquarters.

"Good God! What the blazes has happened to him?" the officer asked the guard who had opened the cell door.

"I believe he tried to escape and had to be restrained," replied the guard.

"For heaven's sake! Some restraint!," said the young lieutenant. "What do you say soldier?" he addressed Mikael.

"Water, water please," Mikael managed to croak through cracked and bloody lips, though he was barely conscious – his body a mass of pain.

"Bloody hell! Take him out, wash him down and give him some water, and let's get going from this place. Is there a shower or a hose or something here?" the young man addressed the guard.

Mikael was carried out into the courtyard where he was undressed, hosed down, and after lying on the floor naked for a few minutes, was given a blanket to wrap round himself. He was totally incapable of standing on his two feet, so he was carried out of the police station and put into the army carriage which was waiting outside.

Mikael himself, startled into wakefulness by the cold water and the movement, kept sliding in and out of consciousness. He barely registered what happened to him during the next 48 hours, and was only able to piece together events much later.

Driven back to the city headquarters of his unit through the streets of Stamboul and out through the gates, he was eventually seen by an army doctor. It was immediately clear to the doctor that the soldier was much closer to death than had appeared at first sight. After careful examination, the doctor diagnosed that apart from the terrible bruises and outward damage, Mikael had a ruptured liver, and his kidneys were not functioning properly. Either way, the army could not possibly have him back on active duty as he was.

The administrative officer of the regiment – the unit and Mikael's commanding officer were already stationed in the Gallipoli peninsula – decided that he should be sent immediately to the military hospital at Scutari. What happened if he didn't die there could be considered later. Thus it was here, some days later, in one of the huge and rather shabby wards, that Mikael eventually first regained consciousness and opened his eyes.

Bending over him, looking anxious, was his old boyhood friend, Loris, dressed in a white, or rather a once-white, coat, obviously a hospital orderly of some sort or another.

"Loris – oh my friend Loris – did you manage to get the

apricots," murmured Mikael with a smile of recognition, and then drifted off into oblivion again.

Mikael recovered very slowly as the weeks went by. His friend Loris visited him everyday and made sure that he got all the attention and medication that the harassed doctors prescribed. Without that personal attention, Mikael would undoubtedly have been neglected, like so many of the others, and would most probably have died.

Mikael later discovered that on being called up, Loris had claimed to be a qualified Vet. He had hoped thereby to be put in charge of the Army's horses and mules – and it was true that he did know something about animals, as his father kept a small herd of cows in their ramshackle old house on the outskirts of Makrikoy. When he was not at school, Loris often went with his father delivering milk to the terraced houses in the town, and the grander houses up the hills above the Valli Effendi racecourse.

However, in true army style, recognisable in armies all over the world, this claim had not resulted in a posting as a vet, but as a hospital orderly attached to a certain Doctor Turhan, who practised at the military hospital in Uskudar. Here, Loris had, with great good fortune, and the support of Doctor Turhan, eventually been allocated a tiny room of his own at the back of the enormous barracks/hospital.

As Mikael's health slowly improved and he became able to shuffle about, he began to spend more and more time in Loris' tiny den. He knew that it was unlikely he would ever fully recover, so spent his time trying to improve his hitherto rather cursory education. He began reading voraciously any book he could lay his hands on.

As there were not, after all, that many Armenians working at the Barracks hospital in Uskudar, it was inevitable that Loris would eventually come across Olga Avakian. Olga used to stay in the nurses' dormitory at least four or five days every week. She returned to Makrikoy for her days off, but even when on duty, there were many moments when the staff interacted. Loris had indeed seen Olga several times, but they had done nothing more than nod at each other.

There was a considerable shortage of female nurses. Normally, these would have been provided by the minority populations – the Greeks, Armenians and Jews. Turks of the old school did not encourage their daughters in this sort of work, and this feeling had not changed much even for the modernisers. However, the news filtering in throughout the summer of the killing fields in Anatolia had left the Armenian community fearful and wary of courting attention, and so there were no other Armenian nurses left. This meant that all the girls were overworked, and that Olga had only Greeks and Jews as colleagues.

It was Dr. Turhan who on one occasion drew Loris' particular attention once again to Olga –

"Loris, my boy, did you know that one of our most conscientious nurses here is an Armenian girl. She's really very good. Every time she works with me, she seems to have learned more than the last time. I understand that she often stays at the hospital in the female staff dormitory. You should make an effort to meet her."

"Certainly, sir, thank you, I'll make a point of it," answered Loris, without any intention of following it up. All his attention was given over to the frail Mikael, whose condition remained critical, even though he had now begun to regain some mobility. Every movement was still painful.

Loris and Mikael had been close boyhood friends in the little Armenian school in Makrikoy. They had clambered over the walls of the wealthier houses, in the Osman Agha area of the town, above the racecourse, and stolen apricots and peaches from the ample orchards there. They had kept watch for each other. They had wrestled together in their early teens, combats which would inevitably be won by the bigger and heavier Loris who would end up sitting astride the frailer Mikael, demanding an abject surrender which would never be given.

Loris had spent Mikael's first month at the hospital feeding him, bathing him, ministering to him on a daily, almost hourly, basis. There was not a spare moment that he did not spend with Mikael; first by his bedside, and then as Mikael began to shuffle about the corridors, alongside each other on the bed in the little room. Here they would reminiscence about their past, and make rather impractical plans for the future. Whenever Loris finished work, he would often come back to his room to find Mikael had been there most of the day reading.

Soldiers from the Gallipoli campaign kept pouring in every day, all with the most horrendous wounds – a new and terrible reality for all the combatants of the Great War. Everyone was overworked and overtired, and thus it was that Dr. Turhan and Olga had worked together since the early morning on the emergency cases flooding into the hospital. All were stretched to their limit. Both Olga and the doctor had been on duty without a break, with nothing to eat for ten hours since their shift began at six o'clock in the morning. The doctor's hand slipped for the second time as he and Olga began stitching up a wound. There was a gasp from Olga and the other nurse as the doctor hastily corrected himself, and finished the task.

"Yes ... Yes ... All right Nurse Avakian. We're both exhausted. Neither of us can do any more good here. Nurse Stefanides, please clear up here and make sure this soldier is given a bed in my ward. I'll get Doctor Fadil to take over – he should have been on duty by now anyway. Nurse Avakian, I believe you know the room belonging to Loris Sarafian. I think you'll find him there as he should be going on duty in an hour or so. Please go and tell him to report to Doctor Fadil immediately. Then you must go and get some sleep yourself – that's an order."

Olga washed up, took off her white apron, dressed and went off rather reluctantly to find Loris' room. Contrary to what the good doctor thought, she had never been invited there, and was not too sure exactly where it was. She had never spoken to Loris except for some cursory professional pleasantries. She was aware that he was not in the slightest bit interested in her, and furthermore, she thought he would already be on duty in view of the current state of emergency in the hospital. So she didn't hurry, but nevertheless trudged up the stairs and knocked on the door. Somewhat to her surprise there was a call from inside –

"Yes. Come in, the door's open."

Olga walked in. She saw a thin, frail man, dressed in the regulation pyjamas and a threadbare dressing gown, lying on the bed, reading a slim book. He had dark and feverish black eyes, with a hard and haughty look in them. Mikael, still on the bed, put down his book, and stared up at the tired looking girl with reddened eyes, still with a remarkable sparkle in them. A girl, whose commonplace, even dowdy dress, seemed to hang on her effortlessly, with elegance and grace.

Mikael struggled to stand up off the bed, and at that point his whole life changed yet again. Olga's face softened, and she gave him a warm and devastating smile, putting forward a firm restraining hand saying,

"Please don't, sir. Lie still. Can I see what book you're reading?"

She leant forward and took the book from his fingers as he sank back on the bed.

"Ah. Namik Kemal – the early poetry. You admire his work? Are you a friend of Loris or a patient? My name by the way is Olga – Olga Avakian." And she held out her hand to the supine Mikael.

Mikael had none of the shyness with girls usual in the young men of the Ottoman world. He sat up on the bed, shook Olga's hand, and moved his feet off the bed inviting Olga to sit on the bed next to him.

Without any embarrassment, Olga sat down.

Working flat out since the early morning, Olga was tired. For his part, Mikael, though on the mend, was always in residual pain, particularly towards the end of the day. Nevertheless they talked together in Armenian for two hours. Only once did Olga get up and go and fetch some water, but she hurried back immediately. They soon discovered that they both lived in Makrikoy. They had even attended the same early primary school, though of course at different times, he in the boys section and she in the girls. As Olga described her house and her life, Mikael thought to himself that she probably lived in one of the grand houses that he and Loris had raided for illicit fruit when they were young.

This inconsequential chat, which they were both enjoying, could have gone on all evening, until, that is, the moment when Loris finally walked in – himself exhausted. Mikael tried to rise, experiencing an odd feeling of guilt.

"Hello – what's going on," said Loris as he took in the sight of Mikael trying to get up, and Olga sitting on the bed, smiling, with her eyes alight.

"Oh, hello Loris, I've been reading in your room. Er ... I suppose you know Miss Avakian ... er ... my friend Loris Temazian ... er ... you must know each other surely."

Olga remained seated on the bed between them as Mikael finally managed to stand up facing Loris.

"Are you well, Mikael, you look tired. Can I help you back to the ward?" Loris asked, ignoring Olga.

Olga scarcely had room to stand – but she did so at this stage, and faced Loris.

"Oh, Mr. Temazian, Dr. Turhan sent me up here to ask you to go on duty early, but you were already on duty when I got here. I've been chatting with your friend – we've discovered we are from the same town – isn't that a coincidence? Anyway, I must go now. Goodbye."

She flashed Loris a somewhat artificial smile and went out.

Loris looked at Mikael. He, too, saw a frail vulnerable body with the far too large black eyes; he too saw the shabby regulation pyjamas and the meagre gown and the fact that this man was still very ill. But Loris was seeing something more. He sighed and clasped Mikael round the shoulders.

"I'll walk you back, Mikael. You look really tired. I hope that girl didn't exhaust you. Please be careful of her, she has a bad reputation, and I believe she's a hopeless nurse – one of those rich spoilt girls playing at nursing. I'll see she doesn't worry you."

Then, he helped Mikael back to the crowded main ward.

Olga could not get the frail and rather prickly Mikael out of her mind. As the days passed, she often encountered Loris in the long, dreary and increasingly dirty wards of the old hospital. Any cleaning that was being attempted was not very effective, and the hospital probably looked little different from the days of the Crimean War.

Olga sensed very quickly that Loris did not approve of her. She began to try on all her rather flirtatious charm, which had been her stock-in-trade prior to her first contact with Selim. To her surprise and irritation, no amount of stunning smiles, sympathetic eye contact, nor any of her other weapons, made any difference. Loris remained indifferent, indeed even hostile, towards her. He never volunteered any information about Mikael, and made a point of telling her that Mikael remained very ill, and needed to be left alone.

Nevertheless, Olga took the trouble of regularly going to the enormous ward in which Mikael languished. She would sit by the side of his bed and chat to him, whenever she had the time. When she was with Mikael, she felt no need to exercise any artificial charm, but chatted freely and with spirit, enjoying the pleasure of mutual discovery. Slowly Mikael began to recover his strength, although Dr. Turhan said that his kidneys had been permanently damaged. Whenever he felt stronger, and if Olga had any free time, they would walk together along the hospital corridors, she in her ugly, regulation uniform, he in his threadbare dressing gown.

A rather unlikely affection began to grow between this aggressive but insecure, lower-class Armenian young man, and this confident, sophisticated, girl from the upper-middle class. Class distinctions in the Ottoman world were never anything like those in the much more class-conscious West. The Turks never had any entrenched, hereditary, ruling elite. Indeed, until the 18th century, most of the Turkish Viziers and ruling Pashas were technically 'slaves' of the Sultan, and rose and fell, independent of family background.

However, there was a considerable difference in education and sophistication between the wealthy professional and merchant classes of the City, and the porters, workers and small shopkeepers. On top of the obvious divisions within the City, neither side took much interest in the vast hard-working

Anatolian peasants of the countryside, of whichever race.

Day by day, regardless of any of these differences, Mikael and Olga became more and more friendly and intimate with each other. Olga, lonely at work, and with the rest of the family at home more and more involved in their own affairs, found a great source of strength in the growing relationship.

It was well into the winter when Loris told Mikael that he would be going to stay for a few days at the house of Dr. Turhan in Stamboul. It appeared that the doctor was due to attend a conference of army medical officers at the War Ministry. He had been asked to bring with him a secretary to take notes of what was discussed, and any decisions that might be taken. He had asked for Loris to undertake this task.

Mikael had continued to use Loris' little room as he grew stronger, although he was more careful to use it only when Loris was on duty, so it was free when he got in from work. On this particular occasion, Loris came in early, insisted on Mikael remaining, and confirmed that he would be away for about a week. When Mikael rose from the bed on which they were both sitting, Loris too rose to say goodbye. Loris held and embraced him fiercely, cheek pressed to cheek. Mikael eventually had to make a physical effort to pull himself away. Mikael turned, slightly taken aback and embarrassed, and opened the door. He looked back and smiled.

"Well Loris – goodbye till next Sunday. Do you realise that we've seen each other at least once, almost every single day, for several months. It'll be nice for you to have a change from my incessant company."

"I don't want a change," replied Loris rather sharply, his eyes smouldering with an emotion that Mikael couldn't place.

"Come, come. Good God, Loris, you must surely be totally fed up with this bloody building. Just crossing the straits is going to be great for you. Look, visit our old haunts, have a good time. Right – well then – till you get back." Mikael smiled, walked out and went back to his ward.

It was two days later that Olga, off duty for a few hours at last, came to Mikael's ward early in the afternoon for their usual stroll and found him already dressed and sitting on his bed.

"Well, well, Mikael – how are you feeling? No dressing gown today – you're dressed. You need new trousers, you know, they're pretty scruffy. Actually Mikael, my dear, forget what I just said, you look better than I've seen you for some time. Your cheeks have colour, and your eyes seem brighter. What has the doctor told you?"

"Hey – Olga hanum – come and sit on my bed for a change," called out the soldier in the bed opposite, who had only one arm and one leg.

Olga flashed him her wonderful, but meaningless, smile and turned to Mikael.

"Well, let's go, or do you want to sit here?"

"No, no, I've got a surprise for you – let's go and have a chat in Loris' room."

"No thanks," replied Olga with a flash of anger. "you know perfectly well that he can't stand me – and for my part, I don't want to have to face up to his snooty disapproval when he arrives."

"No, look Olga, Loris has gone away for a week ... we won't be disturbed, we can have the room all to ourselves."

Startled, Olga looked at him long and hard. Mikael stared back at her – eye to eye – with that slightly dismissive stare of Turkish young men everywhere in the Empire. This was the look which Olga had found so refreshingly absent in Selim. There was a long moment of silence between them, though all the noise and hubbub of the cavernous ward continued, as before, all around them. Olga thought back to her actual words to Nerissa when she had said of Selim, that he had none of that hard arrogance of most educated Ottoman young men.

Olga would be 18 soon – she knew perfectly well that Mikael was not seeking privacy just 'to have a chat' as he put it. Olga saw a tall and thin man, slightly stooped due to the effects of his ruptured insides. His moustache – Enver style – was not now so cock-a-hoop, and his black eyes looked sadder, and had deep lines at the sides. However they still flashed with pride and a latent violence. Olga felt aroused.

"Very well, Mikael; but look I can't be away too long. I have to be back on duty again soon," she lied, without any qualms at all.

Mikael was in a sense cursed with this expression that somewhat belied his real character. He was a good deal more insecure than appeared on the surface, and though he tried to stride out as they walked through the corridors, he soon had to give up and revert to a shuffle. When they arrived, Mikael shut the door behind him as they walked in. Olga turned and found herself clasped urgently and fiercely round the waist. With the one sigh – "Oh Olga," she felt Mikael's thin lips pressed with rough passion against her own full ones.

This was Olga's first real kiss. It was totally different to that wonderful moment when her lips and those of Selim touched and quivered for a second in the basement boiler room at the College. This was passion – she knew it – her body flowed with it, and she wanted Mikael to continue, to force her, to press harder – anything. This was not Mikael's first kiss, nor his first sexual experience – but the emotion accompanying the moment was new for him. His body stirred with urgency, and he felt he would burst with desire. He had experienced these feelings before, and recognised them – nevertheless over and above this, he felt a tenderness and affection which had not accompanied any of his previous experiences.

They sank onto the bed, there was no place to stand in any case. Olga shifted and Mikael naturally came across her. Olga was fully dressed in her Nurse's uniform, and Mikael was wearing a shirt and his own shabby trousers, for the first time since coming to the hospital.

The kiss continued, as Mikael got more and more excited, and as Olga squirmed and felt his pressure on top of her. But as Mikael's hands strayed, and as he began fumbling both at his clothes and hers, Olga came to her senses. A part of her was desperate for Mikael to go on, to loosen her clothing, to impose his will. Another part of her, however, knew it was impossible. She had to hold back – urgently and at once. Already she had allowed matters to go far beyond any reasonable level. A kiss was, in these days, becoming more and more permissible, though even now, not among the circles in which Olga lived. But anything more than that was out of the question.

Olga moved her free hand, and held the busy hand of Mikael hard and tight. Mikael responded at once to her unspoken command. They remained clasped together. They continued to kiss, and explore each other's lips – but it was not going to go any further. Olga sensed in herself both relief and frustration – simultaneously.

Eventually they lay side by side on the bed, and talked about the war, about nursing, about Olga's family, and about Makrikoy. Mikael's feelings got deeper, centred more on Olga, and less on his own desire. They remained together far longer than Olga had envisaged – she seemed to have forgotten having said that she had to go on duty again..

Meetings in Loris' room at the top of the hospital began to take place daily – often only for as short as half an hour. Mikael now came looking for Olga, whereas Olga began trying imperceptibly to cool down the relationship.

After several days of increasing contact between them, Loris returned. The meetings ceased abruptly. For many days there was no question of any meeting between them – even the previous walks together stopped. But Mikael became more and more obsessed with the desire to speak to Olga and touch her – if only just to hold her hand. At last, one day, he caught her in the corridor outside his ward.

"Olga, you've been avoiding me."

"Not at all, Mikael, my dearest. But look, Loris is back and I know I am not welcome – you know that – you know that."

"Olga, my love, my soul. I think of you all the time. I want you – you must know that I love you. I'm getting better day by day. I'll be able to walk out of here soon. Heaven knows what is happening around us, or where we're all going to be when this bloody war ends. But look, sooner or later it will – sooner or later we'll be picking up our lives again. Will you wait for me Olga – will you marry me when I am in a position to marry? I love you, I love you. It's not just desire. I want to live with you always, Say something Olga – for heaven's sake say something!"

Olga looked at this man. She thought of her family – of her parent's reactions. She reflected on her own feelings – on the good qualities of this man almost five years older than her – of those moments of thoughtless anger and violence she knew he was capable of. Then she remembered that no thought of her parents, or her situation, had ever entered her head during the relationship with Selim.

"Mikael, I don't know what to say. My dearest we're living in such uncertain times, and in such uncertain circumstances. Is it right to enter into such long-term commitments? You know we can't marry or even think of that until this war is over, and you get back to full health. All I can say to you is that I have no feelings today for anyone else other than you."

Olga leant forward and gave Mikael a warm kiss on his lips. She then turned and walked away without another word.

That night, as she lay awake in the nurse's dormitory, she reflected that even at that moment, when a young man had bared his soul to her, and begged for a word from her, she had still failed to come out with those vital three words – 'I love you'. Why not? Wasn't that what she had felt during that first passionate kiss? Olga shrugged mentally and turned and fell into an untroubled sleep.

It was on the very next day that Olga's situation became even more complicated. On that day, she was on duty doing the rounds of the officers' wards with the duty doctor – Dr. Fadil. The officer's wards were both smaller and cleaner than the dirty, white-tiled wards of the ordinary soldiers. They moved slowly from bed to bed, as the doctor inspected each man, and Olga took notes or administered the doctor's recommendations. The doctors were efficient, but had no time to say anything to the patients beyond asking the usual questions – most of the nurses did try to say a few words before moving on.

Olga suddenly stopped as they approached the next man. She found herself staring at an officer with one festering and badly bandaged half arm, and whose whole body was shaking with what appeared to be malarial fever. It was Selim Kemal.

CHAPTER 33

Raffi hangs on

When Raffi left his home early in the morning, after the terrifying moment when he had passed in front of the police dressed as a woman, he had no clear idea of where he was going to go. He knew by then that the areas west of Caesaria had not been as badly affected by the deportation and killings as the lands to the east up to the Russian frontier. Furthermore, at the back of his mind there was always the thought of his brother Vahan, apparently completely safe in Istanbul. So his first thought was to go westwards to Konya, which also had the advantage of being on the railway line to the capital.

As so often happens, a minor and purely accidental incident changed this plan. Raffi was 'streetwise' and sensitive to the customs and habits of the town. In particular, he knew how to avoid the unwelcome attentions of policemen and officials. Accordingly, when he got to the dusty square, where the carriages and lorries set off for other towns, he knew how to keep a low profile as he milled about amongst the crowd.

Even at this early hour, the square was filled with horse dung. There were almost as many animals as there were humans – chickens trussed together, donkeys carrying heavy loads, lambs and goats, some of which were about to be loaded on the older carriages that would accompany villagers on their trips home. There were also old, badly maintained, petrol lorries, parked around the square, carrying passengers and yet more animals to destinations further afield. Everything and everybody were all mixed up together in an atmosphere of noisy but friendly confusion.

Raffi had already pinpointed exactly where the four or five policemen on duty were standing. He also noted, thankfully, that he did not recognise any of them. They were ignoring most of the villagers with their chickens and produce, but Raffi could see they were looking at the papers of anyone dressed smartly, or any young men who might be of military age.

Raffi drifted, checking on the destinations and passengers of the lorries and coaches going westwards. It was while at this task, that his eye caught another young man ahead of him who appeared familiar in some way. As Raffi came closer, he saw a thin and very frail-looking young man – scarcely more than a boy, with a pale, almost consumptive, look in his face. The lad was clearly nervous, and sooner or later, thought Raffi to himself, he would catch the eye of one of the policemen.

Raffi was just about to turn away when he heard the boy ask the price of a 'simit', the round hard bagel which was a speciality of the town. At that same moment he also recognised the boy, whose name he did not know, as one who had attended the same school. This lad was, if anything, older than he was, though he looked younger. As he walked forward, he saw the boy's eyes go up under his upper eyelids, and he began to sway, clearly about to faint. Raffi did not hesitate – he was almost alongside by then anyway – but grabbed him as he fell, holding him up and calling out so that at least all those in the immediate neighbourhood could hear -

"Abdul, Abdul – stand up – are you all right. Allah be praised, he's only ill – he just needs a little air."

The simit vendor, who thought he was just about to make a sale, was anxious to help. Holding him on the other side, they carried him and sat him down on one of the rickety chairs outside a decrepit old café on the edge of the square. Checking carefully that the commotion had passed unnoticed, Raffi paid for a couple of simits, and handed one of them to the young man who was recovering.

"I am sorry, *effendi*, to be such a nuisance – I do thank you – I will be all right now, and on my way," said the boy rising to go.

Raffi not only now recognised the lad – but, once noticed, the tell-tale features of an Armenian became increasingly obvious. The lighter hair, wavy rather than completely straight and black, the large round eyes, and the long face – all gave it away. There was also a haunted expression. Before he could run off, Raffi leant forward.

"Hay-yem (I am Armenian)," he whispered – whereupon the lad collapsed back onto the old cane chair, and covered his face with his hands.

Raffi called out for a large coffee, and passed both the simits to the young man, who began eating them eagerly. In a surprisingly short time, Raffi learnt that the lad was already 16, though he looked younger. His name was Dikran. He had left the town with the remaining members of his family many weeks ago, at the time of the first deportation orders. The guards allocated to this particular group had melted away after the first few days, and the wretched column of women, children and old men had been continuously attacked, hunted down, robbed and killed as it made its way slowly through the desolate countryside. In one particularly vicious encounter, Dikran had lost the last of his family, and had decided to escape from the column which was diminishing day by day.

Once on his own, Dikran realised that they had not gotten very far from the town, although they had been walking for days. He had decided to make his way back. He had been sleeping in cellars and the empty houses of the old abandoned Armenian quarter for the past weeks. However, he had no money, and he had been slowly starving, living off what scraps and rubbish he could find. He had not dared to try and get any work as he had no papers at all.

It turned out that Dikran had been told that well to the south of Caesaria, where the main railway line to the Arab vilayets passed through the Taurus mountains, the big German company, still finishing the Berlin to Baghdad railway, were taking on workers without asking any questions. If he could get there, he had been told, he would be safe for the time being, as the Turkish government was anxious to have the railway line completed. All that was needed was for the tunnels through the Taurus to be completed, and the connection would be made between the great Arab cities of the Levant and Constantinople.

Raffi too had heard this, and he was even able to add that the government was even allowing Army deserters to work there unmolested, so important was the project to the war effort. From Raffi's point of view, it was completely in the wrong direction.

But the two boys – for, despite the fact they had been forced to grow up very quickly, that's all they were – talked and made plans together, until Raffi became more enthusiastic.

Raffi felt excited and ready for danger. While not a great thinker like his brother, he had been sensitive to the needs of all the old women in the house, and this had made him depressed and nervous. Now, for the first time, he had a male friend of his own age. They found themselves bouncing ideas off each other in a childish, but natural, manner.

The first task was to get to the railhead. Raffi changed the first of his precious gold coins, and the boys paid a lorry driver who was carrying passengers to Ulukishler railway station. Buying some bread and kebabs for the journey, Raffi and Dikran stood the whole way in the back of the lorry, as it bounced and swayed its way along the terrible roads to the railway line. Without thinking about it, they found themselves chatting together, laughing and giggling, reverting, if only for a moment, to the boyhood they had lost for ever.

When they arrived outside the station, they clambered down from the lorry with most of the other passengers. Raffi had not lost his innate caution, and he looked carefully around, but there were no more than a couple of policemen, leaning against the low stone wall that separated the railway line from the road, smoking and chatting and taking no notice of anyone. The boys were now in an area where there had never been any significant Christian minorities, and the atmosphere appeared much less charged. Nevertheless, there was clearly going to be a problem getting on to a train going to the strategically important Taurus tunnels.

It was Dikran who came up with the bright idea of getting one of the many troop trains, traveling regularly from the capital on their way to the Palestine and Mesopotamian fronts. They would get on by posing as 'simit' sellers, going on to the next station.

"Look Raffi, we go to that bakery over there, and buy up all the simit they've got. We get a pole of some sort – you know the way they do it – drop the bloody things round and down the pole in the same way, get on the train and walk up and down the corridors selling, like all the other kids do."

"It's all very well for you Dikran, you could pass for 13 or 14. But look at me – I already need a bit of a shave, and I shaved last night before leaving."

" Right – we've still got some cash left. We've got lots of time. We go into the town and buy a pair of those dark black glasses that people with poor eyesight wear – you know the kind of thing. I'm sure we can find something. Also to make it look even better we get a stick, white if we can find one, and you hobble along behind me holding my shoulder. What we'll do is go round, up and down the train, doing the selling, and you come along, as my big brother, saying nothing, but taking the money and holding on tight to my shoulder."

There was no way, in normal circumstances, that Raffi would have gone along with this ridiculous plan – but, after all the horrors and tensions of the past weeks, surrendering to childish enthusiasm, overrode his usual caution.

After they had stocked up with the bagels, putting them along two poles, they waited on the platform for the train due from the capital. It was as if the poles of simit, together with the black glasses and the stick, were a passport – they were not challenged. When the troop train arrived, all the wagons were full of soldiers – all the seats were taken, and young, shabbily uniformed soldiers were leaning out of the windows laughing and joking. There were military police all around, who got off the train and stood about on the platform by the doors of the carriages as the train came to a hissing stop.

There were scarcely any 'civilian' passengers getting on the train, and those that were, had their papers carefully checked. Raffi had his papers in the name of Soliman ready, and his heart was pounding with excitement as he and Dikran approached one of the carriage doors. But Dikran, frail and consumptive though he might be, was a natural actor. He grinned cheekily at the two military police at the carriage door, made a breezily ribald remark, offered them each a simit, which they declined and walked boldly onto the train calling out "Simit! – Simit!".

Raffi scrambled up after him with his hand tight clasping Dikran's shoulder, in a state of fear and triumphant excitement, in equal parts. While the train stood, hissing and steaming in the hot and dusty station – whilst guards and police of one kind or another paced up and down on the platform – whilst whistles blew and people in all sorts of uniform shouted – Raffi stood in a sweat of fearful expectation. Meanwhile, Dikran sang out his goods, exchanged rude and sexually explicit suggestions with the soldiers, and made a play of having to hand over the bits of cash to his older, and surlier companion. Then at last, with a great jerk, the train hooted and set off. It was only then that Raffi relaxed, as the presence of the boys, now rather desultorily selling pastry, was taken for granted for the rest of the journey.

On arrival at Belemedik – the end of the line where the tunnels were being constructed – the boys tumbled out with all the soldiers, who cheerfully wished them well as they made ready to march off.

Raffi soon got work with the German engineers building the railway line, which had caused such tensions between the German and British Empires before the war. From the start, it became clear that Dikran was not going to manage to get any sort of employment. Here, Raffi's sturdy masculine frame was what was in demand, whereas Dikran's frailty and his youthful looks, made it difficult for him, quite apart from the fact that he had no papers. On top of this, he was beginning again to look sickly; the weeks of near starvation now coming home to roost.

Raffi, with his false papers, found work as a brakeman for the construction gang trains going through to the tunnels. This was a hard, back-breaking job, which really needed a man's strength and physique. Fortunately for Raffi, one of the German engineers, noting his education, asked him if he could read and write in the Turkish – Arabic script. When Raffi confirmed that he could, he was removed from his first job and taken to work in his office. Meanwhile they both lived in the makeshift shanty town for the construction gangs, alongside the little town in the valley, in a shabby room of their own in a sort of hostel.

Dikran had changed. All those high spirits – that flash of

inspired adventurousness when they had first met – had gone. A feverish, red colour had come into his pale cheeks. He ate badly, and indeed there was always a shortage of food in Belemedik – particularly of fresh fruit or vegetables. Dikran became querulous and fought with Raffi at every opportunity. He stopped going out to buy the food, his only task, and he began staying in bed all day. At night, Raffi would be woken with sighs and whispers as Dikran suffered from terrible nightmares, which he could never recall the next morning.

It soon became clear to them both that Dikran was seriously ill, and that he could be dying. Neither of them had had any experience of medical matters, but as Raffi began asking around, he soon discovered that Dikran appeared to be suffering from cholera, or a severe form of dysentery. Raffi was at his wit's end. There were no doctors or medical services anywhere. He went down to the town one day and sought out an old woman, recommended by one of the maids at the hostel. This decrepit old woman came up one evening, muttered some imprecations over the dirty and sweating Dikran. She then boiled up some foul-smelling herbs and roots, which she forced Dikran to drink. Dikran vomited it all up almost immediately after she left. He had not eaten for days by then. At least Raffi knew how to look after the sick and dying, and he fell back into this routine. But here it was much more difficult – for a start, there was never enough water to keep Dikran clean.

Dikran simply wasted away, and the day eventually came when Raffi returning wearily from work came into the room to find that he had died. Even though he knew it was going to happen, it was still a shock to face – alone. Raffi sat up all through the night by Dikran's body and reflected that they had never talked much about his family. While Raffi had chatted on about his own life, his big brother in Bolis, his mother and father, his trips to the farms in the highlands, he realised that he was not even sure of his friend's surname. Dikran had become simply one of the awful statistics of these events. He held the boy's lifeless hand, and eventually, in the early morning, the tears came as he slept, still holding the hand, and with his head on

Dikran's unmoving chest.

All the joy that Raffi had got in Dikran's cheeky behaviour during the trip from Caesaria and for some time after they arrived, had evaporated. Though now safe enough and able to wait out the end of the war, Raffi became restless. He missed his new-found, and now lost, friend, and this, in turn, made him miss his family. Living alone was not natural to his character, and the death of Dikran began preying on his mind – the room seemed cheerless, and the unmarked grave of the boy, so close by, began to upset him. Even though he was not particularly imaginative, Raffi decided to leave. He left that very night, writing a careful crafted note to his master, who was absent again for a second night working at the far tunnel, explaining that he had had to return home quickly as his mother was gravely ill.

This time he was determined to revert to his original plan of heading back towards Constantinople. Already, there were few Armenians left east of Caesaria, except individuals surviving alone and in hiding. Travel was getting easier and less fraught with the danger of being recognised and killed, as an escaped deportee. The main danger was whether he was liable to military service. Either way, if his true identity was known as an Armenian deportee, death would inevitably follow. But Raffi was now fully experienced in the art of survival. He decided that arriving in the capital suddenly was too risky. Instead, he would go to Konya, where it was known that the current Ottoman governor had not applied the Ittihad deportation orders stringently.

When, after the usual difficulties and adventures he finally arrived in Konya, Raffi decided to retain his identity as Soliman, as set out in his papers. Only two of the precious gold coins were left, and Raffi, having failed to find any risk-free work, took the decision to go into business for himself. He found lodgings with a respectable, Turkish family on the outskirts of town. He invested in a large wheelbarrow, and, getting up very early in the mornings, he would go round to the local farmers who lived closest to the town. There, he would buy their fresh vegetables at a good price as they knew that it would save them a long trek into town, waiting for a sale. He was a good judge of fruit and vegetables and was rarely cheated.

Then he would trundle his wheelbarrow to the central market, where he hired a small wooden platform to lay out his wares like those around him. He was usually sold out well before the end of the day, as his fruit was always fresh. This allowed him to go home in the afternoon with a small, but perceptible, profit on which he could live.

He avoided going to the public baths, where the fact he wasn't circumcised would be noticed, and was always very careful to maintain a strictly Turkish appearance. Soon after he arrived, the old Ottoman governor was unfortunately replaced by another fanatic Ittihad appointee, and once again, the remaining Armenians had to leave. Raffi found that he had done well not to change his habit of hiding his origins to anyone, whatever the circumstances. There were Armenians who still remained, but they were there only on sufferance, and he pretended not to understand the language, even when, as happened once, he was accosted by two men calling out to him in Armenian.

Raffi was lonely – that was his main problem. He couldn't afford to have friends, and kept himself to himself. As the Armenians even here in Konya began to disappear, he knew that the only way to survive was to wait patiently for the war to end. He survived, but that was the best that could be said. He survived.

CHAPTER 34

Olga and Selim

Olga stood transfixed, and stared at the young man lying in the bed. Doctor Fadil was already beginning to gently remove the dirty bandage inexpertly tied round the stump of the arm. Turning to Olga, he said loudly and impatiently,

"Nurse Avakian, what's the matter with you for heaven's sake? There's a job needing to be done here – stop dreaming. This bandaging is terrible – it will need to be replaced immediately, though I suspect the arm is again infected."

Selim was still suffering from the effects of the awful seven-day journey by coach and train all the way from Baghdad. He had been lying feverishly and disoriented for days, and was barely conscious. The words – Nurse Avakian – shouted, rather than spoken, by the irritable doctor – penetrated his hazy consciousness, and he opened his eyes and tried to focus for the first time in many days. There he saw, standing behind the doctor who was fussing over his arm, the girl who had never left his dreams. Olga was tired and somewhat bedraggled from a long day's work on the wards; nevertheless, as always, she carried her regulation hospital coat with style and a natural elegance. Giving him a quick, harassed smile of recognition, she hurried round to help the doctor as he gingerly tried to separate the bandages from the pus and dried blood of the wound, which had not been touched or cleaned for days.

Since he was first wounded, Selim had lived a sort of half-life until this moment. But now, for a moment he forgot everything – his father's death – the war – his pain and the lost arm. He simply gazed at Olga as she came round to his left side; recovering enough to give her a great, beaming, heart-warming smile. Nothing else mattered. Out of the blue, life had suddenly become worth living again, at the same time it appeared to be ebbing away.

As he became more and more conscious of himself and his surroundings, he wondered why he was feverish one moment and his whole body was shivering the next. Then he cried out in pain as the doctor finally tore away the bandage from the stump of the arm.

"Good God – this is getting infected and gangrenous all over again. Nurse – a sedative for this officer right away. Young man, I see you are now fully awake, I'm going to have to cut away some more of the re-infected area and clean up the original wound properly. It's best done right away. It will be painful and Nurse Avakian here will give you a heavy sedative which will send you off to sleep."

"Doctor – I won't need it. I'm sorry I cried out – please just get on with it."

"Son – you may not need it, but I do. I can't do the job properly whilst you are in such obvious pain. Just relax. Now Nurse, get on with it and join me at the next bed when you've done. We have the rest of the ward to deal with, before we can return to finish this, once he's asleep. Get on with it girl. What's the matter with you?"

The fussy little doctor moved on to the next bed, while Olga took the ether bottle and a fresh gauze mask from her trolley and moved to Selim's side.

"Olga – Olga my love, what are you doing here in this soldier's hospital. Oh, my God, how wonderful just to see you. Oh God – let me touch you," gabbled Selim hysterically.

"Hush Selim, my soul, hush. Your arm is really bad, even I can see that. We've caught it only just in time. Don't move my darling."

Olga gently put the gauze mask over Selim's nose, holding his arm tight. Even in these somewhat melodramatic circumstances, she still felt a quiver as she held his bare arm. Looking carefully at what she was doing, she began to drip the ether bottle onto the mask. She was aware all the time that his eyes were burning and staring at her, trying to make vital eye contact, which she carefully avoided.

"Nurse – Nurse – what is the matter with you today? Haven't you finished yet – for heaven's sake it's only a simple anaesthetic. I've finished here already." The troubled and overworked doctor came back to the bedside. Olga finished and closed the bottle.

"Come, my boy – look at me, let me see your eyes – good. Now start counting – yes, yes, just counting."

"One, two threeee, frr ..." and Selim was gone.

When Selim woke again several hours later, his arm was throbbing with pain – but he had been washed – all over – and he had clean white bandages over his stump. Above all the fever seemed to have passed, though he remained very weak. He knew that he would not be able to stand up on his own two feet. But he had not forgotten a single moment, from the instant that he first recognised Olga, to the point that he had again lost consciousness. He waited with increasing impatience for Olga to come and visit him.

Olga got through the rest of her working day by mechanically performing her tasks, knowing that she was not giving of her best. Everything that had occurred a year ago came back to her vividly as if it had happened yesterday – the tea party at Tokatlian's – that moment in the basement of the College – the subsequent meeting in Makrikoy on that fateful day in April. It was not just the memory that returned. That smile – that look in his eyes – as suddenly Selim saw her for that first moment, made her heart leap with a joy that she had not felt for a year.

She was due to return home that evening after work, as she had a full day off the next day, but she knew she wouldn't follow her normal routine. On this night she would again sleep in her bed in the nurse's dormitory. The evening would be for Selim, when he awoke.

The moment that Olga arrived and sat down on the bed beside Selim on his better right-hand side, he grabbed her arm with an intensity that almost hurt her. Olga smiled, leant forward and kissed him on his cheek.

"Oh Olga – Oh Olga, my loved one. What joy, what joy, just to see you. Allah is merciful. I can't believe it. Oh God! Tell me, my love, tell me what are you doing here?" Selim spoke in a hoarse whisper, aware of all the other beds and patients around him.

Several hours passed as they sat like this, with Selim holding tightly on to Olga's arm the whole time. Olga talked quietly and told him all that had happened to her since their parting. Food came and went – nurses on duty moved around – conversation hummed amongst the other patients around them – there were even some visitors, whilst the two talked on and on.

Selim soon began to feel sick – the usual effects of ether. What with that, together with what almost amounted to a re-amputation, though it was only a fraction further up the arm, he kept breaking out in a sweat. However, he would not let go of Olga's arm, and she did not want him to. Olga took a cloth from the side of the bed, and kept mopping his brow, and she occasionally touched her cheek to his.

It was during this period of intimacy – deeply private, even though they were in the middle of a large ward – that Olga felt someone was staring at her. She looked up and saw the figure of Loris by the door, looking at her with an expression she could not immediately place. Later, she realised the look had been a mixture of hatred and triumph. When he saw her look up, he walked away. Olga didn't really care – but it suddenly reminded her, she had promised to call on Mikael before going home that evening. Selim, meanwhile, was still talking urgently and disjointedly. His fever seemed to have returned, and Olga realised that she would have to calm him down, as the excitement was not doing him any good.

"Enough, my darling, enough. I'll have to go now. Tell me, does your mother and sister know that you're here. Honestly, the army's organisation in this kind of matter is hopeless. I've known patients here, whose parents lived almost next-door, but who were never told that they were here."

"Oh, Olga, yes of course. In all my joy I forgot about my poor mother. She may not even have heard about my being wounded in Mesopotamia. My darling – could you possibly let her know? Heavens, they could even visit me here. That would be wonderful – wonderful."

"Of course, Selim, of course. Look, it's my day off tomorrow. I'll go into Bolis, and go and visit your mother."

"Olga – that would be really kind. But listen, do you know where she lives?"

"Come, Selim, of course I do. I passed it every day before the British arrived in Gallipoli. I would look up and think of you inside, I really would. It's that big, modern block almost opposite the Galata Tower, isn't it?"

"Olga – you're a marvel. Remember, it's on the fourth floor – rather a climb, my sweetheart – Flat 8."

"Selim, my soul, sleep now – sleep. I'll come and visit you again tomorrow, as soon as I get back from seeing your mother. I'm sure she'll make an effort to visit you herself very soon."

Then Olga carefully withdrew her hand from Selim's. She

leant forward and gave him a light kiss on the lips. Already the war had changed everything. Only a year had passed since that precious moment when their lips had touched ever so lightly in that basement cellar, but now, even in the midst of a ward full of other men, neither Olga nor Selim thought twice of a kiss, unimaginable only a year before.

The next day, and still in a state of wonder and excitement, Olga took the ferry and crossed over to the Galata bridge on the European shore. She was dressed simply as always, but she knew she was looking her best. Mounting the stairs in Selim's building, she knocked on the door of Flat 8. The door was opened by a young girl with wavy black hair, who looked to be about 12 years-old. She was wearing the uniform of the German Gymnasium, and she looked at Olga questioningly.

"Hello – I am Olga Avakian. I am a nurse at the Uskudar barracks hospital. Is you mother in? I've some news for her."

"Mama," called the girl, and opened the door further to let Olga into the compact hallway.

A woman dressed in black but with a beautiful, diamond brooch on her left shoulder came out of a door. She did not offer to shake hands in the modern style, but bowed her head and nodded, saying -

"I am Halideh – can I help you?"

"Yes, I am sorry to disturb you. I am a nurse at the Uskudar military hospital. I have brought news of your son – Selim."

The excessive and somewhat strained politeness and formality vanished from the woman's demeanour. She took Olga's hand and led her into a small, but neat and tidy, sitting room. This had potted plants, two exquisite Turkish carpets and some low coffee tables, two pouffes, a sofa and a settee. She called out – 'coffee' to the maid who was hovering at what Olga assumed must be the entrance to the kitchen. "Shekerli?" she asked Olga.

"No thank you, I have to return soon," replied Olga, warming to the sign of anxious love in Halideh's eyes. They sat, side by side on the settee.

"I've come at Selim's request to tell you that he is here at the Hospital and that…"

"What's happened, what's happened – is he all right?" interrupted Halideh.

"Yes, yes – he's improving. He has been wounded, but his life is in no danger. However I …"

"Allah be praised, Allah be praised. Now, my dear, tell me more. I won't interrupt again I promise you," and Halideh laughed out loud in relief and touched Olga's hand.

Olga told her quietly all that she had heard from Selim – his experiences in Damascus and along the Tigris facing the British Army. Halideh winced and looked down as Olga came to the wounded and amputated left arm – but she continued to listen carefully to all the news.

"When can we see him, Nurse, when can I go to him?" his mother asked as soon as Olga had finished.

"Well, you can visit officially during the afternoons – but many relations bring food to the men at other times as well, so it is all rather informal."

"Thank you, thank you. May Allah preserve you for ever." "What is your name, my dear, I did not catch it when you first came in."

"Olga Avakian."

There was a long moment of deep silence. Olga felt the woman draw back and freeze. Olga realised then, that knowing this to be a Turkish Hospital, Halideh, not having heard her name, had assumed that she was Turkish or possibly Greek or Jewish.

Halideh stood up from the settee in emotional turmoil. Still not a word was said. Olga sat with her hands clasped together on her lap. Now, for the first time since she had first seen Selim again, all the old problems which had driven them apart came back to her. She suddenly recalled the circumstances in which Selim's father, Dr. Nazim Kemal, this woman's husband, had died at the siege of Van. It suddenly came to her that this was why the lady was dressed in black. Nazim Kemal, for whom this woman was still in mourning, had died at the hands of Armenian rebels, and Halideh hanum, wife of Nazim *effendi* was clearly still bitter. Furthermore it was not entirely clear whether she was aware of the relationship between her son and Olga.

The silence was broken by the voice of the young 12 year-old girl who had been listening intently throughout in the corner.

"Mama – Mama – Selim is here, Selim is here. Let's go and see him now right away," and she jumped up, eyes aglow.

Halideh, with tears appearing in her eyes, which now had a hard glint in them, turned away, as Olga rose in some confusion. Carefully avoiding looking at Olga, she walked to the window, and looked out and down into the street below, with her back to the room, whilst the young girl looked on in some puzzlement.

"Yasmin – yes of course we will go soon. Meanwhile please show Nurse Avakian to the door as she is leaving."

"But, Mama, what …"

"Yasmin! Do as I say. Please tell her, as she goes, that we are grateful for the trouble she has taken in coming here to give us this news."

Yasmin took Olga's hand – totally innocent that there was any problem, though she couldn't help but be aware that her beloved mother had acted in an unusually rude manner to this bringer of good – and bad – news. For the first time since she had seen Selim again, Olga now became prey to all the doubts that she had had a year ago. She squeezed Yasmin's hand, walking out into the hall and out of the front door without saying another word.

Olga was less prone to tears than she had been before entering the hospital, but the humiliation to which she had just been subjected now hit her, and she felt tears trickling down her cheeks. All that unalloyed pure joy that she had felt with the return of Selim, evaporated completely. Selim appeared to have resolved his own doubts, and that had given her enormous satisfaction, but she saw that the problems of a love between her and Selim had not gone away. In many ways they had become even more intractable. Fitted into the equation were now two mothers – Halideh and Armineh – both of whom had lost a husband in circumstances which made it impossible for them to face up to any emotional ties Olga and Selim might feel for each other.

Olga was the last person to board the ferry just before it left the quay, but she could not sit, although several men offered her their seat, she needed to pace to conceal her inner turmoil. On her arrival back at the Hospital, she recalled her promise to Selim to go to him immediately. This was still her day off. But she had no idea what to say.

"Olga, my love, tell me, tell me. How was it?" said Selim as she came along the ward and sat by his side on the bed.

"Selim – yes – yes – calm down my love. I saw your sister, Yasmin. What a lovely girl she is, isn't she? She was really happy to hear that you were here, and they are going to try and come to see you very soon."

Olga held the hand that Selim stretched out to her, but said nothing more. Selim looked questioningly at her.

"Yes – yes, Olga, yes?"

Olga knew that he was disappointed at her failure to say more – to speak more warmly about his mother, his home. However, the days when Olga could cheerfully make up stories and white lies, were over. Olga felt silence about that morning's events was better than giving some false impression – though she saw and felt his hurt.

Olga chatted on about all that she had seen at his home, and all that she had told Halideh about Selim. But she kept silent as to how Halideh had reacted. She saw that Selim sensed she was holding something back. To her deep sorrow, she also saw that Selim believed that it was she who had taken a dislike to his mother. A year ago, Olga would not have accepted that double humiliation, but would have blurted out the truth. Today, she was prepared to take the consequences of appearing in a bad light, in order to save this young man a greater pain.

She felt her tears coming, so she leant forward, kissed Selim on the lips, smiled and got up to go. Selim grabbed her arm, but she moved free.

I'll see you again soon, Selim, but first you must be ready to welcome your mother and sister. I'm sure that they'll come this afternoon."

Olga walked out of the ward, for the first time not acknowledging with her usual smile the friendly, affectionate and slightly ribald remarks directed at her by the other officers in the ward. She suddenly felt incredibly tired, and made her way up to the nurse's dormitory. As she arrived in the corridor leading to it, there, waiting for her, squatting against the wall, was Mikael, fully dressed and with a cheap cloth bag by his side.

CHAPTER 35

Vahan survives

It was one of those wonderful fresh spring mornings, with a crystal clear blue sky and a weak sun shining on the clear dark waters of the Bosporus. the kind of day so beloved by the people of Constantinople – the Bolsetsi.

Vahan sat at his desk in the offices of the main Electricity Company of the town; originally a Belgian Company, now being run by German directors. His job was to go through all the electricity consumption accounts for most of the city, working out the totals and typing up the ensuing invoices on an old decrepit typewriter. There were no envelopes to be prepared, as all the accounts were delivered by the Company's messengers – mostly young boys, but including a sprinkling of elderly men, semi-retired former employees. These messengers milled about the offices all day giving a continual bustle and animation to the surroundings.

The offices, situated on the Pera side, were modern and airy. Every day, Vahan walked from the Patakis house down to the Galata bridge, across and up the hill on the other side. Vahan found the work easy, and, in its way, quite satisfying. It gave him a sense of steadiness and routine, which soothed him, and prevented him from worrying too much about his current circumstances. However, it was hardly mentally challenging, and he would finish his assigned tasks quickly, and was then left staring out of the window, with its dusty slatted wooden shades, into the gardens of the courtyard.

That extraordinarily packed day of the 24th April, now over a year ago, had changed the whole course of Vahan's life. The arrest of Father Komitas, the arrest and deportation of Karekin Avakian, the assault on the boy Haik and his meeting with the Avakians, had all affected him profoundly. However, it was not until he got home that evening and received the letter from his mother telling of the arrest and deportation of his own father – Garabed – that the situation finally struck home with full force. He reflected that it was one thing to read the newspapers, listen to gossip and rumour, or watch terrible events unfolding around you, but quite another when someone you knew and loved was affected.

The news filtering through from the interior, and the reports of the appalling events taking place in the eastern vilayets, made it almost a certainty that his father was now dead. Despite the occasional postcard, it was not clear how long the rest of his family back in Caesaria, would survive. He was particularly worried how his volatile and emotional younger brother – Raffi – could keep out of trouble.

Vahan finished his current task and sat back, musing about the past year and his future prospects. After that momentous day, he had continued drilling at the Harbiye Military Academy and learning the business of being an officer in the reserve.

Like everyone else in the dying days of the Ottoman world, Vahan was politically confused – though from a different viewpoint than his Turkish colleagues. On the one hand, the success of the old Empire, in holding at bay the arrogant self-confident Westerners at the Dardanelles, was a great source of pride to the Ottoman youth –whichever racial divide they came from. Suddenly, their despised country, the butt of so many jokes by the Western newspapers read regularly in the city prior to the war, was fighting back against people who looked down on them, whatever their cultural identity might be.

On the other hand, the minority peoples of Bolis were bit by bit hearing of the horrors inflicted upon the Armenian peasantry of the interior. It might be that those horrors were exaggerated – truth is almost certainly likely to be the first casualty of war –

but the Armenian community in Bolis, had experienced, at first hand, the arrests and disappearance of their own leaders, giving more credence to the news filtering out, not only from Turkish civil servants, but from the European embassies in the city. How then, could an Armenian Ottoman citizen remain loyal to a state which had clearly turned violently against his own people and culture, and even directly against members of his own family?

As he twiddled with his pencils and stared out through the slatted blinds, Vahan recalled how he had continued his training and military service, as last spring had turned into summer, mostly out of sheer inertia, knowing that he would soon have to make some sort of decision. The ordinary soldiers in the army facing the British in the Gallipoli peninsula were becoming less and less ethnically Turkish. Large numbers of Arab soldiers were taking over the terrible gaps in the ranks of the original divisions, which had been plugged into the lines with such distinction by General Mustapha Kemal. Mixed in with the Arab cannon-fodder were Armenian young men from the labour battalions, fed into the front lines and dying in their thousands like everyone else. It was ironic that when the young men on the other side of the lines, from England or Australia, shouted jocularly from the trenches – "Hey, Johnny Turk!" the chances were high that the lads they were addressing were actually Arabs and unlikely to be Turks at all.

The Harbiye military barracks was quite distant from the Patakis house, and Vahan recalled that he would spend many nights, illicitly, in the little sick room at the barracks, to save the long journey home and back again each day. As it happened, just across the fields at the back of the barracks was the house of his violin teacher – a certain Madame Yalbak – a widow of French extraction, who had been the wife of an Ottoman Turkish army officer, until his death years before. Vahan would keep his violin in his locker at the barracks, and would occasionally creep out in the evening to call upon the old lady. She was delighted to be feeding the young man, who seemed to be perpetually hungry. They would discuss politics in a rather desultory fashion and play duets together in her cluttered dark and velvet-upholstered sitting-room, before he clambered back across the wall into the barracks.

Madame Yalbak, now an old lady, wrinkled like a walnut, loved Stamboul and was deeply immersed in Ottoman culture. Vahan had come, not just to admire her, but to love her. She provided an emotional anchor of inestimable benefit to him. Sitting at his desk in the office, Vahan broke into a smile at the mere thought of her.

The good lady pressed him, on a daily basis, to leave the University and the Harbiye, and to hide out until the war was over. She would regularly say,

"My boy, this government has exiled, if not murdered, your father. They are carrying out a deliberate policy of murder against your unprotected people in the east. Your family are barely surviving, living in terror, while all their neighbours are mostly dead. Why – oh why – are you proposing to go and fight for them?"

"Well, because – for better or worse – it is the state in which I live and …"

"But, Vahan, that state has turned against you. You haven't turned against it – nor have most of your people. It's they who have decided to liquidate you. Think, boy, think! For heaven's sake, you know I'm not a pacifist – I married an officer after all – but this is different. Words like 'duty', or 'obligation', don't apply."

"Yes, all right Madame, but what you are suggesting is 'desertion' however you dress it up, and deserting is an immediate hanging offence."

"Ah, so, Vahan, you are scared, is that it? Come, have another cake, my lad."

Vahan recalled that the day had come when he had again stayed one night illicitly in a bed in the sick bay. He had shaved that morning, had given a fond, quick kiss to the night duty nurse who had let him stay, and who grinned at him as she pushed him away. Vahan had run down to have some breakfast in the canteen, prior to joining the morning's first drill in the parade ground. He recalled the moment when the fearsome drill sergeant, with his imperious, great moustache, had come up to him and barked out -

"So, trainee lieutenant Asadourian – you so love the army you stay with us all night do you? The Captain wants to see you now – NOW! – at the double!"

Vahan recalled the sick feeling of terror he'd felt at that moment. He remembered the deep sinking feeling in his stomach, but looking back he could not understand why he had reacted so extremely. He clearly was not under arrest. The Sergeant had shouted and swore at him, but then he had just walked away. His punishment might have been severe, but it was not a life or death matter.

He realised that he had not actually made a conscious decision; all the madness of those past weeks: the terrible news and rumours from the countryside; the continual barrage of words from Madame Yelbak; the probable death of his father, all seemed to have congealed in his mind at once. Pushing aside his meagre breakfast, he had stood up as the sergeant moved away, and without saying a word to those around him, he had gone straight to his locker. There he had taken his rifle, as if he was going out on parade. He also took down his precious violin, and his few personal belongings. He left all his books. Then, with a beating heart, he had gone down to the armoury, handed in his gun, and had walked, not run, through the fields at the back of the barracks, and clambered over to Madame Yelbak's house on the other side of the road.

As he thought back on it, Vahan marvelled at what he had done. Without any real thought, he had cut himself off from all the comforts of conformity, and put himself into the utmost danger – all without any plan or foresight.

Madame Yelbak, over 60 years-old, frail and brittle as she was, had not hesitated for a second when she had opened the door to him at that early hour in the morning. She knew at once what was behind his sudden arrival at her door. She waved away the Greek maid, and took Vahan into the kitchen. At this point Vahan, who had been acting almost mechanically, started trembling. The old lady went upstairs and sorted out some of her husband's old clothes, while Vahan sat at the kitchen table, shivering from a mixture of excitement and fear.

"Take off that uniform, Vahan," the old lady had commanded, handing the clothes she had picked out. As Vahan had undressed in that old-fashioned kitchen, she had picked up the uniform and pushed them, item by item, into the kitchen range. Vahan recalled that the burning cloth made a terrible smell, as he dressed in the clothes that had once belonged to the long-dead Major.

"Have you finished with the first lot of invoices," piped up one of the messenger boys, standing at his desk with a cheeky grin and his hands outstretched. Vahan came to the present with a start. He had actually already completed the whole lot of his assignment for the day, but he carefully picked out about half of them and handed them to the boy, who sauntered off. He carefully left the other half of them on his desk as if he still had to deal with them, and called out to one of the other office boys,-

"Kahve – Osman – kahve. Shekerli please"

Vahan sipped his sweet black coffee as he continued to ponder the events of the past year: the false papers he had obtained soon after leaving the university, were still with him, still giving his age as under 18. It was getting more and more difficult as the war continued to drag on. He had been lucky to get this job so soon after deserting the Harbiye, and for over a year, he had survived just one step ahead of the police.

Vahan sighed and turned his attention back to his work. In the evening, he walked home, down to the Galata bridge where he stopped, as always, for a few minutes and watched the ever-fascinating boats trafficking up and down the Horn, and onto the quays under the bridge. Then looking up at Stamboul hill, to the sun setting behind that incomparable skyline of domes and minarets, he walked home.

On the next day, after breakfast, Vahan walked out of the Patakis house into the little street, which was a cul-de-sac. He saw immediately that it was cordoned off at the far end, and that the police were examining everyone's papers at the exit. Another group of policemen were moving down the street searching the houses. Vahan turned to go back into the house, then reflected that there really was nowhere to hide, and he did not want to get Christina into any trouble. He could see that the police were searching pretty thoroughly, and that this was not just a question of bribing a single policeman.

He walked boldly to the end of the street and handed his papers to the policeman at the gap, who studied them closely.

"*Effendi's* name is Sami – and you are Ermeni and not yet eighteen."

"Yes officer"

"Join that small group of men over there."

Vahan moved over and joined a group of young men, some boys and a couple of older men, standing about guarded by yet another policeman. They were a totally nondescript and disparate lot, with no particular identifying characteristics, save that they were young males.

Eventually the whole group were herded off to the local police station. Here, Vahan found himself locked into a small room with all the others. There was nowhere to sit, and there was a smelly open bucket in the far corner for urinating. No one spoke to each other, and it was unclear why they were there. The door was regularly opened, as one-by-one they were led out and away. About half had gone when it was Vahan's turn.

He knew that they had neither believed his papers, nor that he was under 18 years of age, but he had no idea what was going to happen. With his heart pounding, and in a sweat of anticipation, he stumbled after the policeman who had picked him out, and found himself in another white-washed room which was much cleaner, and in which there was a doctor and a male assistant standing by. Here, he was told to take off his upper clothes. The Doctor carefully examined him, and in particular studied his mouth and teeth. Then he turned away.

"This man is probably 20, but is in any case certainly over 19," then, marking something on the card given him by the policeman, he called out, "Next".

Vahan said nothing, though he was surprised by the accuracy

of the doctor's comments. He was taken to the lobby of the police station, and told to sit down. Vahan was at last caught up in the official coils. The desk sergeant laboriously wrote out the details of the arrest, and indicated to the numbed Vahan that he would have to go to Court the next day. It was at that low point that he heard a cheery voice call out,

"Hello Vahan, what's going on?"

It was Marisa Patakis. The sergeant noted that Marisa, who was now nearly 17, had transformed the atmosphere of the station by her cheerful salutation. He didn't seem to have noticed that Marisa had said 'Vahan' and not 'Sami'. Either way, he smiled at the young girl who smiled back. It appeared that Marisa had seen the arrest of Vahan from her window. Having persuaded her mother, Christina, to give her some money, she had hurried down to the station and waited.

"Sergeant, this young man lives with us at this our address nearby," and she handed over her own papers, which the sergeant carefully perused.

"He won't run away – can we please bail him in the usual way?"

The sergeant considered.

"Very well, mamzelle. He must report here tomorrow morning early to go to the Court in Beyoglu. The bail will be set at two hundred piastres – you better make sure he comes."

Marisa who had brought just enough, handed over the money and they both waited whilst the sergeant wrote out the bail papers, a copy of which he gave to Marisa. When Vahan and Marisa walked home, Christina, who had never really recovered from Elena's sudden departure, said nothing.

Vahan now wrote out a letter of resignation to the Electricity Company, explaining that due to a complication in his affairs he was going to have to resign. He then arranged for a messenger to deliver it. He spent the rest of the day in a state of fear and anxiety as he tried to imagine what would happen to him at the court hearing the next day. Vahan was unable to sleep the whole of that night.

The following day, Vahan took the copy of the bail documents and arrived at the police station early. Here he waited for almost two hours, sitting on a stool by the reception desk, prey to a host of fearful presentiments. Eventually the moment came when a new desk sergeant called over a bored policeman, handed him the documents of the arrest, the doctor's report and the original bail papers, and ordered him to escort Vahan to the district court in Beyoglu.

There was no handcuffs or other restraints. The bail papers guaranteed by Marisa Patakis were still in the hands of the policeman, so Vahan couldn't do a disappearing act. Once again Vahan walked across the Galata bridge by the side of the policeman, looking at the scene with a weary eye, and with the feeling of butterflies in his empty stomach. How different the vivid scene seemed to him this morning. He had no wish to linger – he just wanted to get it all over with.

He had forgotten that the Court was on the same street, a little further along from the Electricity Company offices. They walked into the large and once-imposing marble hall of the Court. It was now looking a bit shabby, but it had previously been a handsome building. Vahan stood well back as the policeman walked up to the busy reception and handed over the bundle of complaint documents, Vahan's papers and the bail papers. Vahan was standing back, still contemplating his likely future.

He watched as the policeman took out his duty book and got a signature from the man at the desk for the papers. Then to his surprise and increasing delight, he saw that the policeman, having completed his duty, his task completed, without saying another word, turned on his heels and walked out. The clerk was still writing something on his desk, at the same time dealing with another person. Vahan suddenly realised that the clerk had no idea that Vahan had arrived under arrest. Vahan joined the queue, and eventually said to the Clerk when he reached the front.

"Ah, *effendi*, I believe that these papers apply to me. Can you tell me where I should go, and to whom I should report?"

The clerk motioned that he was busy and was dealing with several matters. He then gave a quick look at the headings of the papers on the desk.

"Look – take these papers and report to Chavik Bey. He will see to the matter. He's on the first floor, along the corridor to the right as you go up the stairs – the last office at the end."

In disbelief, his heart now pounding with the greatest torture of all – hope – he took the papers and turned to walk up the grand but dusty marble stairs. Once at the top he saw a long corridor with office doors on each side, and many clerks and messengers wandering up and down, smoking and chatting. No one was taking the slightest notice of him. Vahan stopped, surreptitiously taking deep breaths to calm himself down. He looked over the balustrade down into the entrance hall, which had become increasingly busy as the time for the morning petitions and hearings drew closer.

Vahan waited, and then at a moment when the reception clerk was busiest, he walked back down the stairs and straight out of the building. No one challenged him, and with the bail papers and his own documents firmly in his hand he walked back along the street. He knew there was no other documentation evidencing his arrest with the possible exception of a note in the local station records, so he walked along taking great gulps of the suddenly wonderful Bolsetsi air, and turned into the Electricity Company offices.

His boss still had his letter of resignation on his desk when Vahan walked in. Vahan explained that his affairs had all been satisfactorily arranged, and he would therefore like to withdraw his resignation if that was possible. Vahan's boss, who was Jewish, sighed with relief – finding sufficiently educated young men was becoming increasingly difficult. He told Vahan that he had not as yet taken any steps on the resignation letter, and that Vahan could simply go to his room and carry on working – the previous day's absence to be treated as illness.

Vahan sank onto his chair, called for a coffee, and spent a good half hour controlling the trembling, which had taken over his body. He then threw himself enthusiastically into his work preparing invoices, in order to catch up on the previous day's workload. It was nearly lunchtime when one of the old porters came up to him.

"Sami *effendi*, there is a soldier outside who has given us your description and who is looking for you."

Vahan, who had thought himself safe, suddenly felt sick with apprehension all over again. He did not think, he simply assumed that he had been caught out. There was, however, nothing to be done, his colleagues were looking at him curiously as sweat broke out on his brow. The porter waited courteously –

"Ahmed, can't he come up to see me here?"

"No, *effendi*, he insists you come down, and, truth to say, I can see that he can't come up – he has someone with him."

Vahan couldn't make head nor tail of this, but nevertheless, he arranged his desk – most of the work had been finished, took some personal items out of the drawer and followed Ahmed down to the front door. Through the door, out in the street, waiting on the other side of the narrow road, he saw an elderly-looking, unshaven and badly turned out soldier, whose arm was in a sling, standing alongside a young country boy.

Vahan walked across, now no longer quite so concerned that this had anything to do with the morning's events, and approached the soldier. Still not quite yet on the pavement, and ignoring the passing vehicles, Vahan stopped and stared –

"Oh my God – Father – Father, my beloved father – Baba, Baba …" Stepping forward, he clasped the malodorous Garabed in his arms and, oblivious to the surrounding crowds, began at last to cry softly.

CHAPTER 36

Garabed finally arrives

Vahan rarely ever wept openly. But this day's events had finally been too much for him. From moments of deep fear and anxiety when he believed that even death was a possibility, to moments of euphoria when he escaped from the police station, he had been on a roller-coaster of emotions. The sudden appearance of his father, whom he had believed was dead, finally broke his self-control. There and then, standing on the pavement, with all the bustle of the city crowd weaving its way beside and around them, Vahan wept and wept.

It was Garabed who first pulled away and gave Vahan a warm and final kiss on his cheeks, as Vahan swallowed hard and composed himself. Almost immediately, they both started talking at once, and stopped and started again together, and then finally stopped again, laughing as the tension snapped.

"My son – we came to try and find you the moment we arrived in the city and were told where you worked by the quiet Greek lady at your house. We've only been here a few hours."

"Father – look, we can't talk here on the street. Wait a moment. I'll be back in a minute. Are you all right, baba? Is your arm badly wounded or something?"

"No, son – don't worry – it's just a disguise. Off you go, we'll wait here."

Vahan ran back across the street, back into the building. He hurried to obtain leave to take the rest of the day off, assuring his boss that he had already completed most of the day's quota of invoices. He then rushed back out again, marvelling to himself how his life had been turned upside down that day. Garabed was still there, with a young boy standing alongside him, holding tightly on to his free hand. Vahan had no idea who this young boy might be, but it was clear to him that this was not the moment for explanations. While there was no shortage of wounded soldiers to be seen in the streets of the city, this particular soldier, in an extraordinarily ill-fitting uniform far too small for him, and more than usually dirty and dishevelled, stood out rather more than most.

Vahan had spent a lifetime looking up to his father, following his lead and decisions in almost everything. Suddenly, the tables were turned. This was his city – it was he who would have to make the decisions, it was he who would have to guide his father. He didn't hesitate, he only had one small matter to clear up as he motioned to his father to follow him down the street. He look at the young boy, equally dirty and wearing worn-out country clothes.

"Well, baba, who is this young man?"

"His name is Ara," said Garabed simply. "Ara, say 'hello' to my eldest son – Vahan."

"Parev, Barón – hello sir," Ara responded, speaking Armenian, the first time the language was used. Vahan was startled, knowing, as he did, that his father could not speak Armenian. However he held out his hand – then seeing that Ara did not know what to do with it, he took the boy's free hand and shook it.

"Welcome Ara, welcome to Bolis. Come, father, the first thing we are going to do is to get you both cleaned up."

Vahan put his arm round his father, noting that Ara on the other side did not once let go of his tight grip on Garabed's other hand. Strangely connected like this, they walked rather awkwardly down the street. Vahan went straight to the local small hammam, where it was the day for the men. He ordered and paid for a private room.

This was one of the more opulent of the city's baths. Having picked up their thick, warm white towels, and with their white dressing gowns in hand, they went through into the marble courtyard inside. This had a large, green-leaved tree growing in the middle. All round the court were small but comfortable rooms, each with a rattan table and chairs, with lockable doors and a small window looking into the courtyard. There was a small, inner staircase which led up to a first floor which had a balcony running all round the court, with regular, thin pillars holding up the tiled covering. Coming off this wide corridor there was a further line of rooms. These were higher-priced as they had small windows to the outside. Several of the occupants, clad only in their white dressing gowns, had taken their table and chairs out of their rooms and put them outside on the balcon, looking down into the courtyard. Having just come from the baths, they were sitting chatting, drinking gazoz or raki, smoking narghilehs and eating snacks brought to them by white-coated waiters.

Ara, eyes wide with wonder, stared and stared, and clung on

even more tightly to Garabed. Vahan got to their room, tipped the attendant generously and ordered kebabs and bread.

"Come, baba, get out of those awful clothes, and take off that sling. Father, I've forgotten, what's your chest and leg size? Oh ... yes, thank you. Look, you and Ara go into the baths. Have a really good scrub down. Take your time, baba, go into the steam rooms, and when you are in the hot water rooms, make sure that they use one of those really harsh loofahs on you. You too Ara – come on, get undressed, don't be shy – have you never been to a hammam before?"

"No, Vahan," Garabed said rather gruffly, "he's lived in the country all his life – leave him to me please."

"Fine, fine, baboushka. Now look, I'm going to go and get some clothes for you both. They'll be pretty rough, baba, but they'll be better than what you've got on at the moment. We're going to burn this lot – they're not only filthy but they stink. Frankly I'm amazed that you got this far in Pera without being stopped by the police."

Vahan was all hustle and bustle. Suddenly he felt in total control and it felt good. He watched for a few moments as Garabed gently disengaged Ara's hand. Vahan felt a surge of warmth for his father, though he also noted that Garabed had been far gentler with the boy than he would ever have been with his own two sons. Had Vahan or Raffi hesitated to do as he ordered, Garabed would have used harsh patriarchal authority to command immediate obedience. Here, however, to Vahan's surprise, Garabed gently urged Ara to get undressed and to put on his dressing gown and follow him into the baths. Vahan, hurried out into the streets and began searching for the cheaper clothes shops in the back streets nearby.

With Garabed washed and shaved, and Ara, too, scrubbed, and both as pink as babies, they dressed in the clothes Vahan had purchased. They all walked back across the Galata bridge and to the Patakis house. There was no sign of any police, and, in any case, all the trauma of the day had passed out of Vahan's mind in the joyful activity of seeing his father, and dealing with the practical details. Christina was at home when they arrived. She had already seen Garabed that morning when he had first arrived asking after Vahan. After a slightly sticky start, Garabed turned on all the charm he could muster. This was a side of his father that Vahan had never seen. Indeed, Garabed was usually reserved and upright in front of his children. But in these circumstances, he knew that he needed to get on the right side of this lady, and he was accordingly very gallant towards Christina, who lapped it up.

The arrangements were soon made. Garabed was to take the old attic room which André had used, and which had never been re-let after his disappearance with Elena. Ara was to sleep with Vahan, whose room opposite was a little bigger and could take an extra bed.

After an early supper eaten mainly in silence, once Marisa got back from school, Vahan gave a brief account of what had happened to him at Court, and gave the bail papers back to Christina, promising to repay the bail money as soon as he could. He did not elaborate on how they had come back into his possession. Garabed took Ara, who was exhausted, up to bed. There, to Vahan's astonishment, he sat with him until the boy fell asleep. Vahan meanwhile sat on the bed in André's old room. Garabed eventually walked in and sat on the only chair in the room, as Vahan lay back on the bed.

It was still fairly early, and it had only just got dark, when Garabed finally began recounting everything that had happened from the moment that he had been arrested at home. He passed fairly quickly over the things he had seen and done at the farm of Sarkis, and then went on to the difficult and tiring days when he and Ara, together with Ara's sister Anna, and his mother Adrineh had plodded with their two donkeys through the desolate countryside after leaving the farm. Garabed finally came to that last night when he had been attacked by Ara. Vahan noticed that at this point Garabed, who had been pouring out all his feelings as he relived those moments, hesitated, and clearly was not disclosing everything.

"Well, my son, on this particular night, perhaps I was more relaxed as we were getting closer to the Vilayet of Syria, and I could feel that the evenings were getting warmer. Anyway, my soul, in a nutshell I awoke ... er ... I had not been in a deep sleep, to find that Ara had got my knife and was ... er ... looking around wildly. I thought he must have seen or heard something, so I too sat up and looked around. What then happened ... er, in all the confusion in the darkness ... quite by accident ... in all that rush, was that Ara accidentally almost hit his mother with the knife, and wounded me in the arm."

"Good heavens – how extraordinary and what was it that caused all this?" Vahan was plainly puzzled.

"Yes, well anyway, realising his mistake and feeling upset ... you must remember Vahan he is only 12, and think of what he had seen and lived through, and what he had been having nightmares about. Anyway, as I say, realising his mistake, he dropped the knife and ran away into the dark. Well, Vahan, you know how pitch black it can be on moonless nights in the country. So all we could do was to wait until dawn. I built up the fire, so he could see it if he wanted to come back, and we settled down until first light."

"I don't know. Vahan, whether in the end it was the light of the fire, or whether it was fate or what which caused the events that followed but ... Anyway, at the crack of dawn, I left the old pistol that Mustapha had slipped into the bag of onions – fully loaded – with Adrineh. You remember Adrineh, Sarkis' wife?"

"No father – I don't remember – you never took me, you only took Raffi. Have you forgotten?"

"All right, all right. Anyway I told her that if anyone approached, she should stand and tell them to keep away, and fire a warning shot to show she meant business if they ignored her. I never for a moment thought ... Oh God, Vahan, I had so many things to think about all the time. It just seemed to me that the needs of the boy, out alone in that wilderness, frightened, guilty or whatever, were more important at that moment than the two women."

"What two women baba? ... Oh yes of course there was the traumatised sister as well wasn't there."

"I should have thought more. I could have packed everything

up and taken them with me when I went out looking. But I thought, in the pitch dark, the boy couldn't have gone far. Oh, Vahan, how do these things happen? Anyway, after about three hours I eventually found the lad curled up fast asleep against some rocks. He was bruised and dazed – he must have wandered for hours. I picked him up and we started back to where I had left his mother and sister. I don't believe that I was even one kilometre away, when I heard the distant sound of shots in that still morning air. Oh Vahan, my son, I knew that the worst had happened. I tried to put Ara down and told him to follow me, but he clung onto my neck so hard I couldn't shake him off. I began running as best as I could, still carrying him, but it must have taken me almost fifteen minutes before I came in sight of the dying fire. Oh my God, my God."

At this point Garabed buried his head in his hands. Vahan rose from the bed, stepped over and went onto his knees and hugged his father. Even then, with Garabed in extremis, it was not a position that could last for more than a moment. For better or worse, Garabed was unable to draw any comfort in this way from his son. He thought of it as a weakness on his part, and Vahan, too, felt awkward trying to give such comfort to the strong authoritative figure of his father. He rose, stepped away and flopped back down on the bed.

"Continue, baba, what had happened?"

"Well, my soul, I will never know for sure, of course. Lying dead by the side of the remains of the fire was the girl Anna. Her clothes were intact and she looked fairly tranquil. She had been shot at fairly close range by one shot in the heart. Away from her, there was more blood on the ground and signs of a scuffle. The donkeys, our provisions and Adrineh were all gone. I believe what must have happened is that a party of men – who knows – Turks or Kurds or whatever – maybe only three or four – looking, as they all are, for wandering deportees to rob and rape, came upon these two. Anna was already hovering on the brink of madness. I think that after Adrineh fired off her warning shot to no avail, she shot Anna before they could get to her, and then probably tried to shoot herself before she was grabbed. Vahan, I saw no body anywhere. She's gone – gone for good. Who knows where, or what became of her?"

"And what about Ara in all this, in view of what you told me about his reaction to the awful events in the farmhouse?" asked Vahan.

"Well, I don't know, my boy, I just don't understand these things. It needs that man from Vienna we were all reading about before the war – I've forgotten his name – to tell us why. Whatever the reason may be, Ara was fantastic. It was almost as if this last horror kicked him back to reality, whereas until then he had been in denial. Vahan, I had no spade, nothing. We had nothing left – only two gold coins left in my pockets, and the knife which thank god I had picked up quite by chance before setting off to find Ara. Yet we had to bury the poor mad girl somehow. Vahan, my love, it took us the whole of the rest of that day – and even then it was more of a mound than a grave – but we did it. It was a very bare hillside, but we just managed to keep the fire going. That night, Ara crept up after I had gone to sleep, and curled up into my arms. He's still a child, Vahan."

"That was in the summer – what happened over the winter?"

"My son I could go on for ever. The details will have to remain for another time. In a nutshell, I decided that we had to press on into Syria. There was no point in turning back, now that we had come that far. I'll tell you something Vahan, poverty and deprivation in the city is pretty awful, degrading and squalid. Conditions are dirty, you sleep in abandoned smelly corners. You never seem to be able to get clean. But, my soul, poverty in the countryside is worse – desperate. It may be cleaner, but you will starve more quickly. In most towns, however poor you may be, somewhere you will find a tap dripping to get some water. You will usually find some scraps somewhere. Above all there are people around. But that bloody, sparse, barren, rocky, wilderness of a countryside – sometimes with not a soul for miles, and those that you do meet are usually best avoided.

Ara may be a naïve country boy – did you see the wonder in his eyes when we went into the baths – but he was good at scavenging and finding edible things. You wouldn't believe the things we got round to eating. We were hungry all the time. Well, we got to Aleppo eventually, and there, at least, things began to improve. Here I came into my own, and whilst currency is collapsing in value all around us, gold pieces were doing well – and I had two left. This was just enough to get us started, and I found a hovel in which we could hang out. Because I was strong, I was able to get a job humping cotton bales and other goods for a shop in the bazaar. Knowing the trade well, as you know, I was able to give the Arab shopkeeper a lot of help. Eventually he agreed to take on Ara as well – for just the day's food of course – to run around getting coffee and tea, which he would bring on a brass tray for the customers.

My lad, this was just pure survival during that winter. I saw many Armenians – almost all poor peasants – in the town, and many of them simply collapsed and died in the streets. But the richer merchants and professional people who made it that far, moved on to Lebanon or Damascus. We heard, however, that most of the population had either died on the way, or when they made it to Syria, died in the desert.

Vahan, my boy, this was no life, and when the summer came I decided I would try to make my way to Bolis, knowing that you were here, and that most of the Armenian population had not been touched. Caesaria was out of the question. We spent months slowly collecting everything we needed – a soldiers uniform for me – some false papers – that bloody sling – and most difficult of all, but the vital document, a medical pass for a broken arm. Once ready, we travelled by train, walking and more trains. But, my boy, my soul, we made it. We made it! Then to cap it all, you tell me that Mariam, my sweetheart, and my darling daughters are still alive, so far as you know. The Lord Christ be praised, Vahan, we're through. We're here. Who knows, if what you say is true, then maybe even Raffi might still be alive somewhere."

"Father – calma, calma. This war is not going to end just like that. We've got a bit to get through yet. But yes, baba, yes, I think we've a good chance now. Ara is young, and now that he's here, he is out of danger. You too. I will just have to be more careful.

Oh father, father how good it is to have you here by my side. We're going to make it. My God, I do believe that we're going to make it!"

CHAPTER 37

Karekin and Aram return

Seated at a coffee table in a shabby run-down part of Stamboul, close by the Kapali Carsi – the Grand Covered Bazaar – was a tall, middle-aged and bald-headed gentleman. He was dressed in good clothes, which had obviously seen better days. The fez worn on his head was faded and rather shapeless. A careful look at his hands would have shown any curious onlooker that this was a man unused to hard physical labour.

Karekin Avakian sat, eking out his one tiny cup of coffee to make it last, and waiting for the return of his friend Doctor Aram Manuelian, who had left him only an hour ago. He sat pondering all the events of the last year since he and Aram had jumped out of the train in Konya. It had been a time punctuated by short moments of high tension interspersed with long periods of intense loneliness and boredom. He fiddled with his teaspoon as he thought of the last few weeks before they had finally left Konya.

Karekin was now beginning to get anxious as to Aram's failure to turn up as promised. He thought again of that first year in Konya, and how news had begun filtering in of the rape and murder going on in the eastern vilayets. Sivas, it seemed, had been emptied of Armenians. Erzurum had become a ghost town. Everywhere, the news had been of the dead and dying on the roads going south and east.

Karekin knew that the Russians had finally blundered their way into Van, relieving the encircled Armenians, but within the year they were in retreat again. The remaining ordinary Armenian civil population had died in their tens of thousands, while the professional revolutionaries slipped away, as they always do in such situations.

As soon as Djelal Bey, the old Ottoman governor had been dismissed, and the new governor was on the point of arrival, Karekin had realised that their refuge was on the point of extinction and they would have to think again. In their interminable discussions over alternatives, Aram had thought the best place to go was Smyrna, with its largely untouched Greek and Armenian population. It was Karekin who had made the startling suggestion that they should return to Constantinople, under their new assumed names. Karekin recalled the final critical conversation.

"Look, Aram, neither of us have ever been to Smyrna. We have no connections there, we don't know our way around, and being such a sophisticated city we won't find it as easy to meld into the local populace, as we have here. Let's slip back to Bolis. We won't be able to go to our old haunts, but so long as we're not arrested, we're probably safer there than anywhere else. It's a big city, we know how to avoid the police and where to go, and above all there are no deportation orders there."

"You're totally crazy, Karekin, If we're recognised in the streets by any policeman, or even by one of our own Turkish acquaintances, it could be immediate imprisonment or worse."

"But Aram, we won't go anywhere near Makrikoy. In the city, we'll hardly be strolling into Tokatlian's for lunch, or going to places where we would meet business friends. Above all, we would know exactly where to hide out in the poorer quarters of the town."

Karekin reflected that it had not, after all, taken too much argument to persuade Aram on a course of action, so close to his heart. He knew that everyone from Constantinople – the Bolsetsi – always retained an inner love of the city, whatever the circumstances of their departure. Sitting in the café, he also thought of the anxious attempt they had made to persuade the young couple with whom they had been lodging, to come with them.

"Forget your sweet shop, your little house, your friends, everything you hold dear, when your actual lives are in danger," was their continual refrain.

But the young couple couldn't accept that they might suddenly have to leave the place that had been their home all their lives, growing up next door to each other. Karekin reminded them of all the news coming from the east. They merely shook their heads in disbelief, commenting that this was not the Ottoman way, that their parents had lived in Konya all their lives, that they had friends, Turk as well as Armenian, in the town. In the end Karekin sighed, made over his shop and all the remaining goods there to them, and wishing them luck, he and Aram had left.

With a sizeable amount of cash, reconverted into gold coins, and with the battered old suitcases still holding their old, but now cleaned, city suits, Aram and Karekin got seats in a carriage going to Bursa, from where they had then travelled on to Yalova and onwards by boat to Bolis. Karekin recalled that he had spent enormous energy persuading Aram not to go in the train running directly to Constantinople, which would have been much quicker and a good deal more comfortable. Trains, he had pointed out, were always patrolled by efficient police guards, whilst the gendarmerie on the roads were lax and always open to a bit of financial persuasion. Karekin had also made sure that they travelled in a carriage with mainly Turks on board, not that there were many Armenians left in the area anyway.

"Well, well, Karekin, now that we are here," said a voice, "what are we going to do? Our cash isn't going to last for ever, and one thing is obvious – there is no way that you are going to be able to open up a little business here."

Karekin looked up with relief, from the contemplation of his coffee grounds, as Aram, already talking, sat down at the table. The waiter, with his dirty white cloth over his arm, hurried up, thankful for a further order from this table at last.

"*Effendim?*"

Karekin ordered two coffees – one sweet and one without sugar.

"First things first, Aram. Did you get to see your partner, at your old surgery?"

"No, Karekin – it's boarded up and there is a note on the

door saying that the surgery is closed, but that it will be reopening again soon with new doctors. The note looks fairly new, so I suppose Avedis couldn't manage on his own and has sold up. I went off to the library to take a look at a list of current medical practitioners – that's why I'm late by the way – but Avedis is not listed anywhere. I'm supposing that he has either retired or perhaps even died – he wasn't that young. He certainly isn't living in the flat above the practice anymore, as that too is empty."

Karekin nodded and said -

"You know I do agree with you that we're not going to be able to attempt in Bolis what we managed in Konya. Sooner or later, I would be recognised if we opened a shop."

"Yes, but look here, Karekin, what about your family and the business. If I know Armineh, she might well be managing to keep your business going. Now that we are settled in, what about contacting her discreetly."

"Aram, whilst the present situation continues, I simply can't take the chance of putting my family at risk by appearing at home. If they are discovered harbouring a man officially arrested and deported, they too will all be thrown out, imprisoned or worse. No, for the moment that's out. Armineh knows I'm alive and somewhere in or near Konya – that's enough. I must pick the moment carefully to make myself known to them, if that moment ever arrives. I'll do that only when I know there'll be no danger to them."

"All right, I see your point, Karekin. However, honestly, while it seems increasingly clear that the days of our poor old Empire are numbered, the war could still last another year or more, and meanwhile how are we going to manage. Living here in Bolis is a good deal more expensive than it was in Konya, and, sooner or later, our cash is going to run out."

"What about your flat in Makrikoy, Aram. Surely no one will have taken that over. Do you still have your key?"

"Yes, as it happens, but Karekin, isn't that a ridiculous risk? We can't possibly live in Makrikoy."

"No, probably not – but you must have some valuables of one

kind or another in the flat, things we might be able to sell. Your spare cash might still be there."

"I doubt it. I had a Greek maid. She was a nice girl, but if the caretaker has let her in with his master key, believing that I was gone for good, she would probably have taken whatever she could find."

"Yes, perhaps, but we have to find out. We've been here a week already. It's time we began looking about and considering the future. I've grown a moustache and my wispy beard is coming along nicely – I doubt if anyone in Makrikoy would recognise me. Actually, you know, I never had more than a few acquaintances there, not in the same way as business circles in the city."

"Karekin, the position is quite different for me. I might well be seen by one of my several old patients in the town, and they would certainly recognise me, even if I grew a beard. Being arrested a second time would almost certainly mean death for either of us. Think about it – escaped deportees – false papers – there would be no hope at all. Good heavens, the caretaker alone will be enough to ruin us."

Karekin considered for a moment,

"All right – here's the plan. First we buy some flowers from one of those smart shops on the Grande Rue de Pera which do personal deliveries. We get them sent to one of the ladies in your block – you must surely remember the name of one or other of them. Pick one who might not be too curious as to why she has received flowers from an anonymous donor. Fine. When ordering the flowers we ask to speak to the boy who is going to make the delivery on the excuse that the building is difficult to find and we need to give him directions – it's often done. Then, here's the tricky bit, we ask him to find out the name of the caretaker who lives in the basement – and to give us a description if he sees him. We tell him that he'll get a good tip, and that we'll call the next day."

"Where does that get us?"

"Right – first it tells us whether the same caretaker is still there. You know how often they change. If it's the same man it will have to be a risky night job. But if it's a new man, we can bluff our way in during the day. We might even be able to use the flat again if we play our cards right."

"Karekin – you know you've got a criminal mind. I think it's terribly chancy, but then almost everything we've been up to has been risky throughout. All right lets do it. I do in fact have some money hidden under a loose floorboard, which might well still be there. Look – I know that I'll start worrying and thinking of everything that can go wrong if this drags on, so lets start right now this very afternoon, before I start getting cold feet. I know absolutely the right flower shop, and the lively Jewish widow on the floor below mine will adore getting the flowers. She thinks that every male who sees her is immediately smitten and she'll not be the least surprised to get some nice flowers delivered. Come on – pay up, let's go!"

The plan had worked perfectly. Karekin and Aram had waylaid the flower delivery boy on his return to the shop, having already promised him a large tip. The lad had given them the name of the caretaker at the block. As Karekin had thought likely, the previous young concierge was no longer there. It was probable that he had been called up. There was instead a new elderly man, who, if the boy could be believed, was so old as to be almost senile.

Karekin had already grown a fairly respectable beard by the time that they plucked up their courage to make the train ride that had been Karekin's daily trip in happier days before the war. This time, both of them travelled third class without argument. Aram, who had had a local practice in Makrikoy, as well as his city office, muffled himself up in a thick greatcoat even though the weather was fairly warm. Karekin laughed at him, and took nothing but an old scarf.

It was only a few minutes before the train was due to steam into the Cobancesme station that Karakin suddenly thought of a problem, that he had overlooked.

"Oh, my God, Aram, I've forgotten old Abdul and Mustapha – the gharry drivers at the station. They'll recognise me for sure whatever I do. I've used them almost every day for years."

Aram replied a little smugly, "Ah ha, Karekin my dear fellow, so you're thinking about it only now. For once I'm way ahead of you. I've thought of that already. As it happens they might recognise me too, though I rarely took a carriage except in bad weather. Anyway, when I bought the tickets at Sirkeci, I got tickets for the main Makrikoy station in the middle of the town. It's only a slightly further to my flat from that station, than from Cobancesme."

"Well done, Aram, good thinking. You owe me two million or thereabouts so far – I'll let you off a straight million for quick thinking. I'll soon get it back anyway."

Karekin sat back in his seat as the train stopped at the familiar station. They had chosen the middle of the day for their trip, so there weren't many people in the train or on the platforms. He said nothing, making no attempt to relieve the tension and emotions which swirled within him as the train moved on, past the level crossing and on into the town. Three minutes later the train stopped in the main Makrikoy station.

Karekin was not given to indulging in much introspection. He tended to get on with life as it arose, enjoying without guilt its many pleasures, and facing up to its many difficulties, without complaint. But, now, he found himself contemplating the little town with a warm emotional attachment he had not consciously felt before. This was the town in which he had lived and brought up his family for so long – the town which he had feared he might never see again.

Both Karekin and Aram were nervous as they made their way through the main street. They walked past the shiny new shopfronts, alongside the old-fashioned, tiny shops, where people still made, at the back, the goods they sold in the front. Nobody took the slightest notice of them, and they arrived outside the modern block of flats, just behind the main street where Aram used to live.

It was an awkward and decisive moment for them. To get into the block, the caretaker had to open the main door after dark, but the door was usually left open during the day, which it was on this occasion.

"Karekin – I think we should get this out of the way right from the start. We'll contact the fellow now, whilst it is broad daylight and in less suspicious circumstances than if he accosts us coming out," said Aram, knocking at the door of the concierge's little room which faced onto the courtyard, just past the main door. The door opened.

"*Effendim?*" said the man who came to the door, nothing like as old as the flower delivery boy had made out.

"Porter *bey*," said Aram, "I am Doctor Aram Manuelian. I live in Flat 7 on the third floor. I don't think we've met before, I believe you are fairly new. I've been away at the front, and have only just been released. Here is my 'nufus'. And your name is?"

Aram handed the old man his original internal passport papers, which he had been careful to bring with him.

"Ah yes. Er …my name is Murad, Doctor *effendi*. I've been here three months, and this is, indeed, the first time we've met, though I do have your name on my list," said the caretaker looking at the nufus and handing it back to Aram, whose confidence was increasing with each word.

"Well Murad, my good fellow, I'm a doctor and in these difficult wartime conditions I have to spend a lot of time at the military hospital in town. I've been back a couple of times in the last two months, but haven't seen you before. This is my good friend – Mahmud Acimoglu – who will be staying at the flat for a few weeks whilst I am away."

At this point, Aram handed the old man the false papers of Karekin, which they had obtained in Konya. Confidence was what mattered, and Aram found himself oozing assurance. In many ways he was talking to Murad with a haughtiness he would never have displayed before becoming a fugitive. He then clinched the situation by showing the man his keys,

"I have my keys with me, Murad *effendi*, so I can go straight up as always. Has my cleaning girl been coming?"

"Oh no, *effendi*, she hasn't been here at all as far as I know."

"Ah well, never mind," said Aram, holding his hand out for the papers, "I'll find someone else. Meanwhile, Murad *effendi*, this is for all your trouble, and I hope you will be helpful to my friend if he needs anything." Aram gave the man, whose face creased up into a great grin, a large tip – but not too large. He and Karekin then walked up the stairs in a mixture of triumph and excitement.

The keys still fit – there had clearly been no official entry.

Karekin and Aram walked into the empty flat. It was almost a year since anyone had lived there, and although the flat was clean there was a musty, damp, odour about the place. Aram went straight to the main bedroom. Here the bed had been left unmade – the blankets and new sheets folded at the end of the bed. Aram pushed the bed to one side, while Karekin stood at the door watching hopefully. Aram knelt down, feeling the boards, and called out to Karekin,

"Karekin, my soul, go and get me a knife from the kitchen."

When this arrived, Aram began working away at one of the wooden tiles forming part of the modern parquet floor – digging the knife in between the cracks. Eventually he prised it up, and felt down with his hand, and very gingerly brought out a vicious looking mousetrap, which sprang shut as he put it down. He then felt down further, lying flat on the floor.

"Karekin, my friend, Karekin – it's still here."

He carefully pulled out a largish cloth bag. He upended this on the floor and out poured some coins, mostly gold, and some wrapped large denomination notes.

"Hey! Well done Aram. My God! What a lot you've managed to save. I didn't know that you doctors did so well."

"No, no Karekin – this is money left by my father for my mother – which she passed on to me just before she died. Good God, I couldn't have saved anything like this on my fees."

Both men were flushed and excited. Aram admitted that deep down he was fairly sure that the cache would still be there untouched, particularly if there had been no official entry. He said that he had been anxious not to say so, in case they were disappointed.

The two men had discussed for hours exactly what they would do in the event of accessing the flat openly and finding the money intact. It was clearly far too risky for Aram to be seen in Makrikoy. Quite apart from the other residents in the block, who would be certain to recognise him, he had many personal patients in the town, so it would even be risky for him to be on the streets too much. However for Karekin it was different. Almost all his friends and business acquaintances were in Bolis and not in this district. Whilst he had indeed lived in the Osman Agha area for years, he had rarely come down into the little town. He never did any shopping here. There was never any question of accompanying the children to the local schools, and he never used the main station, always going from, and alighting at, the Cobancesme halt.

It had already been agreed that Karekin would stay in Aram's flat, while Aram would take most of the money, and go back to the city and find some lodging where he could have his meals prepared, and less likely to attract police attention, on his own. Neither of them were eligible for military service, and it was unlikely that they would be stopped and interrogated.

The two friends arranged to meet regularly, twice a week on Mondays and Thursdays at a particular cafe in the Stamboul side of the city. This rendezvous was sometimes changed, but usually it was a dilapidated spot beside the old Moslem cemetery above Eyup. This was a quiet area, well away from the traffic and policemen, right at the end of the Golden Horn inlet. Just as Aram could not be seen in Makrikoy, there could be no suggestion of Karekin wandering about anywhere in the Pera side of the city.

Karekin's moustache and beard had soon grown to a respectable size. He fell into a hazy dream-like existence as the spring ended and summer arrived. There was far too little for him to occupy his mind, and, all the time, he was aware that he was within a few miles of his family and all that he loved in the world. When he and Aram met at the café agreed the time before, they would play innumerable games of tavloo, and slowly Aram's debt mounted into many millions of gold or sovereigns – they never specified what currency it was. Aram would always be waiting for him at the same rickety table, outside the old coffee house above Eyup.

Karekin, bored to tears, began taking risks that he had promised Aram he would avoid. Anxious to have a glimpse of some of his family, he began to make a point of hanging about outside the little primary school for girls that Seta attended. On the first occasion, pressed back against the wall of one of the houses across the square from the school, he saw Haik walking along, hand in hand with Seta. His heart lurched as he saw his only son, laughing and restraining Seta, who was skipping rather than walking, and never once stopped talking. Karekin wondered why it was Haik who was bringing Seta to school and not Maric or one of the maids. After seeing Seta into the school gates, Haik would turn and sprint away, and Karekin realised that he wouldn't have much time to get back to his own school on the outskirts.

Karekin began making a point of wandering past Seta's school in the afternoon to watch Haik arrive to pick her up. Karekin could see that Haik was very careful to take Seta by the hand, and he noted that they immediately went off together to walk up the hill past the racecourse without saying a word to anyone. He ached to press them to his chest, and envelop them both in his arms. However they appeared cheerful, and he knew that appearing suddenly before them, would be difficult for them, and dangerous in the long run.

It was well over a year since his arrest, that two events occurred that would once again change Karekin's life. Already several weeks had gone by since he had moved into Aram's flat.

That morning Karekin took the late morning train into the city, and stepped out at Sirkeci station. There were always police about at the station, stopping people at random and asking to see papers as they showed their tickets at the exits off the platform. Karekin had been stopped before – his tall bearing tending to stand out. However, as he was clearly well beyond military age, and his new grey beard made him look even older, their inspection of his papers was fairly cursory. On this occasion he was again stopped, and their inspection was a little more thorough, although they soon waved him on.

Karekin felt an atmosphere of suspicion in the city, and for some reason there were more policemen about. These days of added tension happened fairly often and were usually associated with some news from the front, or scare-stories about spies, or riots of one kind or another in the city. He took the tram that went to the suburb of Eyup. On arriving he walked past the remains of the old Blachernae Palace of the Byzantine Emperors, through the little streets surrounding the Eyup mosque and on up the tiny cobbled street – looking like a country lane – that led up along the old Muslim cemetery. He passed by the old tombstones slewing to one side or the other at crazy angles, and walked round the corner which brought him in view of the simple old round wooden tables with rickety chairs, where Aram would sit in the sun and wait for him to arrive.

The moment he turned the corner, Karekin saw four policemen, all with their backs to him. One had a gun in his hand, and another was waving some papers and shouting. Standing, staring straight at him as he appeared, was Aram, with blood coming from the side of his mouth and from his nose. As he turned the corner into view Karekin saw one of the policemen give another vicious punch to Aram's stomach. Aram doubled up but his face must have shown the light of recognition or something, as two of the policemen began turning to see what Aram was looking at.

The next moments happened in a flash – scarcely more than a few seconds – but it was as if time slowed down as each action and reaction took place. Aram, even in his physical distress, seeing the two policemen beginning to turn toward the corner of the lane behind them, suddenly yelled at the top of his voice into the air, "Pakheh' – pakheh – get away." He then straightened up and struck one of the policemen who was turning – a heavy push really rather than a strike – and began to run away in the opposite direction. He couldn't get far because of all the tables and chairs around him.

Karekin stared for one second, then turned and strode back round the corner, and then started running. Despite the panic and the rush of adrenalin, there was little doubt in his mind that he heard the sound of two gunshots ringing out behind him. He stopped and there was a long moment of silence. For another second he hesitated, but then began walking down the lane and into the busy bubbling streets of Eyup.

He thought of walking straight back to the station. But his legs felt weak, and the moment came when he had to stop. He wandered into a rather rough and ready eating house, ordered he knew not what, and sat staring into space, piecing together in his mind what had just happened. The scene ran back in his mind moment by moment in cinematic detail. He had no idea what the police were looking for, but the blood pouring down Aram's face showed that he had been arrested and repeatedly struck. It slowly dawned on him, that his old friend had deliberately shoved the policeman away in order to distract them from turning towards him. And the two shots ...

A wave of despair swept over Karekin, and tears came into his eyes as he thought of Aram and all that they had meant to each other over the years. Karekin never wept in front of his family, but here, in the midst of a huddle of uncaring strangers, he silently sobbed and sobbed, impatiently wiping away his tears as they sprang from his eyes.

Once again, and without Karekin being consciously aware of it, there were riots erupting in corners and alleys all over the city. Once again, the mindless cries of '*giavours* this' and '*giavours* that' were being shouted by crowds milling about, whose real problem was not the damned infidels in their midst, but the lack of reasonably priced food and the other deprivations caused by the interminable war.

But ultimately this was not Eastern Anatolia. The government was aware of the presence of their Allies' embassies in the city and knew that the Empire could not afford to be seen to be complicit in any ethnic or religious killings. Hence the police were out in force with direct and clear orders not just to stand by, as they usually did, but to control the mobs. The churches, Greek and Armenian, and the synagogues, were well protected and the centre of the city saw no deaths or looting.

Karekin was unaware how long he sat at the little corner table in the shadows. Eventually, however, he rose, having eaten or drunk nothing, left a payment and, walking all the way, made his way to Sirkeci station. Feeling guilty at not having stopped or returned to share his friend's fate, and still in deep distress, he got on his train in a daze.

Sitting in a corner seat, he stared out of the windows as the sea walls passed, and the train went through the gap driven through the great walls of the city. Still not entirely conscious of his surroundings, he got out without thinking automatically at the Cobancesme station, instead of continuing into the town. He was lucky – neither of the carriage drivers were present. However, the mistake suddenly brought him with a snap out of his reverie and back to the dangerous present, as he began walking into the town.

It was then that he first noticed that there was a mob of gesticulating and rough-looking men running past him up the road. Turks, Albanians, riff-raff of one kind or another – where they all came from he could not tell. They were certainly not local Turkish townsmen. He walked on paying little attention, but then he suddenly became aware of what they were shouting. His heart missed a beat as he heard -

"Allah be praised – Allah be praised – the bastards are burning. The filthy *giavour* school has been set on fire. They're going to rot in hell. Come on, come on."

CHAPTER 38

Olga decides

Mikael scrambled up from the floor where he had been squatting as Olga approached down the corridor.

"Olga, I'm leaving the hospital today. I've been given a medical discharge, and I won't have to go back into the army right away. That's the positive side. The negative side is that Dr. Turhan has told me that my kidneys will never recover. He says that sooner or later it will affect my life expectancy."

She was still upset at the outcome of her last brush with Selim, and looked at this man, and realised that he wanted more from her than she could give. Her problem with Selim was a racial and historical divide, whilst with Mikael, it was an educational and class divide. But in the end, it was simply a matter of chemistry. She simply did not feel the same strength of feeling towards Mikael as she felt for Selim.

"I expect, Olga," continued Mikael, "that you knew this when you told me to forget our feelings. But Olga, the doctor said that I could have years of fairly healthy life, and that in all other respects I am cured. Olga – I intend to go far – I know it. Say at least that we'll meet again. For God's sake, Olga, don't shut me out."

"Oh Mikael go home, my dear. Of course we'll meet again, we live in the same small town for heaven's sake. It's unworthy of you to imagine I would reject any idea of marriage based on the state of your health. Really Mikael!"

Mikael's face reddened.

"I'm sorry Olga, my soul. Listen, I was setting out to visit my half-brothers and their mother, my father's – er – mistress, at the moment that I was arrested. I'm going to go back to Yedikule to finish what I started – and then I am going to look for some work in the city before I even consider going home."

Olga leant forward and gave him a gentle kiss, by way of a goodbye. But Mikael was having none of it.

"No, Olga, we can't part like this. I love you – you know I love you. It has only been your presence here that has kept me going. You are going to be mine. We are going to live together once this war is over. Just say it – just say it!"

Olga looked at him – hesitated for a moment – and then speaking softly, without a smile or encouragement, said,

"Go carefully, Mikael my soul. We will surely meet again whether you are in Makrikoy or Yedikule – I know it."

Mikael lifted his hand and touched Olga's cheek, shook his head, and turned and walked away.

Olga soon heard that Selim's mother and sister had indeed turned up, and had sat with Selim several hours that afternoon. It was clear that Selim would be discharged as soon as the stump of his left arm had fully healed. The final defeat and departure of the British and Australian forces from Gallipoli some months previously, had slowly eased the pressure on the military hospital and Olga found more and more time to spend with Selim.

Shortly after Mikael left, Selim had been getting up and about, and now it was the turn of Selim and Olga to walk up and down the corridors and outside in the fresh air. Once again it was Olga who worked hard to reduce the charged atmosphere of their meetings. Meanwhile under her careful and attentive nursing, Selim began once again to take an interest in the difficult and confused politics of the dying days of the Ottoman Empire. Most people were aware that even though the Empire had done remarkably well against the Western Allies, and even if Germany won the war eventually, the Empire as it was currently constituted, was doomed.

For Selim, for the first time, an Arab dimension had been added to the political mix. During his few months in Damascus, Selim had become aware of the latent intellectual ferment amongst the Arab intelligentsia and middle classes. This awareness had been broadened by his experiences on the Tigris, south of Baghdad, where he had commanded ordinary Arab peasant conscripts, whom he had come to like and respect. He poured out all his ideas about the future of the Empire, with enthusiasm, to Olga. While Olga remained an Avakian daughter at heart, ready to question everything and anything, during the past year she had learned how to listen sympathetically to all sides of an argument.

"Olga – you wait and see – although the Empire in its present form is finished, we do have a great future. Djemal has some great ideas, and he's going to be very influential once this war ends – as it will, my love, as it sooner or later must. It was a revelation to me how loyal and reasonable my men in the Baghdad vilayet were. The British can intrigue as much as they like, but at the end of the day the main Arab population of the

Empire would still prefer to be ruled by a Muslim Turkish power, then by a westernised Christian one."

"But Selim, my love, you must have heard that a revolt was declared in the last few weeks by that man who was put in charge of the Hejaz – what was his name?"

"Yes, yes – Hussein. He is a Qureshi of course, of the tribe of the prophet, but he was and remains a mere nominee appointed by Constantinople. Look – it's probable that he has only revolted now, because Djemal was about to depose him, and appoint one of his rivals as Sherif of Hejaz. In any case, what we are talking about here is some miserable bedu tribesmen. Olga, what matters amongst the Arabs, are the opinions in the great Arab cities; in Cairo, Damascus and Baghdad. There is no Arab revolt. It's a myth invented by some enthusiastic young British officers in Cairo with over-wrought imaginations, for the benefit of their own Empire. You just wait and see. When it comes to the crunch – when the choice finally has to be made – you will see that not a single Arab soldier from our regular army will desert. Furthermore, the vast majority of the Arabs will fight to the bitter end for the Ottomans."

"Selim, Selim, my love, calm down. Let's sit here quietly for a moment. Are you saying that there is no such thing as an Arab national movement?"

"Oh no, of course there is, Olga, of a sort. I'm afraid that what is happening is that the more our leaders want to Turkify everything, the more of a reaction is expressed by the other peoples of the empire. Suddenly, the Arabs are being forced to see the Caliph not only as a Muslim leader, but as a Turk as well. Oh dear – Olga, I think that my poor old Dad might have right in his Ottomanist arguments after all."

"Come on," said Olga rising, "let's continue walking. The doctor said that exercise was good for you. What about my people, Selim, what about all the Armenians in the empire?"

"Well, Olga love, here I think Djemal Pasha might have the answer – an Empire of federated peoples, Kurds, Shiites, Sunnis, Christians, Assyrians – whatever – all living under a traditional dynasty."

"Selim, my sweetheart, I recall that long discussion we had over a year ago after you rescued my little brother from those thugs. At the time I thought that chap Vahan – do you remember him – was rather confused about how he thought the Ottoman world would develop, whilst you seemed very clear. But now you seem confused yourself. I know nothing about the Arabs – but surely you can't have a Turkish national state on the one hand, and, at the same time, the old Empire in whatever new form it were to take."

"I know, Olga, I know," burst out Selim. "If only Baba was still alive. He was always so very clear. He was certain that the Ittihad were wrong, and that western-style 'nation-states' are not the answer for the Asian lands of the Ottoman Empire. What I suppose I would like is an all-Turkish modern state in the core lands, and some sort of federal empire for the rest."

"And Constantinople, Selim? Is that going to be part of the core? And if so, is your brave new nation-state going to tolerate all the different minorities, religions and cultures, all the wonderful diversity, like the Ottomans always did."

"Oh God, Olga, I don't know, I just don't know. However, going back to what I said earlier, I am certain of one thing. There is no national Arab revolt. I've been there. I've fought with them against the British on the Tigris. I've spoken with the Damascus intellectuals and so-called revolutionaries. It's all a put-up front, dreamed up by the English in Cairo, and latched onto by Hussein and his sons to save their own skins. It's all got much more to do with British relations with the French and the Russians; part of the carve-up going on, and they haven't even beaten us yet. They don't care two hoots about the Arabs – all they bloody care about is their precious route to India."

Olga put her arm on Selim's shoulder to urge him not get too excited.

"Oh Olga – I do love talking to you. You've changed, you know. I wouldn't have gone on like this a year ago. I suppose we've both changed. Olga – forget the politics – we do have a future together don't we, despite the loss of my lost arm?"

"Selim," said Olga, speaking very carefully, "Unfortunately

we can't forget the politics. Your father was shot by an Armenian revolutionary in Van and ..."

"Yes, but ..."

"Let me finish, Selim my love. A year ago, you wrote me a letter warning me of the insuperable difficulties we faced in developing a lasting relationship. I had to agree, and I tried putting you out of my mind. I have to tell you that I never succeeded and ..."

"Olga, darling, I ..."

"But Selim, listen. It isn't only you who've lost a father – your mother has lost a husband. We both of us live in a society where family ties are vitally important. Have you ever considered what your mother might think of an Armenian daughter-in-law?"

Olga was careful not to say a word about the meeting with Halideh, even though Selim belittled the problem. Then he too made the same comment that Mikael had made many days before.

"It's my loss of an arm isn't it. You think I won't be able to look after you properly, but Olga I'll ..."

Somehow, Selim's comment upset Olga much more than Mikael's had done. She felt the tears coming to her eyes and burst out in a flash of real anger, - "Selim, how could you! How could you! Oh Selim, you know I'm not like that. I won't continue this conversation any longer," and she walked off in a real temper.

"Olga – I'm sorry, I'm sorry," called out Selim. Nevertheless, in a part of his mind he couldn't suppress the thought that his new disability was affecting their relationship.

It was soon time for Selim to leave and return home. Meanwhile, Halideh and Yasmin were now making regular visits to the hospital, and walking out with him into the grounds.

On the day before he was due to leave, Selim had some further minor surgery to his stump, which was otherwise healing well. He was confined to bed when Halideh and Yasmin appeared with a set of clothes he could wear when he left the hospital the next day. It so happened that on that day Olga had occasion to pass through the officer's ward while on duty. Selim saw Olga passing and called out to her,

"Nurse, hello, – you remember my mother and sister?"

Olga stopped and came over.

"Hello – it's Olga isn't it? See I remembered your name – what a wonderful job you do. I'm going to be a nurse when I grow up," gabbled Yasmin, smiling up as Olga approached.

"Hello, Yasmin," said Olga, then turned to smile at Halideh. Halideh nodded, but turned away. Olga blushed, then turned to Yasmin,

"Would you like to come along with me for a few minutes whilst I do some more of my rounds? You must promise just to watch and not to say anything."

"Oh yes please, yes please. Can I?" she turned, not to Halideh who was about to say something, but to Selim. Selim, was oblivious to Halideh's quiet rejection of Olga's advance, beamed with pleasure,

"Yes, of course, off you go Yasmin – be good now."

Olga took hold of Yasmin's hand and they walked off out of the clean and neat officers' ward. They went through to one of the soldiers' wards, where Olga usually worked. Here the atmosphere, and the smells were quite different. There were scarcely ever any visitors – most of these men being from the Anatolian interior. Olga, inevitably was an attraction for these men, though all of them had been brought up to show a deep respect towards her – one of the few positive sides of the 'haram' system in the home.

The presence of Yasmin – a friendly pretty 12 year-old, brightened the whole ward. She walked solemnly behind Olga as she went on her rounds with the midday medications. Her natural bouncy spirit soon broke through her promise to Olga, and she began chatting inconsequentially with everyone.

On their return, Halideh was standing.

"Where have you been, Yasmin? We're very late. You should have been back ages ago."

"But mother I ..."

"Not another word, my girl," and Halideh grabbed Yasmin by

the hand. Turning to Selim she said,

" The military are sending a car – yes, a motor-car – for you tomorrow to meet you off the ferry at the Galata bridge, Selim. We'll see you at home – good-bye till tomorrow."

Halideh walked out without another word, and without even a glance at Olga, who stood by and gave a sad little wave to Yasmin. Selim, sitting up in bed looked at the back of his retreating mother, then looked at Olga, who looked back at him for a second then turned and walked away. She saw that Selim was totally puzzled, with no idea at all of what had happened. However she knew, and she knew that Halideh also knew what was behind all the bad temper.

That night, before she went to the dormitory, she came and sat for a few minutes by Selim's bed. He had been lightly drugged in order to give him a good night's sleep before leaving the hospital the next day. Accordingly, he was only half awake when Olga came, sat by the side of his bed and held his good hand tightly for several minutes. He murmured at Olga, and then fell back into a sleep.

Olga leaned over him and whispered,

"You were right, my darling, you were right after all. We're going to have to part again, at least until the politics sorts itself out. Your mother has to be given more time to complete the grieving process. It's all too soon for her. I love you, Selim – Oh God how I love you – but there is really no hope for us. Oh, Selim!"

Olga leant forward and gave a long lingering kiss to Selim's forehead, and then rose and left as Selim stirred, murmured something, and then turned over onto his other side.

The next day, Selim dressed and then waited and waited for Olga to come and see him off. She never came. No one knew where she might be, and eventually Selim left to go home. That same day Olga applied for and was given a week's leave to return home to her family in Makrikoy.

CHAPTER 39

Makrikoy. The Avakians

Haik had been taking Seta to school every morning and picking her up in the afternoons for months. He was now 13, and the memory of the assault on the 24th April the previous year had faded in the welter of all the other dramatic events which had been taking place around him. While in many respects he remained innocent and naïve, he had certainly become more streetwise. Surrounded as he was by loving and caring females, he was still too young to take on the role of male head of the family. Armineh's decision to make him responsible for the safety of his little sister had been brilliant, but he remained vulnerable and was still immature.

On this summer afternoon, Haik felt the atmosphere was much more tense in the town than normal. His teacher had let them out early due to rumours of riots in the city. The riots were about the price of food and not a display of anti-war sentiment as such, but the continuing death toll undoubtedly aggravated the tensions.

During these more decadent days of Empire, whatever the trigger, riots almost inevitably turned into attacks on the Jewish and Christian communities, and this sometimes spread to the outer suburbs. Haik was now much more attuned to these matters, and he was alert and ready for all eventualities as he trudged into the town to pick up Seta. As he approached the square where the school was situated, he became aware of the running crowds and shouting going on around him.

Meanwhile, this was the same day that Karekin returned from his last fateful rendezvous with Aram at the old cafe in Eyup. As Karekin heard what the crowds were actually shouting, he joined them, running as fast as he could into the town. There was only one *giavour* school inside the town, and this was Seta's. As he ran, he saw, for the first time, the smoke rising up ahead of him over the roofs, and in his fevered imagination he thought that he could smell the fire ahead of him.

Panting, he arrived in the little square – the Nusretiya. Here, in the middle of the square was a dusty area of bedraggled trees and some thin, scrubby bushes, growing out of a sparse grass, which was fighting a losing battle against the dust and the drought. On one side of the square were the buildings of the Armenian primary school and on the other three sides small modest houses. Smoke and flames were billowing out of the centre of the school building.

There was a large crowd standing around the sides of the square. The police were out in some force, and the crowds were being pressed back, away from the fire. Karekin was in a state of desperation. His only thought was – 'first my best friend and now my youngest daughter'. Oblivious to what was happening around him, he thrust himself forward, edging people out of his way, but avoiding the police, and arrived in the dusty area in the middle of the square on the other side of the road, directly in front of the entrance to the burning building across the narrow street. The large main gates leading into the courtyard within, were wide open.

Haik, meanwhile had arrived some minutes earlier. He had no idea what to do. There was, as always, an enormous amount of shouting and yelling, and he saw, too, that there were many policemen about. He remained calm, and noticed that many of the teachers were already outside, with their young pupils gathered around them on the side of the street. They were counting their charges over and over again, and handing over the children to distraught parents. As Haik wriggled forward through the crowd, he recognised Seta's teacher, and pushed his way through towards her.

A strange change of roles was taking place between father and son without them even being aware of each other. Haik with his new-found responsibility, was calm and considered in what he was doing. Karekin, on the other hand, usually so cautious and thoughtful, was at a pitch of emotional conflict as a result of the morning's events in Eyup. He stared in a dazed manner at the burning school, as the flames licked round the sides and began to burn the high wooden fencing which came right up to the main gates.

Then, at the far end of the courtyard, to the right, by the side of the main school building, out of sight of anyone not standing directly in front of the gates as he was, he thought he saw a little girl coming out of the outdoor toilet building, standing confused and too terrified to move. Any restraint Karekin could have mustered, evaporated at the sight. He ran forward across the street, and pushed aside a policeman, trying to hold everyone back. He stared into the school courtyard already filling with smoke.

Meanwhile, Haik had finally made his way to the group standing around Seta's teacher. She had stopped her frantic counting, as all her class was accounted for and grouped around her. Seta was there and ran round on seeing Haik and grabbed his hand.

"Oh, Haik, I'm so glad you came early and you're here. Isn't it exciting? There's no danger, we're all out, or so our teacher says. There was a shout of 'fire – fire' in the school and we all ran outside. I wasn't frightened, Haik, I really wasn't, while we were inside. I didn't really see anything until I got out. But when we did get out and I looked back and saw all the flames – well that did get me a little scared."

Haik squeezed her hand, and they sidled forward to the front of the little group, which was getting smaller and smaller as more and more parents came running to pick up their little girls. It was then that Haik saw a tall man with a grey beard and moustache run forward towards the gates. Seta did not see the man from the front. She looked up only as he stopped, for a moment, with his back to her and pushed aside the policeman at the gate.

Under almost any other circumstances, she would never have made the connection. However, only seeing Karekin from the back, she thought she recognised her father. She screamed out – "baba – baba."

At the precise moment Karekin reached the gate, he heard a voice, a little girl's voice – Oh God, his daughter's voice – cry out, "Baba – Baba!". To his disturbed mind it seemed to come from the terrified little girl that only he appeared to have seen so far, by the outbuilding. With another cry, covering his eyes, he ran through the wooden gates, now also beginning to catch alight, and into the courtyard, where burning beams and other debris were beginning to fall.

Nerissa was also in Makrikoy that morning, giving one of her English lessons to a Greek lady in the town. They didn't hear any of the shouts or noises in the street, but through the window, Nerissa saw the smoke coming up above the roofs a couple of streets away, but became alarmed when the old lady said,
"My, my, that's coming from the Nusretiya Square."
"Oh Madame," said Nerissa, reverting, in her anxiety, from the English in which they had both been conversing, to Turkish. "That's where my little sister's school is. I must go and see she's all right."

Nerissa hurried out, arriving at the Square to find the town's old, and rather decrepit, fire engine was already starting to try and bring the fire under control – starting from the gates at the front of the school. To her relief, she immediately saw the remaining knot of pupils by the side of the square, with Haik and Seta, hand in hand, staring at the front gates. She could see that the flames had taken hold of the wooden posts, and the gates themselves were beginning to smoulder. A group of three or four policemen were standing close together and staring into the smoke filled courtyard, where large pieces of the wood structure, were falling.

Nerissa worked her way round the square to Haik and Seta, and had almost reached them when suddenly there was a shout from the policemen at the gate. The firemen began training their leaky old water-pump hoses onto the gates, and Nerissa saw a young policeman run into the courtyard between the flames. Through the smoke, a middle-aged man with a singed grey beard, and crazed and bloodshot eyes, was staggering out from the flames, holding a weeping child in his arms. He staggered forward and handed the little girl to the young policeman.

To her utter amazement, she saw little Seta, now just ahead of her on the pavement, pull her hand away from Haik and run forward towards the gate. The man, badly burnt but not now in any immediate danger, had sunk to the ground outside the gates, as the school's headmaster came running forward to take the girl from the policeman's arms. Nerissa instinctively moved forward to try to grab and restrain Seta, when she heard Haik, behind her call out,

"Nerissa – leave her, leave her. I don't know, I really don't know, but if she's wrong she has to find out herself."

Nerissa stopped and turned,

"Whatever are you talking about, Haik?"

"Oh, Nerissa, my little sister, Nerissa – just wait a moment, please just wait a moment."

All this happened in a flash – in a moment – all within the time it had taken for Seta to reach the man, who was now sitting, legs outstretched, and with his head buried in his hands. Nerissa saw Seta go down on her knees alongside the man, and put her arms fiercely around him, and press her cheek to his. At that point Nerissa suddenly saw. She saw ... it was her father. Neither she nor Haik moved, as Karekin, wincing from the pain that Seta was causing him by hugging him so hard, turned, and hugged Seta equally fiercely to his chest.

The next moments were chaotic, noisy, and undisciplined, but indescribably poignant. The little girl Karekin had rescued was reunited with someone – it must have been a grandmother, as Karekin, snapped out of his daze. He managed to pick up Seta, and seeing Nerissa and Haik standing side by side across the road, staggered over – put Seta down – and said urgently,

"Come, my lovely ones, come. Let's go before anybody starts asking any questions."

He took Seta's hand and began walking away as the elderly woman approached him. He turned and said to her,

"No, no Madam – that young policeman over there. Yes, he was the man who saved your ... Yes, Madam, do, do ..."

Karekin hurried them all out of the square, and away down the street. Unlike Seta, who had taken in the situation with the clear-sighted clarity of a child, Haik and Nerissa, were both in a state of shock and bewilderment at the sudden reappearance of their father.

Once they were out of the town and on the road by the Valli Effendi racecourse, the questions, the love, the worry, began pouring out. Being Avakians, they all talked at once, with much stopping and starting, touching and holding, so little sense was made. It was also a very inefficient way of making any progress up the hill. Every so often, Seta would demand to be carried by Karekin, and he tried – but was defeated by the rawness of his exposed and inflamed skin. In the end, Haik squatted down, and Seta was hoisted onto his spare but willing shoulders, though she still insisted on holding on to her father's hand, and in this way they continued up the hill towards the house.

The burns he had sustained were causing Karekin spasms of pain, while Haik, with Seta on his shoulders could only walk slowly. Nerissa began to worry how Armineh would react to their sudden, dramatic arrival. Karekin also knew that the dangers, which had kept him away from his family for these past few months, had not gone away. For the moment he was so full of joy – so completely overwhelmed by this unexpected turn of events, which had shattered, in an instant, the terrible isolation of the past year – that nothing else mattered.

The noisy party walked straight into the hall of the Avakian house, Nerissa using her key to open the front door. Haik dumped Seta somewhat unceremoniously onto the sofa, from where she immediately jumped up and ran to fetch Armineh shouting – "Baba's back – baba's back!"

Armineh came running in, then stood stock still, drying her hands on a hastily swept up tea towel. If Nerissa had expected her to faint, or something equally melodramatic, she was disappointed. Armineh just stared at Karekin, and he stared back, both suddenly oblivious of the noise around them – of Seta's chatter, and the arrival of Marie and Shiva in the hall.

Slowly the noise and the chatter died away, as the family stood quietly, each with their own thoughts, frozen by the immobility of Armineh. A rare moment of silence suddenly descended over the Avakians.

No one afterwards remembered how long this lasted, but it was broken as Armineh walked forward and took Karekin by his hand, noting him wince as she touched his skin. Without another word, without waiting for any explanations of what may or may not have occurred, or why her lost husband was suddenly there again after over a year away, she led him up the stairs. Half way up she turned and said,

"Salve, and the burns ointment, Marie please, from the medicine chest. Haik and Seta get a move on – start laying the table for tea. Nerissa, my soul, for heaven's sake close your mouth. See that extra places are laid – remember Olga is back this evening. Come Karekin, my husband, welcome home my darling, let me see to these awful burns."

She lay her hand gently on his cheek, smiled, for just a moment at the children staring up at them from the room below, and then turned and disappeared from view at the top of stairs.